curl up on the sofa? Winter bliss from Lulu Taylor'
Veronica Henry, top ten bestselling author of
Christmas at the Beach Hut

'Pure indulgence and perfect reading
for a dull January evening'
Sun

'Told across both timelines,
this easy read has a sting in the tale'
Sunday Mirror

'Utterly compelling. A really excellent winter's story'
Lucy Diamond

'I raced through this gripping tale about secrets and lies and
long-buried emotions bubbling explosively to the surface'
Daily Mail

'Wonderfully written . . . this indulgent
read is totally irresistible'
Closer

'A creepy story of obsession and deception. Very chilling'
Irish Sunday Mirror

'A gripping psychological thriller'
Essentials Magazine

'This is a fantastic, all-consuming read'
Heat

'[A] gripping story'
Hello!

'The cold, snowy cover and winter setting make
this a great stocking filler for your mum or sister'
thelittlewildwoodkitchen.com

'The book is full of mystery and intrigue, successfully
keeping me guessing until the very end . . . An evocative
read, full of dramatic secrets that will make the reader gasp'
www.novelicious.com

'A poignant, sophisticated and romantic love story'
www.handwrittengirl.com

A
MIDWINTER
PROMISE

Lulu Taylor's first novel, *Heiresses*, was nominated for the RNA Readers' Choice award, and she has gone on to write many more well-received books. With *The Winter Children*, *The Snow Rose*, *Her Frozen Heart* and *The Winter Secret*, she became a *Sunday Times* top ten bestseller. After many years in London, she now lives in Dorset with her husband and two children.

www.lulutaylor.co.uk
@misslulutaylor

By Lulu Taylor

A
MIDWINTER
PROMISE

LULU TAYLOR

PAN BOOKS

First published 2019 by Pan Books
an imprint of Pan Macmillan
The Smithson, 6 Briset Street, London EC1M 5NR
Associated companies throughout the world
www.panmacmillan.com

ISBN 978-1-5290-2965-9

3 5 7 9 8 6 4 2

A CIP catalogue record for this book is available from the British Library.

Typeset in Sabon by Jouve (UK), Milton Keynes
Printed and bound by CPI Group (UK) Ltd, Croydon, CR0 4YY

Visit www.panmacmillan.com to read more about all our books
and to buy them. You will also find features, author interviews and
news of any author events, and you can sign up for e-newsletters
so that you're always first to hear about our new releases.

To my mother

Prologue

It's there in the darkness. Her secret. Her unmentionable.

I must be wicked. I must be terrible. I must be evil.

There's no other explanation. How else could she keep this awful, awful secret?

If I were stronger, I would be able to do what I know must be done.

She could take her secret out into the night, when there is nobody about. She could take it down to the boathouse, where the old skiff lies rotting. She could untie the skiff, climb in and push it out so that it floats silently into the middle of the lake. And then, at the deepest point, where she knows thick, entangling weed lies like an underwater jungle beneath her, ready to snare her and hold her down, she could take herself over the edge, and the secret would go with her.

Then, at last, I would be free.

But right now she is afraid. She is too weak. The secret will kill her somehow. That is the only thing she knows for sure.

1

PART ONE

Chapter One

'Hello, lovelies! Let's see how you're coming along.'

Alex pulled on the dangling light switch, feeling the grit of cobwebs under her fingers, and the drying room burst into a musty yellow light. Now she could see the row upon row of bunches of flowers hanging from the attic rafters, hundreds of tiny petalled heads in shades of red, purple, pink, yellow, orange and white, suspended upside down over the dusty floor. They had been carefully bunched, tied and strung up in the summer, when their petals were full of vivid colour. They were now slightly faded, brittle rather than yielding, and their stems dry and hollow. But they were still beautiful.

'Ooh, you look *gorgeous*!'

She pulled down a bunch from the nearest rafter to inspect. The little starry heads, like miniature chrysanthemums in yellow, orange and magenta, had changed beautifully from silky smooth to straw-dry petals. Lack of sunlight had kept most of the colour intact; the darker ones had lost some pigment, but their colour would be reawakened by putting white blooms among them to bring out their jewel hues, and her careful handling meant that most of the petals were still in place.

Excellent. They're definitely good enough for baubles.

She looked about at her hoard. The other rafters were strung with a bounty of flowers: the white and yellow pom-poms nicknamed billy buttons; long delphiniums in purple, lilac and cream; fragrant lavender in big bunches; hydrangeas with their huge fluttery heads in pale green and soft pink; love-in-a-mist, hollyhocks, roses, baby's breath, lady's mantle. The poetry of their names was enough to make her love the flowers, even without their delicate, dried-out beauty, with its almost melancholy memory of summer now gone.

Taking down half a dozen bunches, she carried them downstairs and out into the potting shed where a long wooden table was ready and waiting. She began to pull her supplies from the row of battered oak cupboards along one wall of the shed – florist's oasis, wires, scissors, ribbons, glue – and made a mental note to order more. As well as making her usual stock, she had promised to supply a London department store with enough floral baubles for all its Christmas windows and that would mean a huge boost to the business. It was exciting, after all these years of slogging, to feel that she was beginning to get somewhere.

The potting shed was always where Alex felt calmest, and today she relaxed into the work, taking the dried heads of helichrysum, snipping them, wiring the stems and pressing them into the sponge orbs that would hold them in place. The work was repetitive but engrossing; simple but creative and satisfying as the bauble took shape. Soon she had several in shades of plum, pink and red, strung with green ribbon and ready to hang.

They're so pretty.

She had a flash of memory of Mum at the top of a ladder, frowning, her tongue between her teeth, as she stretched to hang a canary-yellow bauble on the upper branches of the great Christmas tree that took pride of place in the hall at Tawray.

'There!' she had cried with delight, when it was successfully in place. 'Doesn't that look fabulous?'

It did. Alex had gazed up at the enormous tree with its spectacular load of flower baubles in dozens of gorgeous colours. 'Lovely,' she breathed.

'Who's got the star? Ali Pali?'

Alex ran up the stairs so she could lean over the banister and pass the star to Mum to put on the top. She'd helped to make it: bending coat hangers into the right shape, stuffing them with foam which was studded with dozens of tiny dried daisies. Mum had even let her spray it with the can of paint, releasing a cloud of silver that drenched the petals, giving them a satisfyingly metallic finish. 'Here you are!'

'Thank you, Angel Ali.' Mum took it and with more frowning and tongue biting, managed to get it settled on the top. 'Tiny bit off,' she said, squinting. Her tawny hair was scrunched up into a wild bun, skewered with a pencil and a piece of florist's wire, and she pushed the loose bits out of her eyes. 'But no one will notice! Come on, let's do the festoons.'

That was Alex's favourite bit. The tree looked amazing, of course, but there was something about the festoons that spoke of ancient revels and Christmases past. Mum made them, weaving all the joyous summer flowers into the dark green ivy skeins, putting in holly and old man's beard, and all manner of pagan greenery alongside the delicate beauty of the petals. Alex loved the blue ones best – cornflowers, nigella and delphinium – and after that, the ones that looked like plum velvet: roses, hellebore, dark tulips. But they were all beautiful, how could she pick a favourite? Mum took the ropes of flowers and made a lavish display of them along the tops of the chimney pieces, winding them around thick, waxy church candles; she strung them over the great gilded picture frames in the drawing room, draped them over mirrors, and wound some along the banister of the oak staircase. She even hung garlands around the necks of the suits of armour and put laurel crowns on their helmets.

'There you are, Sir Rupert,' she said, patting one of them on the bottom. 'Happy Christmas.' She winked at Alex. 'Not fair to miss them out,' she said gravely, and Alex giggled.

Every year of Alex's early childhood it was the same: out came the dried flowers carefully harvested in summer, and after hours of careful construction, up went the floral displays. When they appeared, it meant Christmas was truly on its way. Then, when the house was opened up, the visitors came to admire the flowers. When she got old enough, Alex earned a few pounds helping to serve tea in the orangery, and made lots more in tips. Johnnie made his money washing up all the teacups and plates sticky with cake crumbs.

She smiled to think of it now.

But then, the flowers stopped.

After Mum died, there was no one to do the decorations. The flowers wilted in the gardens, turned brown and then rotted. Alex was too young. No one else seemed interested.

Certainly not Sally. She was probably glad not to have the mess – all those dropped leaves and petals. She always liked things nice and tidy.

When Alex was eighteen and languishing in post-exam lassitude, she'd suddenly been inspired to cut the harvest of blooms in the gardens and meadows of Tawray, and set them to dry as her mother had. When autumn came, she taught herself to make the decorations in the old way, and started the tradition again. It was smaller than it had been – Sally wouldn't permit it on the same scale – but the house was still opened for an afternoon so that people could see the flowers in all their glory. And Alex had found her calling.

Alex realised that her fingers were numb; the potting shed's gas heater wasn't really strong enough to cope with the afternoon chill. She put her finished stock carefully into tissue-lined boxes and stored them away, then cleared up her tools. When that was done, she went out, locked the door and crossed the yard to the barn that was now her house. Halfway across, she stopped and took a deep breath of crisp air, inhaling the sharpness of autumn with a sense of pleasure and reawakening. The lazy warmth of summer was all but gone, the leaves were on the turn and she could see copper and russet lights in the trees across the park that stood between her and Tawray. She stared at the gracious house nestled into its nook of green, wreaths of evening mist wrapped around its turreted roof like a veil.

The one benefit to not living there now was being able to see it like this, in a way that was impossible when actually in it.

'Gorgeous Tawray,' she murmured. It was a strange thing to love a place so much, to feel so much a part of it, as though its character and essence swirled through her blood-stream, feeding her cells and nourishing her at some vital level. Perhaps that was why she had never been able to leave, not like the others. They had made their way elsewhere, fol-lowing jobs and studies, and finding new places to belong. But she had always been here, tied to it by invisible ropes of love and longing.

And loss.

The sight of the old house brought an ache of grief: it was there, and yet it was gone. Someone else had possession of its beauty, its solidity and the past that inhabited its walls. Someone else looked out over the gardens, towards the woods, the cliffs and the sea. Someone else walked past the lake, the old tree that overlooked it, the boathouse . . .

But Sally wanted it gone. So that's what happened. Sally gets what she wants, no matter how the rest of us feel – that's just a fact.

Alex pulled herself up, shivering slightly in the chill after-noon air. 'Come on, no point in dwelling on it. Tawray is sold. That can't be changed.' She spoke aloud to make sure she was firm with herself. 'And I don't expect they'll want the flowers either.'

It was years since the family had lived in the house. Long before it was sold, Sally had declared it was too big for her and Pa to live in, with the children grown up and gone. That was fair enough, Alex could see that two people rattling round the great place on their own was not ideal. So it had been rented out to Major Reynolds and his wife, Lady Clare, and their four teenage sons, who quickly grew up, left and, it seemed, began producing grandchildren almost immediately. And they had wanted Alex to carry on doing the flowers.

'It was one of the reasons why we wanted to rent Tawray in the first place,' Lady Clare said. 'We saw the gorgeous Christmas flowers here. We can't imagine the place without them.'

Alex had been touched, and profoundly happy that she could carry on Mum's tradition. It didn't have to end now that they no longer lived at Tawray themselves.

She gazed at the house, with its chimneys and turrets. *But I have no idea if the new owners will want me to carry on. Who knows if they have any idea the tradition exists?* She sighed. *Sometimes it feels as though I've spent all my life fighting to keep something of my past alive, while everyone else is determined to let it go.*

Alex was peeling potatoes for mash when she heard the door open and the clamour of voices and footsteps as the girls came in.

'We're back!' called Di, and she came into the kitchen clutching book bags and a music case. 'Something smells nice.'

11

'Casserole. Where are the girls?'

'Where do you think?' Di rolled her eyes. 'In front of the telly before they had their coats off. They've been very good. No problems.'

'Thanks, Di.' Alex smiled at her. They had a good arrangement of childcare swaps so that they both had clear work days a couple of times a week. As Di's daughters were the same ages as Scarlett and Jasmine, and in the same years at school, it worked well. 'Tea?'

'I won't say no.' Di slipped down into a chair. 'How are you?'

'Fine, fine.' Alex switched on the kettle. 'Same as usual. Trying to keep things on an even keel.'

'How's Tim? Were you right? Does he definitely have a new lady friend?'

'Yup. He confirmed it the other day.' Alex rolled her eyes. 'Exactly as I predicted.'

'You did, you wise old bird.' Di eyed her carefully. 'How do you feel about that?'

Alex chopped another potato and slipped the pieces into the saucepan of water on the stove. 'All right, I suppose. It was bound to happen. He was on dating apps before he even moved out. But the break-up was my call, so I can hardly be angry if he gets a girlfriend.'

She remembered how Tim used to splutter with outrage when she told him he would find someone else.

'No way!' he'd declare. 'That's it for me. I don't expect to find someone else. The failure of this relationship has destroyed me, I'm done.'

'You'll have a girlfriend within six months, I guarantee,' she'd said firmly. 'You'll probably be remarried within eighteen months.'

He'd huffed at that thought. She'd ruined him, that was the implication. He was a broken man. What did he have left to give when he'd given his all to her?

'Well, you should do the same!' Di declared. 'You should find someone else. Have a bit of fun, even. You deserve it.'

'Hmm. Maybe. I'm not sure if I'm ready for all that. I'm still in recovery from relationships. Tim only moved out six months ago. We're still finalising the divorce terms.'

'Yes, but let's be honest. From what you said, it was over for a while before that.'

Alex nodded. The kettle came to the boil and switched itself off, and she went over to make the tea. 'It was. We married too fast and too young, before we really knew each other or ourselves. I just didn't realise how different we were.'

Di nodded sympathetically. 'At least you found out now, while there's still time for the two of you to make fresh starts. You've both been very mature about it – I'm sure you'll take the new woman in your stride.'

'Oh, absolutely.' Alex smiled as she handed Di a mug of steaming tea. 'I don't mind. Really.'

Deep down, though, she wasn't quite so insouciant. Something tasted bitter when she thought about Tim with another woman. *Am I jealous?* She searched her heart. No, it wasn't that. She didn't want Tim back and while she was still fond of him, she had long ago ceased to love him as a husband.

We shouldn't have got married. I was so desperate to

find a home and to be loved, I didn't see that Tim wasn't right for me at all.

The reasons why she had craved a place of safety so much were painful to look at with too much intensity and she pushed that thought away quickly.

I'm not jealous of the new woman. I'm just sad it ended up this way.

Yes, that was it. That was natural, wasn't it? After all, she'd tried for years to make it all right, for the sake of Scarlett and Jasmine. They were so little, still only seven and five, and they deserved that she do everything in her power to keep their family together. But the fissures between her and Tim grew deeper, and the unhappiness more profound. They were two such different personalities and when the excitement of their initial passion had worn off, they'd found themselves mystified by one another. That had grown into baffled resentment and then into undercurrents of hostility that soured life for them all. When Tim went away on a long trip to America, it had been impossible not to see the difference. In his absence, calm had descended on the household, along with the sense that they could breathe, as though the windows and doors had been flung open and fresh, brisk air had flooded in. At first, Alex felt guilty, as though she needed to try harder to accept Tim and everything he wanted and give up her own wants and needs, so that life at home could be this calm and pleasant when he was there. But she knew that was impossible.

When Tim returned and she told him her decision, he'd behaved exactly as she'd thought he might: injured, offended, refusing to listen to her, or to talk seriously and sensibly. He'd shown no regret or sadness for the end of their marriage, just outrage at being 'ordered out of my home', as he put it. She watched him packing, wishing that just once he could act like an adult. She longed to sit down and talk to him, to discuss with him calmly what had gone wrong. Couldn't they treat each other with acceptance and love even as they admitted it hadn't worked out? But the Tim who could do that would have been someone she could stay married to.

In the end, though, he had calmed down and they had handled it as well as they could, considering there were two small children involved, the beings that would tie her and Tim together for the rest of their lives and to whom they owed the utmost consideration. Thinking of Scarlett and Jasmine had kept her together many times when she'd considered drastic options or longed to let rip at Tim in the way that would probably destroy all future relations between them.

And I'm happier now, despite all the pain of splitting up. Tim is too. It's best for all of us.

'The girls seem settled,' she said to Di, sitting down opposite with her own mug, leaving the potatoes boiling in their starchy foam. 'And that's the main thing. That's my focus for now.'

'You'll have to think about yourself too, eventually,' Di said over the rim of her mug. 'Your story isn't over yet.'

Alex smiled. 'Maybe. But I'm not quite ready to start the next chapter.'

*

Alex was clearing up the dinner things while the girls watched television in their pyjamas when her mobile trilled an incoming call. She picked it up, curious; her stepmother rarely made social calls. 'Sally?'

'Alexandra, it's your father. He's in hospital.' Sally's voice cracked suddenly and she croaked, 'It's a stroke. You'd better come as soon as you can.'

Alex listened, dazed, her heart pounding, her hands starting to shake. 'How bad?' she said breathlessly.

'Bad. But he's stable at the moment. Can you tell your brother, please?'

'Are you with him?'

'Of course.'

'When did it happen?'

'Last night.'

'*Last night?*' She was astonished, hardly able to take it in.

'There was no point in bothering you unless it was serious. At first, he seemed to be all right. But he had another attack today. And . . .'

Alex closed her eyes. Was this what she had feared for so many years? That after all this time, Sally would succeed in keeping her and Pa apart just when it mattered most?

'I'll come right now,' she said.

'Tell Johnnie, won't you?'

'Of course I will.' She rang off.

Chapter Two

Johnnie sat on an uncomfortable plastic chair at the back of the community hall, watching Nathan and Joe's judo class. It looked a bit absurd for these small children, lost in their thick white judo suits, to be trying to kick and flip each other, but they seemed to be getting a lot out of it. He watched as Joe danced in front of his opponent, his eyes bright and ferocious, and then dashed forward to grab the other child's jacket and attempt to fell him, squeezing up his face with the effort as he did.

Well done, fella, he thought, as the other child toppled onto the mat.

Johnnie's phone vibrated in his pocket but he resisted the urge to take it out. He'd left work for the day, and now he was watching the twins. He'd resolved not to be like the other parents, ignoring the class and scrolling through their phones. He was here for his sons, and that was important. He'd wished so often that Pa had been around more for him, and so he was determined to be there for his boys.

It is pretty boring, though.

17

He felt guilty for thinking it, and concentrated on watching Nathan attempting a foot manoeuvre. The only other father paying attention looked a bit wild-eyed and kept shouting instructions. 'No, Cameron, *take him down! Down! Oh*, for God's sake, you'll never do it that way, put some wellie into it.'

I don't want to be like that. Joe and Nathan didn't need a commentary. They just wanted their dad there, some praise at the end, and then home for tea.

Johnnie usually relished the evening routine of coming home to find the twins at the table eating their supper. Bertie might be there, but he might not – he tended to come and go as he pleased, eating when it suited him, and he usually had a completely different diet from the other two, now that he was gluten and dairy-free. Netta would be there, busy at the stove and sink, or loading the dishwasher. In no time, she would have fed the boys, overseen homework and reading, got them changed and ready for bed. Sometimes when he came home, they were already in their PJs, all pink-cheeked and warm from the bath, and Netta would be reading them a bedtime story; he would hear the low murmur of her voice from their bedroom. Bertie would be in his room by then, on his swing, or staring out of the window, wearing his noise-cancelling headphones. Johnnie would pop in to say goodnight, and these days Bertie accepted his hug and kiss without demur, which was progress.

It was precious to him, that home. He'd made it his fortress against the world, where he was protected from all the pain outside it. That was why he was feeling unsettled lately.

Things weren't quite right and he wasn't sure what the cause was. Netta was prickly, distant. He had to tackle it.

I need to talk to her about it. I'll do it tonight.

He'd been meaning to sit down with her for ages, maybe cook her something nice, and have a proper heart-to-heart to find out if anything in particular was making her miserable. But life was so rushed and stressful, there was always a mountain of stuff to get through. The time never seemed right for a big discussion and all the heart searching and pain that inevitably followed. He never seemed to have the energy for it.

But I ought to make the effort. I must.

It was why he was less than keen to rush home tonight, though. His phone vibrated again. Wondering if Netta was trying to reach him, he took it out and saw a text from Alex.

CALL ME ASAP. URGENT.

He frowned, his heart instantly accelerating to a faster beat. Alex was no drama queen. She wouldn't send something like this without cause. He got up and headed out of the hall, putting the phone to his ear as it processed Alex's number. A moment later, the ring tone sounded, and then Alex's voice.

'Johnnie. It's Pa. He's in hospital. He's had a stroke.'

There was an invisible punch to his gut and a whining dizziness spun through his head. He fought for control. He had to stay calm. 'Oh no. Oh God. How bad?'

'Sally says bad. I'm on my way to him in hospital now, I'm

just dropping the girls with Tim. I think you should come as soon as possible. I'll text you the details of the ward when I have them.'

Absurdly, he thought of all the hundreds of tiny obligations holding him in place: his job in a high-powered venture capital company, the emails, the phone calls, the meetings, the errands, the places he had to be. He had to get the boys home, for one. 'I don't know if I can get away.' He remembered his important meeting the next day and said helplessly, 'Work . . .'

'Johnnie,' Alex said gently but firmly, 'you can get away. Your father is in hospital, possibly dying. No one would expect you to stay in the office.'

He couldn't speak. *Pa can't be dying.*

'Johnnie? Are you there?'

He managed to swallow and find his voice. 'Of course, you're right. I don't know what I was thinking. I'll get away as soon as I can and let you know what time I'll arrive. You'll call if anything changes?'

'Of course. Drive carefully. I'll see you later.'

He shut his eyes and took a deep breath, realising he was shaking. Then he went back into the hall to collect Nathan and Joe.

'You're early,' Netta said with surprise as Johnnie came into the kitchen with the twins, who immediately dashed off. She turned to look at him, eyes questioning, and then she saw his face and her expression changed to concern. 'Are you okay?'

'Pa's had a stroke.' It came out strangled and the calm he'd managed to assume in front of the boys started to abandon him. 'He's in hospital.'

'Oh love, I'm sorry. That's terrible.' She came over at once and hugged him, with no trace of her coldness that morning. He relaxed into her, finding comfort in the silken touch of her hair against his cheek and the musky rose scent that she always wore. It was so long since they'd hugged like this. Why had they stopped?

'I need to get down to Cornwall right away,' he said.

She pulled away, breaking their hug, but holding on to his hand. 'Do you need me there too?' Her tone was neutral but he thought he could sense her mind whirring over all the dozens of difficulties that would arise if she suddenly had to go to Cornwall.

'No, it's fine for now. I'll go and then let you know what's happening. There's nothing you can do.'

'I'll take care of everything here. Don't worry.'

He knew she would cope brilliantly. She was so much smaller and more fragile than he was, and yet so strong. And he could turn to her in a crisis. They might have their day-to-day difficulties, but Netta made it a point of honour to form a united front when things got tough. In a way, that was the upside of trouble: a sense that they were pulling at the oars of their little boat together, working hard to keep it afloat, to keep it moving forward as safely as possible. It was only when the crisis had passed and they could breathe again that they would turn and look at each other and remember all the other stuff.

Netta squeezed his hand. 'Be careful, love. I'll be thinking of you.'

'Thanks.' He managed a smile. 'I will.'

The traffic was terrible, of course. Rush hour heading out on the M3 as darkness fell, the most unpleasant time to travel. But who got to choose these things? Who knew when the summons would come? As he drove, crawling slowly along the city's arterial roads, he imagined the rupture in his father's head – maybe it had been building up for days, weeks – and the instant when – bam! – something sundered and blood came rushing out, filling up the hemispheres of the brain in dark clouds, like spilled ink, drowning it in thick fluid. If the rupture were small, contained, and if treatment were given fast, then damage might be limited and rehabilitation possible. If it were a big stroke and not treated in time, then . . . well . . . it could mean an infinite number of things, depending on how much blood and where it went, what pathways it flooded, how much of the brain it killed . . .

Oh Pa.

But when he thought of his father, he got the same words in his mind: *Not yet. I'm not ready. It's not time.* As though Pa's stroke was all about him. *Stop being selfish*, he told himself firmly, and noticed his hands clenched so tightly around the steering wheel that his knuckles were dead white. *It's Pa who matters right now.*

Sally had not phoned him herself, he realised. Well, that was hardly a surprise. She did everything she could to avoid him and had done for years. He'd felt the chilly wind of her disapproval for so long that it was hard to remember that there had once been another time when Sally had been a source of comfort to him. He could still remember running to her crying when he'd fallen off his bike, and how she'd wrapped him in her arms, cooing over him, rubbing his sore arm. He'd inhaled the floral scent of her perfume and the warmth of her clean skin and felt safe. He'd felt better.

But it hadn't been like that for years and years.

Just when we needed her most, she turned against us. And then she insisted on moving out of Tawray, renting it out so that we could never go there. And now she's sold it. The house that should have come to me and Alex.

His dark feelings rose up from the depths, the ones that formed a smoky cloud of hatred around Sally, the architect of so much of his misery. He had only tolerated her for as long as he had because of Pa. And now he was on his way towards her, and heading back to the home he'd avoided for years in order to keep away from her.

He shook his head, trying to dispel the unpleasant sensation.

Pa is what matters. He's my father. She's nothing to me. I have to focus on Pa.

Johnnie drove west, the density of London and its satellite towns giving way to the vistas of the countryside: rolling fields and plains bordered by hedgerows, dark stains of copses and woods, the knots of houses topped off with a church spire. The sky turned orange and pink like a tropical cocktail, then dark blue and black. The evening news played on the radio as Johnnie drove on automatic pilot, considering how many times he'd travelled this stretch of road. The first time he'd properly headed away from home had been to take himself to university, vowing he would never come back. He'd thought then that Pa might resist this threat, or at some point come and persuade him to return home at least for a visit, but he never did. Johnnie had gone to King's College London, choosing the big city perhaps because Pa had said how glad he was to have left, how he never wanted to return there.

Maybe I was testing him, Johnnie thought. *Seeing how important I was to him.* Pa's resistance to London had not made much sense. It was hardly a foreign place to him; after all, he'd lived in the heart of it for years. If anything, he was a member of its most privileged echelons, and would be welcomed back into them anytime he wanted.

It was Sally. She didn't want to see me, or visit me, or let me and Pa get close.

He remembered their one visit, Pa and Sally coming to his shared student house when he lived out in the second year, and the distaste on Sally's face at the grot and mess. She could hardly conceal her horror at being in Tooting, with its grimy streets and litter and high street of fast-food chicken outlets, betting shops and Caribbean supermarkets. They hadn't stayed for long.

'We must get home, Johnnie,' Pa had said, but it had been Sally itching to leave, picking up her coat, winding her pink cashmere scarf around her neck. Johnnie had resisted the urge to grab the two ends and pull them tight, but it took an effort. He sometimes wondered how Pa could be so blind to the way Sally treated him. Why couldn't he see that she never smiled at Johnnie, never really looked at him, contradicted him almost every time he spoke? And the way she hustled Pa away, as though he was some kind of rock star who had to be protected from the attentions of the hoi polloi . . . it was ridiculous. It had gone on for so long – through Johnnie's student days, his marriage to Netta, the arrival of the boys and all that entailed. Pa had barely been allowed to be an observer of Johnnie's life, let alone a participant.

Johnnie had not backed down. He refused to beg. He returned coldness with coldness, and gave out as much rudeness as he received. He wouldn't show how deeply it had hurt him to be shut out.

Not like Alex. She tries to please her instead.

Poor Alex had been kicked around by Sally for years, the complicit victim of Sally's relentless games of manipulation. Johnnie had told her over and over not to give in to it but Alex was too scared to stand up to her. She had seen how little effort Pa had made to chase after Johnnie when he vanished, and she was afraid he would be like that with her too.

'Besides,' Alex had said, 'it's different with me. Sally feels more strongly about me because I'm a woman. For some reason, I'm more of a threat than you are. So I've got to be more careful.'

Johnnie wasn't so sure. He sensed Sally's wariness about him just as much as Alex felt it about her. But perhaps the two of them personified different types of threat: Johnnie posing a risk to material security, and Alex to the emotional bond between Sally and Pa.

The mistake I made was underestimating her. I thought she wouldn't dare touch Tawray. I didn't realise I'd have to fight for it until it was too late.

He had not seen how capable Sally was of deviousness and betrayal. He had thought she would be happy just with marrying Pa and taking Mum's place as the chatelaine of Tawray, and he'd imagined Sally merely wanted to swan around the gracious house, perhaps opening the village fete, or showing off to deferential tourists as she led them around the state rooms on open days. He'd thought that being Pa's wife would be enough for her. But he was wrong. She was determined to take everything for herself, and Johnnie had been stupid not to see how far her ambition stretched.

She wouldn't be satisfied with that. She wants everything, every scrap for herself. Nothing for me. Nothing for Alex.

The house had gone, without their even being offered the chance to say goodbye to it, all managed with the kind of secrecy and shutting out that he'd associated with Sally for so long now. She liked to keep him and Alex in the dark, push them away, making it quite clear that their feelings didn't matter to her. They hadn't even been allowed to take anything from the house. What had happened to all the furniture, the pictures, the china and all the rest? Was it in storage, or had it been sold?

It belonged to Mum. It was her house. Johnnie's fingers tightened around the steering wheel as he drove. *Sally had no right to push Pa to sell it. She had no right to shut us out of the decision making.*

What he didn't understand is what she had ever hoped to achieve by this fracturing of their family. Why had she wanted to inflict pain and suffering on Johnnie and Alex, to shut them off from their father?

'She doesn't know she's doing it,' Alex would say, trying to be charitable. When she came to stay in London, or Johnnie was with her in Cornwall, they would sit up late at night when Netta had long retired and all the children were asleep, talking it all through over bottles of red wine. 'At some level she's protecting herself, I think. Trying to keep herself as the focus of Pa's love and attention. She's probably very insecure. Maybe she's afraid that Mum was a hard act to follow and that Pa doesn't love her as much as he did Mum.'

'You're too kind to her,' Johnnie said, shaking his head. 'I think she's monstrously selfish. And jealous of Mum too, I expect – the fact that Tawray was her house.'

'She can be kind,' Alex reasoned. 'I see her more than you do, and she can be perfectly nice and reasonable.'

'Maybe to you. She never is to me.'

'You're pretty cold to her as well.'

'She started it.'

Alex laughed. 'You sound like a child.'

'I *was* a child,' Johnnie said quickly and he felt that familiar shard of pain in his heart. 'I hadn't done anything to her. But she turned against me. Against both of us, when we were suffering the most.'

Alex nodded solemnly. 'Yes.'

'And why?'

'That's the million-dollar question.'

'Come on, we both know why.' Johnnie fixed her a pier-cing look. 'One word. Mundo.'

Alex's gaze sheared away. 'Maybe,' she said. 'I suppose it's the only thing that makes sense.'

Of course it was Mundo, Johnnie thought as he drove into the evening gloom. *She wanted to make sure he always came first. He's the reason she had to banish us – because we threatened his pre-eminence.*

At the heart of it, though, was the man whose love and attention they were all struggling for: Pa. Now lying in the hospital, close to death. The dreadful resolution might already be here.

All the times he'd driven up and down this road, as a student, a young man, newly married with Netta beside him, a father with babies slumbering in the back as they headed down for a visit at Christmas, the boot crammed with the kit children needed – somewhere in his mind he'd known that one day there would be a final journey, when this long story would come to some kind of end.

I don't want it to be now. I don't want it to be yet.

The dual carriageway turned into single-lane road, the street lamps disappeared and he was driving into pitch dark-ness, seeing only what his headlights picked out. He passed the turn-off for Tawray although it was almost invisible in the dark, and felt the bitter pang that now accompanied thoughts of that beautiful old house, gone forever.

Don't think about that now. You have to think about Pa.

Chapter Three

Alex pulled the car to a halt outside Tim's small terraced house in a newly built estate on the edge of town.

'Here we are!' she said brightly, not wanting the girls to pick up on her anxiety, but they were wide-eyed and muted. Hurried evening trips to Dad's house were not part of their usual routine. Jasmine was usually in bed by now and she looked out of place, sitting in her car seat, her pyjamas under her coat and Teddy Weddy under one arm. Alex got them out of the car and the girls stood huddled together in the darkness of the porch as she rang the doorbell. The urge to get to the hospital was powerful, making Alex edgy and breathless. 'Come *on*,' she muttered under her breath as they waited. At last the door opened.

'Oh!' She blinked with surprise at the figure standing in the brightly lit hall. 'Hello?'

It was a woman, small and neat with honey-blonde hair that fell to her shoulders and big blue eyes. Not Tim. 'Hi. You must be Alex.'

'Yes. You must be Chloe.'

'That's right.'

Alex stared at the other woman, feeling Scarlett stiffen beside her and clutch her hand more tightly. 'I was expecting Tim to be here.'

'He just texted. He's been held up at work.'

'I need to leave the girls with him.'

'You can leave them with me. It's fine.'

'Mummy,' Jasmine said softly, and she pushed herself close to Alex's side. She seemed suddenly so small.

'I don't know,' Alex said uncertainly. She knew Scarlett and Jasmine had met Chloe but it was a leap to being on their own with her. *And I don't know her. But what choice do I have?*

'They'll be perfectly okay,' Chloe said.

Alex looked at Scarlett, who was mature for seven years old. She gazed back with solemn eyes. 'Will you be all right here with Chloe till Dad gets back? So I can get to the hospital?'

'Yes,' Scarlett said bravely. 'Won't we, Jasmine?'

Jasmine hugged Teddy Weddy tightly and said nothing.

'Thank you, sweetie,' Alex whispered. Then she said brightly, 'You'll be fine, Jasmine. Scarlett's with you. And Dad will be home soon.'

'I'm not going to bite,' Chloe said with a smile.

'Of course not.' Alex tried to smile back, but she was fighting her own internal battle. Every fibre inside her resisted sending her daughters into the house with a strange woman. She could feel their reluctance and it pained her. In any other circumstance, she would take them straight home. But that was the whole point. She didn't have a choice. 'Go on. I'll come and pick you up as soon as I can. If you have to stay, Dad will get you to school tomorrow.'

'I can make hot chocolate,' Chloe suggested, and Alex felt a small wave of gratitude.

'Thanks, they'd love that. Clean your teeth afterwards, remember.' The girls moved slowly past Chloe into the brightly lit hall. The stairs at the end led up into gloom.

Oh God, I don't want them to go in there alone with her.

But she said, 'Goodnight, sweethearts, be good, I'll be back before you know it,' and turned to leave, hearing the door close behind them with a sense of despair that she couldn't explain.

Alex arrived at the hospital fifteen minutes later, hurrying into the brightly lit lobby, so intent on reaching Pa that she hardly noticed her surroundings. She disliked hospitals and had had both her babies at home. Even going in for a scan had made her palms prickle and sweat break out around her hairline. She knew the work they did was good, but there was something about them that she found difficult to endure.

But this was different. She was heading for a specialist unit devoted to stroke treatments. It was her father's great luck that he lived only a twenty-minute ambulance race to one of the best units in the country. Instead of panic, she felt relief, knowing that all this – the staff, the hospital paraphernalia, the beeps and buzzes – meant they were busy keeping Pa alive.

In the lift, she pulled out her phone and tapped out a text.

Tim, where are you? I had to leave the girls with a stranger. I'm not happy. Please let me know as soon as you're back. I'm at the hospital.

She sent it, wondering if the girls were all right. The way Scarlett had stiffened beside her bothered her. Didn't she like Chloe? If not, why not? So far Alex had resisted talking about this new woman to them; Tim's girlfriend hadn't seemed real until now and, in any case, she might be a flash in the pan. But if she was going to be in charge of the girls . . . well, that was another matter. Just then a text popped up.

I'm home now. All fine.

That was obviously all she was going to get from Tim, but at least she could relax knowing the girls were with their father.

The lift doors opened and she emerged into the stroke unit. A nurse at reception directed her, and she found Pa's room down a long corridor. The first thing she saw as she went in was the back of Sally's blonde head, the frosted high-lights set crisply into place with the usual layer of hairspray. Beneath that was an expanse of sugary pink cashmere cardi-gan; Alex sometimes wondered where Sally went to find such expensive clothes in shades that were so subtly horrible. And she was barely sixty and yet had settled easily into dressing like someone ten years older, as though she was keeping pace with her husband and hadn't noticed that modern sixty-somethings didn't have to set their hair and wear kilts and sensible woollens. Johnnie said she was still stuck in the eighties, her glory years. That was why she liked to clip little velvet bows on the fronts of her black patent shoes. Alex had giggled and said, 'For some bizarre reason, she wants to look like a cross between an aged duchess and Dolly Parton – all blonde hair and pink, but in calf-length skirts, jumpers and pearls.'

'God, you're right,' Johnnie had said with a guffaw. 'I love that. The Queen meets Mae West.'

'The love child of Margaret Thatcher and Patsy from *Ab Fab*.'

Laughing at Sally was one of their mutual pleasures.

'Otherwise we'd cry,' Johnnie would say simply.

'Laughing is better,' Alex would agree. So they did.

I can't laugh about her now.

'Hi,' Alex said quietly, her gaze going straight to her father, lying unconscious in the high hospital bed, connected to myriad blinking machines and a drip of clear fluid.

Sally turned, her eyebrows high, then saw it was Alex, and her face dropped just a little. 'Oh, I thought you were the consultant. You've been ages.'

'I came as quickly as I could. I had to give the girls supper and get them to Tim.' She leaned down as Sally tipped her face up to receive her kiss. Alex brushed her lips over the powdered cheek, smelling the familiar mixture of floral scent, soap and perfumed washing powder. 'How's Pa?'

Sally blinked hard and they both looked over at the prone figure on the bed.

Alex's heart contracted at the sight.

He looks so much older.

Pa lay in his hospital bed, white hair against a white pillow, a light blue hospital gown covering his shoulders, sheet drawn up to his chest. One arm lay on top of the sheet, attached to a snaking clear tube gummed down to the skin by a blue plaster. Pa's cheeks seemed to have sunk in on themselves and they were crazed with red veins – or perhaps it was only that the veins were more visible now that his complexion was a whitish-grey. His eyes were closed and his mouth slightly open, and he lay unmoving as though in a deep sleep. His skin looked thin, his hair wispy, and everything about him seemed worn out and exhausted.

When did he stop being Pa?

Somehow she hadn't noticed him changing from the father she adored: the tall, vital man with the dark thatch of hair, the jet-black colour she had inherited, and the deep blue eyes that made him look like some dangerous Irish gypsy hero from an old romance.

Fear seized her, potently mixed with love. Was she really about to lose him? *No. Not yet. I'm not ready.* She had thought there were years left. He was still young, only just seventy. He was fit and healthy, he loved to walk and play golf and enjoy life . . . *This wasn't supposed to happen.*

'We're waiting on the scan results. And the consultant is due anytime. Meanwhile, he's stable.' Sally's voice had a touch of a tremor in it.

Alex dropped her bag and went over to Pa's side. She put her hand on his, noticing the purple blotches and liver spots and the thick blue rope of vein running over it. It was cool to the touch and for a moment she felt a rush of panic that he was dead, then saw he was still breathing. 'But you said he was taken ill yesterday?'

'That's right.'

'Sally, why on earth didn't you ring me then?' Alex said, looking over at her stepmother, bewildered.

Sally's voice took on a note of steel. 'My first priority was David, not you. I did what was best for him.' She gave the little sniff Alex knew well, the one that showed offence had been taken. 'I'm sorry if you feel that wasn't good enough.'

Alex reached inside herself for calm. Her mantra was 'don't let her hurt you' and she muttered it mentally a couple of times, finding it helped. She wasn't going to rise to it. It always felt as though Sally was spoiling for a fight, ready to take offence, keen to be outraged. Alex coped by never responding but skating over it lightly as though she hadn't noticed the haughtiness, the warning tones, the lifted chin. 'I've called Johnnie. He's on his way. You can tell us all about it when he gets here.'

Sally's lips tightened slightly. She was no fan of Johnnie's. She liked to keep him as far away as possible. Alex had a sudden flashback to a summer holiday, when Sally had laid a large lunch for everyone on the table in the garden – there must have been visitors that day, because there seemed to be lots of places. But when Johnnie came up to sit down, there was no place for him. Sally had said something poisonously sweet in that way she had: 'Oh, I'm so sorry! I thought you preferred to eat your lunch inside. You seem to enjoy your own company so much these days. I've left yours on the kitchen table.' That was how Alex remembered it. Johnnie's face and its stony expression, her own sense of being stabbed in the heart on his behalf. Sally had always been kinder to her than to Johnnie, knowing how Pa adored her. Sally was far too smart to hurt Alex in the way she liked to punish Johnnie. She had her own secret, hidden ways of doing that.

Alex gazed at her father, then sighed and bent down to kiss his cool cheek. 'I'm here, Pa,' she whispered. 'Johnnie's coming too. You'll be all right. You're going to get better.' She squeezed his hand, as though wanting to send some of her own vitality through the barrier of their skin and into his bloodstream. 'You can do it.'

'Of course, David does too much,' Sally said mournfully. 'He takes on far too many commitments, and he won't listen. He just accepted the role of Chair of Governors at Cheadlings Prep. I said it was more than he could manage, but he won't have it.' She shook her head, her green-blue eyes sad, and took out her make-up bag, snapped open a compact and inspected herself. She patted away a non-existent shine with a small make-up puff. 'What with overseeing the clubhouse renovation at the golf course and sitting on the board of trustees for the hospice . . .' She pulled out a lipstick, twisted up the pale pink stick and applied it over her lips. 'I warned him, I really did.' Her eyes filled with tears as she put her make-up away. 'And now look . . .'

'I'm sure you did, you've always looked after him,' Alex said softly. She sat down in the chair next to Pa's bed, still holding his hand.

'Yes,' Sally said, but as though she were contradicting Alex, not agreeing with her. 'He's my world.'

Alex nodded. She knew what was coming: the familiar litany of everything Sally did for Alex's father, as though it were some huge gift to Alex herself, for which she should be endlessly grateful. From Alex's point of view, it was a little different. She thought Sally had done quite well from marrying Pa: her life was hardly onerous; it was comfortable, ordered and looked very satisfactory from the outside. She seemed to get her own way most of the time, and she and Pa lived the enviable life of prosperous pensioners in good health, with plenty of holidays and outings and treats.

Alex sat there quietly as Sally talked about her many duties and obligations and how hard she worked to look after Pa, but she wasn't really listening. Instead, the fact that Sally hadn't called her immediately when Pa first got ill was running round her mind, making her nervous.

Why didn't she call me?

Alex had long learned to trust the prickles of instinct that warned her trouble was in the offing. Like a farmer who could sniff a storm in the air, she had discovered she had an internal warning system that pinged loudly when things with Sally were veering off course and appearances were not to be trusted. Sometimes Sally could be outwardly happy to see her but the faintest chill in a kiss on the cheek, or a swerved glance, or the tiniest change in tone of voice could tell the real truth: something was badly wrong and Alex was going to be punished for it. They would set off down the well-trodden path, its every step familiar. First, Alex would have to find out what had upset Sally, whose modus operandi was pretty familiar after all these years. The almost imperceptible chilliness was the first sign. Then the freeze set in: phone calls unanswered, lunches or meetings cancelled without explanation, sudden illnesses that meant she had to retire to bed like a Victorian matron with the vapours. Goodness only knew how long that state of affairs would continue if Alex didn't step in to end it, but she always did; she suspected Sally was quite capable of keeping it up for years, if she wanted to. Her next step in the face of Alex's questions about what was wrong was to deny everything for the first dozen times of asking, before finally beginning to hint at the problem. Then, when Alex stumbled on it – the throwaway comment, missed call or unthinking action that had caused the offence – the sniff and averted glance would announce that the source of all the trouble had been found. After that, it was time for humble apologies, flowers and promises to be good.

She had been talking about it only this week, when she and Di had gone out for their weekly drink at the bistro in town. The arrangement had started as a book club with half a dozen others who had all gradually dropped out, so it ended up just the two of them no longer discussing books, but talking about their lives and sharing their problems.

'Why do you do it?' Di had asked, astonished, when Alex poured it all out about her latest transgression. It had turned out that Sally was offended she had not yet been told anything about the girls' school carol service, which, for some reason, she seemed keen to attend despite never being interested in previous years. Only once Alex had worked out the problem, apologised, explained that she hadn't yet been given the official form to fill in for seats and promised to include Sally and David when she did, had Sally thawed. Then Sally revealed that she'd heard the mayoress was expected to attend and she was hoping to ensnare her in a friendly chat.

Alex rolled her eyes at Di. 'Nothing to do with watching the girls.'

'Tell her to get knotted!' Di said indignantly.

Alex shook her head. 'Can't do that. I have to keep her happy.'

'Really? Why?'

'She's my stepmother. My father's wife. I don't have a choice.'

'I still don't see why you have to be pushed around. How long has she been married to your father?'

'Since I was nine. But she's been around as long as I can remember actually.' Alex frowned. Yes, there had never been a time when she hadn't known Sally. That was an odd thought. 'She lived near us before my mother died.'

Di raised her eyebrows. 'Your mother knew your father's second wife?'

'Yes. Very well.'

'Oh.' Di looked a little awkward, and then said positively, 'So maybe she'd be happy your dad ended up with her.'

'Maybe. I don't know.' Alex still found it too painful to think about. Going into what her mother's mental processes might have been all those years ago was not something she could do.

Di took a sip of her wine and said, 'It's odd because the way you talk about her, it seems like you two don't know each other awfully well. But she's known you since you were a child.'

'Yes.' Alex stared at the table. It was hard to explain the strange currents of emotion that ran between her and Sally, and the way their relationship had developed. *Because I don't really understand them myself.*

'So you shouldn't have to play her games,' Di said firmly. 'Don't humour her, you're just encouraging it. Tell her frankly she's being passive aggressive and you'd appreciate some honest communication.'

Alex sighed, thinking that only someone as good-hearted and uncomplicated as Di could think it would be so simple. 'You don't understand. I can't afford to piss her off. I think she might be capable of getting me banished.'

Sally must always be placated. She was the gatekeeper to Pa, and Alex had understood from early on that she must pay the gatekeeper for entrance to the fortress that was Pa. If she failed, the gates would slam shut, possibly forever.

'So she's a textbook evil stepmother? A stepmonster?'

'No.' Alex shook her head. 'Nothing so black and white. I'm very fond of her in lots of ways. But she's got this power in my life and it's as though she's always testing it to keep me in line.'

'What's the worst she can do? You've got power too. Don't forget that. And she couldn't stop you seeing your father. He adores you. He'd never allow that to happen.'

'Don't be so sure. He might not like it, but he'd always choose her over me. I just know it.'

'Why should he have to choose?' Di made a face. 'He's a grown man, surely he can see that he can love Sally and you at the same time and without the permission of either of you. Maybe he could even mediate between you.'

Alex stared into her glass of wine, gazing into the honey-coloured depths, helpless to explain. The idea that Pa might broker an accord between her and Sally was impossible. If Sally was his gatekeeper, then he was hers at the same time. If Alex asked him what she had done to offend Sally, he would prevaricate, tell Sally's own lies for her – 'She's really not well, Alex, she has a terrible migraine' – and be as adamant as she was that there was nothing wrong. When things were finally set to rights, his relief would be obvious but still, he would say nothing about it.

'No,' she said finally to Di. 'It just doesn't work like that. Trust me.'

Has Sally finally slammed the gate shut?

As she sat now by Pa's hospital bed, his cool hand still in hers, Alex realised that all that placating, all that humility and backing down and refusing to fight had had one purpose – to ensure that she was never shut out at a moment like this, when the crisis came.

She felt a stab of pain in her stomach. Was Sally so unforgiving after all? Would everything Alex had ever done – as a thoughtless child, a hurting teenager, an impetuous young adult – be held against her? Sally had the greatest weapon still in her hands, and might desire to wield it while she could.

41

She might keep me away from Pa, even now. The pain was bitter in her mouth. Maybe Sally had already succeeded. *What if Pa never regains consciousness? I'll never get the chance to say goodbye. How would I cope with that?*

She was afraid of how that would make her feel and what she would feel towards Sally. And Johnnie too. He already loathed Sally far more viscerally than she did. The sale of Tawray had filled him with cold fury. If Sally had prevented their saying farewell to their father . . . She shivered internally, and her gaze went towards the door as if expecting it to open, but nothing happened. She bent down to take her phone out of her bag, not hearing anything but the drone of Sally's voice, to check for a text from Johnnie.

But just as she was doing that, the door swung open, and he was there, her older brother, his tawny hair windswept, his eyes full of anxiety, bringing the cold air of outside with him on his coat.

'Johnnie!' she said, jumping up, full of relief to see him.

'I'm here,' he said, coming in, gazing at Pa with frightened eyes. 'Am I in time?'

'Yes, yes,' Alex said, going to hug him. 'He's stable, there's no change. The consultant is due any minute.'

Sally said in a cool voice, 'I think he's here now. Yes. He's just outside. Stand back, Johnnie, let's give him room to get to your father.'

The door opened, and the consultant came in.

Chapter Four

Inside David Pengelly's brain, a mass of blood has drowned a huge proportion of his grey matter. The scans, already pored over by experts, are being shown to the family, held up against a light box so that they can see the damage: the great black blots that reveal where the brain has died.

His wife gasps with horror at the sight, her hands pressed to her cheeks, her mouth a round O of despair. She can see without being told that the damage is extensive. The children, when they speak, sound stunned. Johnnie's voice is low, a rolling deep bass, and businesslike despite the shock. He asks for exact details, for facts. Alex's is higher, melodious like her mother's, despite the note of sadness and disbelief. She wants to know what hope there is, what can be done.

The consultant is talking. He's telling them gently that there is little hope. He doesn't go too far; he doesn't say the nerve endings in the damaged areas are extinct, the neurons inactive, the neural paths that once flashed instructions now mere stagnant canals of fluid. But he lets them know that the chances of David recovering are very slim indeed.

David, deep inside himself, knows it must be true. Darkness is falling, his spirit is disconnecting from his physical form, or perhaps is in retreat to the last living areas of his brain. Gradually he has closed down the bits of himself that are no longer needed: he has almost no movement, his eyes are closed and will never see again, and his body is powering down, conserving its last remnants of energy for breath and heart beats, for swallowing, for the warmth in his core that even now is ebbing away.

He is not afraid. He is gently letting go, slipping softly under the water and far from everything, back to the silent darkness from which he came seventy years ago. In the depths, he is still there, though. He knows that he has lived a life and that it is nearly over. Like a diver spotting the phosphorescence of deep-sea creatures, he sees lights in the darkness that swirl towards him and become pictures.

The children.

There is Johnnie, just born. And then a giggling toddler, tottering past. Here is Alex, wide-eyed, sucking her thumb, watching, adoring her brother. Now she is a girl, poker-straight dark hair, skin tanned from the Tawray summer. In seconds, they are growing, they are adults. Here are the grandchildren, new sources of pleasure, but less visceral, less immediate, less intense. And here is Sally. Oh Sally – sweet and shy, no one at first and then the port in the storm he needed so badly. His sun and moon. Oh the love, the restorative, life-saving love she gave him.

Dearest Sally. I want to stay with you.

The thought gives him a moment of longing, regret and

grief and he fears he is about to be engulfed by utter, desperate and unbearable despair. But the soft silence of approaching death soothes him, as if to say, 'What does it matter now? There's nothing you can do. Just accept.'

So he does. Calm returns.

Tawray.

His consolation comes: a visit, as he floats like an angel or a sprite across his beloved home, through its doors and into its rooms, out again to soar over the land towards the sea, and then back to the dear, familiar view of the turreted roof, the arched front door in the tower.

But someone is missing from his memories.

What about Julia?

Her name conjures her, like the spell that summons a djinn. Her face appears before him, then her body, youthful and beautiful, and for a moment he remembers the deep, profound pleasure of being flesh, being alive, hungering for her and finding total satisfaction and joy in possessing her. *Oh Julia.* She smiles that bewitching smile; she is as she was and he can recall her in utter clarity, down to the scent of her hair and the taste of her mouth, and he wants to reach out and hold her.

And then he realises with something like happiness: *Everyone is coming to me. But I am leaving. I am going to Julia.*

Chapter Five

1975

'It's very tiresome, but there's not much to be done about it.'

The voice was quite nearby and it startled Julia, who looked up from her book. Gran was coming into the drawing room with someone, talking as she went.

'Harry wants to send her away to St Agatha's. He's asked me to pay for it as he is so short since the divorce.'

'Still? He's got a bit of a nerve. After all, he divorced Jocasta seven years ago.' That was Aunt Victoria, Daddy's sister, who was always staring at Julia with her cold fish eyes, as though inspecting her for signs of incipient madness.

Gran passed by the window but didn't notice the tips of Julia's sandals poking out from behind the curtain. 'Jocasta cost rather a lot to get rid of. That flat in London nearly wiped him out for five years. And St Agatha's is going to mean quite a commitment.'

St Agatha's. They must be talking about me.

Daddy had been telling her only recently about the school she was going to be sent to in the autumn and how blissful it was going to be to play with lots of other girls and learn hockey and French and Latin. Julia was looking forward to it. Her ears pricked up.

An impatient sigh and Aunt Victoria said, 'Why go to the trouble? When Julia's only a pup from the second litter.'

I'm WHAT?

In her hiding place behind the curtain in the drawing room, Julia's mouth opened in an expression of silent outrage. *A pup from the second litter?* She wasn't exactly sure what that meant, but her aunt's tone was unmistakably scornful. She drew her skinny legs up under her chin and bit her knee to stop herself squeaking in indignation.

Gran didn't know about Julia's little hidey hole. She didn't know that sometimes, when the sun was out, this corner became a blazingly warm nook, extra cosy from the radiator that had been installed underneath the little window seat. There, with a delicious view out over the gardens towards the woods and the cliff, Julia hid herself away on the old tapestry cushion, the heavy curtain providing extra insulation, and read her books, a store of apples and sweets by her side.

Aunt Victoria added, 'A bitch pup, at that.'

'Please, darling, don't remind me. If we've been through all of this, and can't even get a boy out of it, then I just don't know. But don't take it out on Julia, Vicky dear, she's a sweet little thing.'

'She's a terror. Always getting into trouble. It wouldn't matter so much if she was a boy, but she's not.'

'Perhaps we'll be lucky this time,' Gran said consolingly. 'And if we're not, well, so much the better for Quentin.'

Aunt Victoria said lightly, 'Well, there is that. One hardly knows what to hope for. Quentin could make something of this place.'

Julia thought of Quentin, her cousin. He was all right, she had nothing against him, but she did think he was boring. Even though he was eighteen, he seemed more like thirty-five. He was tall, thin, and supposedly very clever, but he had no capacity for jokes, and that always made people seem dull. Books didn't seem to give him the kind of pleasure they gave Julia. It was obvious that if the new baby was a girl, Quentin might be the one to get Tawray but she couldn't see what he might make of it when he'd never shown even a scrap of awareness of Tawray's magic. He didn't run across the gardens, into the woods and down to the sea, glorying in the buffeting wind and the tangy salt air; or lean on the old brick walls of the kitchen garden, soaking up their warmth, before hunting for fruit in the orchard. He didn't like hiding in the many delightfully dark cupboards, or dressing up from the old trunks in the attics, or scaring himself stupid in the dusty cellar by going to the furthest, blackest, dankest vault where the spiders lived.

He doesn't love it like I do. She sighed. Violet, Quentin's younger sister, was no better. She was timid and so literal it was impossible to talk to her. The thought of Quentin and Violet in charge of Tawray was a miserable one. *Oh, why are babies so much trouble?*

Mummy was in bed again, just like all the other times when a baby was on the way. They never told Julia what was happening, but she knew well enough by now because it always went the same way. Mummy would get sicker and sicker, vomiting and fainting, suffering so badly that once Julia had heard her declare with passion that she wished she were dead. It had made her clammy with horror to hear it.

It was Lorraine, the nanny, who confirmed what she'd already guessed, sitting by the fireplace in the nursery, one of her favourite magazines on her lap, smoking Silk Cut. 'Your mum's pregnant again.'

'Why is she so sick?'

'That's morning sickness. Your mum gets it worse than anyone I've ever seen. And it never seems to end. My sister never had anything, my other sister was sick in the morning for six weeks and then fine. But your mum suffers something rotten.'

Julia found it terrifying that Mummy was possessed by this dreadful sickness, so severe that even a drop of water was enough to send her gagging and retching to the loo. She would get thinner and paler and more utterly miserable until she couldn't move from her bed, but lay there, grey-faced and weak, a big bowl beside her to be sick into. She looked to Julia as if she might die, and when she smiled wanly and said in a voice reedy with suffering that she was going to be fine, Julia found it hard to believe her.

'Why is the baby doing this to Mummy?' she asked Lorraine, but Lorraine didn't have much in the way of answers.

'Dunno,' she would say with a shrug. 'My mum says it's because your mum is too grand to be up the duff. You know what I mean?'

Julia was baffled but it was often hard to get much sense

out of Lorraine, who seemed to talk another language most of the time.

It would be worth all the suffering, Julia thought, if there were a baby at the end of it. But after weeks of being sick, Mummy would get better and that would be that. No baby ever appeared. It had happened twice now, and it was happening again. Julia wondered if this time, there would actually be a baby, and if anyone would ever tell her what on earth was going on.

So now, she shrunk down behind the curtain and listened hard.

'I don't think that woman is capable of bearing children,' Aunt Victoria declared.

'She must be. There's Julia.'

'Yes,' Aunt Victoria said darkly. 'There's Julia. And yet there hasn't been another since.'

'It's not unknown, is it? What are you suggesting?'

'Nothing, nothing. Only that Harry hasn't been able to father a child with her successfully, not since the wedding. And Julia followed hard on the heels of the honeymoon.'

Gran tutted. 'Come on, Vicky, she loves him, you have to give her that.'

'Maybe. But she wanted this. Like they all do. Jocasta was the same.'

'You're too cynical.'

'I'm not, Mother. It's the truth.'

'Well, I can't help feeling sorry for her, I've never seen anyone have such an awful time in pregnancy. But she keeps going through with it for Harry's sake.'

A sniff from Aunt Victoria. 'It's the price she's chosen to pay, for this. For Tawray.'

I hope they go away, Julia thought. She didn't want to hear any more.

Luckily they didn't stay for long, and when they'd gone, Julia whisked out from behind the curtain, pushing her book and apples under a cushion, and ran down the corridor and out of the side door, onto the mossy gravel near the leaky drainpipe, and then sprinted out and across the velvety green lawn. It was June, and oh, the sense of beauty and freedom at Tawray. It fired something in her blood: the heady mixture of open sky, the cool dark wood, and the glittering crystal of the sea in the distance. Life flowed around her; it sang in the throats of birds, it radiated from the acid green grass and in the melting beauty of the summer blooms: mountains of mop-headed roses, huge drooping pom-poms of white hydrangea, purple blades of rhododendron. The gardens were a riot of colour and scent, everything thrusting upwards towards the life-giving sun, or splaying out to the cool grass and the baking gravel of the paths. Lavender in purple starbursts lined borders, each plant alive with a cloud of murmuring bees. White butterflies shimmered among the yellow-flecked *Alchemilla mollis*.

Poor Mummy, to be in bed, sick, when there was here, there was outside.

Julia ran through the series of walled gardens, the ancient bricks warm as bread ovens, and out though the last door with its great iron latch into the wilderness behind. She raced through the wild grass, letting the little fat grass heads whip across her legs as she went, sometimes grabbing one and pulling it through her fingertips so that the furry softness came off in a bunch and then floated away in a tiny silvery cloud when she splayed her fingers out.

If she carried on straight ahead, she would enter the woods, take the shady, steep path that twisted downwards, with ropes set at the steepest places to hold on to, and sometimes even steps cut into the hillside, and then emerge suddenly on the path that led along the side of the channel to the sea. The path had a sea wall along it but when the weather was rough, the waves would curl over it and land in huge, splattering, watery explosions. Julia had never been there when the weather was really rough, it was far too dangerous; Daddy had said she could be swept out to sea if the waves were big enough.

But she wasn't going to the sea today. Instead she veered to her left through the wilderness and down a small slope to the lake, which was the latest place of fascination for her. Last year, it had been the roof, where she had set up a hideaway in one of the towers. In the old days, apparently, ladies and gentlemen had walked around upon the roof, to enjoy the views and gaze out to sea. There were two hollow towers on opposite corners, just big enough for a small supper table, where refreshments could be laid out for them. Julia had turned one into her special place, with blankets and books and supplies stolen from the kitchen, and spent hours there on her own. Once the weather turned, it had been too cold to stay in the tower for long, and the rain blew in through the opening and spoiled things.

This year, she had discovered a platform in a tree by the lake, put there years ago from the looks of it, built firmly across a sturdy branch that stuck out over the water. Julia had persuaded Tom, the gardener, to hang a knotted rope for her to climb up, and she had created her own pulley system with a basket so that it was easy to lift her things up there. Now it would be her place for the summer. The only bother was the midges from the water, which liked to feast on her bare legs and leave her covered in itchy spots, but Lorraine had given her a strong-smelling citrus oil to rub into her skin and keep them away. From her platform, Julia could see the rotting old boathouse with the skiff in it. She'd had a look in there a few times, but didn't like the darkness and the dingy, weed-filled water beneath the boat. She was not tempted to try and row out into the lake, even with her father's warning to stay off the water.

'That boat hasn't been looked at since I was a boy with Uncle Reggie. Don't get in it, Julia, do you hear me?'

Julia nodded, and meant it. She loved the sea, icy and alive, but she didn't much like the look of the lake, so still, so full of dark fronds and little flicking shadows. It was slimy and grotty, and the surface was flecked with insects, dead leaves, waxy water lilies and floating detritus.

The platform was romantic, though, hidden among the branches, with a pleasing sense that she was on board a private ship, sailing down a jungle river, or hidden among the tribes of the Amazon.

Now she reached the rope hanging down the tree trunk and heaved herself up it, quick at grasping a knot, walking up the trunk until her feet hit the platform and then swinging the rest of her body up afterwards, and she lay, panting, on the smooth planks.

'Pup from the second litter!' she said aloud. *What does it mean? I need to ask Lala.*

Lala was her older half-sister, the daughter from Daddy's first marriage to Jocasta, the ex-wife who was only a name to Julia, always mysterious and absent and a little scary. Lala was not scary – quite the opposite. She came for a couple of weeks last summer, as she usually did, because that's when her mother went to France, to spend June to early September at her large house in Provence with her second husband and their family. Lala told her all about it: the jade-green lizards that lay in the sun and then flicked out of sight when you tried to get near. The blazing hot summer days full of the sound of crickets and the scent of hot rosemary . . . but no sea.

'No sea?' Julia demanded, outraged. 'That's terrible!'

'It's too far away for every day. There are swimming pools,' Lala said and, seeing Julia's face, 'Good ones, honestly.'

'But it's not the same.'

'No. Not the same. But it's pretty nice.'

'Can I come?' Julia would ask, more in a show of support than any real desire to go there. She wouldn't want to leave Mummy, or Tawray, and most certainly not the sea in summer, the only time worth living for in the entire year.

'Of course,' Lala would say breezily, even though they both knew it wasn't possible.

Julia didn't mind not going. It was wonderful to have Lala, who was older and might have been a complete rotter, but was instead the reverse: a kindred spirit, a fellow romancer who understood all the millions of magical possibilities at Tawray. The five years she had on Julia might have made her a tiresome would-be grown-up, but she wasn't even jealous about the fact that Tawray had once been her home and now was not.

'This was my bedroom before, you know,' she said to Julia when they'd gone in to lie on the very hard mattress of her canopied bed.

'Really?' Julia looked around, trying to imagine Lala sleeping here and not in the Pink Bedroom, which was hers when she stayed.

'Yes. Nicer now. I had the oldest curtains on this bed; they smelled mouldy. These ones are lovely and new. Your mother must have insisted. Daddy listens to her, doesn't he? He didn't listen to my mother much. They fought instead.'

Julia looked anxiously over at the older girl, worried in case she was angry about the situation, but Lala didn't seem to care. She was nice to Mummy, and nice to Julia, and she seemed perfectly happy with the way things were.

She loved the tower on the roof. 'You've made this brilliant, much better than I did,' she said excitedly when she saw it. 'I didn't think to bring anything up, not like this. They wouldn't have let me in any case.'

'Lorraine doesn't mind what I do,' Julia explained, and it

was true. As long as Lorraine was left in peace with her magazines and the kettle, an ashtray and the nursery television, then she was happy for Julia to do exactly as she liked.

Lala looked very pleased at everything Julia had assembled in the tower: the rugs, the boxes of keepsakes and books. 'But we can make it even better,' she said. They raided the house for things to create a tiny but magnificent boudoir: the smallest paintings, filched from shadowy alcoves or back passages; embroidered cushions and velvet footstools to sit on. A miniature carved trunk, a tiny guest room bookshelf filled with Tom Thumb volumes from the nursery. That was where the world began to take shape: Morotania, their country, ruled by them. The tower was their palace where they were both queens; the house beneath was their kingdom, the gardens part of their spreading domains and the neighbouring kingdoms, both ally and enemy. But there were enemies within the kingdom. Aunt Victoria, or the evil fairy Malatrix, as they called her, whose oozing flattery towards Lala and chilly critical demeanour towards Julia marked her out as a bad 'un. Gran was their aged Lady Chancellor, in thrall to Malatrix. Mummy was the Fairy Queen – beautiful, fragile, adored – and Daddy the Grand Vizier or, sometimes, the Old King, but actually the Old King was supposed to be dead, so he was mostly the Grand Vizier. Everyone in the house had a role, whether they knew it or not, and hours passed by in playing Morotania, drawing its maps and naming its places, creating its laws and rules and geography, chronicling its history and sending its fleets to sea and its armies to war. The joint queens ruled over it benignly, wisely and justly, riding out on their white horses to survey their kingdom and greet their people, or retiring to their palace to eat teacakes and drink lemonade.

When Lala's stay in the house was over, and it was time for her to take the ferry across the sea to France to be with her mother, Julia was bereft. It was no fun to be the Queen of Morotania on her own. The kingdom lost its colour and vivacity and faded to a silly parlour game without Lala there to help create the magical alchemy that brought it to life. She moped after Lala left, unable to find pleasure in anything, until the vividness of her presence wore off and life went back to normal, with Julia doing things mostly on her own.

Lala would be visiting again soon, once her final school exams were over, and Julia could hardly wait, but she wanted some answers before then, so she wrote to Lala, who replied in a very Lala-ish way.

Hail my sister Queen!

How go the affairs of the kingdom in my absence? I hope that scurvy wench Lorraine of the Silken Cut has not caused thee anguish. If she hath, I will condemn her to the stocks when I return and we will take much pleasure in smashing her in the boosh with rotten tomatoes.

Meanwhile, thou askest what meaneth the phrase 'pup of the second litter'. Dear Queen, don't give this another thought. Methinks thou has listened anon to Malatrix

and this is part of her game as an agent provocateur. It is
true that you are fruit of the Old King's second marriage,
but that is much as Elizabeth I was, so don't let it worry
you. If they think it means you don't matter, you just
prove them wrong, that's all.

Mummy said your mummy is having another baby.
I hope she's all right.

See you soon, O royal sister. I hope the raspberries
will be ripe when I get there, so we can have a proper
feast.

Love from Queen Lala the Lackadaisical

The letter made Julia laugh, even though she didn't understand some of it. And, she decided, if being from the second litter made her Elizabeth I, then so much the better. Sometimes she tried to make herself look like the queen in her coronation portrait, which she'd seen in a history book. She made a cloak from an embroidered bedspread in one of the grand bedrooms, a crown from gold paper, and an orb and sceptre from a small cannonball from the display in the hall and the nursery poker wrapped in more of the gold paper. Then she spread her long tawny hair out over her shoulders and sat dead still in a chair opposite the mirror taken from the bathroom wall, practising her Elizabethan look.

'You look proper royal,' Lorraine said admiringly when she came in and saw her. 'Your hair looks lovely.'

The long red-gold locks were what made her look like Elizabeth; she didn't share the queen's almond-shaped eyes, but had large, round greeny-brown eyes flecked with gold.

She took after her mother's side of the family. Her father's family were fair, with long, bony noses and high foreheads, like Aunt Victoria, with her eyes the colour of watery sky. Lala was like that too, sharp and intelligent-looking, fair and blue-eyed.

But I am a pup of the second litter, Julia reminded herself as she looked at her own face and saw the drama in her eyes and mouth, and knew she wasn't like the portraits in the gallery – prim and controlled and proper. She was something altogether new.

The screaming rang through the house. Julia woke and climbed out of bed, her heart hammering with fear. There was scuffling and noise downstairs, footsteps on the staircase, voices raised. She peered down over the banister and saw that the doctor was hurrying up the stairs, carrying his bag.

She knew what it must be: it was Mummy and the baby.

She already hated the baby, just like she hated the other ones, for making Mummy suffer so much torment. She could hear Daddy on the telephone, calling the local hospital and asking them to send the ambulance as quickly as possible.

Julia sat on the stairs, shivering despite the warmth of the summer night. The noises subsided; they were all in Mummy and Daddy's bedroom. Then the screaming, muffled now, started again, coming in waves, then quietening.

All she wanted was for the terrible noise to stop, for every-thing to be safe and normal again, for the baby to go away like all the others had. But it was beyond the time when babies simply vanished and were never spoken of again.

Mummy was too large and swollen for that, there was most definitely a baby and something had to happen.

Daddy came running out, bounded down the stairs and picked up the phone again.

'Listen, where is that blasted ambulance? This is an emergency, don't you understand? . . . All right, all right. Just come quickly!'

He ran back to the bedroom, slamming the door behind him to cut off the wailing inside.

The house was empty at night. Lorraine went back to her house in the village, and the housekeeper lived in the cottage on the other side of the grounds. Julia went downstairs, a small white figure in her nightgown. She opened the large front door and went out through it into the navy night. Stars glittered hard far above her; a slip of a moon, like a fingernail in the sky, curved silvery white. She went down the front steps to the gravel and crunched across it in her bare feet until she found the cool damp grass of the verge. She began to walk down the drive, not sure of where she was going or why, but impelled by a sense that she must do something to help and this was all she could think of.

I will open the gates. I will wave when the ambulance comes.

The drive seemed long when she was in a car. On foot, it was never-ending. She felt as though she had been walking for hours and still there was no sign of the gate. Behind her, the house loomed as large as ever, lights showing behind one or two of the windows, the rest dark. On and on she padded, wishing that Hattie, her terrier, was with her.

She had reached the stretch of lime trees when she heard the roar of the engine, the whine of the alarm and saw the flashing lights.

'It's here!' she said, relief washing over her. The gates must already have been open. They knew what to do. She didn't have the burden of responsibility after all. The ambulance flew past her in a flash, and disappeared towards the house, covering all the ground she had so laboriously walked in just an instant.

With nothing more to do, she couldn't think of anything else but to turn around and begin her march back to the house. She was almost there when the ambulance was leaving. Daddy stood on the doorstep, watching it pull away, his face white and anxious. Then he saw Julia, picking her way over the gravel in her bare feet.

'What are you doing?' he cried. 'You should be in bed!'

'I woke up. I wanted to help the ambulance driver.'

He rushed over and picked her up so he could carry her back to the house. 'You silly thing, your feet are frozen. You didn't need to do that, sweetie. They knew the way.'

'Is Mummy all right?'

He paused, hugged her tighter. 'She is going to be perfectly all right.'

'Is the baby here?'

His arms squeezed her tighter. 'Yes, the baby came. But it's not very well, I'm afraid. We must all be very brave. Now, shall we put you back to bed?'

*

61

When Mummy returned a week later, there was no baby with her. One day not long after, Mummy and Daddy went away dressed in black and came home sad and sombre. Mummy went back to bed and didn't get up for three months. By then, Julia had been sent to St Agatha's and a new chapter of her life had begun. Sometimes she wondered what had happened to the baby, and where they had put it. She knew it must be dead, but she wasn't absolutely sure, as no one had said.

We're not allowed to talk about dead babies. That must be the rule.

Chapter Six
1976

It was Daddy's idea to have the mural painted. Years before, the huge old drawing room had been divided in two and the back half had become the library. The wall that was built to divide them was not panelled like the others, and had been left quite plain by the ancestor who had decided on its construction. He had painted it brown to match the panelling colour and hung some paintings on it. At each end stood a suit of armour, a shield propped against its shins. Both suits were quite small, and so were not at all frightening, especially as up close it could be seen that they were etched with vines, flowers, bird and animals, rather lovely and unwarlike things. The suits had been stuffed with material to keep them upright, the hand pieces filled out by dark gloves that had been stuffed and stitched to the arm material, and under the helmets was scrunched-up brown paper, just visible behind the visor. Julia had amused herself by drawing faces for each of them on pieces of card – one blue-eyed with cherry-red lips, the other brown-eyed with a black moustache – and she stuck them under the visors, calling the blond one Sir Vivien and the other Sir Rupert. They were her knights, the knights of the kingdom of Morotania, charged with protecting it and its queens. Julia had found she could move the gloves a little so that the knights changed their hand positions from time to time, which made them seem a little more real, and she liked to imagine them chatting to each other when they were left alone at the end of the day. At almost thirteen, she was getting a little big for the Morotania game now, and was embarrassed even to mention it to Lala, who was so grown-up these days, but she was still fond of her knights.

Then one day, Sir Vivien was standing by the fireplace and Sir Rupert had moved to the hall.

'Why are the knights in different places?' Julia demanded breathlessly, having run into her father's business room without knocking.

Daddy looked up at her from his desk, a pen poised in his hand. 'What on earth are you talking about?'

'The knights! The suits of armour. They've been moved.'

His face brightened. 'Ah, yes. I've had a rather brilliant idea. I'm going to paint the drawing room wall.'

'What colour?'

'Not a colour.' He smiled at her, pleased with himself. 'You'll see. It's going to be a trompe l'oeil.'

'A trump loyal?' That sounded very knightly, something Sir Vivien might toot on his bugle as he rode into battle.

'It's French and it means to fool the eye. It's a wonderful plan. You'll see. Now leave me in peace, cabbage, I need to work.'

*

Julia could not think what he meant, but it became clearer when the artist arrived, a handsome and diminutive Frenchman with a small black moustache just like Sir Rupert's and who looked like he would be able to fit easily into Sir Rupert's armour too. The drawing room furniture was moved out of the way and covered with dust sheets, and Monsieur de Pelet took up occupancy in there, with various stepladders, cases of paints and brushes, tubs of pencils and sharpening knives, and jars of oils and mediums. Julia, away from school for the Easter holidays, was drawn to the room to watch what was going on, but she wasn't supposed to enter and distract Monsieur de Pelet, so she peeked through the gap at the door, and watched him bustling about. He was always nicely dressed in dark brown moleskin trousers, a smart shirt with a fashionable long collar and a tight russet jersey that never got any paint on it. Most of the time he had a cigarette clenched between his lips as he climbed up and down the ladders, working on the wall; a little tinny transistor radio played constant pop music, which he hummed to as he worked.

'You won't make too much of a mess, will you?' Mummy said anxiously, looking around at the room. Julia hovered behind her, watching.

'Assuredly not, madame,' he replied, calm and in control. 'I'm quite used to working this way. I have painted in many grand homes and am still received in them. You mustn't worry.'

'I can't help it.' Mummy looked pale and tired, as usual. She put a hand into her thick tawny hair that was held away from her face by a broad dark headband.

'Are you all right, madame? Do you want to sit down?'

'No . . . a headache, that's all. I'm fine.' She sighed. 'I'm sure I can trust you, monsieur.'

He was looking at her quizzically and said softly, 'I will try to make the sessions easy for you when it's your turn.'

She didn't seem to hear, but turned to Julia. 'You won't disturb Monsieur de Pelet, will you?'

'Of course not,' Julia replied.

'Then I'll go and lie down.'

Julia watched her walk slowly out of the room. She had not been the same since the baby died. It was as though her life force had been drained away and now she was a pale shadow of her old self. Julia remembered that once she had been vibrant and gay and playful, bursting with energy and rushing about the house, full of enthusiasm for it and the great task of its management. There had been visitors, busy weekends, large dinners for important people. But she had retired from all that, and Aunt Victoria was busy being the hostess of Tawray in Mummy's place. She was the one doing the tours for interested visitors, or opening the fete, or presiding over luncheons and dinners, and it seemed sometimes as if she had taken up residence in the house and would never leave.

Why, Julia wondered, in this huge house did it feel as though there wasn't room for her when Aunt Victoria was here? That was the mystery. She concentrated on keeping out of her aunt's way, and observing the artist at work in the drawing room.

*

Then Lala arrived, driving up in her red Mini in a whirlwind of luggage and wearing a bright orange coat. She was like a glorious punch of colour in their muted world, and glamorously independent now that she was eighteen and at art school.

'Lala!' Julia flung herself at her older sister, delighted to see her after what felt like an age. 'No one said you were coming.'

'Didn't they? I've been summoned,' Lala said with a laugh, hugging her. 'Daddy told me I had to get here. Apparently I'm being painted!'

'Yes, come on, you must see. It's going to be brilliant. Come and look. Monsieur de Pelet has gone out so we can sneak in and take a look.'

Julia had made friends with Monsieur de Pelet by the simple expedient of moving a little further into the room each day so that he became accustomed to her presence, and now she was allowed to perch on the window seat for as long as she wanted. She had grasped the idea of what he was doing and it fascinated her to watch how he was conjuring what looked like three-dimensional reality out of the flat wall, even though he was just sketching out his scheme for the moment. He was re-creating the room behind the wall on its surface, as if the wall itself had become transparent. The drawing of the library beyond was almost to scale, the perspective perfect so that it extended, completely plausibly, into the distance to the windows on the other side, where the garden outside could be glimpsed. In the room, members of the family would be placed. They were just outlines at the moment, and each would sit in turn for their own portrait.

Julia was almost jumping on the spot with excitement. 'Look, isn't it fabulous?'

Monsieur de Pelet had completed the under-drawing, with spaces left for the figures, so it was quite possible to get the idea of what he was creating.

Lala gazed at it, her mouth open. 'Oh my goodness. You're right. It is fabulous. How clever, it's like looking into a real room. And it looks exactly like the library.'

'I'm going here, at the front,' Julia said proudly. 'Monsieur de Pelet told me. Look – he's putting a stone balustrade across here and I'm going to be sitting on it. I'll have my favourite books next to me, and my sketchbook, and apples, and Hattie is going to be sitting down there by my feet. Isn't it marvellous?'

Lala laughed. 'Yes, it is. How talented he is. Who else is in it?'

'Daddy is going to be there, standing by the fireplace. Mummy is going to be sitting in that chair by the writing desk. Aunt Victoria will be standing by that vase of flowers, pretending to arrange it. Gran is by the window, talking to Violet, and Quentin is inspecting the books.'

'And where will I go?'

A voice behind them said, 'You, mademoiselle, will go here, in the middle. That is the best place for you, I think.'

They turned around to see Monsieur de Pelet had come in, his brown eyes sparkling. He gave a little bow to Lala.

'I'm not sure my aunt will think so,' Lala replied with a laugh.

'She must defer to youth and beauty. It is the way of things.'

'Gosh,' Lala said, flushing.

Julia thought that Lala did look beautiful. She was wearing a denim skirt with a mustard-yellow blouse and her fair hair fell in a swooping fringe over her blue eyes, and she looked fresh and young in the panelled room with its ancient furniture and dusty pictures.

'I want you to wear exactly that. It is just right. In fact, I want to start right now,' declared Monsieur de Pelet.

'I think I'll put my coat down and get a cup of tea first,' Lala said with a laugh.

'Of course.' He bowed again. 'You must be comfortable. That is the first rule of being painted. We will start in one hour. Is that acceptable?'

'Yes . . . yes, that's fine.'

'Ooh,' Julia said as they went out into the hall. 'He likes you.'

'Does he?' Lala said casually but she seemed pleased. 'At least I can practise my French while he paints me.'

'Mmm, yes, I suppose you can. French *kissing*,' Julia said, and went off into a peal of giggles while Lala swiped at her playfully with her coat sleeve.

The next week Julia spent sitting on the window seat, watching while the artist drew Lala into her position in the mural. He had created a frame for the painting, a stone surround with a balustrade and a doorway through into the room beyond. Lala was standing just beyond the doorway, almost life-sized, drawing the eye to her elegance. Julia could see that the fairness of her hair and the yellow of her blouse would make a point of light and interest when the colour was added to the painting. Monsieur de Pelet frowned as he drew, smoking constantly and humming along to the music from the radio. Lala tried to speak French to him occasionally but he was too distracted to hold a conversation for long, his concentration elsewhere. Nevertheless, his attention was constantly on her and Julia was sure she could sense some kind of connection between them. She did hope so – it would be lovely for Lala to have a romance, she never seemed to have a boyfriend. At first, Julia had wondered if she, Julia, might fall in love with Monsieur de Pelet and was rather hopeful he might try and seduce her, but he obviously saw her as a little girl and treated her with nothing but amused friendship, so she gave up on that. But if he were to fall in love with Lala, that would also be very satisfying. She hoped to be able to witness the birth of a great love affair but although there was some gentle flirting and Monsieur de Pelet was lavish with his compliments, nothing seemed to kick off between him and Lala, much to Julia's disappointment.

Lala's portrait took over a week to complete. She was the first element to be properly painted, and Julia watched, fascinated, as her sister's likeness emerged from the flat white of the under-painting, first in a sepia study that caught the proportions, and the light and shade, and then, bewitchingly, in oil paints that glowed with colour and magically bestowed life onto the portrait as skin flushed, eyes became moist, and breath appeared to enter the body.

'It's amazing,' she said, when Monsieur de Pelet had declared Lala's portrait done and allowed them to stand in front of it and look for as long as they liked while he cleaned off his brushes.

'It is,' Lala agreed, staring at herself in stunned amazement. 'Look at me, standing there like that!'

'Yes,' Monsieur de Pelet said, wiping a brush on a rag. 'I'm pleased with it.' He smiled at Julia. 'And you are next, mademoiselle.'

'Oh good,' Julia said happily. 'I can't wait.'

Lala came down with her to see the platform by the lake, and happily climbed up the rope to sit with Julia and gaze out over the water.

'It's just a relief to be out of that skirt and blouse,' Lala said, stretching out her legs in her blue jeans. 'I had no idea when I put them on how long I'd be wearing them for.'

'What shall I wear when I'm painted?' Julia asked.

'Something you won't mind looking at forever.'

'Then I'll wear my cord skirt and the cream jumper I got for Christmas. I'd like to wear my boots but I should think I won't be allowed, so I suppose it will be my school shoes. Can I borrow some lipstick?'

'You don't need it. Monsieur de Pelet can paint some on, I suppose. But he probably won't, even if you wear it.'

'I haven't got any make-up at all. I'm such a square. Millicent at school has all her sister's old stuff, masses of mascara and lipstick and blusher. I've got nothing.'

'You don't need it yet. We can go shopping for some when it's time.'

'I wish I was grown-up like you. You'll be a proper woman in the painting. Monsieur de Pelet has made you look magnificent. But I'll be stuck as a girl.'

'Perhaps you won't mind that so much when you're older. You're only a child for a short time, you're a grown-up for the rest of your life.'

'Childhood takes *forever*,' Julia protested. 'And I can't wait for it to be over.'

'Why?' Lala looked at her. 'Are you unhappy?'

Julia stared out across the lake and watched the coot swimming on its surface, sometimes bobbing down under the water. 'I don't know. Perhaps. It's lovely when you're here. But I'm on my own so much.' She turned to her older sister. 'Aren't you ever lonely?'

'Not really,' Lala said, after a moment. 'But I have brothers and sisters from my mother's other marriage. And now I'm at college for three years with lots of friends. But I can see that you are all alone here. Isn't school fun?'

'Oh yes, it's fun, I like it. And I love it here, of course, there's nowhere like Tawray. But there's no one to share it with.'

'What about Cousin Violet?'

'She's a lump, like Quentin. And Aunt Victoria keeps her away from me in any case. She hates me and thinks I'll be a bad influence.'

Lala said nothing but Julia could see she knew that was true.

Julia said wistfully, 'I loved it when you were here and we could play Morotania.'

Lala took her hand. 'I know. But we're too old for Morotania now.'

'That makes me awfully sad. Nothing was so real as that. I want to grow up, but I also wish we didn't have to.'

Lala squeezed her hand comfortingly. 'We have to. But there are consolations in getting older. And you'll always have me, I promise.'

Once Lala had gone, it was Julia's turn to sit for Monsieur de Pelet, and she enjoyed the whole process of being painted. Observing him at work was absorbing, and she didn't mind sitting still and listening to the music while he looked at her, painted, looked again, painted again. He stopped to mix paints or change brushes, and to look for his matches, which he was constantly losing. Julia collected as many boxes as she could and put them around the room so that he could find some wherever he was. At first he thought he kept finding the same box, but then realised what she had done and laughed.

Then he began to talk to her, asking her questions about the house and her family and her time at school. She chattered away, full of stories and conversation, and he turned off the radio to listen to her. He occasionally asked her to stop talking and stay still, but most of the time he was content to let her chat while he concentrated on painting other elements.

'Tell me about your mother,' he said. 'She has come in a

few times, and she is so full of sorrow. I'm not sure how I'm going to paint her without making her sad.'

'She lost a baby the summer before last,' Julia told him. 'And it wasn't the first one. But it was the worst.'

He whistled softly under his breath. 'I'm so sorry to hear that. A terrible thing.'

'She's not like my mother anymore,' Julia said, finding she could say these things to this man, things that she couldn't even say to Lala. 'The baby sort of killed her. She used to laugh and be interested in me. Now she can hardly manage anything.'

'Ah, now, she will get better, won't she? Perhaps she needs to have another baby to replace the one she lost.'

Julia felt a stab of cold fear at the thought. 'No. No! Not another one.'

Monsieur de Pelet looked up from his palette, surprised by her vehemence. 'But a new baby is a good thing. It might make her stop mourning the lost ones.'

'No.' Julia shook her head. 'I don't believe she is supposed to have any more. Or it wouldn't be this hard. I don't want her to. I just want her to be the way she was.'

'I see.' Monsieur de Pelet considered as he swirled a dot of red paint into the skin tone he was mixing. 'You are very sad about this, I can tell. Your smiles have gone, and you smile all the time.'

'I wish I was enough for her, that's all. But I'm not.'

'I'm sure she loves you.'

'Yes. But I'm a girl. If I was a boy, she wouldn't have to

have more babies. She knows Daddy doesn't want Quentin to have the house, that's why she feels she must keep on.'

'Boys are overrated,' Monsieur de Pelet said with a smile. 'Girls are much better. But the answer is simple: you must have the house. Why not?'

'Me?'

'Yes.'

She blinked at him. It seemed impossible. Easy enough for him to say, but something that could never really happen. *Imagine if Tawray were mine.*

Aunt Victoria would be sent away, and Mummy would be happy again, once the burden of providing an heir had been lifted. Quentin could go and be a lump somewhere else. He didn't deserve this place; he would never get the joy from it that Julia would.

'I'm painting Quentin next week,' Monsieur de Pelet said, as if reading her thoughts. 'I do not think he will be quite as much fun to paint as you are.'

'I'm afraid you're destined for boredom with Quentin. You'd better make sure you have lots of batteries for your radio.'

'Why don't you tell me about him?' suggested Monsieur de Pelet.

She knew he was moving her away from the subject of her mother and she didn't mind. 'Glad to, and about Violet too. I'm not allowed to play with her because I'm a bad influence. Shall I tell you all about it?'

'Excellent. This I will enjoy.' Monsieur de Pelet looked around. 'Now, where are my matches?'

*

Her portrait was done but the painting was not finished when Julia went back to school. It wasn't until she returned at half-term that she was finally able to see it completed, with all the protagonists painted in. Monsieur de Pelet had just put the last touches to it and was preparing to clear up his ladders and equipment when Julia came dashing in to see it.

She gasped. 'Oh my goodness! It's amazing! It's completely transformed since I last saw it.'

The effect was so startlingly realistic, it was as though her family really were standing in the library, just through the stone doorway, above which busts of her parents seemed to sit in little alcoves on either side of the family coat of arms. The huge painting glowed with colour and was dazzlingly rich in detail. At first Julia could only look at the amazing portraits – Lala in the middle drew the attention, but there they all were: Quentin frowning over a book he had taken from the library shelf, Violet sitting primly next to her grandmother, Aunt Victoria with a pair of scissors in her hand, about to snip the end off a lily stem with an air of formidable authority. Lovely Mummy, wistful in black, sitting at the writing desk, a pen in her hand, staring into the fire, where Daddy stood, leaning against the chimney piece. And here she was – Julia, exactly life-sized. She was sitting on the balustrade, her legs crossed at the ankle, Hattie just below her gazing up with adoration. On her lap was an open book – 'My favourite book, it's *Treasure Island*!' And beside her some more of her favourites in a haphazard pile. Her sketchbook lay open, weighted down by a glass of lemonade. A glossy apple sat next to her on the balustrade, and a discarded core lay on the ground near the edge of the painting. She was gazing out, straight at the onlooker, her tawny hair spilling over her shoulders, a smile playing on her lips. Of all of them, she seemed to be the only one who knew they were being painted, the only one who was in on the prank.

'Do you like it?' asked Monsieur de Pelet, smiling at her dazzled expression.

'I love it. I adore it.' And then she began to see all the jokes that Monsieur de Pelet had put into the painting. Throughout the library were boxes of matches – on the chimney piece, on the table, on the bookshelf, even up high on the stone surround. There was a small green parrot sitting on the curtain pole at the back of the room, and Julia remembered she had told him the story of *Swallows and Amazons* while they were sitting there, so he must be Captain Flint's parrot. The more she looked, the more she saw: tiny flourishes that would be invisible to most but were little messages to her. Quentin was reading a book called *Great Personalities of Today*. Violet was wearing a charm bracelet with little objects hanging off it, all connected to stories Julia had told him. Mice were nibbling at the corners of books, and scuttling to a hole in the wainscot. A butterfly wearing a tiny crown sat on a petal in the vase of flowers. One of the pictures on the wall was a tiny facsimile of Elizabeth I's coronation portrait. In the bookshelf was a history of Morotania. The more she looked, the more she saw.

She started laughing.

'You see, I do listen,' Monsieur de Pelet said. 'Even when I appear to be distracted, I'm listening.'

'You're wonderful,' she said sincerely.

He went to pick up a case of paints. 'I'm told so. And your father is happy, that is the main thing. It has worked rather well. I'm having it photographed next month so it can be recorded for my portfolio and a magazine wants to publish it, if your father allows.'

Julia said nothing. She was looking at her mother's portrait. She had just seen that her mother was writing a letter and it was addressed to *My darling Julia*. Beneath that it said *You are my joy*, before the writing was concealed by the fold of the paper.

'Oh,' she said weakly. Tears sprang suddenly into her eyes. 'Oh.'

'Are you all right?'

'Yes. Yes.' On an impulse, she rushed to him and took his hand. 'Thank you,' she said, gazing into his candid brown eyes. 'Thank you. It's just right. It's just as it should be.'

'I know truth when I hear it,' he replied softly. 'This is your vision, my dear Julia. It is the true story of life here.'

'Yes. I know. You've got it.' She smiled.

'It will be our secret.' He put his finger to his lips. 'And now I must put my tools away. I need to do something other than paint for a while.'

Chapter Seven

July 1981

Lala and Julia sat in the small sitting room at the back of the house, unglamorous but cosy with its mismatched furniture and the sofa with cushions sinking into the springs. They were crossed-legged on the floor, a packet of cigarettes each – Silk Cut for Julia, which she'd grown a taste for since she'd started nicking Lorraine's a few years back, and strong Gauloises from France for Lala, the same as Monsieur de Pelet had smoked. Julia thought smoking Gauloises was incredibly sophisticated, although she found they made her dizzy and a little bit sick when she tried them herself. She suspected that Lala had had some kind of relationship with Monsieur de Pelet after the mural had been finished, though she had never quite dared to ask about it.

Julia admired Lala even more now that Lala was almost twenty-three and had developed a style of her own, a mixture of English and French influences that was, to Julia, hugely chic. Today Lala wore jeans and a black and white striped top, and looked effortlessly elegant. Her fair hair was in a beehive and she wore frosted white lipstick and had batwing eye liner painted on her lids. Julia was in a gauzy old tea dress she'd found in a trunk in one of the attics, and she'd pin-curled her thick tawny hair into tight waves and put on red lipstick. The girls couldn't have looked more different.

Lala reached for another Gauloise and sparked it up with the lighter. 'It's practically child abuse, that's all,' she said, breathing out a cloud of fragrant smoke.

'Is it?' Julia, at seventeen, thought that twenty was a decent age.

'Er. Yeah.' Lala laughed. 'It's bloody weird if you ask me. He's – what? – thirty-two. Twelve years older than she is!'

They were watching the royal wedding on the television, just the two of them in the empty house, trying to see if they could spot Daddy, who was one of the many thousands of guests. Mummy had gone with him to London but she wasn't likely to be in the cathedral. She found it hard to be outside her safe places. She would be in the London flat, no doubt, watching it all on the telly, as they were, despite the engraved invitation from the Lord Chamberlain on the chimney piece and her hat in the striped box, in case she'd changed her mind and decided to go.

'Is that Daddy?' Julia said suddenly as the camera panned the congregation as it waited for the arrival of the bride.

'Is it? Blast, I missed him. We aren't likely to see him. Look how many people there are! We're only going to see the ones in the best seats. He's bound to be tucked away behind a pillar.'

'Still. Lucky thing. I wish I were there.' Julia sighed. She had begged her father to take her instead of Mummy, but he'd said the palace wouldn't allow it. Security or something. It was a bloody bore. Julia liked saying things like that. 'A bloody bore!' It sounded very grown-up.

Lala laughed. 'You're so sweet! I bet you think Lady Di is amazing.'

'No!' Julia protested, blushing a bit because, secretly, she did think that Lady Di was both amazing – so pretty and so stylish – and incredibly lucky because now, for the rest of her life, she was going to matter. She would be loved and adored and feted, and live a life that was the closest to a fairy tale that was still possible in the world. 'I'm interested, that's all. Everyone is. Look at the crowds!'

Lala shrugged. 'I suppose so. France has done away with all of that, you see, so I don't really get it. I suppose I find it kind of funny.'

Lala was completely and utterly Frenchified now. She had even gone to live in France, doing a further degree in fashion and design at a college in Paris before looking for work in the ateliers of the design houses.

'Funny?'

'It's all a bit hilarious from the outside. I couldn't believe the state of the village!'

'What's wrong with it?' Julia was slightly indignant. The village looked wonderful, a riot of red, white and blue. There was bunting everywhere, and huge Union Jack flags were draped over hedges or hung from flagpoles. The pub was practically hidden under the fluttering flags and rosettes and posters celebrating the royal couple and their big day. Later, after the ceremony – which was being broadcast in the village hall for those who didn't have a television or who wanted to be with others at the big moment – there would be a party in the village, food and drink served on trestle tables, a bonfire and fireworks once darkness had fallen. After all, it was the first marriage of a Prince of Wales for seventy years, or something like that. Everyone thought it was worth doing properly when the opportunity came along.

'Nothing wrong with it,' Lala said, sucking on her Gauloise. 'It's just funny. Sweet but incredibly feudal.'

The excitement on the television stepped up a notch. The glass carriage had left Clarence House and was rolling along the Mall on its way to St Paul's, policemen riding alongside it, two footmen standing on the back plate, resplendent in red and gold. The crowds cheered and waved their flags, and the camera moved in on a sweet face obscured by a cloud of white veil, a smile and a waving hand.

'There she is!' Julia breathed, enraptured. Even Lala was interested, leaning forward to get a closer look. 'Gosh, she looks amazing.'

'The dress will be interesting,' Lala allowed. 'That's why I'm watching it. Research.'

'Keep telling yourself that,' Julia said, and they watched as the carriage rolled through the streets of the city past hundreds of cheering onlookers before it drew up at last in front of the cathedral, where two bridesmaids waited on the steps. Then the door was open and the cheers increased as the bride descended in a mass of crumpled ivory and lace, her train following endlessly, the bridesmaids bustling about attempting to straighten it.

'Oh,' sighed Julia, drinking it all in: the fluttering veil, the great puffed sleeves, the vast bell of crushed silk. 'I love it.'

'It's all creased!' cried Lala, pointing her cigarette at the screen. 'They'll have to shake it out as fast as possible. What silk have they used? It's like tissue paper! What a confection, she looks like a big cream bun.'

'She looks amazing,' retorted Julia. 'Like a perfect princess.'

Lala gave her a sideways look. 'You're a romantic. Like she is.'

'Aren't you?'

Lala shrugged. 'I like to think there's an ideal attitude that mixes pragmatism with romance. Marry well, be a perfect wife – and take a lover.'

'What?' Julia was appalled. 'Lala, how can you? You should marry for love alone. Your husband should be every-thing to you.'

Lala looked wise and mature. 'That's far too much to ask of any man. Even a woman finds it hard to be everything, and she makes it her life's work.' She paused, pleased with her aphorism, then laughed again. 'Ignore me. I'm cynical in my old age. Oh look, at least they're getting her straightened out now.'

The bride was standing by the cathedral door, hands fuss-ing and primping around her, while she glowed with youthful beauty beneath her veil, gazing up the aisle to where her future awaited her. The trumpets sounded. Everything was ready. She folded her arm inside her father's, and began her advance as he shuffled beside her, smiling and nodding at the congregation.

'It's weird,' Julia said, her head on one side. 'It's like she's not just marrying him, the prince. It's like she's marrying all of us, the whole country. That's why everyone's so happy. Now we get to keep her.'

'That sounds romantic, but really she's just there to provide an heir.'

'Is she?' Julia frowned. A chill settled on her shoulders and she shuddered involuntarily. She thought of her mother, pale and worn out, increasingly unable to go out or do anything, oppressed by being unable to fulfil her own duty. 'But it doesn't matter if she doesn't have a boy. Girls can inherit. Not like it was in France,' she added quickly, glad to have something to say in favour of her homeland.

'I suppose that's something,' Lala said. She pointed her cigarette at the screen, where the white-clad figure was still walking slowly down the aisle. 'Look at that. On her way to the scaffold. Poor child. Someone ought to come down from the ceiling on a wire, like James Bond, and snatch her away. Save her before it's too late.'

'Don't say anything else,' Julia commanded. 'You'll spoil it. I want to watch it properly, so shh.'

They watched the entire service but Lala was bored after that, and went outside. Julia stayed glued to everything, watching the carriage ride back, the veil now lifted to reveal the new princess in all her glory. She watched the appearance on the balcony, the kiss, and all the highlights they showed and reshowed. It was everything everyone had wanted: full of pomp and ceremony and youth and beauty and romance.

She was still there, dreaming, when the newlyweds emerged from the palace in an open landau, on their way to Waterloo Station, a handwritten sign reading 'Just Married' on the back, and blue and silver heart-shaped balloons bobbing over them.

Later, Julia and Lala went down to the village and joined in the street party. Everyone was there – villagers and the people from the big houses – eating, drinking and celebrating. Julia drank two pints of cider and felt as though her stomach had swollen as tight as a drum, but she also felt wonderfully carefree and elated, and when the band started up, she jumped and hopped and swayed with the best of them.

A handsome boy took a shine to her and started dancing with her, grabbing at her hands and holding them, smiling at her and flashing meaningful glances in his liquid brown eyes. When they both were puffed out, he walked her into the darkness off the main street and, to her surprise, kissed her passionately behind the telephone box. It was her first kiss: smoky, sweet and astonishingly intense. The touch of his lips, his mouth opening against hers, seemed to take her on a direct route into herself, awakening sensations she'd never felt before. It set new nerves jangling and buzzing.

A royal wedding. My first kiss. She wondered if the princess was being kissed like this right now, feeling the same thrill of awakening desire mixed with a strange rush of power that came from the sense of being wanted.

They kissed for ages and then he muttered, 'I wanna get to know you better. Wanna meet me tomorrow night?'

He had the village burr, the soft twang of the locals.

'I don't know,' she whispered back. 'Maybe. I don't even know your name!'

'Paul. What's yours?'

'Julia.'

'That's a nice name.' He was nuzzling at her, breathing heavily, eager for her lips again, and she let him kiss her, falling into it as though plummeting through the rabbit hole into a maddeningly blissful world of darkness, desire and the urgent, pressing, primitive sense that she needed to get somewhere, to some kind of resolution, and soon.

She pulled away at last, longing and yet also sated. 'I have to go now.'

'So, you gonna come tomorrow?'

She gazed at him in the summer darkness. He was beautiful and the kissing was divine and she wanted more of it, more of whatever he might like to share with her.

'I'm not sure,' she said slowly. 'Maybe.'

'Come here at nine o'clock tomorrow,' he said. 'I'll be waiting for you.'

He took her hand and they went back to the melee. He let go of her and she lost him in the crowd.

'There you are!' It was Lala, looking anxious. 'Where've you been? I've been looking everywhere.'

'Just around,' Julia said. She felt grown-up suddenly, worldly and experienced, closer to Lala than she had before.

'Come on then. We'd better go home. It's late.'

Paul, Paul, Paul.

His name whirled around her head and his taste was still in her mouth.

I'll see him tomorrow night. Or maybe I won't.

He was sweet, he was exciting. But he wasn't her prince, she knew that for certain.

And when he comes, I'll know. Because it will be perfect.

Daddy was not a good reporter, it turned out. In response to Julia's fevered questions about the royal wedding, he was vague and generally useless at remembering anything important. The bride looked 'very nice' and the atmosphere had been 'jolly'. He'd been more interested in the difficulties of getting to the cathedral and home again afterwards. 'Crowds everywhere like you wouldn't believe. What a scrum it was.'

Mother was calm and strangely happy, despite being pale and sickly. Julia saw the signs with a horrible prickle of fear. It had been so long, she'd almost forgotten the special kind of terror that her mother's pregnancies engendered.

Surely it can't be true . . . she can't be pregnant, not now.

How could it be possible? *Surely they don't do . . . that!* But once Mummy had retired to bed, gagging over sips of water, it was unavoidable. Her mother was pregnant again.

Julia took fresh water and small bowls of food up to the bedroom for Mummy to attempt. She held Julia's hand and gazed into her eyes, her own expression so pathetically hopeful, Julia could hardly bear it.

'It's going to be all right this time, darling. You'll see. I'm going to do it this time, I just know it.'

Chapter Eight

Present day

They got back late to the Old Barn, Johnnie pulling in to park beside Alex's car and then getting out, agitated.

'Are you hungry?' Alex asked, opening the front door and switching on the lights. The house always felt different without the girls. Hadji, her Jack Russell, came trotting out of the kitchen and barked happily to see her. Hadji walked with a sideways twist as a result of a run-in with a car door in which he had come off the worst but it never seemed to bother him. 'Hello, Hadji, my love.'

Johnnie walked past her into the kitchen and went straight to the fridge. 'Do you have anything to drink?'

'Open the wine in the door. I could do with a glass myself.' She followed him into the kitchen and put her bag down on the counter. 'So, are you hungry?'

Johnnie shook his head and opened the drawer for the corkscrew. 'No appetite at all.' A moment later, he was pouring two large glasses of wine and sliding one over to Alex. 'So the old cow's won at last.'

'What do you mean?'

'Pa's going to die. She had the chance to call us when he was conscious and she didn't.'

Alex sighed, took her wine over to the sofa and sat down. When the barn had been converted, the vast old doors that had once let in tractors and lorries had been turned into a wall of glass and now the kitchen overlooked the rolling fields towards the woods. It was pitch black outside, and the whole room was reflected back at her, lights gleaming, Johnnie at the counter, herself on the sofa. After a moment, she jumped up and pulled the curtains shut.

She looked over at Johnnie. She could see that his grief and fear about Pa was coming out as anger towards Sally. *Just like it always does.* 'I don't expect she thought that it was going to be this serious.'

Johnnie frowned. He looked much older suddenly. It wasn't always easy to see the changes in a familiar face, but the light overhead showed the furrows in his forehead, the lines between his brows and the fan of wrinkles at the edges of his eyes. He still looked like the handsome Johnnie of his youth, but he had that tired look, the one that never went away after a certain age. He took a gulp of wine and said, 'Don't stick up for her, Al. I don't know why you do it when she's always been so horrible to you. It wasn't for her to decide whether to call or not. As soon as Pa got sick, she should have been in touch.'

Alex said nothing as she went back to the sofa. He was right. As usual, Sally had placed herself firmly between the children and their father. It had been that way for so long, it was hard to remember a time when there hadn't been that frosted pink and white figure between them, giving orders disguised as gentle suggestions: 'Children, your father is tired now. Perhaps you should think about making a move and letting him get some rest?'

Or: 'Would it be a good idea to cancel our little get-together on Sunday? We're so frightfully oversubscribed with social duties at the moment.'

Alex remembered how, after Scarlett was born, Sally kept ringing with excuse after excuse, all delivered with the same rueful tone, of how they were simply too busy to come and visit because of all their many obligations. Participation in the local bridge tournaments, games of golf and a commitment to the choral society's performance of *The Messiah* were, apparently, more important that meeting the baby. When Pa and Sally finally came to the Old Barn, it was all Sally could do to drag her eyes away from the clock. She cooed over Scarlett for about two minutes, before handing her back and looking ready to leave. All the way through the childhoods of Johnnie's children and Alex's daughters, Sally had kept the same air of vague interest as though her husband's grandchildren were really not her concern. Alex knew it would be quite different if Sally had grandchildren of her own.

Oh yes, quite a different kettle of fish then.

Johnnie came and sat beside her, hunching over his wine glass. Alex put her hand on his arm.

'Are you okay?'

He glanced up at her. 'It's just a lot to take in, that's all. For all we knew, Pa was fine this morning.'

Alex nodded, wondering why she felt so numb. *Pa is dying. He's had a fatal stroke. It's all over.*

But another voice came in firmly behind that one, a voice that sounded like Sally's. *Oh no. He's going to get better. The brain is capable of amazing things. A baby with only ten per cent of normal brain grew up and learned to windsurf, I read it in the paper. Of course he'll come back. This isn't the end. It can't be.*

'We've got to be positive,' she said firmly.

'What good will that do?'

'I don't know, but it's all we've got. How long can you stay?'

Johnnie shrugged. 'A few days, I suppose. I can do some work on the fly, and Netta can cope without me, but I'll need to get back before too long.'

'Of course. Listen, I can heat up some casserole I've got in the fridge, and we'll have some supper. We'll feel better after that.'

'Okay.' Johnnie took a big gulp of his wine. 'Thanks, Al. That's probably what I need.'

They ate together, swapping their news as they did. They were connected, as most people were, by webs of social media. Alex saw pictures of Johnnie's three boys at their various schools and football matches, and he saw Scarlett and Jasmine's progress; he liked their World Book Day costumes and their baking attempts and their sporting triumphs. He wrote encouraging comments under photos of them playing their recorders or singing in the choir and said well done when Alex flagged up another achievement.

And yet, the pictures were curated highlights, not the real story.

'Scarlett isn't coping with the divorce as well as Jasmine,' Alex confided. 'She's been a bit tearful lately, and she's getting anxious about moving between the two houses for some reason. I'm trying to help her, Tim's being good about it too, but I suppose she'll take time to settle. It doesn't help there's a new woman on the scene.'

Johnnie raised his eyebrows. 'Really? Quick work. He's moved on then?'

'Yes – and that's fine. But I'm worried that's the cause of Scarlett feeling uncomfortable.'

'I suppose it might be,' Johnnie said. He smiled at his sister. 'You're so much happier without him, Al, you definitely did the right thing. But I get how she might make things awkward. Have you met her?'

'Just once, last night. She seemed all right.'

'It had to happen. And it will definitely happen for you too, at some point. As long as you and Tim can reassure the girls they'll always come first, I'm sure they'll cope. They might even thrive.'

A wave of melancholy swept over her. 'Of course. That's what I need to do.' She smiled at him, not wanting him to see how sad she suddenly felt. *He might think I'm jealous, or that I regret splitting up with Tim, and it's not that.* 'How's Bertie?'

'He's okay.' Johnnie picked over his casserole with the tines of his fork. 'Well . . . you know.'

Alex nodded. 'But he's still in his school, right?'

'Yup. We won that battle, thank God.' Johnnie and Netta had recently taken their local council to court when it proposed moving Bertie from his current school, where he was happy and settled, to another that was much closer, saving on his travel costs, which were publicly funded. They had won, but the whole thing had been exhausting and fraught with worry. Johnnie had suspected that it was a ploy to get out of paying for Bertie's schooling altogether, and landing the cost of his education with them. The special school that Bertie attended, with one member of staff for every pupil, cost about sixty thousand a year. Impossible. 'But one day he's going to be out of full-time education.'

'That's a way off, though.'

'Yes, but the law might change, funding might stop. We have to think about the future. Once he leaves school, there are various options for a couple of years after that – then we're on our own. It's up to us to occupy him and look after him for the rest of his life.'

Alex didn't know what to say. When she told friends that she had an autistic nephew, they often had stories of autistic children they knew, usually those who were in their child's class at school. She had to explain that Bertie was a bit beyond what was normally understood by autistic. He wasn't ill at ease in social situations, or unhappy with overstimulation, or obsessed with numbers, or any of those things. He was non-verbal and would never speak, and had no need of anything much beyond his basic wants. Music, pictures, people meant nothing to him, he was far away inside his own head and without inhibitions or a sense of danger. He had to be locked into his bedroom for his own protection and that of the house, and the family, because there was no telling what he might do left to himself – without malice, but also without awareness. He still required, at twelve, to be taken to the loo, and cleaned up afterwards. He needed stimulation, but not much: staring out of the window, clicking his fingers, could keep him happy for long stretches, punctuated by dashes to the sink to run taps, and drink from them. Even so, he needed constant supervision. Alex had watched as, over the years, Johnnie and Netta had realised the extent of their son's condition. Their first impulse was to fight it. They'd invested all their savings and a great deal of time in therapy and education for Bertie – Netta gave up work and trained herself as a therapist – believing at first that they would be able to overcome his autism, which stood between them and him like a steel door. All they had to do was fight hard enough, and in the end, the door would open. Their delight over progress was infectious, and Alex had begun to believe too that one day Bertie would communicate with them.

It was true that he had changed a little. The therapy did make inroads into his condition. He learned to understand certain things and obey some instructions, with the help of many rewards and positive reinforcement. He was able to recognise his family, though he ignored his brothers for a long time, only acknowledging them when they were about four. He knew what home was. Most of all, he loved food and was clever at finding it, and operating anything to do with it, and had limitless appetite for cereal, cheese, chocolate and ice cream, which had to be locked away in case he gorged on them. But in the end, all of them had quietly accepted that there was not much point in going on trying to make Bertie speak. He was happy, he was loved and he was well looked after. There wouldn't be any more than that.

Johnnie leaned back in his chair. From that angle, he looked suddenly like the photograph of their mother that Alex, as a girl, had taken and hidden in her room in case it was made to disappear, like all the other pictures of her mother had been. Johnnie's hooded green-brown eyes looked like the ones in the photograph, and so did his thick hair, blond with a touch of ginger. Alex had longed for years to look like her mother – so striking and beautiful – instead of her boring dark hair and blue eyes. But then, as she grew older, she was glad to have her father's colouring, as a kind of reminder to him that she was his daughter, his real family, not his pretend family. Perhaps if Johnnie had looked less like Mum, Sally might not have disliked him so much.

'So Bertie will live with you and Netta once he leaves school,' Alex said. She said it as a statement because she didn't see any other alternative. Bertie would never grow up and leave: he was a lifelong commitment.

'It's what Netta wants.'

She gave him a questioning look. 'Don't you?'

Johnnie took another swig of his wine and sighed. Then he looked up at his sister, his eyes troubled. 'I wish I could say I do. I love Bertie, of course, and I'll provide for him as long as he lives. The thing is, he isn't a baby anymore. When he was a child, it was easier – he was beautiful, and small, easy to pick up and carry, and when people stared in the street, they thought, *That kid's a bit badly behaved*, and then moved on. But now . . . he's growing up, Al. I can suddenly see the man he's going to be. He's already tall and getting stronger. Soon he'll have hair and hormones and all the rest of it. People look wary or even scared when they realise he's different. What's okay in a child is not in a grown man.'

'What are you saying? That he's dangerous?'

'He doesn't mean to be, and he doesn't intend any harm. But you should see Netta try and restrain him when he's going for the cereal or wants to get outside when he's not dressed. She almost can't anymore.'

Alex could imagine that: Netta was tiny and birdlike, small-featured with close-cropped dark hair. Alex thought she could put her hands around Netta's middle and her fingers would meet. The strain of looking after Bertie for so long probably had something to do with Netta's slenderness; she hadn't taken much time for herself, even to eat, for years. 'Yes,' she said slowly. 'I see that.'

'He's got everything a young man should have, except the ability to understand anything at all.' Johnnie brushed his hand over his face. 'I thought we'd been through the worst. But seeing the beginnings of the man he could have been if it weren't for whatever is wrong with his brain . . . God, it hurts.'

Alex reached over and took her brother's hand and squeezed it. 'You've made such a good life for him. He's happy.'

'He is. Yes.' Johnnie sighed again. 'But what about the rest of us?'

'How are the twins coping?'

Johnnie bit his lip. 'Fine. They accept him, I think they even love him, but they also shut him out of their world sometimes. Thank goodness they have each other. And I worry that they'll have the burden of caring for him if something happens to Netta and me. But all in all, they just get on with it.'

'They're wonderful boys.' Alex got up to clear the plates. 'But you're worried about Bertie staying at home in the future?'

'I don't see how he can. He's going to need proper carers. Netta just won't be able to cope. And it's not fair on the twins. But she can't see it.'

Alex started to load the dishwasher. 'It sounds like you think he needs to go into an institution or something.'

'We have to think about the future, that's all I'm saying. Bertie is strong and healthy, he's going to be around a long time. We might not be equipped to give him everything he needs.'

'Does Netta know how you feel?'

Johnnie felt uncomfortable. 'I'm not sure. Sort of.' He knew that wasn't really true. 'We do need to discuss it.'

Alex sighed. 'You've all had such a hard time.'

'I'm not the only one. You've been through a divorce, for God's sake.'

'Yes, but that's over now. I'm through the worst. I thought it was time something good happened. And now there's this.' She turned around, leaning against the kitchen counter. 'We've got to get Pa through it somehow. We will, won't we, Johnnie?'

He looked up at her and smiled, though she could see it was an effort for him. She sensed the inner struggle. Johnnie was known for being smiling and good-tempered but she knew that inside, he was constantly fighting against a dark gloominess threatening to engulf him. 'Yes. We're going to do our best, that's for sure.' He emptied his wine glass. 'Oh, and just to put the icing on the cake, Sally said she's rung Mundo. She said she had to let him know.'

'Bloody hell.' Alex said it without thinking, and it came out with sharp-edged vehemence. 'That's all we need.'

'I know.'

Neither of them liked Sally's son, who sat between them in age, and who had grown up at Tawray with them once Sally moved in for good. They each had their own reasons for disliking Mundo so much, but they were united in the emotion.

'I can't bear to think of him sliming around here,' Johnnie said.

Alex gave a grimace of distaste. 'He's not coming, is he?'

'Bound to be. If Sally has told him how serious it is, he's going to be on his way.'

Alex went to the window, lifted the curtain back a little

and stared out at the night. She could see the lights of Tawray glowing in the darkness. That was where it had all happened: the dramas of their lives, the interactions and the events that had brought them here, with Pa in hospital, Sally at his side, and Mundo on his way back.

She dropped the curtain and shut out the night.

Chapter Nine

It was always strange to wake up without the girls at home. Alex missed the sounds of their voices, and the bustle of their activity. She got up and showered, thinking about them over at Tim's house. Had Chloe stayed the night? Maybe she was pouring juice and making toast for the girls right now. Something about that left a bitter taste in her mouth. But it wasn't so bad imagining her looking after the girls. Harder was imagining Chloe ignoring them, or even treating them badly. It churned her up inside and set all her protective impulses firing off. *Calm down*, she told herself. *It's okay. They're fine, Tim's there.*

But as soon as she got downstairs, she texted Tim and didn't feel happy until she'd got a reply.

They're fine. Jazzy's having muesli, Scarlett's eating toast. I'm taking them to school in a minute. How's your father?

Alex replied:

He's okay for now. I'll tell you more later. Thanks for taking them. I might need to call on you a bit, depending on what happens with Pa.

She was tempted to ask how Chloe had coped with the girls, but resisted it. She'd made an internal promise that she would stay mature over all the future arrangements with the girls. There were several years ahead when they would need their parents to be there for them, stable and secure and focused on their needs. Alex couldn't risk sparking off trouble between her and Tim just when things ought to be calm, and she felt that, in the aftermath of the divorce, it wouldn't take much to set it off.

Johnnie came in, sniffing appreciatively at the scent of freshly brewed coffee in the air. He looked better after a sleep, his tawny hair still damp from the shower. 'Are the girls home today? I'd love to see them.'

'Yes, I'll get them after school. I'm going to have to tell them about Pa's condition, maybe take them in to see him. They're going to be really cut up.'

Johnnie nodded. 'Nathan and Joe as well. They all love him, don't they?'

Alex poured out the coffee for him. 'I think it's easier to be a grandparent than a parent.'

'You said it.' Johnnie took the mug. 'Thanks, Al. You must miss the girls when they're away.'

'Yes, I do, of course. But the peace and quiet isn't so bad. It gives me a chance to get some work done.' She told him about her contracts for the Christmas decorations. 'The only thing I'm not sure about is if I should schedule in some time for doing the Tawray display.'

Johnnie frowned. 'Are they going to keep the tradition going?'

'That's the thing, I don't know. Perhaps no one told them about opening the house so people can see the flowers. I think I'll go up there and ask. I ought to introduce myself in any case. They've been in a few weeks now.'

Johnnie looked grim. 'Don't remind me. There's a lot I'll never forgive Sally for, but selling Tawray has to be at the top.'

'She couldn't have done it without Pa's say-so. He was the owner.'

'What about us? That was our house. It was Mum's so it should have come to us, not gone to Pa.'

Alex shook her head, wrapping her hands around her steaming mug to warm them. 'Don't go down that path, Johnnie, it's not worth it. It's all been done. If Mum had lived, it would have been different, but she didn't.'

'And we know why,' Johnnie said with a kind of growl in his voice.

'Yes. She was ill.'

'Come on, Al. You don't believe that, do you? That's Sally's line!' Johnnie pulled a face and made a mocking attempt at Sally's voice. '"Your poor mother, we loved her so much! But she was ill. Depression is a terrible thing!"'

'Of course it was depression, you know that. Pa told us that from the start.'

'Yes, but why was she depressed?' Johnnie leaned towards

her. 'It must have been kind of depressing finding out that your best friend is sleeping with your husband.'

Alex went still and stared at him, a coldness settling round her shoulders. He'd never said anything so stark before. Once or twice he'd made barbed remarks about the speed with which Sally had moved in on their father once he was widowed, but not this. 'You mean . . . you think Sally was having an affair with Pa? While Mum was alive?'

'Come on, Al! Of course she was. Think about it.' Johnnie jabbed his finger onto the kitchen table for emphasis. 'She lived about two minutes away, she was always at the house. And Pa was barely with us that last summer, remember?'

Alex tried to remember, but she'd been so young. That summer was fuzzy, distant. It only came into focus with Mum's death.

Johnnie went on: 'Sally came onto the scene far too fast. She was in like Flynn.'

'She was Mum's friend, she already knew Pa. She came to help him through it all. That's how it started.'

'But she moved in almost immediately. Come on. She must have been sleeping with him. I bet that's what made Mum do it. She found out, and she couldn't stand the betrayal.'

Alex stared at him, her mouth open. Johnnie had never talked like this before. The emotion of the last twenty-four hours must have got to him. He had always found it difficult to deal with his feelings about Sally, and now they had boiled to the surface in this ugly accusation. 'We don't know that,' she said slowly. 'We really don't.'

'You don't have to be bloody Sherlock to work it out,

though.' Johnnie shook his head. 'She's ruthless, she always has been. She wanted Pa and she got him. She wanted Mundo to oust us and she almost managed that too. That's probably why she's getting him back here – so that if Pa recovers consciousness, guess whose face he'll be staring into? Dear old Mundo's. Forget the fact that we're his actual children and Mundo is just the cuckoo in the nest.'

Alex put down her coffee cup. 'But you don't know for sure, and we never will. Come on, we'd better get to the hospital now. I really need to see Pa.'

Alex drove them both to the hospital and they went up to Pa's ward. He was just as he'd been yesterday, lying motionless in his bed, hooked up to his trolley of machines and drips, with no discernible difference at all. They sat by his bed, Alex holding her father's cool hand and occasionally rubbing her own over the back of it.

'He could stay like this for a long time,' Johnnie said gravely, looking at his father's still face. 'Weeks even.' He glanced over at Alex. 'I'm going to have to make some decisions about how long I stay.'

'Let's wait until we've spoken to the consultant again,' Alex said. 'There's no need to decide right now.' She didn't want to talk like this in case her father could hear and got the impression that they wished he would hurry up and go either to recovery or to death, so they could get on with things.

A few minutes later, the door opened and Sally came in, well wrapped up in an overcoat and untying a scarf.

'Ah, what joy,' Johnnie said under his breath, then more jovially, 'Hello, Sally.'

Sally didn't reply, going straight to David's bedside to take his other hand while gazing mournfully at his face. 'Good morning, my darling. I haven't slept a wink thinking about you. I don't want you to worry, I was fine driving myself in to the hospital even though I was feeling so dazed and exhausted.'

'Oh Sally,' Alex said at once, contrite, 'you should have said, I could have picked you up.'

'Please, it's fine.' Sally held up a hand and smiled mournfully. 'I'm perfectly all right. I may have to get used to looking after myself a little bit more.' Her blue eyes filled with tears. Despite her state, she was still immaculately turned out, her hair blown out into its usual silvery-blonde frosted cloud, her eyelashes spiky with blue mascara and rimmed in blue eyeliner, and her lips shining candy pink. 'Where is that consultant? Honestly! Johnnie, go out and ask for me, will you?'

Johnnie got slowly to his feet and went out into the corridor to the nurses' station. As soon as he'd gone, Sally turned to Alex.

'How long is he staying?'

'As long as Pa needs him.'

'He doesn't need him, dear. What bothers me is the energy Johnnie is bringing into the room. It's very negative. I think David can sense it. It's making me awfully uneasy.' Sally's lashes fluttered and her lips trembled. 'Quite upset, if I'm honest.'

'Oh dear.' Alex felt the usual pull between her stepmother

and Johnnie. She had always been in the middle of them, like a rag doll held by the arms between two squabbling children. *Sally wants me to tell Johnnie to go home. But I'm not going to.* 'He's just really worried about Pa. We both are.'

'I appreciate that.' Sally sniffed and tightened her lips. 'Well, I'll feel better when Mundo gets here.'

Alex felt a strange sensation over her back, as if someone had just drawn an icy finger across her skin. 'Is he on his way?'

'Oh yes. He wants to be here for his father, just as you do.'

His stepfather, Alex wanted to say, but she didn't dare. It was Sally's way to act as if Mundo was David's actual son, and he'd called him Pa, just like she and Johnnie did, almost as soon as he arrived all those years ago. Once, years ago, Alex had actually ventured to ask Sally who Mundo's father was. Her expression had closed like a portcullis slamming to the ground.

'I don't talk about *him*,' she'd said with vehemence. 'He doesn't exist as far as I'm concerned.'

Alex had felt almost sorry for Mundo, who never saw his real father, except that he didn't appear to mind at all, or consider himself deprived. He had Pa, and that seemed to be enough for him. Johnnie disliked the situation immensely, but it had been harder for him. Sally had constantly tried to manoeuvre Johnnie out of the picture and Mundo into the frame instead. It was so brazen at times that Alex couldn't believe her father was unaware of what she was up to. There was the year that Sally held Mundo's birthday party on Johnnie's actual birthday – because it was the only Saturday the marquee suppliers could do, Sally said – and Mundo had got the cake and presents and singing, while Johnnie's birthday was barely mentioned. It went on throughout their childhoods, with Mundo always getting a little more than the others: the special music lessons, the skateboard (when Johnnie had longed for one), the pocket money, the expensive school trips. The only upside of the special treatment was that Mundo was sent off to a grand boarding school while she and Johnnie went to local schools, which meant they got a bit of relief from him, and as he got older he went off on skiing trips and rugby tours in the holidays. They couldn't exactly forget him, though. A portrait of him hung in the drawing room and there were photographs of him everywhere, often flanked by Sally and David, as though he was their only child. She and Johnnie used to laugh about it, but actually it had hurt. Of course, it wasn't Mundo's fault that Sally had so blatantly favoured him, but he didn't help himself because he seemed quite happy with the situation and took advantage of it whenever he could. So Alex and Johnnie kept him at a distance and made sure he didn't know when they were slipping off to the platform by the lake to spend time without him.

Johnnie came back in. 'The consultant's just coming,' he said. 'A few minutes away.'

'That means at least ten,' Sally said with a martyred look, and she settled herself on the chair Alex had been on, taking her husband's hand. She glanced over at Johnnie. 'How are you? How is the family?'

'They're fine, thanks.'

'Your wife is a marvel. I don't know how she copes. With

Bertie's . . . *needs* . . . and the other boys, and her career.' Sally shook her head. 'She's a superwoman.'

'I know. I'm very lucky.'

Sally put her head on one side, and blinked at Johnnie while she smiled, a tight-lipped, sad little smile as if to say that she knew how much they suffered. It was her little habit, Alex knew it well. What happened next could not be predicted; Sally's brain was usually moving in a mysterious way while she nodded and smiled and blinked.

'Of course she needs to be careful of osteoporosis,' she remarked.

'Sorry?' Johnnie looked bemused.

'Netta. She doesn't eat enough. You ought to make sure she gets more calcium. Otherwise her bones can suffer in later life; it's the little-known curse of women. I'll send her some nice yoghurts.'

'Okaaay.' Johnnie sent a look to Alex, and he rolled his eyes lightly.

'I expect she'll need you home soon,' Sally said. 'We'll understand if you need to get back. Alex and I can take care of David, you know.'

'Yes, I know. But Pa's not out of the woods yet, is he? I'm here until we know more.'

Sally sighed just a little. 'Of course. Ah, here is the consultant now, thank goodness!'

The consultant talked them through the situation, which was more or less unchanged. David was stable. If he went through the next forty-eight hours without further strokes, they would reassess him. The risk was high, and the next stroke would most likely be the last, but every hour that went by was a good sign that he was hanging on.

'I can't say for certain what a long-term prognosis would be,' the consultant told them gravely. 'But you can't hope for a total recovery. I'm afraid that's a vanishingly small possibility.'

'But not impossible?' Sally said brightly.

The consultant hesitated. 'We never like to say impossible. But it's very remote.'

'As long as there's a chance,' Sally said, and tightened her grip on David's hand.

When the consultant left, Johnnie went after him into the corridor and said, 'My stepmother is clinging on to the hope that my father will pull through. He won't, though, will he?'

The consultant shook his head. 'We can't talk in certainties but I'm as sure as I can be. I'm sorry to say it but I have no hopes of recovery. The most likely situation is that your father will hang on until another stroke or an infection gets him.' He gave Johnnie a sympathetic look. 'I'm sorry.'

'That's okay,' Johnnie said. A horrible sensation of something burning hot and dry in his belly flew upwards and seemed to fill him with a pain he hadn't known before. The agony over Bertie was something different. This had within it a core of angry regret made acute by the knowledge that things between him and Pa could, so easily, have been different. *If only . . . if only . . .* But he managed a smile and said, 'Thank you.'

'We'll talk about options in a day or two. Until then, there's not much you can do.'

'I see.' Johnnie nodded briefly and turned back to the room. Through the glass panel to one side of the door, he saw Alex sitting against the wall, looking over at Sally. The expression on her face made him stop: it was a mixture of her own misery and a kind of apprehension that was close to fear as Sally talked. Sally was leaning over David, holding his hand, everything in her showing that she was defending her property. Alex, as usual, kept at bay, pushed into second place.

What the hell has Sally been so afraid of all these years? She got Pa, wasn't that enough? Why did she have to push us away? There was enough of him to go around. Why couldn't she share? The thought was amplified by the pain still burning through him. *She can't be allowed to get away with it. I'll stop her.*

He burst through the door into the room and Sally looked up at him, startled. He'd intended to shout at her but as she looked up, she seemed suddenly vulnerable and old, a sixty-year-old woman clutching the hand of her unconscious husband. He couldn't do it.

'Is everything okay?' Alex asked.

Johnnie nodded, unable to speak. It seemed so awfully sad: Pa there, the three of them wanting him back so badly, wishing now that things could be put right.

'Johnnie?' Alex looked worried.

'Yes. There's nothing more to add. Look, Pa is stable. I'm going to think about heading back.'

'That's a good idea,' Sally put in. 'If you go early, you'll miss the worst of the traffic as well.'

'Yeah. I think that's what I'll do.' He bit his lip. Tears, unexpected and unwelcome, had rushed into his eyes. He blinked hard. 'I'm just going out for a moment. I'll be back.'

He walked through the hospital corridors, seeing little through the blurriness in his eyes, avoiding the shapes coming towards him and trying to find his way out. By the time he got down to the ground floor and made his way out of the huge glass doors, he had tears flowing freely down his face. No one paid much attention; tears were not unusual in a place like this. He made his way past a couple of smokers, one in a wheelchair with a cigarette in one hand, the other clasped around the pole of a drip stand, and found a space where he could sob quietly. It lasted only a moment but the weeping released some of the pent-up pain. He felt a hand on his arm.

'Johnnie?'

It was Alex, her dark blue eyes concerned. 'Are you okay?'

Johnnie nodded. 'Just felt the strain there, that's all. I'm fine.'

'You're not really going, are you?'

'If he makes it to tomorrow, then I'll go home. I'll come back as soon as I'm needed.'

Alex looked anxious. 'Of course. It's just . . .'

'What?'

'Nothing. You're needed at home, I know that. At least you'll see the girls tonight.'

'Yeah.' He smiled. 'That's good. I'll look forward to that.' He sighed. 'I just don't know how much of Sally I can take.'

'She's being poisonous,' Alex agreed.

'No change there. I just wonder why she can't let up, even now.'

'I don't think she sets out to hurt us, I honestly think she doesn't know how it looks and sounds.'

Johnnie smiled at his sister, full of affection for her. 'You're too kind to her.'

Alex shrugged. 'Come on,' she said. 'Let's go back in. I'll treat you to a coffee from the shop if you want.'

'Can't resist that,' Johnnie said, and they went back in together.

They sat together around the bed, drawn by the man who lay there. Nurses came and went, and they went out for soup at the canteen for lunch. Then, in the afternoon, conversation faded and they sat in their own thoughts.

When did I last see him? Alex wondered. She had driven around the previous Sunday with the girls, to Pa and Sally's new house, a smart red-brick on the edge of the village in a development of similar houses, aimed at the prosperous retired: easy to maintain, with traditional looks and generous gardens and garages. Sally had brought out lemon drizzle cake and made tea, and they'd sat in the kitchen, talking about this and that. She remembered now that she'd asked him about the new arrivals at Tawray and he'd been very vague. Scottish people, he'd said. With a funny name.

'I'd like to do the Christmas flowers,' Alex had said. Sally had gone upstairs to make sure the girls weren't in her sewing room and they were on their own for a moment.

'Oh yes, dear, you must,' Pa had said. 'I can't imagine Tawray without the flowers at Christmas.'

'You'll have to come and see them,' Alex had said.

'Oh no.' He'd shaken his head slowly. She'd noticed again the way his hair was now almost entirely white, and how his face had hollows in the cheeks and was loose at the jaw – as the padding of youth had vanished, it had fallen in and down. He was not just middle-aged now, but elderly. 'I don't think I'll go back to Tawray.'

'What, never?' She'd given a laugh of disbelief.

'I don't think so.' He'd looked up and, to her surprise, his eyes were sad. 'I don't think I'll ever go back again. My time there is over. To be honest, it was over a long time ago. I've just been a caretaker. I wasn't really supposed to live there, not after you children had left.'

She hadn't known what to say; too many questions rolled around her mind to find the one that was most important. And then Sally came back in, and the subject changed. Sally wasn't keen on talking about Tawray, except in tones of relief that they didn't have to be bothered with it anymore.

I had no idea that was the last time I would talk to him.

They'd parted as they had so many times: kisses in the hallway, a promise to see each other soon. He'd slipped the girls a five-pound note each. Then he and Sally had stood on the front step, waving, as they drove away. She'd quickly forgotten the afternoon, thinking about what needed doing in the coming week, simply trusting things would go on as normal. Instead, everything had changed.

We never know when that moment will come.

She had the strongest impulse to run over to Pa, shake him, beg him to come back. She could hardly believe he wasn't going to wake, blink, cough and say, 'Goodness, what on earth am I doing here?'

That isn't going to happen.

She thought of the girls and looked at her watch. She'd said she would pick them up from school today, as they had their bags from the night before to bring home.

'Shall we make a move, Johnnie?' she asked.

He started. 'What? Oh yes. Come on.'

'Can I give you a lift home, Sally?'

'Oh no. I'm staying here until they throw me out,' Sally replied, smiling. 'I can't think of leaving him.'

'I'll bring the girls back later if you want a break.'

'I can't leave him,' she said in a dramatic tone. 'I can't bear for him to be alone.'

'Of course.' *Why does everything she say sound fake, even when I think she means it?* 'Well, please call me if I'm needed.'

'Yes, dear.' Sally looked over at Johnnie. 'And you're going home?'

'I'll come in the morning,' he said quietly. 'Then I'll go back.'

'I see.' Sally brightened perceptibly. 'Of course, Mundo will be here by then.'

Alex swapped a look with Johnnie.

'Come on, Al,' he said, holding out his hand. 'Let's go home. That's what I need right now.'

Chapter Ten

1985

'Everyone is worried about you, Julia,' Lala said. She waved at the waiter, who hurried over. 'Two glasses of Sancerre, please,' she said, 'and a dozen oysters.'

Julia said quickly, 'Can't I please have something else?' Unusually, she was starving, and the idea of oysters was not just repellent but pointless. She needed substance. She'd already devoured all the bread in the basket and was hoping they would bring some more.

'Of course – but what?' Lala said with an air of faint surprise as though she couldn't imagine anyone wanting anything other than oysters.

Julia looked enquiringly at the waiter, who passed her a menu. She searched for the heartiest dish. 'Oh, steak, please, with frites. And mash.'

'*And* mash?' echoed Lala, then looked at Julia as if for the first time, seeing her thin face and skinny arms. Worry crossed her face. 'Absolutely. Mash too. Whatever you want, darling.'

They were sitting on the ground floor of a very smart

restaurant. Above them was a hushed and luxurious dining room where a famous chef with a Michelin star served French food, but they sat downstairs in a brightly tiled bistro. Lala had brought Julia there for what she said was a treat but now, Julia saw, it was going to be a talk.

The price of a decent meal.

'More bread too, please,' Julia said quickly as the waiter departed. 'God, I'm famished.'

'You look like you haven't eaten for a week,' Lala said, her expression still worried. 'In fact, you look terrible.'

'Well, thanks very much.' The bread basket was empty, so Julia took out a cigarette and lit it, hoping that Lala wouldn't notice the faint tremor in her fingers.

Lala sighed. 'You know what I mean.' She looked suddenly sad. 'Julia, this is awful. I hate seeing you like this.'

'There's no need to worry.' Julia shrugged. 'I've grown up.'

'So I see.' Lala obviously wanted to say more, but lit herself a cigarette instead, pulling the zinc ashtray across the table towards her. After a few puffs, she tapped her ash and said slowly, 'You've had a horrible time, Julia. I'm so sorry about what happened. It was terrible.'

'Mmm. Thank you.'

Aunt Victoria had said quite plainly that it was a doomed venture to try for a baby so many years after the last one. It was bound to end in tears. As though it was all Mummy's own fault, and she deserved it. Julia had been alone in the house except for her mother when she heard the shriek and cry from upstairs. She'd run up the stairs, pelted along the landing, pushed open her parents' bedroom door and seen no one. Then she'd heard the moan from the bathroom. Crossing the bedroom seemed to take forever, the pounding of her heart deafening her. She'd gone in, terrified, and seen . . .

She puffed quickly on her cigarette while she looked for the waiter. 'Where is that wine?'

Lala moved slightly towards her, her pale blue eyes sorrowful. 'It must have been awful for you.'

Julia didn't say anything, barely looked at her, but a bitter voice in her head replied, *Of course it was. I'm tormented by it all the time. If Lala can't see it, then who can?*

'I'm worried about you.' Lala was more chic and Parisienne than ever, her fair hair in a neat bob with a feathery fringe sweeping over her forehead. She wore a striped blouse and a white skirt, and looked more elegant than anyone else in the room.

She looks happy, Julia thought, her gaze pulled to the shiny red lipstick her sister was wearing. There was a man in Paris, she remembered, a much older professor who worked at the Sorbonne. Lala didn't live with him but they were a couple. At least, she thought that was right. Time and distance had loosened their bond, and Lala seemed so very grown-up now. 'Did Daddy send you?'

'He's worried too. We all are.' She emphasised the 'all'. No one knew why Julia would barely speak to her father. After what had happened, after Mummy was buried, Julia disappeared into a black hole of depression. Her school work stopped abruptly and she plummeted out of St Agatha's sixth form like a stone sinking without trace in the sea.

'We would like to help Julia, Mr Teague, but I'm afraid

that she is a little beyond us now,' the headmistress had said gravely, as though Julia hadn't been sitting right there, staring mulishly at the carpet. 'We suggest she takes a long holiday to put recent events behind her and perhaps an independent therapist may be of some help in a case like this.'

No one is going to mention Mummy, Julia had thought, furious. When Julia went away to the funeral and then returned, no one so much as asked her how she was. She was expected to behave quite normally, as though she hadn't seen what she had seen, done what she had done. That was some kind of dirty secret, that she must keep to herself and not bother anyone else with.

Daddy insisted on the therapy, so she went, but it made no difference. When she told the therapist outright that she felt that Daddy and the family had murdered Mummy by forcing her to get pregnant, the therapist had found it all so interesting that she had ended up agreeing with Julia that perhaps he had. That was when she found she could barely look at her father, let alone touch him or smile at him, or beg him for the comfort she wanted so desperately.

Fix this! she wanted to yell. *Bring her back!*

But there was no mending it, and Daddy seemed entirely ignorant of the pressures he'd put on his wife, and the fact that she'd carried the weight of Tawray's future on her shoulders. So Julia wouldn't stay.

She'd demanded to go to London and try her luck as an actress, and Daddy let her go, helpless in the face of her determination, just when she most wanted him to hold her close and tell her he needed her and loved her, and he was sorry. But Daddy was lost in his own grief, and around him fluttered Gran and Aunt Victoria, like a pair of anxious pigeons, and he couldn't seem to see out from the whirring of wings flapping and snapping around him.

The acting course Julia took at a theatre school in north London was not a particularly good one – it didn't have the cachet of RADA or the more well-known schools – but it was something, and it was there she met Mark, a tall, round-faced old Etonian who was passing time until he inherited a baronetcy and a country house in Yorkshire. They seemed to recognise something in one another – a desperate nihilism disguised as an appetite for fun – and they started spending all their time together. Mark kissed her one night at a party and the next day he casually asked a barman for a glass of wine 'for my girlfriend' and Julia realised that they were a couple. She liked that. She liked him kissing her, although it was usually when they were both very drunk and it was hard to remember much about it afterwards. It didn't take much to persuade her to leave the respectable house she was lodging in and move into his place, a shabby old townhouse in Stockwell that had once been grand and imposing but was deteriorating slowly, its stucco crumbling, the roof slates sliding off, the chimneys growing crooked. Mark's other friends were a mixture of public-school boys and anarchic students, dropouts and addicts he had met in local pubs and offered rooms to. They all had one thing in common: drugs.

Julia was innocent of everything but cigarettes and the occasional drink, but she soon learned that Mark wasn't fussy: he took anything and everything he could get his hands on – mostly pills, weed and coke when he could get hold of it. The house reeked with cannabis smoke and was covered in the detritus of drinking, smoking and drug-taking. It was seedy but Mark lent it a rakish glamour.

It must be all right, if Mark does it.

She smoked her first joint with Mark the day she moved into his house, both of them sitting cross-legged on the floor-boards of his bedroom, and then he suggested they have sex.

'All right then,' she said, shrugging, as though it was some-thing she'd done many times, not never. *I've got to some time. Maybe being a bit dizzy will help. They say it's always horrible the first time. First joint, first shag. Might as well get it all over at the same time.*

It was the afternoon, the window half obscured by a piece of tie-dyed cloth nailed to the frame. On Mark's bed, the mattress was only just covered by a sheet of uncertain clean-liness and a duvet without a cover. Julia lay down, hoping that Mark knew what to do and that he would be able to transport her with the kind of raptures she'd read about in forbidden books at school, but she felt nothing except dis-comfort, while he panted and groaned, evidently getting something from the whole process that she did not. She couldn't lose herself in it. It wasn't anything like the excite-ment of kissing the boy in the village that night of the royal wedding. There was nothing of the urgent, pleasurable rush, the strange need to complete the act she'd felt then. But that was only kissing.

Is sex always like this for us? For women? she wondered. She wrapped her arms around him and tried to make a connection with him as he heaved on top of her, but into her mind flashed the terrible picture of her mother, lying on the floor of her bathroom in a pool of scarlet, and she remembered scrabbling with towels, shouting for help, slipping in the blood, seeing that awful sight on the tiles . . . She knew suddenly and without a doubt that it was her lot to suffer too. That's what happened to women. There was the blissful time when they were children – happy, unselfconscious, natural – before the gruesome transformation into the beings desired by men, and then they were slaves – not just to men but to these bodies, full of the mysterious and bloody machinery that created life.

Gripped by panic, she pushed Mark away suddenly, with a strength that she hadn't known she had.

'What?' he said groggily, confused.

'I won't get pregnant, will I?' she demanded, urgent and breathless.

'I don't know. Are you on the pill?'

She shook her head, eyes wide and frightened.

He grumbled as he disentangled himself from her, and crawled over to his trousers to retrieve a small foil packet. 'S'alright. I've got a johnnie.' A moment later, he was crouched over himself, pressing on the small slippery disc and rolling it down. 'There we are. You're safe now.'

She didn't really want to carry on, but he assumed it and she didn't feel she could call a stop to things now. She stared at the patterns on the ceiling until it was, at last, over.

'Did I leave you high and dry?' he said, rolling off her.

'Oh no, I had a lovely time, thank you,' she said politely, though she wasn't really sure what he meant.

The next day she went to a clinic in Clapham and got herself on the pill. After that, she felt all right when they had sex, although she never seemed to get as much from it as Mark did. Another couple in the house couldn't keep their hands off each other, and sounds of enthusiastic congress emanated from their room at all hours – groans and screams and thuds and poundings – after which they emerged looking dazed and euphoric. Julia wondered what on earth they could be up to. Could it be so very different from what she and Mark did? Surely there were only so many permutations available in the basic biological process. How could it be blissful for some people and not for others? It was a mystery.

But still – sex and drugs. This must be living, at last, Julia thought. It was exciting: endless parties, music and dancing, the oblivion of cheap white wine, vodka from the corner store, and the fuzzy numbness from smoking joints. She dyed her hair peroxide white and put another piercing in her right ear. She bought clothes in the markets and charity shops, and changed her look entirely. When Mark offered her pills, she said no, but she drank hard, smoked weed and snorted coke, quickly loving the buzz, the rush, the mania it gave her. With coke she could stay up all night, drinking and dancing, losing herself in the frantic rush for pleasure.

It helps.

But it wasn't really pleasure, she knew that. It was valuable because it made her feel hyper-alive while numbing the pain. When she wasn't in the grip of chemically induced excitement, she felt she was existing in a world full of cotton wool, removed from the rest of the human race, as though she was opting out of all that. She was never hungry, and either slept very little or else for long, dead, dreamless hours. She lost weight, smoked too much, flunked her course and dropped out, living on the allowance Daddy gave her. Two years had gone by and she had nothing to show for it.

'But we're having a marvellous time,' Mark told her, so she tried to believe him. When his friend, a marquess who spent thousands a month on heroin, took them to his stately home in a helicopter and they spent a weekend utterly out of it, high, sick, drunk and in a state of dazed depravity while surrounded by priceless works of art and magnificent furniture, Julia felt that something was terribly, awfully wrong, even when Mark told her that they'd had the weekend of their lives.

What was the answer then? It seemed clear. She should surrender to drugs entirely, like Mark, let go of her old life, and forget all the misery and pain. Would it be so bad to accept this strange muffled netherworld? To stay forever huddled up to Mark, both of them out of it, living on in this broken-down house in a grim part of town?

Under the influence of his grand, addicted friends, Mark had gone from weed and coke to using heroin. Julia was becoming accustomed to finding him dazed and bleary-eyed, totally out of it, the nasty paraphernalia of tubes and needles scattered around him. He was slipping away from her into a closed-off, utterly personal existence. He wanted to inject her too, and she'd refused. But lately she was finding that heroin was on her mind more and more. Now, every day, she wondered if today she should ask him to shoot her up too, to give her a taste of the marvellous escape he had told her about, the warm, all-enveloping euphoria that melted pain and trouble away. She yearned for it in a primitive, infantile way, but Mark's evident physical decline stopped her from taking the step, along with her certainty that she would surrender instantly and completely to it. Then they would be addicts together, egging each other on until they grew scarred, pocked, thin, grey. That image of the future frightened her. But she still wondered, every day, if today would be the day.

How did I get here?

Now here was Lala, a person from that old life. Julia knew Daddy had sent Lala to find her and talk her round.

He can forget about it. I'm not going back.

Tawray was like a dream, a world that she had inhabited in another existence, or a place in a story she had once read that was so vivid it had been like living there. In her heart, though, she yearned for home: the familiar beauty of the old house, the garden that spread down the cliffs to the sea with its ever-changing moods, the lake and the roof and all her secret places. Here, in London, she was nothing – a tiny speck of pointless humanity in a seething city. She couldn't see a time when this wouldn't be her lot: struggling on, trying to get through another day with as much pleasure and as little pain as possible.

The waiter brought the wine and Julia drained hers in two gulps. 'Can I have another?'

Lala nodded. 'I mean it, Julia. You're not looking your

best.' She watched as Julia smoked nervously, waiting for the waiter to bring her refill. 'Your hair . . .'

'I love it. It's like Debbie Harry,' Julia said quickly. She touched her hair, which was rough and straw-like from the peroxide.

'It's not just the hair. You don't look well.' Lala put her hand out and rested it suddenly on Julia's, quelling the nervous tapping, and gazed into her eyes. 'I haven't been around for you, I know that, and I'm sorry. My life has been so busy – but that's no good as an excuse, I know that. I want to make it up to you. Why don't you come with me to Paris? You could sleep and eat and rest. I could look after you.'

Julia shook her head. 'No,' she said vaguely, 'I'm too busy.'

'Doing what? Daddy said you're not acting anymore.'

'I might take it up again. The course was no good. I'm thinking of doing some fringe theatre.' Julia stubbed out her cigarette and lit another immediately. 'Someone I know is putting on a rehearsed reading in a pub. I might audition.'

Lala looked doubtful. 'A pub?'

'I've got to start somewhere.' Julia smoked crossly. 'All right. I won't bother.'

'Darling, I can see you're not happy. Let me help you. Come to Paris. Get away from here for a while. You might see things differently after that.'

Julia blew out a plume of smoke and tapped her foot anxiously. 'Maybe,' she said. 'I'll think about it. My boyfriend might not like it.'

'Your boyfriend?' Lala looked interested. 'Who is he?'

'No one. Just a boyfriend.' She shrugged. She didn't have

the energy to tell Lala all about Mark. She couldn't begin to describe how the house was deep in squalor and how she was afraid of being sucked under, taken down into the murky depths of the place where Mark now lived. She wanted to, she longed to, but she didn't know where to start. Lala would be horrified, she would try to take Julia away from Mark and the filth of the Stockwell house; she didn't understand that it was something bigger than just where she lived and who with. It was something inside herself, a monster that wanted to pick her up and throw her into the fire and watch her burn.

They ate lunch together, Lala trying to get as much information out of Julia as she could, until it became obvious that Julia intended to be uncooperative, and then she changed the subject entirely. By the time lunch was over, Julia felt happier, blurry on four glasses of wine and replete from an unaccustomedly huge lunch, so she agreed to wander with Lala along the Brompton Road. They stopped to look at the clothes in the windows of the exclusive dress shops and Lala talked to her about her work in Paris and her dreams of designing and perhaps having her own atelier.

Lucky Lala. She sees something in the world that I don't.

It felt like almost everyone else was absorbed in this strange existence, acting as though it wasn't the temporal, brief little dream she knew it to be. They lived as though now mattered and as if they were going to live forever. Try as she might, Julia couldn't see it. The knowledge of the short flicker of existence dominated everything for her. What could last? Only places, like Tawray, and the seasons, and the sea.

'Come and stay with me,' Lala said when they reached Knightsbridge underground station. 'I mean it. I think it will help you.'

'I'll think about it,' Julia promised. She imagined leaving her dark, grubby world and going to Paris, for light and life and rehabilitation. It sounded inviting. Perhaps it was possible. She trembled on the brink of saying a decisive yes, giving herself over to Lala's vision, and then she pulled back, not quite ready for that commitment. Instead, she let Lala kiss her cool cheek. 'Bye, Lala. Thanks. Give my love to Daddy, okay?'

She turned and descended into the dark warmth of the underground.

Chapter Eleven

The invitation was completely unexpected and arrived with Tawray's address crossed out by one strong blue line and the Stockwell address carefully printed next to it.

Julia stared at it, blinking.

'What's that?' Mark asked. He was lounging on the sofa, feet crossed on the coffee table, an overflowing ashtray next to them. The television was showing some daytime quiz show but he was waiting for the lunchtime edition of *Neighbours* to start.

'An invitation from a girl I knew at school,' she said. 'Look.'

He took the stiff card from her and looked at it. 'Mr and Mrs Jardine for their daughter Seraphina. Birthday party at Annabel's. How nice.'

'Do you know her?'

Mark shook his head. 'I don't believe I've had the pleasure.' He tossed it down onto the coffee table. 'It's for tomorrow night, that's a bit sudden.'

'It was sent home. They've only just forwarded it. Do you want to come with me?'

'You're not going, are you?'

'Well . . . I don't know.'

'You don't want to be with that lot anymore, do you? It's much more fun here.'

Julia looked around the dirty sitting room, with its broken furniture covered in cigarette burns and stains, the filthy carpet, the fireplace full of fag butts and the bare bulb dangling from the ceiling. She knew Mark was high. It was only ten in the morning, but his gear was on the table – burned tin foil, a spoon, a cigarette lighter – and his face had a bleary quality that showed he was half lost to a world of oblivion.

She stared at him in a rush of sadness. He hadn't been like this when they'd met; he'd been plump-faced, not gaunt, his eyes clear, his voice strong. He'd been warm and funny and sweet. She'd been fond of him and then grown to love him. The sex might have been less than earth-shattering, but it was affectionate and friendly, and she'd come to like the nearness to him and the comfort his body offered her. They rarely did that now. Mark didn't have the energy or the inclination. He was thin, full of anxiety when he wasn't smoking heroin, and then utterly zoned out, until the effects wore off and the anxiety returned. Julia saw suddenly and clearly that Mark would probably not survive and that if he was going to be saved, she wasn't the person to do it. He would, inexorably, take her with him and something small and persistent inside her told her that, despite everything, she wasn't ready to go under. Not yet.

She picked up the invitation. 'Well, I think I might go. I always liked her.'

Mark shrugged. 'Whatever you want.'

By the following afternoon, she was feeling nervous about going, and would have pulled out if Mark hadn't annoyed her by teasing her about it. She half decided just to pretend she was going, and then wander around for a few hours, get a coffee somewhere and come home.

Nonetheless, she spent the afternoon getting ready. She put on a slinky dress of purple silk that Lala had sent her, and a pair of high heels borrowed from one of the girls in the house with a higher glamour quotient than her own. Her peroxided hair was backcombed and hairsprayed until it stood out in a white halo, and she went to town with cheap make-up from Boots, her eyelids thick with glittery purple shadow and her mouth scarlet and glossy. Over the top she slung a fur coat she'd picked up in a charity shop on the Clapham Road. Once she'd finished and was ready to go, she certainly didn't look anything like Miss Julia Teague, late of St Agatha's convent school.

Maybe I look a little bit like Debbie Harry. Just a bit.

She hoped so. Thinking of Debbie gave her confidence.

'You look good,' Mark said when she came downstairs, all ready for the party. He was sitting with four other housemates, preparing for an evening in. 'Watch out, though, you could get mugged around here, looking like that.'

One of the other housemates, a tough bloke from East London, eyed the coat. 'Is that real fur?'

'Antique.' Julia did a twirl. 'No animals in living memory were harmed. Why don't you walk me to the station if it's dangerous out there?'

'You'll be fine.' Mark was preparing to roll a joint and didn't want to put down the paraphernalia that was carefully balanced on his knee. 'Don't get too pissed or you'll fall over on the way home.'

'Thanks for that. See you later.'

She tottered to Stockwell station, not used to walking in heels, clutching a plastic carrier bag with a gift for Seraphina in it, and felt as if everyone she passed was staring at her.

Do I look great? Or like an idiot?

On the train, she kept her eyes fixed to the floor to avoid the gaze of the other passengers, but once she emerged at Green Park, she felt better. It was a March night, dark and cold after a briskly sunny spring day, and Piccadilly was dusky, the blackness brightened by the lights of the Ritz, the shops and the glow from headlights and traffic lights. Other people in smart clothes walked past her: men in dinner suits and dark overcoats, women in glittering dresses with shoulder pads. As she walked past one man, he whistled gently under his breath and she felt a strange rush of pleasure at his approval. She pulled her fur coat closer and walked slowly towards Berkeley Square, smoking a cigarette to calm her nerves. She still half intended to go past Annabel's and find somewhere to sit quietly until it was time to go home, but somehow she ended up making her way to the western side of the square to the little canopied tent behind the railings that covered the staircase down to the club. On the pavement was a liveried doorman, keeping out passers-by and letting the favoured ones pass down the steps and into the hallowed depths.

'Evening, miss,' he said as Julia approached. 'Are you a member?'

The tone of his voice made it quite clear that he did not believe for an instant that she was. She lifted her chin and tried to sound authoritative.

'I'm here for the party. Sardine's party.'

The doorman frowned. 'Who?'

'I've got a card somewhere – Sardine's party . . .' She scrabbled in her pockets, flustered. 'Ask Sardine, she'll know me.'

He took in her peroxide hair and her shabby fur coat, and seemed to make a rapid judgement about her. 'Look, love, you need to move on. You're not coming in, understand? This isn't your kind of place. You try one of them places up on Oxford Street, eh? You'll get business there.'

Julia gaped at him, searching for words to explain herself. Her cheeks flooded red.

'Come on now, on your way.' He went to take her arm and move her aside.

'It's all right, she's with me,' said a voice and Julia turned to see a tall man in a smart dark suit. 'We're here for the Jardine party – Seraphina Jardine's birthday.' He held out a stiff card, the same as the one she had forgotten to bring with her.

The doorman was suddenly all courtesy, smooth and welcoming as though he had never questioned Julia at all. 'Yes, of course, sir, miss. Please go in.'

The man smiled at Julia and gestured for her to lead the way down the iron staircase. Julia went past the doorman, saying, 'Thank you,' and the man followed.

When they got to the bottom, she turned and said, 'Thank you so much. He wasn't going to let me in! He thought I was a prostitute or something!'

'Sardine?' he said quizzically.

'That was Seraphina's nickname at school. Seraphina Jardine – Sardine. You can see how it happens.'

'*I* can. But you can hardly be surprised when the doorman doesn't get it.' He led her towards the tiny reception window. 'Come on, let's get our names ticked off, then you can leave your coat.'

In the ladies' cloakroom, she smiled at the attendant and checked her appearance in the mirror. She looked good, she thought, despite the gauntness in her face, and the peroxide hair looked punky and rebellious against the purple silk of her dress. She hummed the tune of 'Heart of Glass' under her breath as she applied another slick of blood-red lipstick, and went out to see if her friend from the staircase was there, but he was gone, and she had to make her way through the low-ceilinged, vaulted basement rooms of the nightclub on her own until she found the private room where Seraphina's party was being held. Inside were a crowd of smartly dressed people, talking and drinking, and they turned to look in surprise as she came in, familiar faces among the strangers.

Think about Debbie.

She put her chin in the air and held out her bag. 'Where's Sardine, then? I've got a bloody present!'

They gaped at her. Not so long ago she had been just like these girls, her erstwhile friends and schoolfellows, with their long hair, Alice bands, ribbons and floral dresses. Now they were a notch or two above that in glamour, but not much, in sensible heels, smart dresses and strings of pearls. From the looks on their faces, it was obvious she'd taken another path and it had transformed her, so that she was an exotic bird among a flock of pretty, plump domestic chickens. They surrounded her, shrieking and fascinated.

'Oh Julia, you look so different! Doesn't she look amazing? Your hair, aren't you brave! I wouldn't dare, Mummy would have a fit. Oh goodness, where did you get that dress? *Paris?* How glamorous!'

They were sweet, well-brought-up girls, doing secretarial courses at Lucy Clayton, or working as personal assistants in banks, law companies or publishing houses. They lived in Chelsea and Kensington and went out to Harvey Nicks, Dickens & Jones and a few other acceptable haunts. They expected to marry soon, and quite well, then settle down to life as wives and mothers, raising their own broods and chivvying them through the same old rituals. The men were at university, or in the army, and would soon be the bankers, lawyers and consultants with young Sloaney secretaries of their own.

Why am I not like this? Julia wondered. *It seemed to be my destiny. But I'm different. I don't belong in Stockwell, and I don't belong here either. Where do I belong?*

She took a glass of champagne from a passing waiter and

slugged it all back at once. 'Happy birthday, Sardine, darling!' she said, offering her bag with a bright smile to Seraphina, who was in raptures over everything. Then she took another.

I'm drunk.

She blinked lazily and nodded at the young man talking to her, plump in a striped shirt with braces, his jacket abandoned somewhere. He was pink in the face from lots of champagne and weekends spent outdoors, and chattered away with an almost endearing mixture of bluster and nervousness.

'Oh, I say, your hair,' he would exclaim every now and then, and chortle. 'It is brilliant, it really is.'

Julia sipped her champagne. It was late. They'd eaten canapés and drunk lots of booze and nearly everyone left seemed to be smoking. The birthday cake had been cut, the birthday girl had been cheered, and now plates of half-eaten cream sponge with vivid pink icing were abandoned around the room. Somewhere, she could hear music pounding, and she was drawn to the beat, her feet itching to dance.

Oh yes, I want to dance!

When had she last danced?

I'm young. I'm drunk. I want to dance. Fuck this lot.

Her companion was talking earnestly about his work at Schroders. She looked around the room from beneath lowered lids. Over there, Sardine was talking tearily to one of her friends, clearly pissed and overemotional. A couple was snogging wildly in a corner, as though they were invisible to the rest of the room. Others were in small gaggles. The party was officially at an end and there was talk of going to a favourite pub near Sloane Square. She noticed a tall, broad back in a smart charcoal flannel jacket and recognised her friend from the door. He hadn't crossed her path all evening, and she'd forgotten about him.

Bloody rude. He was supposed to be my friend. He told the doorman we were together – well, we weren't, not one bit. Rude.

She put out the cigarette she was smoking, grounding it down into an ashtray. 'I'm just going to the loo,' she said firmly to the braces boy.

'Oh, yeah, sure. See you in a bit,' he said as she walked off, trying not to sway on her heels. Out of the small private room, she could hear the thud of the music, louder and more enticing than ever, and turned away from the cloakroom to follow it. It led her through another bar and into the restaurant, a barely lit space full of tables and punctuated by glimmering brass pillars, the diners just dark shapes with faces illuminated by the table lamps. Beyond it was what she was seeking: a dance floor sparkling with tiny stars, a shadowy DJ booth at the far end. People were dancing, girls grinding and bopping, most of the men grooving clumsily with suit jackets flapping and ties flying. Julia made her way through the restaurant, stumbling slightly as she manoeuvred around chairs and pillars, until she reached the dance floor just as one of her favourite songs came on. It was Blondie. 'Rapture'.

She shrieked with pleasure, though she couldn't be heard, and began to dance. Her purple silk dress gleamed in the flashing lights, her hair was a white cloud, and she moved with an elemental connection to the powerful beat, singing along and whirling about the floor. It was blissful. Everyone and everything else fell away: the dreariness of her life with Mark and her abandoned dreams of acting; the dark misery that had hung around her heart for so long. She rode the wave of drunkenness and music, feeling elated and liberated, alive at last after so long feeling dead.

She didn't know how long she danced but each song set her off on a fresh wave of excitement and connection to the music, and after a while she realised that a man was dancing with her; she was happy that someone else shared her joy and desire to let go and she smiled and danced alongside him, though she could see that he wasn't all that good at it. He was fat and his belly hung over his trousers and juddered as he moved. But they were joined in the pleasure of movement and so she wouldn't hold that against him.

But then, she found he was too close, and suddenly his huge hands were on her, stroking the purple silk and rounding the curves of her behind, and the big belly was pressing against her, his face brushing hers. She tried to push away but he was insistent, pawing at her, grinning and singing loudly, 'Pretty lady, pretty lady!' in her ear. 'Why don't you come with me, pretty lady, huh?'

'No thanks,' she shouted, and pushed at him again.

But he didn't hear her, or pretended not to, crooning at her and pushing himself against her, edging her away from everyone else. She thought, dimly, that he would soon have her off the dance floor and into the shadows at the side.

Suddenly a warm hand took hers and a voice said loudly over the music, 'Do you mind?'

The next moment, she was being pulled out of the fat man's grasp, and she saw it was the man from the door. 'Oh, hello,' she said cheerily. 'Do you want to dance?'

He ignored her but instead said insistently to the fat man, 'I think you'd better leave her alone.'

The fat man shrugged, laughed and flapped his hands as if to dismiss Julia, and turned to look for someone else to try his luck with.

Julia grabbed the other man's hands. 'Come on then!' She started to dance, laughing. He took a step or two with her, and then shook his head, smiling.

'I'm not drunk enough.'

'Come on!'

Her enthusiasm was hard to resist. The Rolling Stones came on and he seemed to find a new confidence, moving in time with the music.

'You're not bad actually,' Julia said, but he didn't appear to hear her. They danced to the insistent beat, Julia singing along, making him spin her around. When it finished, they were breathless and laughing. The music started up again, and she went to carry on, but he shook his head and beckoned to her to come away.

'I want to dance!' she protested, but she let him lead her through the restaurant and out into the bar. 'Oh, are we having another drink?'

He turned to her as they went. 'We could. But it's late. And I think we've both had plenty.'

'Thanks for getting rid of the slimeball.'

'This place can attract a certain type, I'm afraid.'

'Dirty old men?' She giggled.

'And willing young ladies.'

She pouted. 'That's not me. I just like dancing.' She cast a wistful glance over her shoulder to the crowded dance floor and the fainter pounding of the music.

'I can tell.' They were in the bar now, and he stopped and turned to look at her. He was tall, she had noticed that right away, but now she saw a firm gaze, and a determined mouth. He had intensely blue eyes, and his dark hair, almost black, was cut regulation short. 'I don't mean to boss you about, but don't you think you ought to go home? You're more than a little pissed.'

'Do you mind?' she said, indignant. 'I'm a bit sloshed, yes, but . . . well.' She felt very grown-up and sophisticated suddenly, a girl who had seen the dark side of life. 'I can take it. My boyfriend is a drug addict.'

He raised his eyebrows. 'Well, I'm not sure that means you have a limitless capacity for booze. You should go home. I'll put you in a taxi. Where do you live?'

'Stockwell.'

He looked surprised. 'Really?'

'I know! Horrors! Not in Chelsea! Yikes.' She hiccupped gently and said, 'Or we could have a drink here.'

'We'll be lucky to find a taxi that will take you to Stockwell. Do you really live there?'

'Yep. With my boyfriend.'

A worried look crossed his face, and two lines formed between his dark brows. 'The drug addict?'

'Yes. You name it, he takes it. Speed, acid, charlie, heroin.'

She felt almost proud of Mark's prodigious appetite. 'Not everyone can manage all that, you know.'

'Heroin? Where are your parents?'

'Dead and buried, darling,' she said dramatically. 'Dead and buried.' Then added, 'Well, one of them. But my father is in Cornwall so that's a no-go.'

He fixed her with a hard stare. 'Are you going to be all right? You . . .' A bewildered look crossed his face. 'You look too utterly fabulous to be going to some drug addict in Stockwell.'

She laughed, flattered, and then the laughter fell away and she was staring at him, almost embarrassed by the knowledge that he was right, she shouldn't go back there to Mark and all the grime and misery. She wasn't happy there. She didn't want to go back. *I don't love Mark. Not really. He'll never change. He'll sit on that sofa and take drugs for the rest of his life. I don't want to watch him kill himself.*

He seemed to read it all in her face. 'Come on,' he said decisively. 'You're coming with me.'

A whoosh of something elemental flooded through her, a kind of fizzy joy mixed with a sense of absolute rightness, as though she had somehow, against all the odds, managed to get herself to the right place at the right time, and destiny had been fulfilled.

'I'd better get my coat then,' she said.

She woke in a strange bed in a strange room and the first thing that struck her was how comfortable she was. The mattress was soft, the sheets crisp and clean, and everything smelled lovely. The air was fresh, with no bitter tang of sweat, dirt and smoke.

Am I home?

Then she remembered. She was in the flat of the man in Annabel's. David, he'd said his name was. He had given her his bed, insisting on putting on fresh bedding for her, and he had taken the sofa in the small sitting room.

She came out wrapped in the dressing gown she found on the back of the door, and he was in the tiny kitchen making cups of tea, already showered and dressed in a suit and tie. He smiled at her as she came in. 'Good morning. How are you feeling?'

'All right.' She winced. 'Well, not all right. But I'll live.'

'Glad to hear it.' He handed her a cup of tea. 'Sugar?'

'At least three.'

'That bad then?' He passed her the jar of sugar and a spoon.

'Just need to stabilise. Then I'll be fine. Goodness, I must look a fright.'

'You look amazing,' he said softly, and she looked up at him properly.

'You're not so bad yourself,' she said, and the moment turned electric, and then awkward, and she bustled about putting the sugar in her tea.

'I have to go to work in a moment,' David said, sipping his own tea. 'But you're welcome to stay here as long as you like.'

'Where am I?'

'In a little street between the Strand and Covent Garden.'

Julia nodded, sipping the hot, sweet liquid. 'And where do you work?'

'St James's.'

'Stockbroking? Finance?'

'No. The palace. St James's Palace. I'm on leave from the navy working as an aide.'

Julia blinked. 'Gosh, how grand.'

He smiled. 'It is, and it isn't. You'd be surprised. Very ordinary in lots of ways. Didn't you say last night that your father lives in Cornwall?'

'Yes. A place called Tawray.'

'Tawray?' He looked surprised. 'I know it. I'm from Cornwall as well. My surname is Pengelly.'

'Don't tell me our parents are friends or something.' She grimaced. 'That would be a bit too close for comfort.'

'I don't think so. We're Falmouth way. And I've never seen Tawray.'

'It's beautiful. In fact, there's nowhere more lovely.' A longing for home swept over her. 'I'd love to be there now.'

'I know that feeling.'

She felt another bond of connection linking them together. He knew Cornwall. He understood. The sense of rightness grew firmer. She had felt it since the moment she woke up; everything seemed to be in its perfect place. There was order here. There was calm and the comfort that came from things done right. She had the strongest sense that this was where she was supposed to be, and warm relief that she had made her way through the storm to a place she belonged.

'Can I stay here?' she said suddenly.

'Of course. I was going to ask if you would.' He smiled. 'Stay all day. We can go out for dinner tonight and you can tell me all about yourself. Will you do that?'

'Yes please.' She smiled back. 'I don't want to frighten you, but I don't think I'm ever leaving.'

'I won't let you,' he said softly.

'How funny,' she said with a laugh. 'We both know, don't we?'

'Yes. Yes we do.'

Chapter Twelve

Present day

'Your home is so calm compared to mine,' Johnnie said to Alex the next morning, as they prepared to go into the hospital.

'Girls,' Alex smiled. 'That's the answer.'

'Yeah, there is that.' He smiled back, thinking of his energetic younger sons and the way they raced around, noisy, scatty, unable to concentrate for long, and signally unable to do anything for themselves. He thought of breakfast at their house; he tuned out the chaos as much as he could, munching cereal and sipping coffee while he read the news on his tablet. Netta rushed about, getting the boys everything they needed, asking them about swimming kit, instruments, homework, missing socks and all the rest of it. Then there was Bertie. She'd already got him up, washed and dressed him, and brought him downstairs, settling him before the younger ones arrived. Bertie's car and chaperone would arrive to take him to school, and Netta would see him off before driving the boys to their school and then heading on to her workplace. By then, Johnnie was on the train into London, his headphones

145

on, listening to music or the radio and thinking about the day ahead.

He had accepted it as the natural order of things. But here was Alex, free of nearly all of that. Scarlett and Jasmine poured out their own cereal and milk, cleared away their own dishes. Jasmine, at only five, could even put things in the dishwasher. It occurred to him that maybe he could do a little more to help Netta in the morning, and he felt suddenly ashamed. He considered himself an enlightened, modern man. He'd changed nappies and bathed babies, and he made a mean pasta with tomato sauce.

But do I, deep down, feel entitled to be looked after by my wife?

He'd thought he was helping by looking after himself. But then, he never wondered if his cereal would be in the cupboard or coffee in the pot, or milk in the fridge. It was just always there, without any effort on his part. He had clean shirts, pants and socks in the drawer; loo paper, shampoo and toothpaste in the bathroom; lightbulbs and Hoover bags and washing powder and dishwasher tablets – all there, as if by magic. Needs he didn't even know he had were constantly provided for.

He pictured Netta, in her pyjamas while the rest of them were dressed, drinking coffee on the run and skipping breakfast while she unloaded the washing machine, made toast for Joe and told Nathan where to find his PE kit, while he, Johnnie, scanned the news and thought he was helping by putting his plate in the dishwasher before sauntering out.

And was he training the boys to be just as entitled, to

expect someone to run around after them, sorting them out
as well as herself?

He knew the answer.

At the hospital, Johnnie observed sadness descend on Alex.
She had been strong the night before with the girls there,
giving them the most positive spin on their grandfather's condition, but now they were at school, she could show her
misery and anxiety.

As they stood in the lift going up to Pa's floor, he put an
arm around her and gave her a quick hug. 'It'll be okay.'

She nodded, her eyes glistening. 'Yeah. Maybe.'

'Come on.'

They walked the already familiar route to Pa's room. Sally
was sitting by the bed, looking more drawn than the day
before, but managing a smile as they came in.

'He made it through the night, so that's a very good sign.
Do you know, I think he'll be right as rain by Christmas!'

Her brittle cheerfulness grated on Johnnie and he said
brusquely, 'I don't think so.'

Sally frowned. 'What do you mean? The nurse says it's
very good that he hasn't had any further strokes. He's almost
out of the danger zone, they said.'

Johnnie stood by Pa's side, looking down at him, his
expression grim. 'They're soft-soaping you, Sally. It's obvious
Pa isn't going to get better. It's a question of when, not if.'

Sally's blue eyes filled with tears, and she lifted one trembling hand to her face. 'How can you say that, Johnnie? How
can you condemn your own father to death?'

'Don't be ridiculous, it's nothing to do with me. It's just the truth. I'm sorry if you don't like it.'

'Alexandra!' Sally turned to his sister. 'Don't let him speak like this, I won't allow it.'

Johnnie felt the return of the same strange inner burning he'd experienced the day before. Every muscle seemed to tighten. 'You can't change the truth, Sally, just because you don't like it. I know you've tried to do that our whole lives, but it's got to stop. I won't put up with it anymore. I've done it in the past for Pa's sake, but that's over now. We've gone along with your stupid pretences, and your desire to wipe out the bits of the past that aren't convenient, but that isn't going to happen any longer. Do you understand?'

Sally gasped and stared at him through watery eyes, both her shaking hands on her powdery soft cheeks. She said nothing.

'Johnnie,' Alex murmured. 'That's enough.'

He turned to her. 'You know I'm right, Al. No one wants it to be true, but it is. I'm going now – I've got to get home. If Pa really is out of the danger zone, then good. I'll wait to hear from you and I'll come straight back if I'm needed.'

Alex went over, hugged him and kissed his cheek. 'Yes. Go home to Netta and the boys. Give everyone our love. I'll keep in touch.'

He felt comforted. The burning sensation died down a little. 'Thanks. See you later.'

As soon as Johnnie was out on the open road, heading back eastwards, the fury returned as he replayed everything.

Sally, Sally, Sally.

He'd never wanted her in their lives. She'd been forced upon them without so much as a vestige of an explanation or a question about how that made him feel. He remembered the dark, evil days after Mum had died. Life divided into a sunny, carefree time before, and the terrible morning when Pa had come to see him and Alex in the playroom. They'd been watching Saturday morning television, noisy, silly cartoons, and he'd come in, white-faced and red-eyed.

'Johnnie, Ali, turn that off, please.'

She was still Ali then.

He'd been going to protest but something in his father's face frightened him, and they sat on the sofa as Pa told them in a shaking, halting voice that Mum had died.

'How?' Johnnie had said at once, while Alex sat there, frozen and aghast, trying to comprehend the magnitude of what she'd just heard.

Pa had looked agonised. 'She . . . had an accident. At the lake. The boat she was in overturned and she drowned.'

'Then it can't be her,' Johnnie said with ten-year-old confidence. 'Because Mum can swim really well.'

'I'm sorry, Johnnie. It is Mum.'

'Can we see her?' He was sure that if he could just see whoever it was, he'd be able to tell them it wasn't Mum. She could swim. And she told them never to go on the lake because it was dangerous. She'd said the boat was leaky, unsafe. It just wasn't her to do something like that. It wasn't something she would do.

Pa shook his head. 'No. You can't see her. Grandpa and

Granny are coming to take you to stay with them for a few days.'

'Can't I stay with you?' Alex asked in a small, stunned voice.

'It's best if you go where they can look after you. But I'll bring you home soon, I promise. Now go and pack your things, they'll be here in half an hour. Don't forget your tooth-brushes.'

The children stood up, dazed. Alex was starting to cry, but Johnnie couldn't, not until he was sure it was true. Five minutes before their world had been normal, ordered, dominated by concerns like not missing the cartoons. And now it was all utterly, nightmarishly changed.

That's when Johnnie saw her in the doorway, watching, half silhouetted, the flicked-out ends of her blonde hair standing out black against the light behind her. He couldn't see her face clearly, and there was no telling what she was thinking. But the sight of her stamped itself on his memory. Sally had been there right from the start, from the first moment that he'd known he'd lost his mother, and she was inextricably bound up with it. He had to go away, and she stayed. When the children came back after a few days with Pa's parents, Johnnie still not believing that Mum was really dead, Sally had already moved in. She was at the funeral, holding their hands while Pa did the speech, even though Johnnie didn't want her to. Her boy, Mundo, was there too, kicking the pew all the way through the service, clearly bored. And by the graveside, he pinched Johnnie hard as if wanting to make him cry out. Johnnie endured it, pinching his lips together and ignoring the stinging tears that jumped into his eyes as Mundo dug his nails into the tender skin on his arm, beginning as he would mean to go on. Sally and Mundo. Neither of them had ever gone away.

And now Pa's gone too, and Sally is still here. And I think I'm right. I think Sally drove Mum to it by stealing Pa.

He drove on, his fists clenched around the steering wheel, feeling the car pulse and thrust forward under him as he pressed his foot down. He crested a hill and saw a lumbering tractor on the road in front of him.

Oh shit. This isn't the time of year for tractors. What the hell is it doing?

He slowed down. Ahead of him, the road stretched out like a dark silver ribbon, undulating through the green fields on either side. The morning sun had come out unexpectedly and illuminated it into a dazzling line. In front of the tractor, it was clear in both directions.

Fuck it, I'm not sitting behind this guy for miles on end. I need to get home.

Johnnie flicked on the indicator and pulled out to his right, pressing down on the accelerator as he went to regain his speed. As he began to pass the tractor, he saw suddenly that the road ahead was not a straight line after all, but that he was on the crest of a small hill, the road dipping down ahead before rising up again in the distance, creating the illusion of being level.

The very moment he realised this, he saw a car appear directly ahead of him.

Oh shit.

Instinctively he pressed down hard on the brakes and glanced to the left to see if there was room to pull out of the way, but the tractor driver, seeing the situation, was slowing too.

Speed up, you idiot.

Only if the tractor went faster as Johnnie slowed would he have room to pull over in time. A mere few seconds had passed. The driver in the opposite car had seen him and was braking too, but Johnnie saw, with a strange slow-motion clarity, that with no way of pulling to his left, his fate was now in his brakes and the brakes of the car opposite.

He was horrified yet calm, oddly removed from the situation. He was either going to be involved in a terrible head-on collision in a matter of moments, or he wasn't. There was nothing to do now but wait, his foot pressed to the floor on the brake.

Johnnie's car stopped. The tractor had stopped too. The car opposite pulled up violently only a few feet from Johnnie's bonnet. He stared, stunned. He was alive. They hadn't hit.

The man in the car opposite opened his door and got out. Johnnie was flooded with relief. He wanted to get out, run to the other man, throw his arms around him and thank him for saving their lives. Then he saw that the man was red-faced, furious, shouting and swearing, and gesturing at the lines on the road that clearly showed no overtaking.

Johnnie had no memory of seeing them. But he must have checked, surely? Surely he had when he had started his manoeuvre? Or maybe not . . .

He was still stunned, but he could see there was going to

be no tearful act of gratitude and he couldn't face a confrontation. He started the engine, and pulled forward, driving slowly between the tractor and the other car, mouthing an apology at the yelling man as he went. Then he drove slowly away, shaking, unable to believe how close he had come to dying on the road, maybe killing someone else in the process. He thought about Netta, Bertie, Nathan and Joe, and his life with all its myriad stresses and strains, pleasures and joys. *I nearly left it all forever.* Five minutes later, he pulled into a lay-by and sat, dry-eyed but shaking, until he felt calm enough to continue.

We never know. We never know when it's going to come.

Sitting by Pa's bedside, Sally was complaining about Johnnie. 'I don't know how he can be so negative! Poor David, I'm just glad he can't hear what his son is saying about him – that he'll be dead in no time!'

'He wasn't saying that,' Alex said. She had quietly consulted her phone and found several emails about work, asking her when she would be delivering the London-bound decorations, as well as an enquiry for a winter wedding. She was also painfully aware that she had not been keeping her social media accounts up to date, and she had learned lately how much she relied on them for publicising her business and bringing in new clients. As the reality of Pa's new condition had sunk it, the panic of the last two days had begun to lessen. It was now harder to imagine him up and about, walking and talking, than it was to picture him in this supine position, unconscious and completely unresponsive.

Life would have to go on, no matter what. She had orders to fulfil, bills to pay. Tim's monthly payment helped with the mortgage and things the girls needed, but she still had to find the lion's share.

I must see about whether I'm going to get the Tawray contract.

Sally's voice was still quavering in the background of her thoughts.

'That boy has always been ungrateful! David's looked after him so well, and when poor Bertie came along, he was very upset. We all were. I don't know why Johnnie has to be so obstreperous, I really don't. He's been spoiled all his life.'

Alex tried to tune it out. How was it possible for two people to have such diametrically opposed versions of events? It was like they were members of political parties who could never credit their opponents with a shred of human feeling or a single decent motive. Their take on any situation was always that the other had acted badly, unfairly, true to form.

But Sally's wrong. Johnnie wasn't spoiled. Not in the sense she means.

She tuned her out by scrolling through a news feed, reading people's comments about the things going on in the outside world.

She heard the door open, but didn't look up, assuming it was a nurse, come in to check the monitors or replace a drip bag. Instead, a deep voice filled the room.

'Mother, hello. I came as soon as I could.'

She looked up, and Mundo was already in the room, dressed in an expensive camel-coloured coat, every inch the

154

successful lawyer. She was struck by how handsome he looked: his dark hair was cut short, and he had blue eyes, like Sally's but just a little lighter. A slightly pudgy face and an underbite that pushed out his lower lip were balanced by a strong Roman nose. He went to Sally, took her hands and bent over her, kissing the top of her head. Like her, he had a turn for the dramatic that had the effect of sometimes making everyday actions look stagey and insincere.

He stood back, his brow furrowed. 'I'm so sorry. What a bloody tragedy.'

Some people had told Alex that Mundo had a beautiful voice. It was certainly deep and mellifluous, with rounded vowels as a result of his grand school, and she could imagine it sounding imposing in a courtroom. But it had always left her cold.

Sally's face was instantly bright. 'Oh darling, you're here.'

'I'm sorry it's taken so long. Work's been manic. I got away as soon as I could.' Then he looked over at Alex, and smiled, one edge of his mouth pulling up further than the other. 'Alexandra. How delightful to see you. I'm sorry about the circumstances, that's all.'

'Hello, Mundo.' She stood up, not feeling strong enough to face the two of them together. 'I'm so sorry, I have to go.'

'That's a shame,' he said, 'when I've only just got here.'

'Sally will tell you everything.'

Mundo looked mournfully over at David. 'How's Pa?'

'Oh darling!' Sally said, and buried her face in her hands, sobbing. 'It's all too awful.'

'I'm here now, don't worry.'

Alex said briefly, 'I'll be in touch, Sally,' and headed out into the corridor. As soon as she got outside, she took a deep breath and muttered, 'Oh God.'

It had been some time since she'd seen Mundo. His London life and legal career kept him busy. He lived with a younger woman, a leggy Spanish beauty who was a model or an actress, or a combination of the two. He was not a part of Alex's present, beyond the odd shared Christmas lunch or family gathering, but he had been a part of her past, his arrival tied up with that awful time when life had changed forever. Mundo had seemed quiet at first, but she soon learned that he was simply observing, biding his time before he made his mark in the family. Slotting neatly in age between her and Johnnie, he seemed to fit easily between them and he soon made it his hobby to try and cause mischief. Johnnie was his main target, and Mundo was adept at the art of annoyance. Besides nasty little tricks, the pinching and sly kicks, he liked to niggle, prickle and torment in tiny ways that gradually became unendurable, until his victim exploded with rage, and became the object of parental wrath. It was hard to explain that Mundo was doing whatever it was on purpose simply to provoke. The answer would usually be to put up with it.

Pa would say crossly, 'Why can't he touch your football?'

'You don't understand,' Johnnie would say, red-faced, 'he keeps picking at it just to annoy me, even though I asked him to stop.'

'Ignore him.'

But Mundo didn't want to be ignored. He desired a reaction. His games with Johnnie were straightforward – he liked to pitch Johnnie into a fury, then sit back and watch him get punished for reacting to his slow-acting torture. Later, he would lord it over Johnnie about just about everything: exams, girlfriends, clothes, music, possessions. Whatever Johnnie had, Mundo had better and liked to make sure Johnnie knew it. Johnnie learned to ignore him, but his confidence was badly undermined.

His games with Alex were more subtle. He had been a dark force in her teenage years and she tried to do what Johnnie had done: wipe him out of her mind. She gave him barely a thought, hardly spoke to him when she saw him, determined to keep him at a distance.

That's not going to be so easy if he's staying here. Let's hope he has to get back to his work soon. I don't know how I'll cope if he's around.

She shivered as she headed back to the car.

On her way to the Old Barn, Alex obeyed an impulse and drove past her gate, taking the road onwards, skirting the old wall of Tawray until she came to the entrance, then made her way between the old gates. The drive was bumpy, the pot-holes having been crammed full of gravel rather than properly mended, but it was still impressive, taking the curving road round to the house. It was so familiar that it was hard to believe the old house was no longer her home, that she couldn't run in and up the stairs to her old bedroom with its wallpaper of oranges and lemons and the rattan lampshade, left over from the summer she demanded to be allowed to decorate it. Sally hadn't wanted it but Pa had persuaded her, one of the few times he'd taken Alex's part against his wife's wishes. Sally's condition was that Alex move into what had been the nursery and make that her room instead of the large room she'd had at the front of the house. Alex hadn't minded, she preferred her new room, and Sally got to redecorate the old one just as she liked, in tones of peach and beige, with swagged, tasselled curtains, and a chintz bedspread with a mound of lace-edged cushions on it.

But it's not our house anymore, she reminded herself, and she wondered if the new owners would strip off her old wallpaper and make it all sleek and modern. *I hope not. I hope they don't start knocking through and making spaces that shouldn't be there. The bones of it are just right. At least Sally never did anything to those.*

She parked on the gravel next to two other cars, and went quickly up the stone steps to the front door. The old bell chimed inside when she pressed the button, and she waited patiently, remembering how long it could take to answer the door if you happened to be upstairs when the bell went. After five minutes, she rang again, and waited some more. She was on the point of giving up when the door opened a small way and a woman's face appeared in the gap. She was frowning and looked suspicious.

'Yes?'

'Hello, I'm sorry to bother you. I'm Alex Pengelly. I used to live here, years ago, before it was rented out and then sold. In fact, I grew up here.' She waited a moment, expecting a reaction or an expression of interest, but there was nothing. If anything, the woman looked even more suspicious.

'So . . .' She smiled brightly, trying to cover her awkwardness. 'I don't suppose you know, but it's a tradition to decorate the house at Christmas with dried flowers, and let people in to see it, and I wondered if you might consider carrying it on. I can tell you all about it, how it works, all that. I realise it's a big ask, but I do the flowers; I run the Tawray Flower Company, we're based over there' – she pointed in the direction of the Old Barn and the flower fields that lay to the east of the house, away from the sea – 'and I'd be happy to do them again. In fact, I'd like to.'

'No thanks.' The face disappeared and the door started to close.

'Wait. Are you sure? I mean, it's a real tradition, it would be a shame to lose it . . .'

The face reappeared, blank and uninterested. 'We're not going to be here at Christmas,' the woman said. 'We spend it in Antigua. The house will be shut up, I think. Sorry. Bye.' The face disappeared again, the door closed firmly.

Alex stood staring at it, unexpectedly upset.

'You don't have to be so rude about it!' she said loudly, then turned on her heel and ran off down the steps. She realised that she'd been expecting to be asked in, welcomed almost, and that the new people would be interested in the history and traditions of the house.

As she drove out of the gates, she realised she was crying.

'Idiot,' she said aloud. 'You're a bloody idiot.'

She meant herself.

Chapter Thirteen

On the way to the hospital the next day, Alex noticed that all the festive lights were up. Christmas was coming, and quickly. The girls had been talking about the various concerts and activities that would be going on at school. They were worried about their grandfather and yet they seemed to have a blithe confidence that everything would be normal by the time it came to Christmas.

Usually, they were either with Sally and Pa, or at the Old Barn, but Johnnie and his family always stayed with Alex. Last year had been particularly awful, with her and Tim hosting the whole thing but barely able to speak to one another. Sally had been bright and cheerful, acting the part of the perfect guest, while delivering barbed compliments or asking innocently skewering questions. Alex had done everything necessary: the tree, the presents, the decorations, the food and drink, the stockings and mince pies, and ticked all the dozens of boxes that had to be ticked; she stayed sane by holding on for Tim's departure to America in January. She hadn't known it was going to be the last Christmas they spent together, but she would not have been surprised if someone had told her. The communication between her and Tim, never wonderful even in the first flush of their relationship, had grown weaker and then eroded away to nothing. He'd seemed bored by her, uninterested in her work, her friendships, her life. He shared little of his own life with her, determined to focus only on the practical as though that was the measure of a relationship: being able to make a timetable and stick to it.

I probably would have been relieved if I'd known it was coming to an end. But I would have been heartbroken if someone had told me it would be Pa's last Christmas.

Pa had kept out of everyone's way, usually nursing a glass of something by the fire with a newspaper or a book, coming obediently when summoned to the table, contributing just as much as was required. He loved the girls, and they gravitated to him quite naturally. Sometimes Alex found him engrossed in a card game or in front of a Ludo board with one or both of them, usually when Sally was out of the way doing something else. It reminded her of the Christmases at Tawray, which now were such vague memories, they were more like dreams.

At Tawray, the huge tree in the hall reached up nearly to the landing, decorated with the flower baubles. There hadn't been many presents under the tree, nothing like the mass of stuff that seemed to collect there these days, and stockings had been Pa's old socks mostly full of fruit and bags of nuts, along with chocolate and a book. Christmas lunch, after church, had been a simpler affair as well, without the astonishing array of extras a modern Christmas seemed to require. A quick walk and the giddy excitement of the afternoon film had completed the day, and then it was all over and back to normality. It hadn't been the great month-long festival she had to endure these days. The only real extravagance was the glorious bounty of dried flowers adorning the hall, the drawing room and the state rooms, exquisitely pretty with their vintage colours and fragile petals.

But whatever the factual accuracy of her memories – had Mum appeared with a roasted goose on a platter, a paper crown falling over one eye as she shouted, 'Ta dah!'? – the emotional truth was the one she clung to: it had been the happiest of times, with the four of them full of joy and togetherness, living at Tawray even though it was so shabby and far too big for them. Life had been as close to perfect as Alex could imagine. And, if she remembered their last Christmas together rightly, then she'd got the skipping rope with red handles she'd wanted so badly, but better than that, her own gardening set and packets of seeds, and a patch of ground of her own in the walled garden.

And that was her legacy to me – the flowers.

The following year, Sally had been there. No more dried flowers until Alex had taken over the job again for herself. Now, whenever she was hanging her baubles on the tree, she felt close to her mother again. It was the only time she ever did.

A bitter taste came into Alex's mouth as she remembered

the peremptory refusal of the new owner to have anything to do with the arrangement.

I've lost that connection. It's gone forever.

The consultant had a talk with her and Sally that morning. Mundo had not accompanied his mother; Sally didn't say why.

'My husband should be at home with me,' Sally insisted, though her voice was tremulous with emotion. 'You say he's been through the worst on the one hand, but you also say he's not going to improve. I don't want him lying here indefinitely when he could be at home where I can look after him. And if it's all going to end in any case, I know he'd prefer it to be at home. Besides which, we'd be freeing up this bed for someone else.'

'Arrangements can be made,' the consultant said, 'but you'll have to make some provision for him.'

'We're in a position to do that,' Sally declared.

'You'll need a ground-floor room. We can supply a hospital bed temporarily. But a nurse will also be required, there's no way you can care for him alone.'

'That's not a problem. I told you, we can make the arrangements.'

Alex felt that, for once, Sally's obstinacy and insistence on her own way were a good thing. She would get what she wanted, and Alex agreed with her: Pa would be happier at home. If he regained consciousness, then he'd be somewhere familiar. If not, they would all have the comfort of being in his environment, not here, with its notes of urgency and temporal care. You were on your way somewhere in a hospital: to recovery and departure, or to the morgue. At home, you had arrived and no one would be hurrying you out to somewhere else. There would be peace and calm and time at home.

'Alex will help, won't you?' Sally said, turning to her, her eyes enquiring.

Alex stared back at her. She had never heard a note like this in Sally's voice: beseeching, almost a little pleading, with something humble in it. *She needs me now.*

Suddenly she saw herself and Johnnie as standing together at a crossroads. They'd arrived here after a long and difficult journey, and they'd been badly treated by others on the road. Now they were in a position either to repay cruelty with kindness, or to take pleasure in refusal, perhaps even in revenge. Johnnie, she felt, would be tempted to take the latter course.

She thought suddenly of Johnnie's suggestion that Sally and Pa had been having an affair, and that had caused Mum's death. *No wonder he hates Sally, if he thinks that.* But could it be true? It was a monstrous thought. Alex had always taken it for granted that the order of things had followed correctly: Mum dying, Pa grieving, Sally supporting, a love affair beginning. It seemed too awful to consider that she might have got it all back to front. But watching Sally talking to the consultant, adamant and single-minded in pursuit of what she wanted, Alex considered for the first time that perhaps it could have happened that way.

But that's too awful. She searched her memory. She had always believed in the love that Pa had for her mother. If he hadn't loved her, he would never have broken down the way he did when she died. *No. I'm sure Johnnie's wrong. Pa was devastated. Sally put him back together. That's the way it was.*

Sally hadn't waited for Alex's reply. She and the consultant were discussing the practicalities of transferral, the necessary equipment and all the documentation that would need to be approved and signed before David was released to their care.

They're going to let him come home. That means they think he's going to die. She looked at her father. *Oh Pa. I wish we'd had the chance to talk – really talk – before this happened.*

Pa was going to be wrenched away without warning, just as Mum had been. Alex was gripped by a convulsion of grief. The house was gone, her parents were gone, her husband was gone. She still had her girls and her work, and the Old Barn. But she felt like she was standing on the deck of a ship abandoned by the rest of the crew, gazing out into unknown and stormy waters. The sky was dark, and she was afraid.

'What are you doing?' Netta asked, exasperation in her voice. Johnnie was in the utility room, hanging wet laundry out on a rack.

He looked up from where he was carefully draping a pair of underpants over a rail. 'I heard the washing machine finish its cycle so I thought I'd unload it.'

'Right.' She came over, sighing a little. 'That's very nice of you, but you need to hang it like this.' She took the pants, whipped them out so the creases fell away and then placed them neatly over the rail. 'Or else they dry sort of crunchy.'

Her eyes travelled over the rest of the haphazardly placed clothes. 'But obviously . . . I appreciate it.'

'Okay,' he said, feeling foolish. 'I was . . . just trying to help.'

'I know.' She looked as if she was going to say something else, then turned and went back into the kitchen.

Johnnie stared at the rack. His experience of a near-miss on the road had shaken him. He hadn't felt so grateful to come home in years; walking through the door had felt like a miracle. The ordinary things in his life appeared like magical blessings, and the sight of Netta and his sons had inspired a deep and powerful joy. That night, pressed against her warm body in bed, he had inhaled the scent of her skin and hair like a drowning man gasping in sweet air. She was life, and he was life. They had made life together, and they were present, on earth, right now: hearts beating, lungs inflating, synapses sparking, blood pulsing around them, *alive*. There was Pa, cold and unconscious in a hospital. There was the alternative Johnnie, dead in a smash on a Cornish road, an RTA statistic. There were all the people who'd gone before who'd had their time and were now dead. But he and Netta were alive, still young, still healthy, still here. He'd kissed her until she woke up, drowsy, warm and welcoming, and he'd made love to her, feeling everything with such intensity it was almost like some kind of acid trip. He never wanted to feel numb to life again, even though he knew it was impossible to exist permanently in such a heightened state.

I want to make it up to her. I want to be the best husband I can be, while I still can.

He was guilty sometimes of sleepwalking through life, and he wanted to open his eyes, see and participate. He'd come so close to death, he had to grasp life, live it well and make up for his failings so he could show Netta how much he loved her.

Johnnie hung out the rest of the laundry, trying to imitate Netta's method but finding that the wet garments didn't behave for him as they did for her. Then he went back into the kitchen. Bertie had already gone off to school with his driver and the twins were upstairs, doing their teeth. Netta was sitting at the kitchen table, wrapped in a towelling robe, her short black hair wet, and she was crying.

'What is it?' he asked, concerned, coming over and sitting next to her. 'What's wrong?'

She lifted reddened eyes to him. 'I'm stressed, Johnnie. I've got a hell of a day in front of me, a big presentation to a load of tax lawyers, I've got to leave early for Joe's nativity play and I'm supposed to take Christmas treats for everyone as well. Plus Nathan's got football later and his kit is wet, and I don't know how I'm going to pick him up from that, and get Joe fed and be back in time for Bertie, because Lydia can't come today. And now' – tears welled up and flowed down her cheeks, turning her brown eyes hazel and making her nose go pink – 'you've hung the laundry all crooked.'

'I'm sorry. I was trying to help.'

'I know. I can't explain.' She began to weep hard. 'I mean, it just . . . I hate seeing it like that, all wonky, knowing it will dry wrong. But how can I complain when obviously it's nice of you to make the gesture?'

'Sorry,' he said. It was frustrating that his efforts had back-fired and he seemed to have made things worse when he wanted to make them better. He tried to stay sympathetic. 'I know you're under a lot of pressure. Christmas is tough, and you do such a lot to keep everyone happy. Can I do anything to help you with the day?'

'What can you do?' She shrugged. 'You're at work in town.' Her shoulders slumped. 'I just feel that . . . the work of the family, the work of the house . . . that's all on me. You let me do the lion's share with Bertie, you know you do. I'm the one who copes with him most of the time. And I have a job. Your job seems to excuse you from all that other stuff, and when you do a bit of it, you don't even know how to do it properly. And what does it matter to you? You won't be ironing it, or putting it away, so what it does matter if it dries wrong?'

'I want to help,' he said plaintively.

'Help. Help!' Netta cried hard. She took in a deep breath and tried to control herself. 'I have a cleaning lady. She helps me. I have people come in to help me with Bertie. They don't owe me anything, and when they help me, I pay them. But you . . . you shouldn't *help*. This is your house too, your children, your life. You're telling me that this is my job but you're prepared to help me with it, when you're in the mood. When did you last really do anything – I mean the shit stuff like cleaning the loo or hauling hair out of the shower plug? You still use the satnav to get to the children's schools, for crying out loud.'

'I know that.' He felt guilty and ashamed. Was he acting

like some kind of overentitled male, the kind that everyone hated so much these days? He'd thought he was a kind, empathetic, supportive husband. He'd certainly tried to be. 'I know I don't do as much at home as you do. I suppose I bring in the money.'

'Not all of it,' Netta said. 'I work too.'

'But I pay for most of it – this house, our holidays, the car. For the children. For Bertie.'

Netta sniffed and wiped away some of her tears. She was staring at the oiled tablecloth, one fingertip tracing its way around the polka dots. She looked up at her husband and Johnnie had a sudden flash of her as she had been when they met: a glamorous half-French student he saw at some university event and couldn't stop thinking about until he'd tracked her down in the library and struck up a conversation with her. She'd been elfin, so delicately pretty and so graceful, he'd almost been afraid to touch her. Those fragile looks had been deceptive. She was strong, immensely strong, hugely strong. He'd seen it first when she gave birth to Bertie: fighting with all her strength over four days to deliver him before they insisted on a Caesarean. And then, when the diagnosis of autism came, and they realised that the life they'd dreamed of for Bertie would never happen, that he might never recognise them or call them Mum and Dad, her raw grief had swiftly been banished as Netta reached for her strength and started fighting. She'd inspired him, motivated him, when he felt floored by the reality of Bertie's condition. She took on their houses and made them homes. She said they should have more children when Johnnie was terrified any other children might have Bertie's autism too, and she cared for her babies while looking after her desperately needy son, simultaneously training herself to be a therapist in the new developments in autism treatment. And then, when Nathan and Joe started school, she'd returned to a career in accountancy, as though she didn't have enough on her plate. But she'd said she needed an identity that wasn't just being a mother and a carer.

Yes, Netta was strong all right.

So how can she be crying over some pants hung wonky on a laundry rack? He put a hand on hers. 'What is it? What are you thinking?'

Her brown eyes rose to his, still swimming in tears. 'I suppose I was thinking . . . about you providing the money, and what I do . . . And if we add it up . . . if we really add it all up, and if adding it up is important and will give us some answers . . . what will the answer be?'

Johnnie felt a prickle of apprehension. 'What do you mean, add it up?'

'The labour. The time, the work, the effort. If it matters who does what, what will it tell us?'

He saw anger in the set of her mouth. 'What's wrong, Netta? You seem very cross with me.'

She got up and started putting breakfast things into the dishwasher, and said nothing. He watched her. The silence between them grew longer and more intense. With everything loaded, she closed the dishwasher and padded to the door on bare feet. There, she turned and looked at him. 'I'm just wondering about our future, that's all.'

'Our future?' he said, surprised. He'd expected her to say that she was undervalued, unappreciated, in need of recognition. She was right about that, he would concede it graciously, offer a dinner out, a trip somewhere nice, a weekend away. He'd already made a mental note to ask his assistant to arrange some flowers.

'I don't know if I can make you happy,' she said simply.

She turned and walked out, leaving him watching her in astonishment.

Make me happy? He felt an odd, unsettled sensation, as if he was in a lift that had plummeted too quickly. There hadn't been time for their own happiness for years and years; they had been coping. Happiness was for the children. For them, the blessed relief of a few hours' quiet, an early night, a glass of wine and telly. That had been Johnnie's idea of happiness ever since the children came. Of course there had been plenty of happy moments, but did Netta make him happy?

Of course she does.

He couldn't imagine being with anyone but Netta. They'd lived a life, raised children, got used to each other. They were *married*. Happy or not. Hopefully happy at least some of the time. But they just got on with it and hoped that happiness would come along occasionally. Didn't everyone?

He had a feeling, a horrible feeling, that Netta meant something else. But what, he wasn't entirely sure.

In the hotel car park, Alex checked her reflection in the mirror on the back of the visor in the car. She looked all right but suspected that the dim lighting helped mask a multitude of sins – sins like sleepless nights, wine, and failure to remove make-up adequately before bed. She was also feeling agitated, churned up by the sight of Chloe sitting in the passenger seat next to Tim when he arrived at the Old Barn earlier to collect the girls. There was something about it that upset her, seeing that shadowy shape in the darkness as the girls got into the car.

'Enjoy yourself,' Tim called out, and then drove away. They looked like a family, Alex realised, and the unpleasant feeling washed over her, the one that always came when she saw Scarlett and Jasmine disappear with Tim. She went back inside to get changed for the reception, and now here she was in the car park of the Manor Hotel, about to go inside to schmooze with other local business owners in a celebration of local enterprise. Not exactly her idea of fun, but important for the Tawray Flower Company. If she could pick up some work from the hotel, a favourite for weddings and parties with locals, then it was worth it.

She got out and went inside, hoping she was smart enough in jeans, high boots and a plum velvet jacket over a plum silk shirt. Lipstick and dangly earrings did most of the work in making her look in party mode. Inside, she took a name badge from the table and a glass of white wine offered by a waiter, and wandered into the reception. It was already crowded and she recognised plenty of familiar faces from the village and the surrounding areas, owners of small businesses who'd recently banded together to try and combat the power of online shopping and the out-of-town trading estates. They had come up with new payment and loyalty schemes, joint promotions and marketing events.

'Hello, love!' A tall woman, owner of a local wine business, came over and gave her a smacking kiss on the cheek. 'How are you? Any nice plans for Christmas?'

Alex smiled. 'Hi, Pam.' She paused for a moment and then said, 'Nothing really. Just the usual family affair.' News of David's stroke had not spread then, and she didn't want to spoil the mood. 'How are things? Gearing up for your busy time?'

'The Christmas season is the goose that lays the golden eggs, it's true. But have I told you about my plan for some tasting evenings at the warehouse?' Pam was off, and they were soon deep in discussion about possible joint ventures, joined from time to time by other local traders who wanted to contribute to the subject of business rates.

Pam, on her fourth glass of white even though she'd declared it rubbish, suddenly called out, 'Oi, Jasper, over here!'

A man across the room turned around, his eyebrows raised.

She waved at him. 'Come here!' Pam leaned into Alex confidentially. 'He's just spent a wedge at the shop, restocking his cellar, he said. Here he comes.'

The man came over. He was tall, with short, ruffled brown hair and blue eyes, and casual in jeans and a red hoodie top, faded, which advertised the Penrith Tea Rooms. 'Hi, Pam,' he said. 'How are you doing?'

'Good, thanks, Jasper. Have you met Alex?'

He looked at her, his eyes bright and intelligent. 'I don't

believe I've had the pleasure.' He held out a hand to her. 'How do you do?'

'Fine, thank you.' She shook it, noticing that he had a rich Scottish accent.

'What's your business then?' he asked. 'You must have a reason for being part of this jolly event.'

'I grow flowers.'

'Oh, right.' He looked interested. 'Is there much demand for that?'

'You'd be surprised. People just think of weddings, but there's a huge gift market and I'm moving into doing flower growing and flower arranging workshops.' She launched into her familiar patter; people usually asked a variation on just a few questions. Jasper nodded, listening intently.

'Fascinating,' he said. 'You have my respect – it sounds like hard work.'

'It is.' She smiled, pleased. People seemed to think flower growing was ladylike and elegant, as though she spent her time wafting around roses and dahlias, snipping their pretty heads into a willow trug, when the reality was hard work, filthy wellies, cold and lots of dirt. *He's attractive.* She liked his short, feathery haircut and the slightly rugged look he had. *And that accent.* It was rich and fluid, a soft Highland brogue. She glanced down at his hand to see if he sported a wedding ring but it was at the wrong angle and she couldn't see. 'What's your business?'

'I haven't decided yet. I'm thinking about weddings, in which case we might have a bit of an overlap.' He smiled. 'It's all to play for right now.'

'Oh?' She frowned, confused.

'Jasper's just moved to the area,' Pam said. She looked suddenly wary, as though she had just realised a connection that bothered her. 'In fact, you should know—'

'I've taken on an old wreck,' he said. 'Lovely place but really broken down. I'm just considering what to do with it – gut it, turn it into a hotel, set it up for events . . . not really sure. It's got a listing, so planning will be a bit of a nightmare.'

'Which house is it?' Alex said, interested. 'I've lived here all my life, I'm bound to know it.'

Pam tried to cut in before Jasper spoke, but it was too late and he said, 'Tawray. Crazy old house, almost a castle with the turrets on the top. A crusty old major and his wife lived there before we moved in, and they've let it go over the years. So I'm coming up with ideas to revitalise it.'

Alex stared at him, her mouth open, stunned.

Pam said, 'Alex knows it, don't you?'

She nodded.

'Oh yeah?' He smiled at her then his face changed. 'Hold on, you're not that flower farm on the far side of the park, are you?'

'Yes.' Her voice came out frigid and cold. She was remembering the woman at the door of Tawray, the way she wouldn't open it, her refusal to consider continuing the Christmas flowers, her closed-off expression. *That must be his wife.*

'We're neighbours then,' he said cheerfully. 'And you've lived here all your life, have you?'

Alex paused, then said with faux brightness, 'Would you

175

excuse me? I'm really sorry, Pam, I've just remembered I have to get back home.'

'Sure.' Pam looked sympathetic while Jasper was evidently taken aback.

'Oh, right,' he said. 'Well, see you soon.'

'Yeah.' She put her glass on the tray of a passing waiter. 'Goodnight then. Happy Christmas, Pam.'

Then she hurried out, not wanting to spend another moment in his company.

Chapter Fourteen

1985

Three months to the day after Julia's meeting with David, he asked her to marry him and she said yes without thinking twice. They were in a dream of love, barely able to function apart, yearning for one another at every moment. She'd never known anything like it, and if she ever thought of Mark at all, it was to be grateful that he had given her the means of appreciating the contrast between the grinding on his Stockwell mattress with the utter delight she found with David.

Everything about him pleased her, from the way his dark hair curled softly on his neck and on the curve behind his ears, to the shape of his hands. She loved his warm, sweet smell, and the feel of his strong body when he wrapped his arms around her. His voice was the loveliest sound she could imagine, and everything he thought and said seemed right.

This is how it's meant to be. This is what it means to be in love.

So when on a lazy Sunday morning, only a few weeks after they had collected her things from Stockwell and she had said goodbye to Mark, who seemed quite unfazed by the fact she was leaving him for good, David pulled her to him under the sheets and said seriously, 'I think we ought to get married as soon as we can, don't you?', she had said, 'Yes, yes I do,' and meant it utterly.

What was the point in waiting, when life was to be grasped and taken? David excited and thrilled her, but he also made her feel safe. He was older, wiser. He seemed to quieten the voices that told her insistently that life was brief and full of suffering, and that she must find her joy where she could, in dancing, drinking, and whatever hedonistic oblivion appeared. She felt, almost without knowing it, that he would keep her away from all that, and in his safe, sober world, she would be all right.

'But first,' she said, lacing her fingers through his, 'we need to go to Tawray.'

Julia had been away too long, she felt that as soon as they neared the house. Something in this place fed and nourished her. It had been self-punishing to stay away from it.

'My goodness, look at that!' David exclaimed as they came up the driveway and he saw the house for the first time. 'What a place!'

Julia felt a rush of pride and love at the sight of the old house, sitting in its hollow surrounded by mellow parkland. 'And look – the sea!' She inhaled deeply. 'Oh, I can smell it. I love that smell.'

'What period is the house?' David said, interested.

'It's a bit of a mishmash,' Julia said. 'Bits from different times, stuck on by different ancestors. But somehow it works.'

Her heart swelled with love for it – the strange Gothic towers on the roof, the battlements and turrets, and the dark Cornish stone of the main house.

David brought the car to a halt in front of the broad shallow steps that led to the front door. 'I can see why you need to come back here.'

'Come on, let's go in,' she said, her eyes shining. 'There's something I want to show you.'

They stood in front of the mural, David exclaiming at its lifelike quality. 'And this is you,' he said, reaching out to touch the tawny hair of the twelve-year-old Julia. 'You look like a young witch.'

She gave him a sideways look. 'Really? Is that a good thing?'

'Oh yes. You're brewing enchantment. It's a wonderful picture of you. And I love the apples.'

'That's my mother,' Julia said, pointing at the wistful figure by the writing desk. 'It's just how she looked in real life.'

He stared, solemn. 'She looks lovely. Very sad.'

Julia nodded, biting her lip. 'She was. Very, very sad.'

'When did she die?'

'Four years ago now.'

'Here?'

She nodded, unable to say more, and he saw that she couldn't, so said quickly, 'And who's this?' He gestured to the girl in the middle, a bright spot of yellow and soft blue eyes. 'Fantastic seventies outfit.'

LULU TAYLOR

'That's my sister, Lala.'

'I didn't know you had a sister.'

'Half-sister, if we're being pedantic. She lives in France. I don't see her much these days but we used to be close. You'll meet her at the wedding, I'm sure she'll come over.'

'I'll look forward to it. I hope she wears those shoes. And who is that hatchet-faced woman?'

'Oh, that's my rather poisonous—'

'Well, well!' Aunt Victoria's voice cut through the air, and she advanced towards them, stately in a tartan skirt, navy jumper and pearls, followed by two fat waddling spaniels with drooping brown ears. 'Fancy arriving and not even ringing the bell! We didn't know you were here, darling.' Then she stopped and put her hands to her face. 'Oh Julia! Your hair! Your lovely hair. What on earth have you done to it?'

'Just a spot of hair dye, you know, to ring the changes. Nice to see you too. Sorry not to announce ourselves. I wanted to show David the painting.'

'David!' Victoria's face softened as she inspected him and she smiled. 'Welcome. You're Julia's new friend?'

'Her fiancé,' David corrected as she offered a cheek for him to kiss.

Her eyebrows shot up. 'Really? How unexpected. Isn't that rather sudden?' Her gaze went at once to Julia's middle. 'And you haven't even met Julia's father.'

'I intend to remedy that as soon as possible.'

Julia said lightly, 'We don't live in the Dark Ages, for Christ's sake,' and enjoyed the expression of distaste that crossed her aunt's face. 'I'm perfectly capable of making my own decisions about who I'm going to marry without Daddy's permission.'

'But,' David said quickly, 'I appreciate it's the correct gesture to make.'

'I'm glad one of you knows how things are done. So, a wedding. What fun. I can't wait to hear all about it.'

'Has she always lived here?' David asked as they went upstairs to put their bags in their rooms – David having been put firmly down the hall in one of the guest rooms.

Julia slapped her hand lightly on the banister as they went up. 'No. She's actually got a house nearby but I suppose she as good as lives here now my mother's dead. She made Mummy's life a misery, that's all I know, and she's always treated me like shit.' Julia grinned at him. 'She never liked my mother. Something about not trusting second wives. As though someone might want to get their claws into her horrible old husband. Goodness knows what's happened to him, he's not been seen for years.'

'He's not in the portrait.'

Julia shrugged. 'Too out of it on whisky by eleven a.m., I think.'

David looked around as they reached the upper landing and the long red carpeted corridor that stretched away, lined with family portraits. 'This is a big place to grow up all alone.'

Julia smiled at him, taking his hand. 'Most people say how lucky I am. But I was lonely. I longed for nothing so much as a parcel of brothers and sisters to share it with.'

'But none came along?'

Julia shook her head sharply and opened the door in front of them. 'Here you are. The Acorn Room. All yours.'

'Won't I be with you at all?' he said wistfully.

'Darling, this place was made for corridor creeping. No point in having a corridor like this and not using it. I fully expect you to come tiptoeing down as soon as you can.' She hugged him quickly and they kissed softly. 'Now, get changed, I want to show you the outdoors, it's really the best.'

David was awestruck by the beauty of Tawray's surroundings. 'I can't believe it,' he said as she led him through the walled gardens. 'It's exquisite.'

Julia skipped with pleasure, delighted at his praise and bursting with pride. 'I have to admit that Aunt Victoria is rather good at gardening. She's the one who's the force behind all this, and she's trained Daddy well.'

'But you've got everything!' David turned to look at the vista spreading out before him, the wind ruffling his black hair. 'These gardens, the view, the lake, the sea . . . It's amazing.'

'You must be used to Cornwall, you live here too!'

'Not quite like this. On a much smaller scale and without the sea to lend it magnificence.' He turned to look at Julia, his expression amused. 'You don't seem to realise what this place is, sweetheart. It's not like most people's houses, you know! And certainly not like the small place I grew up in – a perfectly nice cottage but nothing like this.'

'No.' She felt sheepish. 'I do know that. Really I do.' She

shoved her hands into her coat pockets against the chill wind. 'I'm spoiled.'

'No, you're not. You can't help growing up in a place like this. Of course it's normal to you.'

'I want to see where you live,' she said quickly. 'And meet your parents. And get to know all about you.'

'I know you do. I love you for it.' He dropped a kiss on the end of her nose. 'We've got all the time in the world, Julia. That's the marvellous thing. We've found each other and we've got the rest of our lives to enjoy together.'

'Yes.' She was filled with excited warmth by his words and threw her arms around him to hug him. Then she pulled away, worried. 'But, darling, you know, I won't get this house. It's going to go to my cousin Quentin. We won't be able to live here.'

'Do you think I mind about that?' He laughed and squeezed her tightly. 'I didn't even really know what this place was like until today. Besides, my work will keep us in London a while longer.'

'Mmm.' She pressed in close to him, pushing her cheek against the coolness of his coat. She had already discovered that his work required him to be away for long hours, and there was a foreign tour coming up that he had to prepare for, and go along on. But if he weren't working at the palace, he'd be back in the navy, assigned to a submarine and gone for months at a time. 'What a shame we're not rich, then you wouldn't have to work.'

'I need to work, darling. You know that, don't you?'

'Of course.'

'Good.' He smiled at her and there was perfect serenity between them again.

She pulled at his arm, happy once more. 'Come on now, I want to show you the lake. I wonder if my platform is still there.'

It was, though covered in moss and lichen, and the rope looked a little slimy. Julia grabbed it and heaved herself up onto it. 'Yuck, it's a bit grotty. It needs a scrub.'

David found it easier to get up with his long legs and strength. 'You used to sit on this?'

'For hours. When the weather was good, that's what makes the difference.'

'It's a lovely spot. What a pretty lake.'

'Yes.' Julia looked out over the water. Aunt Victoria's influence didn't seem to extend down here; it looked neglected and overgrown at the sides. The murky water was thick with algae and the fleshy saucers of water lily pads. She could see their stems snaking away into the depths like pale coils of rope. What on earth had drawn her here so much? It really wasn't very nice at all.

'Come on,' she said, grabbing the rope to descend. 'Let's go down to the cove. Much more interesting.'

Dinner with Julia's father passed off perfectly well, and David's excellent manners and conversation were shown to their best advantage. Daddy was impressed to hear that David was a naval officer, and Aunt Victoria quite excited to hear that he worked at the palace.

'But how thrilling,' she said, leaning towards him over the

184

polished mahogany of the dinner table. 'You must know all the inside gossip. Is it true about the Waleses? My friend Monica knows someone who's a good friend of his, and apparently they're having a frightful time.'

David smiled blandly. 'I'm afraid I couldn't possibly comment.'

'Of course not. Discretion is the thing, isn't it? But you can trust us. We wouldn't breathe a word, would we, Harry?'

'No, no . . .' said Julia's father, looking flustered, and he took a quick sip of his wine.

'She's very difficult, we hear. Quite hysterical most of the time!' Aunt Victoria shook her head. 'Poor man. What he must be going through.'

Julia said loudly, 'David's going on tour next year, to Saudi Arabia. Isn't that interesting?'

'Goodness!' Aunt Victoria blinked with surprise, evidently impressed that David was important enough to accompany royal personages to the Middle East.

David quickly picked up the conversational baton. 'That's right. I'm going over to do a recce quite soon, as it happens. It will be fascinating; I've always wanted to visit the East.' He set off chatting happily about his knowledge of the desert and oil-rich countries, and Aunt Victoria was successfully diverted. After dinner, he and Daddy went off to the library to smoke cigars and have their talk.

'I thought we were the ones who were supposed to retire,' Aunt Victoria said acidly, watching them go.

Julia picked up a decanter and helped herself to a good measure of dark red wine. She gulped half of it back in one go, then pulled out her packet of cigarettes and tapped one out onto the table.

'Oh Julia, no.'

'Why not? You wouldn't mind if it was David.'

'Well, it's not.'

'Hard cheese.' Julia put one in her mouth and lit it from one of the candles.

'David seems very nice,' Aunt Victoria said pointedly. 'You'll have to behave once you're married, you know. Once you move in royal circles.'

Julia snorted. 'I won't move in them! It's David's job, you know. He's not their friend.'

'Still.' Aunt Victoria sniffed. 'No doubt you'll have to go to the odd function. It won't do to knock back the wine and smoke at the table.'

'Then I'll pop outside and have a fag with Fergie, won't I?' Julia grinned. 'If you think marriage is going to make me respectable . . . well, you'll just have to think again.'

It wasn't quite true, though. She did think marriage would make her respectable, because she was sure that with David, she would be so happy it would be impossible to be anything else. They would be everything to one another. He would give her the love she wanted so desperately and fill the black hole of need she'd felt for so long. He'd quieten the voices that terrified her, the ones that warned her of pain and loss and despair, and agonies of suffering.

She lay in bed that evening, longing for him, and when she finally heard her bedroom door open and felt him climb in beside her, warm and infinitely comforting with his strong embrace and eager kiss, she found that she was weeping.

'What's wrong?' he asked, when his lips encountered the salty wetness on her cheeks. 'Are you crying?'

'I missed you so much,' she said, sniffing. 'I was so afraid that you'd not come, and I'd be alone here in the dark.'

'But, darling, this is your home. Nothing can hurt you here.'

You're wrong, she thought, as she kissed him back. *It's my home, and I love it. But it's here that I hurt worst of all.*

Aunt Victoria declared their wedding date to be the most inauspicious she had ever heard. She came up to town to take Julia for lunch in Kensington to find out all about the arrangements and was aghast when she heard. 'It could only be worse if it was Friday the thirteenth, not Saturday the thirteenth.'

'If you believe all that nonsense,' Julia said as calmly as possible.

'Why not postpone until the spring? It's virtually the middle of winter! Getting married in December, how ghastly. Dark and dank and horrible.'

'Or sparkly and festive and lovely,' Julia countered. 'We want to get married as soon as we can; this works around David's commitments. He doesn't have to go away.'

Aunt Victoria wasn't really listening. 'The thirteenth of December – that's ringing a bell. Goodness, I think it's St Lucy's Day.'

Julia stared at her, bemused. 'So?'

'There's a poem by John Donne, set on St Lucy's day. He calls it the year's midnight. Isn't that a rather chilling thing? Who would want to get married at midnight?'

'Is the thirteenth of December the year's midnight?' wondered Julia. 'Isn't that the thirty-first?'

'I think he means the shortest day, like the solstice. On the old calendar it was probably the equivalent of the winter solstice on the twenty-first.'

Julia shrugged. 'I haven't read it.'

'Oh, it's awful, all about death. *I am every dead thing.*' Her aunt shuddered. 'What a horrible date to choose, Julia. Can't you find another one?'

'Because of a spooky poem? I don't think so. And it's too late, I'm afraid. We've booked Chelsea town hall.'

'Not a church?' Her aunt was even more scandalised.

'No. We don't want a big fuss. Just a few friends and family at the register office is fine.' She took a gulp of her wine, and pushed her salmon mousse around her plate. 'Lala has said we can have her flat in Paris for a honeymoon.'

'Well.' Aunt Victoria's mouth had tightened into a straight line, her eyes flinty. 'You must do what you want, of course, but your father will be disappointed. We imagined you'd be married at Tawray in May or June.'

'David's in Canada and Japan in the spring. And he's terribly busy all summer, he wouldn't be able to get the time off.'

'The year after then.'

'We can't wait till then. We don't want to.'

'We thought a lovely marquee on the lawn. The village

church. That's where I got married and it couldn't have been prettier.'

All the more reason to avoid it then. But she said nothing.

'A midwinter wedding,' Aunt Victoria said mournfully. 'I just can't help thinking it's bad luck, that's all.'

It was indeed dank and dark on the thirteenth of December. It rained all day in endless grey sheets of icy water, and it seemed as though the sun never bothered coming up at all.

'What a shame!' Lala said as she and Julia took a taxi from their hotel to the register office. 'It's a miserable day.'

'I'm happy, though,' Julia said firmly. 'I don't mind the weather at all.'

Lala smiled at her. 'You look radiant. Such a beautiful outfit.'

'Thanks to you.' Julia looked down at the exquisite Paris suit in a cream tweed shot with silver which Lala had brought over, wrapped in tissue, ready for the big day. Her mother's diamond earrings sparkled in her ears. 'I feel like a million pounds, I really do.'

'You look very chic. Not at all like a big choux bun. I like things simple and elegant, not all fussy. It's how we like to do things in Paris, but the English much prefer the old style – flounces and frills.'

Julia thought back to the royal wedding they had watched together only a few years ago, and how back then she had dreamed of sailing down a magnificent aisle in acres of silk and veil, sparkling with diamonds. She had remembered it only last night, when David unwrapped the wedding present he had received from the royal household – a signed photograph of his employers in a beautiful silver frame. 'So they can keep their beady eyes on me,' he had joked. But Julia had stared at it: the image of togetherness, the glossy, glamorous outside that concealed a less palatable truth. Not that David would ever speak of it – he was famously discreet. It was only something she picked up from his occasional throwaway remarks, his evident tension, the telephone calls he had to take, the miserable exhaustion that possessed him at the end of a long day.

'Sometimes you wonder why people have to be so bloody-minded,' he once said. 'Why they can't bring themselves to cooperate with each other, when life would be so much easier all round if they did.'

'Is there trouble?' she'd asked, and he'd gazed at her sadly.

'I can't tell you, but it's tragic.' He shook his head. 'Just tragic all round.'

Tragedy is everywhere, she thought now, looking out of the taxi window at people as they went slowly down the King's Road towards the town hall. They were hurrying along, hunching under umbrellas, trying to keep out of the rain. The Christmas lights shone out valiantly against the darkness, their colours spinning out through the raindrops. *Everyone I can see has a story with sadness in it. We are all here to suffer.*

She thought of the John Donne poem that Aunt Victoria had told her about. She had read it and afterwards had almost told David that they ought to change their wedding date. She would have, if it hadn't sounded so silly even to her. But the lines, once read, kept floating through her mind like some kind of bad omen.

I am re-begot
Of absence, darkness, death: things which are not.

She shook her head to banish the words. *I mustn't think about that now. It's my wedding day. It's a day of happiness and promise, not . . . not those other things.*

But her mother wasn't there. She was absent, lost in the darkness of death.

She pushed that thought away, and clutched her bouquet of cream roses and pale pink spikes of Cornish heath from the gardens at Tawray, nurtured in the greenhouse just for her.

David would keep it all away, she was sure of that. He was her champion, her real-life knight, not just a stuffed suit of armour with a scrawled-on cardboard face. He would banish all the monsters.

The taxi drew to a halt in front of the town hall. Her father was waiting outside, scanning the traffic for her from beneath his black umbrella. Julia noticed with amusement that he had put on morning dress, although no one else would be wearing it, and was holding the brolly high over his silk top hat.

'Oh Daddy,' she said, her heart softening towards him for the first time since her mother's death. She had told him he wasn't to walk her down the small aisle in the Rossetti

Room, and he had agreed. But there he was, waiting in the pouring rain to escort her inside. That was something.

'Are you ready?' Lala asked, smiling. 'Are you sure you want to do this?'

'Oh yes,' Julia said. 'I will never be more sure of anything.'

Lala grabbed her umbrella. 'Then let's go.'

Chapter Fifteen

The honeymoon in Paris was sheer delight, a great deal of it spent in bed, or else in marvellous restaurants, sparkling cocktail bars or earthy little places with carafes of rich red wine and plates of gamey terrines and slippery confits. They ate and drank, slept and made love as though the most important thing was to experience their physical forms as elementally as possible.

'We need to bath together as well,' Julia said, as though that would complete some kind of important set. So they climbed into the small but very deep bath, splashed and laughed and slid over each other's limbs until they were unable to resist making love again.

'I love being married,' she said to David, gazing into his eyes, touching his skin and inhaling his scent. 'It's everything I hoped it would be.'

'This is our honeymoon,' he said with a laugh, nuzzling into her neck. 'It's supposed to be bliss.'

'Do you mean it won't carry on like this?'

'It's generally supposed to wear off.'

She stared into his dark blue eyes and thought how much she loved him. 'Not for us.'

He laughed again. 'Maybe we'll be the first to experience honeymoon rapture all our lives.'

'Why not?' she demanded, a little petulant but smiling through it. 'Don't spoil it! Why can't it carry on like this?'

'I don't know. Life, I suppose. You'll get tired of me.'

'I'll never get tired of you. Never.' She pulled him in for another kiss, feeling as though he was her oxygen, her engine, her everything.

They came out of their bubble of love to see Lala on Christmas Eve. She had moved into the flat of her boyfriend Denis, a craggy-faced, grey-haired professor who looked exactly like someone who wrote learned theses. Julia and David went round for dinner to the bright little flat opposite Saint-Sulpice. It was small and crammed full of books, paintings and oversized sculpture.

Julia begged them to open their Christmas presents first: beautiful editions of Thomas Hardy novels that she and David had bought at an antiquarian bookshop for Denis, and a 1920s lamp from a chic shop in the Galleries near the Louvre for Lala.

'Wonderful!' Lala said, beaming. 'I will put it in my new studio.'

She had recently been taken on as a designer for the venerable fashion house of Ducroix, and was excited about what lay ahead.

'And now,' she said, 'your presents.'

There was a bottle of good single malt for David, and a scarf of finest silver cashmere for Julia, so soft that it seemed to be spun from clouds.

'Come and see my new designs,' Lala said to Julia, and they left Denis preparing the Christmas supper of guinea fowl stuffed with boudin blanc, while David sipped on some whisky and read the opening pages of *The Woodlanders*.

'They're fantastic,' Julia said, admiring the vibrant sketches of colourful puffball skirts worn with jackets in exuberant checks. There were silk tuxedoes in jewel colours worn over camisole tops in clashing hues of neon pink, orange and yellow, and sexy evening dresses slashed to the thigh and glittering with sequins. 'Wow! I can imagine these on a supermodel. You've really developed your look.' She smiled at Lala. 'How clever you are.'

'You're developing your look too,' Lala said. She reached out and touched Julia's hair. 'You're growing out the white.'

'David wants to see my natural colour and maybe I'm tired of peroxide.' She put her hand to her hair, feeling the difference between the silkiness of her natural hair and the strawish consistency of the dyed portion. 'Shall I get it cut off? There's nothing I can do with it otherwise, it has to grow out.'

'Maybe. When your natural hair is longer. It would be too short otherwise.' Lala looked at her thoughtfully. 'You know, marriage suits you. You look so much happier.'

'I do?'

'Your eyes were dead before. He's brought you back to life.'

'Yes, he has. I thought my life was over, and now it's started anew.'

'I'm so pleased for you.' Lala hugged her tightly. 'I've been so worried. I was afraid you were lost.'

'I'm fine, really. I promise. I've got David now, it's going to be all right.'

Julia had finally learned to master the steel stove-top coffee pot in Lala's flat. 'With only one day left in Paris, I manage it!' she said, putting a cup of espresso in front of David.

'Better late than never.' He took a sip. 'Oh yes, that's good. Let's get one of these little pots and take it home so we can have this every day.'

'Honeymoon magic,' she smiled. They were trying to come up with little things that would ensure the continuation of their happiness beyond the time when they had to return. 'But it isn't quite over,' she reminded him.

David's employers were away on their Christmas holidays and not expected back for another fortnight, so he had taken some extra leave and they had arranged to go to Tawray for a while, to walk and sleep and read and explore.

'I'm glad we've got that, or it would be just too bleak leaving Paris,' David replied.

Julia was looking at the coffee pot. 'I think that if I added hot water to this coffee, and some cream, it would be just like a *café au lait*. I'll try it.'

The buzzer by the door went suddenly and they both looked up in surprise. No one was expected. Who would be visiting them? David got up and went to the intercom phone. 'Yes?' He looked over at Julia as he said, 'Of course, Lala. Come on up.'

Julia stared at David, who looked bewildered as he replaced the handset. 'Surely she has a key,' he said. 'It's her flat.'

'Oh my God,' Julia said flatly. She felt the colour drain from her face and she clutched at the table for support.

'What?'

'Don't you see? Don't you understand? There's only one reason she would come.'

David shook his head just as Lala pushed open the door. She was white-faced, her eyes reddened, and she stared at Julia, her expression agonised.

'It's Daddy, isn't it?' Julia said in the same flat tone.

'I'm sorry, darling. They had Denis's number. They rang me there.'

'Is he dead?'

Lala nodded, her eyes filling with tears. 'Yes. I'm sorry.'

'Well.' Julia looked away from David's sympathy and Lala's sadness. 'That's that then. I suppose it had to happen sooner or later.' Then she looked at David, a wave of sudden grief sweeping over her. 'But don't you see what it means? Tawray. We're going to lose Tawray.'

The honeymoon was over and they went home. Tawray looked exactly the same. That was both the painful thing, and the comforting one. They had not gone directly there in the end, but had returned to London and prepared to go back, not to complete their honeymoon but for a funeral. Julia stared at the old place as they drove down the avenue towards it, watching it expand to fill the windscreen as they approached, until it towered over them.

Do we change anything? Do our lives make any difference at all?

Daddy was gone, and that was terrible, though Julia still felt untouched in some deep part of herself, as though the loss of Mummy had inured her against further pain for her father. The house he'd loved and lived in all these years was still here, just the same, untouched by his loss. It even felt the same, she thought as they went in, just as it had when Daddy went upstairs for a sleep in the afternoon.

But then, she remembered, it had been full of loss and grief. That was the whole point. It didn't need to change.

The family were all there, even Aunt Victoria's husband, his face wrecked from decades of hard drinking with a nose that was swollen, pocked and purple. The funeral would be soon, Aunt Victoria said, there was no point in waiting. The death was natural, there were no question marks: a man whose heart gave out one night as he slept and was found cold in his bed the next morning.

'I'm an orphan,' Julia said sadly as she and David sat outside on the terrace, wrapped up against the bitter January wind. She'd needed to step out of the house, away from the crowd inside, people murmuring solemnly while they emptied the decanters and sought seats close to the fire.

David looked at her with sympathy. 'I know. It's horrible. After this, I thought we could go to my parents for a while. They'd love to see us. We hardly got to speak to them at the wedding. We can be looked after there.'

Julia nodded. She'd liked David's parents on the few occasions they had visited them at their cottage. They were kind, unpretentious and adoring of their only son. They'd welcomed Julia with warmth and happiness. 'We shan't be able to stay here anyway.'

'Are you sure?'

'Of course. Quentin will get to say who stays here now, and he's bound to want the place to himself. I'm an orphan, a homeless orphan.'

'Darling.' He pulled her to him and hugged her hard. 'It's not quite that bad, is it? Your father will have made a provision for you.'

'I expect so,' she said, pulling away from the waxy surface of his jacket. 'We'll find out after the service tomorrow. But I'm still an orphan.'

'You've got me, you know that. I'm your family now. And we'll have our own children, we'll make our own family. It'll be wonderful, you'll see.'

She turned away, not able to show him the truth.

I'll change. I'll be able to face it. It will be all right.

The funeral itself passed in a blur; the church was full to bursting, the music was beautiful, and the vicar spoke movingly. Lala and Quentin did readings. There was no eulogy and the coffin was placed in the crypt at the bottom of the church. Julia refused to go down there. She stayed up in the church and lit a candle instead.

Afterwards the congregation walked the half-mile back to Tawray and then along the drive to the house, a long procession of black-clad mourners, the older ones returning by car. Sandwiches, cake, tea and whisky were laid out in the dining room, and the ground floor was soon full of murmuring vis-itors while the immediate family were called into the library for the reading of the will.

Afterwards Julia came out, flushed and breathless. 'Well, that's that. We might as well go now.'

'What's happened?' David had been waiting in the hall and now he grasped her hand. 'What is it?'

'Quentin gets the house,' she said, 'but it's all held in trust. Lala and I get lump sums and some of the trust. Poor old Cousin Violet – remember her from the wedding? Quen-tin's little sister – she gets a bit of cash. Everything stays here; it can't be sold off, not yet, unless the trustees deem it neces-sary. Once I'm thirty, I get a say. Quentin's bit will come to me and Lala if he doesn't have children.'

'Quentin doesn't get it all then, does he? That's good.' David was trying to read the expression on her face. Julia could see the confusion in his eyes. 'Are you pleased?'

'Pleased?' She gave a dramatic laugh. 'Hardly. It's the end of Tawray for me, just like I said. Quentin will marry some-one, have children, and I'm out. He'll give me the piano or a table or something, and think he's done pretty well by me.' She laughed again. 'A bitch pup. And one from the second litter at that. Well, perhaps it's for the best. Maybe I'm not supposed to be here, in this house. Perhaps it's bad for my health.'

But all she was thinking was, *Poor Mummy. She died trying to give Daddy a boy. And it's all gone to Quentin after all. She might as well have lived. Then she'd still be here. I'd still belong here.*

David said urgently, 'Then let's go. Let's go to my parents – we can nestle in and see out this miserable week before I go back to work. We can live very happily in London, can't we?'

'Yes, of course we can,' Julia said brightly, her eyes glittering. 'We're young. What do we need with a place like this? We should be having fun in town, not be lost down here. You're right. Get me out of here, David. Right now.'

The strange feverish excitement brought on by her father's funeral didn't leave Julia for some time afterwards. She felt constantly agitated, as if on the brink of a big adventure, and wanted to hurry back to London as soon as they could get there. After a week with David's parents, kind though they were, she was even more restless and eager to be off. She talked the whole way back to London.

'I've got some money now. There's my mother's jewellery too – we can sell some of that if we want to. Where shall we live? Richmond is lovely. But perhaps you should be closer to the centre, for work. I suppose it depends what we can afford, I've no idea what things cost.'

She knew she was rambling but she couldn't seem to stop. It was important to keep talking, and to keep her energy up, to stay focused on the future. She was Mrs Pengelly now, and her childhood was a closed book.

I must look to the future. She was afraid of that too, but perhaps by talking and talking, she could hide it, and distract David from her evident fear by making him think about houses and locations and all the rest.

It seemed to work. He focused on all that practicality as

well, frowning as he navigated through the traffic back on the M3.

'That's a good question. I'm sure we'll be able to find the right place, and I do think that being close to work is probably best. But there's no hurry. We can stay where we are for now, in the flat.'

'Yes,' Julia said brightly, but she fully intended to start looking for a home as soon as they returned to London.

The reality of the demands of David's working life was not so bad at first. He disappeared off early in the morning and tried to be home at a decent hour but he often had evening functions and what he called 'away days' that meant staying away from home. He could, at a moment's notice, be summoned all over the country to any number of different houses, and he seemed constantly to be heading to airports and helicopter dromes and then there were the trips abroad, which necessitated two visits – one to recce and plan, and one to accompany the principals and stage-manage the actual event. It would have been easier if he was able to talk about the intimate details of his job, but he was utterly discreet, almost to the point of not mentioning names at all.

Julia didn't mind at first, with the distraction of looking for a house for them. Once she realised quite how much David's job would occupy him, she decided that they must live as close to his work as possible and she found a small house on a cul de sac in Kensington, close to the park and a short drive to St James's. It was expensive but her legacy from her father paid for most of it, and she occupied herself decorating and furnishing it, feeling quite grown-up as she made the perfect home for the two of them to share. But there came a point when the house was finished. They were one year married and David had been away for almost two months of that. She was happy when he was with her, but lonely in the many hours she spent by herself. The people who lived around her seemed so much older than she was. She had lost touch with her friends during her months in Stockwell and it didn't seem an easy thing to get them back. She began to mope, feeling her spirits sink.

I'm too young to be shut away like this.

Julia was in Harrods food hall, staring at a display of cheeses and wondering what David might like. Her basket was full of things she wasn't even sure she wanted, but it was passing the time and she liked the beauty and drama of the hall: mounds of chocolates and sweets, baskets of bright fruit and vegetables, picturesque arrangements of bread, cakes and pastries. She couldn't really cook, but she liked shopping for food.

'Julia? Is that you?'

She turned, startled, and saw a woman she vaguely recognised standing beside her with an enquiring expression, one hand held out in a tentative gesture. 'Oh. Yes.'

'It's Sally. Sally Grigson. From school.'

'Of course!' She smiled. She could see now that in this older face, with its carefully applied make-up and neatly brushed hair, there was the younger one she remembered:

round blue-green eyes, round face, short button nose – sweet but unremarkable. And it was still unremarkable, the kind of face that wouldn't draw the eye twice. Nice, normal. 'Hello, Sally, how are you?'

'You look exactly the same,' Sally said, shaking her head. 'Just the same!'

'So do you.'

'What are you doing now?'

'I'm married. I live not far from here, about five minutes away.'

'Lovely.'

'And you?'

'I'm a secretary, I work around the corner. I come in here sometimes for a treat, when I'm feeling low. Nothing like Harrods to lift the spirits.' Sally smiled again. 'If you don't mind the tourists.'

'Well. Quite.'

'You do look well, Julia. How lovely it is to see you again.'

It came out in a rush before she even thought it through properly. After all, she had barely swapped a sentence with Sally at school. 'Have you had lunch? We could have some together if you like. It would be good to catch up.'

Sally's eyes widened and she looked pleased. 'What a nice idea. Why don't we go upstairs to the bistro? They do sandwiches there at lunchtime, quite reasonable. I've got forty minutes of my lunch break left.'

'Wonderful. Let's. I'll pay for this and we can go straight up.'

*

By the time they were settled at a table, with chicken sandwiches and glasses of Perrier, they were chatting away like
old friends, swapping stories of St Agatha's and the girls
they'd known there.

'Are you married?' Julia asked.

Sally shook her head, chewing on her sandwich. When
she'd finished, she said, 'I've got a boyfriend, he works in the
City. I'm living in the spare room at my aunt's house in Pim-
lico. It's not so bad.'

'And you've got a job.'

'Oh yes. Nothing fancy but I quite enjoy it. It's a small literary agency, just two agents, about fifteen authors, and me.'

'Well, that sounds interesting.'

'It can be. I like the authors, most of them anyway, and
I sometimes get to read manuscripts.'

'Anyone famous? Jilly Cooper?'

'No one so glamorous as that. Most are academics, actually.'

'Do you want to be a literary agent?'

Sally laughed. 'Oh no. Bill – that's my boyfriend – and I
might get married and then I imagine I'll stop work.' She
smiled. 'I should think married life is marvellous.'

Julia thought of David, and her heart swelled with love for
him, and their life together. 'Yes, it is. It's wonderful.'

'Any children?'

'No. But I'm thinking of getting a dog.'

'Really? What kind?'

They talked away for half an hour, when Sally checked her
watch and said, 'I must get back. They're not too strict but
we open again from two, so I'd better go.'

'It's been lovely seeing you,' Julia said, surprised to find she meant it. 'We must do it again.'

'I'd like that.' Sally took a scrap of paper and a pen from her bag and scribbled quickly. 'There's the number of the agency. Ring me if you ever fancy lunch again.'

'I will.'

They kissed their goodbyes and Julia watched her go. *I've got a friend*, she thought, almost with surprise. *I will definitely ring her. She could be just what I need.*

A week later, David came home with a box containing a wriggling, wagging, licking bundle of black Labrador puppy.

'To keep you company,' he said, as she squealed with delight, lifting the creature from its box and hugging it. 'I know you're alone so much and you said you were thinking about a dog.'

'David! It's adorable!'

'She's twelve weeks old. You can choose her name.'

Julia laughed as the puppy snuffled and licked and jumped up to nuzzle her neck. 'She's lovely, thank you.'

'Something for you to look after. Until we have a baby.'

Julia was still for a moment. Then she laughed again. 'Oh, what shall I call you, you rascal, eh? Thank you, darling. I love her. I really do.'

Chapter Sixteen

1986

The arrival of Greta the puppy brought energy and focus to Julia's days. Now she had a companion to care for and quite a few weeks were spent training her, taking her for walks and being diverted by the puppy's antics, as well as whisking David's smart shoes out of the reach of her gnawing teeth and trying to stop the table legs being chewed.

'I love her so much, thank you for getting her,' she said to David over the breakfast table, as Greta watched them from her bed by the door, head resting on its cushioned side.

'It's wonderful to see you happy again.' His eyes twinkled at her over the top of his coffee mug as he took a sip. 'I've been worried about you since we moved house – that you're lonely.'

She laughed. 'I've got Sally now, you know that. We meet practically every other day.'

'Yes. She seems nice.'

'Nice? Hmm, I know what that means. You think she's a bit boring.' They had gone out with Sally and Bill a couple of times – to the cinema on Kensington High Street, and to the pub on Edwardes Square, where the men talked politely about cricket.

David shook his head. 'She's perfectly pleasant, and so is Bill.'

'Pleasant also means boring.'

'Well . . . all right. Neither of them exactly sets the world alight. You're not like them, so I suppose I don't quite understand what you see in her.'

She smiled at him. 'Flattery. Well, I like Sally, and I've got Greta too, so I'm quite sorted out.'

'Good.' David put down his empty cup. He was neatly dressed as always in a perfectly pressed, fluff-less dark suit, crisp shirt and neat tie in a Windsor knot. 'Right. I must get to SJP. I've got meetings all morning. No doubt I'll be crossing the park this afternoon.' He adopted a martyrish expression and raised his eyebrows.

'More gin and tonic to mix,' Julia said lightly. It was a joke that all David did was make drinks and carry flowers, but she knew it was more than that. The reality of keeping a senior branch of the royal family working smoothly, with its myriad needs and activities, meant that he was not only extremely busy but also often tense and worried. He wouldn't have any newspapers in the house first thing in the morning.

'I'll see them soon enough when I get to the office,' he would say. 'And I'd like to enjoy my coffee in peace at least. The phone doesn't ring here, thank goodness.'

David kissed her goodbye and went off into the bright morning to walk down to St James's Palace, and Julia watched him go. She never asked him anything about what went on in

his job and he offered very little: just snippets of unremarkable news, such as the fact that he had sat that day in the
Buckingham Palace staff canteen with the Captain of the
Queen's Flight, or had discussed pictures with the Keeper of
the Royal Collection. Just those few scant details made her
aware of the huge operation and the dozens of people who
kept the machinery of the monarchy moving smoothly. David
was just one more cog in it, and yet his proximity to the most
glamorous of all the royal figures gave him a particular
importance, at least to Julia's mind. He didn't want to see the
papers because his boss was most likely to be featured, and
most likely to be talked about. It was just a fact that women
drew more attention and inspired more debate than men. No
one was much interested in suits and ties, a balding head or a
military uniform; dresses, shoes, hats and jewels were another
matter. Feminine hairstyles, make-up, weight, moodiness, and
attributes as a mother were fascinating to the public, it
seemed, and the state of relationships within the crystal gold-
fish bowl of royalty were the most sublimely interesting of all.
Julia herself was not immune. If the papers were anything to
go by, there was trouble in paradise, and she knew that David
must be keenly aware of anything going on behind the elegant
windows of Kensington Palace. He knew the truth of all the
gossip and speculations. But he never said anything.

Julia's interest, perhaps piqued by David's reserve, in
what was going on behind the closed doors began to grow.
She took Greta for walks in the park and imagined David
in the grand red-brick Queen Anne house at the far end of
Hyde Park – she knew he spent a great deal of time travelling

between St James's Palace, where he had his office, and Kensington Palace, where he would be summoned for meetings by his boss, who was reluctant to venture into the heart of operations at SJP, that bastion of the old guard. Julia threw sticks for Greta and imagined David in a cosy, intimate, feminine sitting room, gazing into the famous blue eyes under the sweep of fair hair, and wondered if he would be able to resist that charm, heightened as it was by royal star power.

His mood – usually one of exhaustion and worry – seemed to indicate he could. But what if his natural chivalry was being roused by working for, protecting and representing a magnetically attractive woman? What if he simply couldn't help it?

Then she would tell herself not to be so stupid: how ridiculous was it to be jealous of someone like that? It was pathetic and pointless and she gave herself a mental shake. *Stop it, Julia. Just stop it.*

But she walked Greta one day through the park to the outskirts of the palace, and found herself standing at the gate staring down a long driveway to another gate where a security guard waited to vet anyone trying to gain entry to the maze of courtyards, apartments and flats that lay beyond.

David might be in there.

She felt a huge longing for him, like a physical pain in her gut, and had the wild impulse to run down the driveway, calling his name. *They'll think I'm mad. They might even shoot me or something.* No, she mustn't do that.

Then she saw a movement: the navy-blue bonnet of an expensive sports car edged to the security gate, stopped

momentarily and then purred down the driveway towards
her. Julia watched as it approached. It stopped beside her,
engine thrumming, as the driver waited for a gap in the traffic. At the wheel – *yes, that's her* – a flash of blonde hair,
determined eyes, a delicate yet strong-willed chin. The driver
was partially obscured by a protection officer in the passenger seat, who stared out at Julia, baleful and suspicious. A
second later, the car edged out onto Kensington High Street,
and joined the flow of traffic, and was lost.

It was the strangest feeling. The other side of David's life,
utterly oblivious to her, had just passed her. She was as closed
off from it as any other person wandering through the park
that morning, and as firmly shut out. And yet, her husband
spent more time in there than he did with her. His duty to all
of that, and to the driver of the sports car, seemed greater
than his loyalty to her.

You're being stupid, she told herself as she walked home,
Greta bounding around her. But the mood of deep gloom
that had settled on her was hard to shake.

When David came home and told her the he'd soon be away
for the best part of a fortnight for work, Julia nodded and
seemed to accept it but within half an hour they were having
a terrible row. It started over something tiny, then grew as
Julia found more fuel to add to the flames of her indignation
until she was in a high state of anger. David, always unflap-
pable, became more distant the more emotional she got. As
she worked herself up into a tearful fury, he stared at the
floor and went cold, refusing to respond to her, which in turn

drove her into greater turmoil. Then at last, she got to the heart of it.

'You don't care about me! You don't love me!' she screamed. 'Or how could you leave me?'

He looked at her, his blue eyes cold, his face set. 'Don't be ridiculous, Julia! It's my job, you know that. You knew it when we got married.'

'You care about *her* more than you care about me!'

His expression went stony. She hated to see it, and she knew it wasn't true, but she couldn't help herself. She needed his reassurance so much. The sense of being shut out of his life, an outsider, had stayed with her ever since she'd glimpsed the woman in the car, and had sat in her mind like something noxious.

David got up. 'There's no talking to you when you're like this. I'm going out.'

'No, don't go!' She followed him down the hallway to the front door. 'Don't leave me, David, please!'

Why couldn't he understand that leaving her was the worst thing to do? She wanted his strong arms around her, the murmuring of calm words, the insistence that he cared about her.

'I'll be back later,' he said, not looking at her. 'I hope you'll be a bit more reasonable by then.' The door slammed shut behind him and she sank to the floor, sobbing.

He did not come back until much later, when she was in bed staring at the wall in darkness and he smelled of whisky and the smokiness of a pub. He sat down on the bed beside her and reached out to stroke her hair.

'Darling,' he said, his voice soft and just a touch blurry with drink. 'I do love you. If you knew how much . . .'

She said nothing, afraid that if she spoke, she might say the wrong thing. She wasn't sure if he even knew she was awake.

'You need something else,' he said. 'More than Greta. You need a baby.'

Her blood turned to ice. She closed her eyes and bit her lip. *No. Not that. Never that.*

David kicked off his shoes and lay down beside her. He gave a great sigh and the next moment was asleep, his breathing loud and slow in the quiet room.

Julia lay there, paralysed with fear. She'd known this would come, it had to. How on earth would she tell him the truth?

'But you and David seem so happy, such a perfect couple.' Sally's gaze was frank and concerned. 'I always think how absolutely right you are when we see you.'

They were in an Italian cafe they had found in the mazy streets behind Harrods and which they had made their regular lunch place.

'We are happy.' Julia gazed at her sandwich: ham and mozzarella with spiky peppery lettuce leaves. 'Very happy. I'm just alone so much, that's all.'

Sally nodded. 'I know. You do put up with an awful lot. But just think, if he was still in the navy, he'd be gone for much longer, and submarines are a bit more dangerous than palaces.'

Julia nodded. 'I feel as though something is always going to take him away from me.'

'But, darling, isn't that life? Isn't that what happens?'

There it is again, like David said. Life is awful. Just accept it. I don't know if I can.

Sally brightened and she put her sandwich down, hit by an idea. 'I know! You should get a job!'

'Me? What am I good for?' Julia shook her head. 'I didn't even finish St Agatha's. I dropped out of my acting course. I'm completely unqualified for anything.'

'So get a qualification. Go to secretarial college like me, it opens up a lot of avenues.'

Julia thought for a second and then said, 'I'm far too stupid and lazy.'

'Then maybe David's right and you need to have a baby.'

Julia looked away, staring out of the window to the road beyond, where she watched a street sweeper slowly sweeping up litter and depositing it in his trolley. 'No,' she said at last. 'Not yet. I'm not ready.'

'Well, you are still very young. But honestly, Julia, you're bored, can't you see that? You need to do something. I'm worried about you. Why don't you and David meet Bill and me for dinner or something?'

'David's going away,' Julia reminded her.

'When he's back. Oh goodness, look at the time, I must get back to the office.' Sally gestured for the bill. 'Let's do something nice together at the weekend. You shouldn't be alone so much. It's not good for you.'

*

Sally was kind, Julia thought as she walked back to the house, Greta gambolling beside her. *She's a good friend to me. It's odd because we never really spoke at school.*

Julia had been loud, well liked, though sometimes in trouble, and often the centre of attention. People seemed to be drawn to her and her vivacity, her jokes and her sense of fun. Sally had been a subtle character, quieter, more observant. It was odd because she often started off on the margins, but then, slowly but surely, made her way into the heart of things so that she was always in on the action if not one of the main players. She had been the kind of girl who made her mark later in her school career, who came from nowhere to be head girl or captain of something, or won the biggest prize on Speech Day, and surprised everyone.

She felt envious of Sally in a way she never had when they were schoolgirls. Sally had finished school, got her qualifications, bagged an interesting job. She might pretend not to be ambitious, but Julia suspected a steely spine and an iron will behind the round blue-green eyes and the gentle smile. *I'm sure she knows how to get what she wants.*

But she felt safe with Sally. *Yes, safe. She doesn't pry about David's job. She doesn't try and get me to tell her what I don't want to. She's kind. And I like Bill.*

Bill was a sensible man, without any of David's dark glamour. He would be a reliable, steady sort of husband. No nasty surprises there.

Julia felt a longing to be satisfied with less, the way everyone else seemed to be. She wanted so badly to be like Sally and Bill. No doubt they would get married, have a family, and be resolutely, comfortably ordinary. She suspected Sally was the kind of woman who would make it her life's mission to look after her man and not make demands.

Why can't I be like that? Why?

The letter from Quentin was completely unexpected.

Dear Julia,

I wonder if you would meet me for lunch? I want to talk to you. I'm coming down from Cambridge in a fortnight for a conference and I'd be much obliged. If possible, shall we say the 28th at 12.30 p.m. in the Oxford and Cambridge Club?

Affectionately,

Quentin

She stared at it, surprised. Quentin had never been in touch with her before, not even so much as a birthday card. When she thought about him, it was to imagine him ensconced in her father's favourite armchair in front of the fire at Tawray, sitting there as the lord of the manor, delighted at how it had all turned out. But the reality was that he was in Cambridge, pursuing his academic career. She'd even seen his name in the paper, when he was appointed as a fellow at Trinity.

Wondering what on earth he might have to say to her, she wrote to accept the invitation and went along a fortnight later, walking down St James's, eyeing the palace as she passed it with something like suspicion, and making her way up the stone steps to the club entrance. Quentin was waiting for her in the lobby, inspecting notices pinned to the green baize board, a tall and gangly figure in a baggy tweed suit.

'Ah, hello,' he said awkwardly once he'd spotted her, and kissed her cheek with over-pursed lips. 'So glad you could come. Let's go straight to the Coffee Room, shall we?'

She accompanied him along the short walk to the Coffee Room, which was actually the club's restaurant, a grand room with red silk walls and huge portraits of kings and queens gazing down upon the diners. They were seated by the tall windows overlooking Pall Mall, and Quentin was given the menu with the prices, while Julia was handed one without.

'Have whatever you like,' Quentin said beneficently. 'The pigeon is very good.'

Julia made her choice and Quentin filled in the little order slip which he gave to the waiter, who brought over water and a carafe of ruby-red wine. She asked polite questions and he talked about life in college and his research into Scottish medieval history, but they both knew they were skirting something. When finally, over their half-finished lunches, he asked her how married life was, she said, 'That's all fine. But what's this about, Quentin? Is it Tawray?'

He coughed a little awkwardly and blinked behind his tortoiseshell-rimmed glasses. 'Well . . . yes, as it happens. It is.'

'What about it? Is everything all right?' Cold fear pierced her at the idea that something might be wrong with the old place. Already she was fretting that Quentin would tell her it was to be sold, but she was sure that wasn't possible without her and Lala's permission.

'Yes, yes. Listen, Julia, I need your help. I don't want Tawray, I never did. My mother was intent on my having it. I don't know why, as I never showed the slightest interest in it. My bent is for study, and the university, and I want to make my life and career there. I thought it would make no difference to have the house and that I might even like it. I thought Violet might enjoy it but she loathes it. And it needs proper care, it turns out. There's always so much to be done.'

'So what are you suggesting?'

'Something very straightforward. I'll make my part over to you and Lala. The trust can pay me something for it one of these days. But I'll surrender all my interest and it can be yours. What do you think?'

'I . . . Yes, I . . .' She struggled to find the words. She had not expected this: that Tawray might return to her, and she to it. Happiness rushed up through her, like a geyser bursting up from the ground.

'You'll need to talk to your husband first, of course. Get his advice.'

'Oh no. I know what I want. I want the house. I can't think of anything nicer.' *I've been sick*, she thought, *because I miss home so much. Once I'm back in Tawray, it will all be better. Everything will be all right.* She beamed at him. 'Oh Quentin, thank you. I mean it. Thank you.'

'You're welcome.' He smiled. 'I'm glad you're happy. My mother won't be, but there we are!'

'She doesn't like me.'

'Perhaps not. I don't know why. Perhaps it was because she thought your poor mother was not up to the task of looking after the house. It always meant more to her than to me. I shall get in touch with the trustees and we can set the whole thing in motion as soon as possible.'

'Of course I'm happy,' David said slowly, when she told him in great excitement that evening about what had happened. 'And I can see you are. But be realistic, Julia – what are we going to do with that house?'

'What do you mean?' She stared at him, her smile fading.

'How on earth can it fit in with our lives now? I have to be here, you know that. My work is here. Cornwall is not easy to get to from London. How on earth will we manage?'

'I don't know, but we will,' she said stubbornly. 'I can't turn it down, David, you know how I feel about it.'

'Yes, I do.' He sighed. 'Oh God, this is not going to be easy, is it? Let's go and see the old place first. Then we can have a proper talk about it.'

She hugged him hard. 'Thank you, darling. Let's go as soon as we can. I'm longing to see it again.'

They drove down that weekend, when David's employers were out of town, though not together, and he had the whole of Friday to Monday to spend as he liked. As soon as they were out of London and on the road heading west, Julia felt her spirits lift. Once they were past Basingstoke and Andover, and she could see the miles to Exeter melting away, she began to feel quite joyous, as though the wind blowing against them was breathing life back into her. She could hardly stay still in her seat as they got closer to Tawray, and once they were though the gates, she couldn't stop herself shrieking with her first glimpse of the house at the end of the drive.

'Oh David. We're home!'

He glanced at her, unable to stop smiling at her enthusiasm but with an air of apprehension. 'Yes. We're back.'

When the car stopped, she leapt out and opened the boot for Greta to come out as well, and the dog jumped about with excitement at being set free among so many interesting sights and smells. Julia stood on the gravel drive, looking up at the old house. It already seemed more dilapidated than she remembered. *It's lonely too. Like me.*

She searched in her pocket for the key to the front door. 'Come on. I can't believe it's really mine. And Lala's too, of course. But mine.'

David went to the back of the car for the bags. 'Not quite yet. There are papers to be signed, aren't there? The money to be decided.'

'Yes, yes, you literal thing. The papers aren't signed yet, but it's all agreed.'

She pushed the old door open, hearing it creak on its hinges, and stepped inside. It was dusty and cool within, everything the same and yet lacking lustre, as though even furniture took its gleam from the activity of human life around it. Julia saw dozens of things that needed doing just gazing from the top of the staircase to the hall and back. A pile of post lay on the mat and in a heap on the side table. Someone was coming in then, from time to time. She saw that the drawing room door stood ajar and that Greta had disappeared in there, so she followed her as David came up behind with the cases. As soon as she was inside, she screamed.

'What is it?' called David, and he dropped the bags to hurry in after her. 'Are you all right?'

'David – look! Oh look!' She pointed with a trembling finger.

'It's gone,' he said with surprise.

Where the wall and the mural had been there was only space, and the drawing room now opened seamlessly into the room beyond. Where there had been the illusion of the library, the real thing now occupied the same space. The effect was eerie, as though half a dozen people had simply vanished. Their absence seemed to echo in the air.

'He's destroyed the mural,' Julia said in a broken voice. 'It's gone. My mother. Her letter to me. Daddy. All gone.' She looked to David. 'Couldn't he have left me that?'

David hugged her. 'I'm so sorry.'

'Couldn't he have left me that? Out of all of it?' And she burst into tears.

Chapter Seventeen

Julia couldn't bring herself to ask Quentin why he had destroyed the mural and broken down the wall into the library; she had a feeling he would not even know and that would make it worse. It was too terrible, that it had been destroyed for no reason at all. But it had gone and there was nothing she could do about it, though the pain of absence did not diminish; she felt it every time she went into the drawing room and saw it wasn't there.

Another thing to go, to disappear without trace, with no questions to be asked.

She and David spent a long weekend going over the entire house from top to bottom, making lists of what needed to be done. By the end of the process, David's expression was grave.

'It's an enormous project, Julia. Huge and expensive. And for what?'

'What do you mean, for what?' She gazed at him, bewildered. 'What choice is there? It's Tawray, and that's that. It needs to be done. The money will come from the trust, I suppose. The house makes a bit of an income.'

'I'll bet you it costs a lot more than that to run and maintain.' David looked about sadly. 'These places are a relic of the past now, more of a burden than anything else. It would make sense as a school or a business or even a museum. You should think about selling it, darling. Lala won't want it; she lives in Paris and her whole life is in France. How are the two of us going to manage this?'

She laughed as though he were joking. 'Sell it? No! I can never do that. We'll make it work. It's going to be my project, my thing.' She hugged her notebook to her and spun around on the spot. 'Sally is right, she said I needed something to do, and here it is – my purpose. My reason for being here.'

David half smiled but his expression was apprehensive and his brow creased with a frown. 'You say that, but how on earth is it practical?'

'I'll make it happen,' she said with determination. 'Just you see.'

David said no more, but she knew that he was against the idea of Tawray. She suspected now that he'd been glad when it was left to Quentin rather than to her. But he said nothing and mucked in just as hard as she did. They spent a busy weekend, getting filthy in jeans and shirts, as they cleared and cleaned, with Julia getting progressively more enthusiastic and her lists longer and longer.

They went back to London exhausted but Julia was sure that David was glad to see her mood so much improved and her old energy and verve returning. The strange, bitter jealousy she had felt towards his employer seemed to have disappeared and they didn't speak of it.

'I've been in a slump,' she said that night in bed, as they hugged in the darkness before sleep. It was always easier to talk then, close together, just bodies and voices. 'I've been really low.'

'I know,' David said sleepily. He yawned. 'I love you, you know that. More than anyone in the world. I just want you to be happy.'

'Tawray makes me happy.'

'You say that but I find it hard to understand. In the past, you've said it scares you and makes you miserable.'

'It does both, I suppose. Like family. Sometimes you hate it and other times you need it. I think I need it right now, and it needs me.'

'It's going to be a massive bloody problem. It's a five-hour drive away from here.'

'We can do it,' she said obstinately. 'I know we can. And you're away so much, so it will stop me feeling lonely.'

'It'll be worth it if it makes you happy.' He hugged her tighter. 'And besides, there will be all the more reason to fill it with scampering children, I suppose.'

'Yes! What a lovely idea.'

For a moment, in her joy at having her home restored, she really thought it was.

Sally was impressed. 'How extraordinary to have the house handed back to you like that.'

Julia nodded, the wind whipping her tawny hair over her face. They were walking in the park, slowly making their way towards the Albert Memorial while Greta raced about,

224

exploring. 'I think my cousin had grand ideas of using it as a place to work when he wasn't at Cambridge, but the reality of looking after it put him off. Notoriously lazy, academics.'

'I've never seen it, of course,' Sally said. Her fair hair was pulled tightly back into a ponytail against the wind. 'It sounds glorious.'

'It is. You and Bill must come down.'

Sally looked gloomy. 'That's all off, I'm afraid.'

Julia stopped short and gaped at her. 'What?'

'Yes. We broke up at the weekend.'

'Why?'

'I did it. I suppose my heart really wasn't in it anymore. Bill is lovely, but he's not very go-getting, not very . . . well, he's lovely, but not really for me.'

'What a shame, I liked Bill,' Julia said lamely, wishing she could offer more; but she couldn't really protest that Sally was wrong when she felt just the same about Bill's niceness and general all-round dullness. He didn't have David's brooding dark handsomeness or quiet magnetism.

Sally pulled her pink tweed jacket a little tighter around her against the blustery April wind. 'He was a bit cut up but he'll get over it. So I'm young, free and single again.' She grinned at Julia. 'Know anyone you could set me up with?'

Julia laughed. 'I'll do my best! David's got some friends but most of them are in the navy, and head off on service for months at time.'

'Naval officers are sexy, I quite like that idea. Prince Andrew – yum.'

'Shame he's already taken.'

'More's the pity. Oh well, you'll have to get on the case and find me someone like David: handsome and imposing and successful.'

'I don't know if being an equerry is all that successful, is it?'

Sally looked surprised. 'Oh yes, it's a real feather in the cap. David will be able to get a fabulous job once he's finished that, if he doesn't want to go back to the navy. Has he talked about that?'

'No. He seems rather addicted to this job, I'm afraid.'

'It must be fascinating. I'd love to work in the palace.'

'Would you? I can't help thinking it must all feel rather silly once you get close up.'

'Silly?'

'Princes and princesses, bowing and scraping, footmen and ladies-in-waiting and all the rest of it. David doesn't tell me much but he's given me the distinct impression that it's all as camp as Christmas.'

Sally looked shocked and frowned at her. 'That's awful, Julia – that's our monarchy! Our royal family. We should be terrifically proud.'

'Yes . . . yes, of course,' Julia said quickly. Sally evidently took the whole thing very seriously. 'Well, I'm sorry about you and Bill, but if it wasn't working, it wasn't working. Let's see if we can find you someone else.'

Sally had gone back to work and Julia was on her way home, Greta pulling at the lead like crazy whenever she saw another dog she wanted to befriend. She saw a Scottie dog padding towards them along the pavement and made a dash for her before Julia knew what was happening and the next moment, she'd been pulled headlong into the owner.

'Oh, goodness! Sorry, sorry! Down, Greta!'

'Well, hello,' said a drawling voice.

Julia looked up and blinked with astonishment as she realised she was looking at Mark. 'Oh!'

He grinned. 'This is a surprise. Fancy crashing into you like this. You do look respectable, Miss Teague. And is that a wedding ring I spy? So you're not Miss Teague at all. Who are you then?'

'Mark! I can't believe it.' She gazed at him. He looked quite well, in comparison to how he had been a few years before in the Stockwell house. 'I'm Julia Pengelly now. But how are you?'

'I'm all right actually. You?'

'Fine, fine.' She could feel herself flushing with a mixture of embarrassment and pleasure at seeing him again.

'Are you busy? Why don't we pop to The Antelope, and you can tell me all about it?'

'Well . . .' She thought about the rest of her day, and how little she had to do apart from chores and lists. 'Yes. Yes. That would be lovely.'

Twenty minutes later, they were sitting in the pub, which was quiet with only a few lunchtime drinkers left, and Julia had a gin and tonic in front her, while Mark had a pint. Greta curled up at her feet and went to sleep.

'I don't usually drink at lunchtime,' she said, as he shuffled himself into the tight space of the wooden bench they were on.

'I expect you don't, not these days. You used to be quite the party queen.' He grinned lazily and she remembered his slow charm, the way he talked in a drawl that meant his sharp wit was all the more surprising and amusing.

She said jokily, 'Well, you can talk! You used to be absolutely out of it most of the time. What's happened? Are you better?'

'Better?' He raised an eyebrow at her, which made her laugh.

'Off drugs.'

'Not exactly off, dearie. Let's just say I've got things a bit more under control. My dad sent me to rehab, if you must know – three weeks in a godawful place in America, and another three in a nicer place in Surrey. I think it cost him about fifteen grand.'

'Really?' Julia's eyes went wide. 'And it helped?'

'It helped a bit.' Mark lowered his voice conspiratorially. 'Now I only take heroin at weekends. I stick to coke and speed the rest of the time.'

Julia laughed despite herself. 'Oh Mark. Honestly.'

'What about you? Married, of course.'

She nodded.

'Well, that's a damn shame,' he murmured. 'I always rather hoped you'd come back to me.'

'No you didn't, you old charmer. I bet you never gave me a second thought.'

'That's not true. I was heartbroken. So, who stole you

away? Was it that rather stiff-looking type who was with you when you moved out?'

She nodded.

'I could see you'd got it bad, so I'm not surprised. And now you're busy living happily ever after.'

'Yes, that's right.' Mark was staring at her and she took a nervous sip of her gin. 'What?'

'Are you really?'

'Of course. Why on earth would you say otherwise?'

'I know you, Julia. I've seen you at your absolute lowest. We're alike, you and I,' he said slowly. 'We don't battle our demons, we make alliances with them. We join in the fun. That's why we're both headed the same way.'

She felt a chill of fear prickle over her at his words. 'That's awful. Of course we're not. We're quite different now, aren't we? I'm happily married, you're recovered. We've got everything to look forward to.'

Mark shook his head. 'Bottomless pits, that's us. You can pour love and hope and life into us and we will never fill up. We escape from time to time, and think we'll be happy, but then it all comes back, doesn't it?'

He pulled a packet of cigarettes out of his pocket and offered it to her. She took one, even though she'd almost given up as David didn't like it, and was surprised to find her fingers trembling. Mark lit it for her, and then his own.

'That's a very bleak prognosis,' she said, exhaling her first drag.

He shrugged. 'Just realistic. I know better than anyone that I'm not going to be clean for long. It will take more strength than I've got to stay away from the lusciousness of my favourite mode of escape.'

'I'm going to be all right,' she said firmly. 'And you could be too, if you want.'

'I'm glad to hear that about you, but I don't share your confidence about me. Fancy another drink?'

Julia got home late, her head swimming with gin, and with Greta ravenous for her supper. The house was dark and she remembered that David was at a function that evening. He was on duty so would probably stay on afterwards for some whisky with some of his colleagues. It was one of the perks of his job he enjoyed: the excellent food and the supply of very good single malt and vintage brandies that were made available when the work was done.

When Greta was fed, Julia went and stood in front of the mirror over the fireplace in their small sitting room. She saw suddenly the face of the girl who'd lived with Mark: gaunt, hollow-cheeked, eyes rimmed with kohl, white hair. Now she was a respectable wife, just as he said, with her thick, natural hair held back by clips, pearl earrings glowing in her lobes, her face peachy and healthy. For a moment she felt nostalgic for the crazy, hedonistic world she'd once lived in. After a moment, she went to the drinks table and poured herself a large gin and tonic, and fetched herself a cigarette from an old box in a handbag, and put on some music. She sat alone in the sitting room, drinking her gin, singing to Blondie and smoking, and wondered if what Mark had said was true: that she'd never escape the darkness inside her. It would always, always call her back.

A week later, Lala was waiting for her at Charles de Gaulle airport, waving hard as soon as she spotted Julia among the arrivals and then pulling her into a tight hug.

'Oh darling, I'm so happy to see you! Come on, the car is just outside, we must go before I get a ticket.'

On the drive into central Paris, Lala chattered away, telling her the latest news. Although they talked from time to time on the telephone, they hadn't met since their father's funeral.

'I'm so busy, that's the problem,' Lala said. She seemed to have the faintest French inflection these days, as though she had taken up residence in the space between the two languages.

'That's good, isn't it?' Julia asked, with a laugh. She was proud of her sister's success, her promotion to Head Designer, and she understood that the frantic pace of the fashion year meant that Lala was hard at work all the time.

'Oh yes, very good! I'm loving it, to be honest.' Lala slid a look at her. 'And you? How is married life?'

'Wonderful.'

'I'm pleased to hear it. But I think you're here to talk about Tawray, aren't you?'

'Yes, but . . . let's wait until we're settled.'

Lala managed the feat of driving through the madness of the city without a collision and they left the car in a private courtyard near her apartment, before walking to a nearby cafe. It felt perfectly Parisian to sit outside on cane bistro chairs in the sun. The waiter brought *café crème* accompanied by tiny bitter-sweet biscuits and Lala lit a Gauloise.

'Now I know I'm in Paris,' Julia said, sniffing the air. 'Coffee and cigarettes.'

'And the bloody drains,' Lala said, laughing.

'I can't smell that.'

'Maybe it's the river.'

'Greta would go mad with all these fascinating aromas. My dog,' she added, seeing Lala's bafflement. 'I've left her with a friend, and I'm rather missing her.'

'A dog?' Lala raised her eyebrows. 'I suppose you need the company, with David away so much. Where is he at the moment?'

'Abroad for a fortnight. One of his trips. He left a week ago.'

'So you thought you'd come and see me? That's lovely. I've arranged to take a day or two off, and we'll do sightseeing. I need an excuse to see some art and pictures.'

'That would be fantastic. I'm definitely your partner in crime. But I do need to talk to you about Tawray.' Julia pulled a letter out of her handbag and smoothed it down on the table in front of them, putting the ashtray on it to act as a paperweight. 'I got this. From Quentin's lawyers.'

'Oh?' Lala squinted in the sun. 'What does he say? My reading glasses are in the office.'

'Only that he's terribly sorry but he wants to buy a house in Cambridge, and he'll need the value of his share of Tawray. Or he'll force a sale of the whole place.'

Lala turned to her, frowning. 'Can he do that?'

'The trustees seem to think it's a possibility.'

Lala was quiet for a moment, taking a thoughtful drag on her cigarette. 'I see. And I think you don't want to sell.'

'No. I don't. I really, really don't.' Julia leaned eagerly towards her sister. 'I've felt alive again since I've been going back there. I want to make it my home, where David and I can live properly once he's finished his time at court.'

Lala said nothing for a while and then, 'I know it means a lot to you.'

'It means everything.'

'But Julia . . . it's so big, so costly to maintain. I would be happy to be rid of it, if I'm honest. I've never felt the same about it as you do. In fact, I wouldn't mind if I never went back there. I would rather it's sold, if I'm brutal about it.'

'No, Lala! I can make it work. I've got so many ideas and plans. I'll tell you all about them, and you'll see.'

'You could be happy somewhere else. Somewhere smaller.'

'No!' Julia's voice came out so strongly even she was surprised. 'I mean it, Lala – I can't be happy anywhere else. It's my lifeblood. Don't take it away from me, please.'

'All right,' Lala said slowly. 'I can see you mean that. Then what's the plan?'

Julia paced up and down the same length of blue carpet in their small Kensington sitting room, waiting anxiously for David to return from his trip. When he arrived at last, a black cab pulling up outside and David climbing out with his suitcase, she was outside, jumping into his arms almost before the taxi had pulled away.

'I'm so happy you're back! I've missed you so much!'

He laughed and kissed her strongly. 'Good. I've missed you too. But shall we go inside before we get carried away and shock the neighbours?'

Inside they abandoned his luggage in the hall and ran upstairs, eager and laughing, kissing and pulling each other's clothes off as they went. Their reunion was swift and blissfully enjoyable.

'I've missed you,' he said, pulling her close. 'I've been longing for you for days.'

'Me too.' She snuggled into his embrace and revelled in his nearness. 'How was the trip?'

'Difficult. Very difficult.' He made a pained face.

'Are relations chilly?'

David was silent.

'You might as well tell me,' Julia said. 'The papers are full of it. They were all over the fact that there were separate sleeping arrangements on the tour you went on, the German one.'

'Do you read that stuff?'

She said nothing, not wanting to tell him that she read everything she could find, poring over tabloid news stories as well as glossy magazines and high-society journals.

He sighed. 'You're right. I know everybody's talking about it. The gossip vultures are circling.'

'They say that they're practically living separate lives, and she's got a string of other men.'

'I know what they say.' David's expression hardened just a little. 'They don't know what they're talking about. I don't like this gossip, Julia, I really don't. If you knew what it's like up there . . . Not just chilly. It's an ice storm. And it would make your heart bleed to see it.'

'Whose fault is it? Hers or his? I bet it's his.' She thought of the glimpse she had seen of the blonde hair, the blue eyes, strong and yet somehow fearful at the same time. What was there to be afraid of? A small part of her wanted to get David to say something about the owner, so she could gauge the strength of his feelings about her. Would he leap in to defend her, be her champion? That would surely be telling.

'Oh darling, that's the worst of it. Fault? It's both and neither. The dreadfulness of it is what an amazing partnership they make, how powerful they are together. But it won't work. I've never seen two people make each other so miserable.'

Relieved at his even-handedness, Julia ran her finger over the smooth, warm skin of his arm. *We're so lucky that it's not like that for us.* 'The poor children.'

'The children are both loved, that's the main thing. But even though they're so young, they must have a sense of what's going on. We all do. I can't help feeling there's a crisis in the offing, and we're wasting all our chances to avoid it.'

'So you're not on her side?' Julia asked.

'I want the best for her, but I'm the first to say that she's no angel.' He kissed her head and she felt a burst of relief. 'But I don't want to talk about that. How have you been without me? Have you been lonely?'

'A bit.'

'Didn't you see Sally?'

'Oh, yes, once or twice.'

'And you went to Paris to see Lala. How was it?'

'Wonderful. A tonic.'

'Really?' A smile broke over his face. 'I'm so pleased you had a good time. How is she?'

'Very well. Blooming. Busy and creative and successful, just as you'd imagine.' Julia hesitated. She hadn't intended to bring up the subject so soon, but as they were in the lovely post-reunion haze, perhaps now was the best time after all. 'There's a bit of an issue with Tawray, and I talked it over with her.'

'An issue? You haven't said anything . . .' David turned to her, his dark blue eyes enquiring.

'No.' He was right. During their regular phone calls, she'd not brought it up, wanting to sound Lala out before she took it any further. 'I wanted to be sure I knew the facts. The thing is, Quentin wants me and Lala to buy out his share right away so he can get the cash. But Lala doesn't want Tawray either. So . . .' She hesitated again. It had all seemed perfectly clear and right when she'd made the decision in Paris but now that she had to say it out loud to David, it didn't seem so obvious.

'Yes?'

'Well . . . I said I would buy them both out.'

He blinked at her, evidently thinking it through. 'Buy them out? How can you do that? Do you want to raise a mortgage on it or something?'

She shook her head. 'I thought . . . I'd sell this place and use the money to buy them out. It should be just about enough, and I can borrow the rest.'

David pulled away so that he could see her properly. 'Then where would we live?'

'Tawray.'

He sighed impatiently. 'We can't, Julia, you know that! My work is here.'

'We can rent something small where you can stay when you're working.'

He took this in, and then said slowly, 'You mean live apart?'

'Only some of the time. But it's the only way.' She clutched at his arm, digging her fingers into the flesh. 'I've got to go back there, David, I mean it. I won't make it here in London.' She couldn't tell him about Mark, about the siren song of oblivion he poured into her ears, and the temptation to give up all that was good in her life and surrender herself to it. Already there was a stash of empty wine bottles in the bin, and a plastic bag full of cigarette butts and cloudy soft ash tucked in there too. Already she'd thought about going to Mark's house – not to be unfaithful to David but to find that welcoming numbness that was always on offer there. She needed to get away from that as soon as possible, or she knew that one day soon, it would all start again.

David looked sad. 'I can't bear the thought of us being apart. I love you. I want you here with me.'

She pulled him close and pressed her face into the warmth of his neck. 'I love you too. Please, darling, I wouldn't ask if it weren't important. We can make it work, it's only another year or two and you'll be retiring from the palace in any case. I just feel the need to be at home, at Tawray.'

A picture of her home floated into her mind: the familiar rooms, the beautiful gardens, the sea. She needed it like she needed her own blood.

He said nothing for an age, and she waited, feeling the thud of his heartbeat against her own chest. At last he spoke.

'All right, Julia. We can talk about it. But I have my own price – it's only fair you know that.'

She nodded. She had thought as much.

Chapter Eighteen

Present day

It was a little too early for Christmas parties, but there seemed to be a celebration going on in the far corner of the restaurant.

'I'm sorry we didn't come somewhere quieter,' Johnnie said apologetically across the white linen tablecloth loaded with china and glass.

'It's fine,' Netta said, pushing her fish around her plate and eating a tiny morsel when she finally speared a bit on the end of her fork.

'Not exactly conducive to conversation, though,' Johnnie said with a smile. She smiled back, her eyes glittering in the candlelight. She looked wonderful, he thought, in a drapey black silk top, silver necklaces of different lengths, and with glittering dark eyeshadow and red lipstick. He'd always been attracted by her easy elegance and her muted style. Showy women didn't really interest him, he preferred Netta's quiet self-possession, her maturity. What always astonished him was that she had fallen in love with him; he'd hardly been able to believe his luck. His sense of disappointing her was one of the worst aspects of their current situation but he didn't seem to be able to change himself enough to satisfy her. The words she'd said to him in the kitchen that day – 'I don't know if I can make you happy' – had resonated in his mind and he felt it was urgently important that he make sure she knew how happy he was, and how lucky he felt to have her. So he'd booked this dinner in an expensive London restaurant and wanted to tell her his plan.

Netta took a sip of her wine. 'They're not too loud. I'm not really bothered.'

He eyed her cautiously. She seemed perfectly calm and happy but he knew this mood – it often concealed something. Real happiness in Netta meant a liveliness, an eagerness to talk and listen, an enthusiasm for everything. When she became removed and closed off, it meant she was making distance between them. *You're not my friend*, she was saying. *I'm angry with you and I'm going to take away the things you like about me, and we'll see if you notice.*

'I spoke to Alex today,' he said conversationally.

Immediately she softened. 'Oh right. How is your father? Any change from yesterday?'

Johnnie shook his head. 'No. No change. He hasn't had any further strokes, but he's not responding to much. Sally is in the middle of arranging to get him home.'

'Is that wise?' Netta looked doubtful. 'Isn't hospital the best place for him?'

'Sally wants him home, and Alex thinks it's probably for the best as well.' He held up his wine glass and watched the red liquid glow in the candlelight as he tipped it back and forth. 'She said she thinks it's an indication of what they think the outlook is.'

'Oh Johnnie. I'm sorry. This is awful for you. And I'm so fond of your father.' She looked sincerely sad. Johnnie knew she had always liked Pa, and they'd got on well. Sally was always lovely to Netta, as though extending her endless sympathy for the misfortune of being married to Johnnie. She also respected Netta's style and obvious intelligence, and often gave subtle hints that she thought Netta could have done a bit better in her marriage. 'Will you go back?'

'Well . . . I had a thought about that actually. You said you had some holiday owing that you have to take before the end of the year.'

'Yes. I was going to take that when the boys break up for Christmas.' She looked wary. Johnnie coming up with plans always seemed to make her nervous. 'You know how absurdly early their holidays begin.'

'Sure. So here's what I'm thinking. Once I explained that Pa isn't going to make it, Sanwa said I can take advantage of some compassionate leave. A month or two months.'

'Right.' Netta slowly ate a piece of her fish, waiting for more.

'So I thought . . . let's go down to Cornwall for the whole month, as soon as the boys break up, or maybe even before, and take some time to be a family all together.' He smiled at her, hoping his enthusiasm for the idea would be catching. It had come to him in a flash and he'd thought it was a brilliant plan for reuniting them, giving them some quality time together and taking off the daily pressures of school and work

241

for longer than just the standard holiday break. They needed it, he was sure.

'Where would we stay? With Alex?'

She hasn't dismissed it at once. That's good. 'No, I think that would be tough on her and anyway, we need our space. I spoke to an old school friend who has a house down there. He's not using it right now and wouldn't mind renting it out to us. It's really close to Alex, not far from Pa and Sally's. I think it would be great.'

He watched Netta's reaction carefully, hoping she wasn't annoyed. She looked thoughtful, taking her time as she pondered what he'd said. After a few minutes, she looked up at him. 'Okay,' she said. 'I can see that might work. I don't want the boys to miss school, though.'

'That's fine.'

'Maybe it would do us all good to get away for a bit. And I appreciate that you want to be close to your father. So if you want to, I think we could make it work.'

Johnnie knew that she was, without mentioning it, giving up her original plan to see her own parents over the holidays, and he appreciated it. 'Thank you. I'll tell Robert we'll take the house and we can start to make the arrangements—'

Netta held up her hand. 'But.'

'Yes?' A flutter of nerves went through his stomach.

'I think it's only fair to tell you that I saw a solicitor today.'

The flutter turned into a full-scale wrench, a sickening somersault, and his fingertips prickled. 'What?'

She sighed. 'I've been doing a lot of thinking. About our future. About our happiness.'

He felt sick, his head suddenly swimming as though he'd been punched. A second ago, they'd been unified in their plans for a family Christmas, and now this? 'I don't understand.'

'I told you I don't know if I can make you happy.'

'You can,' he said. 'Why have you seen a solicitor?'

'I'm considering everything, that's all. And maybe this holiday will be a good time for us to talk about it.'

Oh God. He'd thought she'd agreed because she liked the idea of some time together as a family. But actually, she wanted to talk about divorce.

She saw the look on his face and her expression became sympathetic. 'I know it's a shock, but I haven't made any decisions. We just need to talk about it, that's all. Things can't go on as they are.'

Can't they? That was precisely what he'd thought would happen: muddling through, going on.

'Okay,' he said. He needed to move carefully, think hard and not just blunder in and ruin it all. So he made an effort to keep calm. 'We'll talk. All I ask is that you keep an open mind.'

'Yes.' She lifted her own wine glass. 'That's fair. We both keep an open mind.'

She sipped the dark red liquid, her brown eyes watching him over the rim of the glass.

Alex drove up to the house, where a private ambulance crew was busy unloading the equipment onto the driveway. Other people were taking it into David and Sally's house,

243

and Sally was hovering anxiously in the open doorway, directing operations.

'Into the room at the back, please, and stay on the plastic matting!' she called, as two men went past her carrying the upper part of a hospital bed. She looked older than usual, in a blue kilt and a pink cardigan over a frilly-necked blouse, her hair tied back instead of frosted into place with hairspray, but she still had big pearl clip-on earrings and shoes with bows on the front.

Classic Sally. Still dressing in the fashion of her youth.

'David's arriving soon,' Sally said, excited, as Alex came to greet her. 'I'm so glad to have him home.'

Alex nodded and let Sally lead her down the hall to where their study had been made into a temporary bedroom. Sally had evidently taken care over it: it was bright, clean and made cheerful with flowers, a television and radio – though Alex doubted her father would need them much – and cosy armchairs. The strange note was the large hospital bed with its moveable mattress set in a sitting position, and the drip stand and machinery nearby.

'A nurse is coming to stay,' Sally explained, as Alex looked at the kit. 'She'll be able to manage all of that. David's fed by a drip, and she'll empty the bags, and keep him clean.' She clasped her hands together like a giddy girl. 'I'm so happy to have him back. It's been awful without him.'

Alex patted her arm. 'I know.'

She saw, quite suddenly, Sally in relation to David, and not to herself. They had been married for nearly twenty-one years – a second marriage longer than many first – and they had barely been apart in all that time. Sally had stuck to David constantly, putting his welfare at the very heart of her existence in a way that had seemed to Alex hopelessly old-fashioned. Sally made no secret of the way she devoted herself to David, looking after him in what was sometimes an almost maternal fashion. Although she certainly expected plenty in return, she nevertheless was firmly of the opinion that her version of traditional roles was the right one. It was her wifely duty to gaze in moist-eyed adoration when her husband spoke, to oversee all his domestic needs, keep his house clean and his stomach full, and to appear perfectly groomed at all times. While she could chivvy him, she also coddled him – babied him, Alex thought – and treated him like her own personal hero in a way that Alex and Johnnie had laughed at privately, making sick faces and pretending to vomit when she said something particularly nauseating. To Alex, it also felt insincere, somehow, as if Sally were acting her devotion instead of feeling it. But Pa hadn't seemed to mind. In fact, he had let Sally do everything she wanted for him, and he became her creature, eating her favourite foods, sharing her hobbies and interests, taking up her friends, dressing in the style she preferred. Alex supposed that was all part of becoming a couple, but it hurt. It seemed as though the real Pa was being lost inside this new, docile one who was happy to surrender his old vibrant self and become Sally's creation; and that Pa put Sally first, before his relationships with his children.

Alex remembered the wedding, in the village church where

Mum was buried in the graveyard. Sally had wanted her to be a bridesmaid, in a candy-pink taffeta dress and a headband of yellow and white roses. Alex – *no, I was Ali then* – aged nine and confused by the emotions Pa's wedding was inspiring, had said she didn't want to wear the dress but Sally wouldn't hear of anything else and had made it clear what she expected. On the day itself, a bright May morning, Ali sat in her room in Tawray, the hated dress laid out on her bed, and set her chin against it. She wouldn't wear it.

When Johnnie came to check on her, sent by Sally, she told him that she refused to put it on. He shrugged and went away to deliver the news. The next moment, Sally came rushing down the corridor, in a bathrobe and a veil, her make-up half done, maddened with rage.

'What do you think you're doing?' she yelled, her eyes blazing. 'You put on that dress right now!'

'No.' Ali crossed her arms and narrowed her eyes at the vile pink of the ruffled dress. She hated it and she wasn't going to wear it. If that meant they would cancel the wedding, then good. She knew that down the hall, the daughter of Sally's best friend was obediently getting into her pink monstrosity. Sally wanted two bridesmaids and Ali was going to do it.

'Put it on!' Sally shrieked and picked up the dress.

'No.' Ali had never felt more sure of anything in her life – she wasn't going to wear that dress and be Sally's bridesmaid. Mum was there, in that churchyard, and to put on the pink silk horror and walk behind Sally as she married Pa was a betrayal Ali couldn't bear.

'Yes, yes!' Sally was frantic. She dropped the dress and hauled Ali to her feet by one arm, her grip vicious with the painted red fingernails digging in. 'Take those things off.' She started clawing at Ali's T-shirt, pulling it up and over her head while Ali struggled and shouted.

'Get off!' she yelled. 'Let me go!'

'You little . . . *bitch*,' Sally cried and she tore the T-shirt away, leaving Ali bare-chested and shaking. 'And the rest!'

She grabbed the waistband of Ali's jeans and her anger made her perfectly able to keep Ali where she wanted her, despite the struggling. Then Ali, seeing Sally's arm in just the right position, bent down and sank her teeth into the bare flesh. Sally screamed, drew back her hand and slapped Ali hard around the face, sending her to the floor.

'What's this?' Pa was standing in the door in full naval uniform, white-faced and shocked. 'What's going on?'

'She bit me!' howled Sally, rubbing her arm. Her veil, tugged in the struggle, was half off her head, her newly done hair messed so that it stood out in frozen sprayed strands. 'Ali won't wear her dress and she bit me!'

Pa stared, taking in Ali, who was on the ground, one cheek scarlet with finger marks clearly visible, not crying but wide-eyed and stunned; and Sally, eyes full of tears and outrage, on the brink of hysteria.

'Sally, go and get ready,' he commanded.

'Make her wear the dress,' Sally said, a whimper in her voice.

Pa said nothing and Sally sniffed, pushed up her veil and

went slowly out. Ali still half lay on the floor, shivering slightly and wrapping her arms around her bare chest.

'What's all this about?' Pa said, coming in. He put out a hand and pulled Ali gently to her feet. He took a small blanket off the bed and put it around her shoulders. 'Why won't you wear the dress?'

She stared back, not sure if she was brave enough to defy Pa. She would happily fight Sally to the death and never surrender, but Pa was a different matter. He was looking at her face, his lips turned down, his eyes sad, but he said nothing.

'I don't want to,' she said. She longed to tell him that was code for the fact she didn't want him to marry Sally. That she missed Mum so badly, and wanted their old life back so desperately it made her cry into the night. She wanted to tell him that her heart was broken and Sally didn't care and Sally was coming between her and Pa and the grief they shared and the restoration they might be able to give one another. She wanted to say that if only Sally knew how to love her, it might be all right. But she had no idea how to say any of those things. She just wanted Pa to understand, without her having to tell him that she needed him, and she wanted him to tell her that he loved her and would always be her Pa, Sally or no Sally.

'All right, old chum,' he said, using their nickname for each other. She felt a rush of desperate need. He had been her Pa, the centre of her world, the one who adored her. Then Mum had died and the games and smiles and laughter had stopped. Pa had vanished into a locked room of grief, and only Sally had been able to bring him out. To hear the old name reminded her of the bond they had once had and it was both a comfort and a painful reminder. He smiled at her. 'I know that dress is not the loveliest thing in the world. But it means everything to Sally. I want you to wear it and be her bridesmaid. Do you understand? I'm afraid you don't have a choice about this. It's an order.'

Ali's eyes dropped to the floor. She couldn't disobey Pa, she wasn't strong enough. She needed him too much.

He spoke again, his voice stern. 'And did you bite her?'

'Yes.' She looked up from under her fringe, wondering what would happen now.

Pa said nothing for a moment but his eyes went to Ali's cheek again. After a moment, he said, 'That was very wrong. But we'll overlook it this time, if you put on the dress and behave yourself today. Will you do that?'

Her shoulders slumped. She was defeated. At last she said in a very small voice, 'All right.'

'Good.' He patted her head. 'Thank you, old chum. Now, let's get going, we're going to be late if you don't crack on.'

So she had walked up the aisle behind Sally, whose good humour was restored, and who was smiling beatifically as she floated along in a vast white dress, adorned with lace and ruffles, next to the other girl bridesmaid and in front of Johnnie and Mundo in their sailor suits, which they were far too old for, really, with Johnnie big for twelve and Mundo a chunky ten-year-old. She had watched Pa marry Sally, while Mum lay dead in the churchyard, feeling that Sally had won and Pa had let her, and that this victory would set the tone for years to come.

She had been right. Not long after the wedding, Sally said that Ali needed to change her name.

'It's so silly!' she said brightly, as though it was the funniest thing in the world. 'We can't have Ali and Sally in the same family. It sounds too comical. We're going to call you Alex from now on.'

She couldn't even let me keep my name. Mum called me Ali. Ali Pali. Angel Ali.

But from that time, she was Alex, and that was that.

Alex was in the kitchen to make cups of tea for the ambulance crew when Mundo came in. 'Alexandra,' he said loudly, coming in just as the kettle was boiling.

'Hello,' she said briefly. Only Sally and Mundo called her Alexandra, and Sally only did it when she was being lofty. The name made her skin crawl just a little. Mundo always said it in a tone of voice that implied some kind of intimacy whereas she felt it only emphasised how foreign they were to each other, even after years of living in the same house.

'We didn't get much time to catch up,' he said genially, leaning against the kitchen table and watching as she made the mugs of tea. He was looking casual, which in Mundo's book meant perfectly pressed chinos, a crisp shirt and an immaculate jumper. 'How are you?'

'Fine, thank you.'

'Busy?'

'Yes.' She thought of how much time she'd had to spend in the potting shed over the last week, working into the night to keep up with her orders, boxing them up carefully for the couriers arriving each morning. Her regular helper, Gary, tended to the greenhouses during the day and she'd had to book extra hours as she was at the hospital so often. That would put a strain on profits, but she'd counted on the Tawray contract to cover some of it. *That won't happen now*, she thought darkly.

'Lovely business, flowers,' Mundo said, a dreamy note in his deep voice. 'It must be like working with poetry.'

'Something like that,' Alex answered dryly, and she noticed the rim of dried mud under her fingernails as she fished out the teabags. 'And how are you?'

'Very well! Very well. My work is fascinating. I've just won the most extraordinary case. The first time I've ever had to go to the judge and ask him to name my own client as a hostile witness.'

'Really?' Mundo worked on big criminal cases at the Old Bailey and liked to regale people with stories of the more gruesome or celebrated ones.

'Yes. Her husband had clearly tried to kill her and she had only just escaped with her life, but she didn't want to believe him capable of it. So, on the stand, she started changing her story to make him appear innocent.' Mundo laughed. 'I had to put a stop to that. She was in danger of getting him acquitted.'

'It sounds very stressful,' she said politely. 'Did you win?'

'Happily, yes. So I can afford to take a bit of a break and help Mummy through this awful time.' He shook his head gloomily, his expression grave. 'It's terrible, isn't it? I'm in pieces, to be honest.'

'Yes.' Alex didn't feel convinced for a moment, even though she could understand that Mundo was very likely sad about Pa. It just didn't touch her. His emotions didn't ring true. *He's like someone playing the part of being a caring human. Like what I imagine a psychopath must do.* Perhaps Mundo was a psychopath. He had always seemed chilly to the core to her, even though other people spoke about his charm and intelligence.

Mundo went on: 'That's why I thought we ought to have a conference. You, Johnnie and me.'

'Really? Why?' She went to get the milk from the fridge, taking the long way around the kitchen table so that she could avoid passing him.

'Why?' He blinked as if in surprise. 'I know it's not pleasant, but we're going to have to face some truths. If Pa dies . . . well, Mummy is going to be on her own and she's going to need looking after.'

'Will she? She seems very capable to me.' Alex got the milk and headed back to the mugs. 'She's still young.'

'My theory is that she'll age quickly without Pa to look after, and she'll be lonely. I'm in London, too far away to help much. But you're here, right on the doorstep.'

'Oh, I see. You want me to look after her. Take on the job of her carer.'

'No, no. Not that. But you are the closest.'

'Convenient.'

'So you can look in on her, keep me informed if she needs anything. You know the sort of thing.'

'Right.' She poured out the milk, added sugar where

needed, and began to load the mugs onto a tray, seething inwardly at Mundo's arrogance and bland assumption she would take on caring for his ageing mother. After everything that had happened.

'But that's not the only thing we need to discuss.' His tone was portentous.

'What do you mean?' She picked up the tray and turned to look at him. His eyebrows were raised meaningfully.

'The three of us have to talk about what's going to happen to Pa's assets.'

Alex stared at him and then understanding dawned. 'So that's why you're here. You want to know what's going to happen to any money. I might have guessed.'

'I'm looking after my mother's interests,' he said, suddenly icy, and she got a glimpse of what he could be like in the courtroom. 'If that's all right with you.'

'I'm sure Pa has provided for Sally perfectly adequately,' Alex said tartly. 'And everything will go to her as a matter of course, I think, if I understand the legal position.'

'Unless he's made other arrangements, and we won't know that until the will is read.' Mundo's eyes had gone a chilly blue.

'Doesn't Sally know?'

'She doesn't. And I don't want to talk to her about it at a time like this in any case; it hardly seems appropriate when she's grief-stricken.'

Alex looked at him, nodding. *I might have known that would be his main concern. He just wants to know what he's going to get out of all this, and make sure he's not cheated out of whatever he thinks he's entitled to.*

Entitled. That was Mundo, all right. Always thinking he could have whatever he wanted.

'I'll talk to Johnnie,' she said, not wanting to tell him that Johnnie was planning to come down soon in any case. He might not want to see Mundo, though it would be hard to avoid him, as he was staying in Pa's house.

'Good. You do that.' Mundo's eyes softened. 'And we need to catch up, don't we? It's been a while since I heard your news. You're divorced now, aren't you? I was sorry to hear that.'

She said nothing, not wanting to discuss her personal life.

He smiled, one corner of his mouth going upwards in that way she suspected he thought was charming. 'And also not sorry.'

A pang of disgust stabbed her.

Sally came bustling in. 'Where's the tea? You've been ages.'

'Sorry, Sally, here it is. Bringing it now.' Alex went out as quickly as she could, leaving Mundo watching after her.

Chapter Nineteen

Johnnie was still reeling from the idea that Netta wanted a divorce. Or, perhaps did not actually want one – she hadn't decided. But she was thinking about it. He was in shock. He'd had no idea that she felt so strongly that their marriage was going wrong.

He pondered it when he went for his Saturday morning run down to the river, along the towpath and back via the park, in the company of dozens of other middle-aged weekend runners.

She feels like she does all the work and I don't appreciate her.

But he did appreciate her. And the money he earned helped pay for the big house she wanted, the childminders, cleaners, gardeners and all the others who made their lives run as smoothly as possible, who enabled their standard of living. She was financially secure; didn't that count for a lot? Johnnie worked bloody hard to make sure his family could enjoy a comfortable life, and he was focused on making sure he did his absolute best for them all. If that meant he couldn't clean the damn shower, then he couldn't clean the damn shower. They had a cleaning woman for that.

But . . .

He tried to be fair. It was more than that, he knew. He'd read an article lately on something called the mental burden, and how women shouldered it and how it added hours of invisible work to their already considerable load. He hadn't entirely understood it but it seemed to be things like remembering birthdays, running calendars and writing thank you letters. All the social grease and family admin. But men didn't care about all that. Johnnie couldn't honestly say he'd mind if he never got another birthday card, he had no interest in receiving thank you letters, let alone sending them, and he felt that it was Netta who crammed the diary with activities, holidays, get-togethers, dinners, parties and all the rest, then complained that they were so busy. And if he tried to intervene and start organising things himself, she'd be furious.

Johnnie checked his tracker and saw he'd run over six kilometres so he took a pit stop at the park cafe to drink a coffee before he returned to the mad house. No school on Saturdays, so Bertie would be there, needing constant supervision and holding back from stealing the cereal. Johnnie found it upsetting in a way he couldn't articulate when, every five minutes, Bertie would rush to the nearest tap, turn it on and drink from it. Life was dominated by 'Where's Bertie?' and 'Is Bertie all right?'

The truth was that Bertie had a life that Johnnie sometimes envied. He had no obligations, no demands, and he pleased only himself. He didn't care what anyone thought of him, and his needs were simple: to be outside occasionally, to be warm, clean and fed. He did whatever he wanted: he watched the garden for hours on end, like a cat, bounced on his trampoline and swung in his swing. He adored swimming pools and theme parks. He ate and drank what he wanted when he wanted, slept and wandered about, then watched the garden again. He was utterly unselfconscious.

Not such a bad existence. In days gone by, he could have been shut in an asylum or allowed to die through neglect. Now, he would always be cared for, and surrounded by the love of his family. He would never be bothered by world affairs, taxes, bills or whether he'd find a parking spot in town. On the other hand, he would never be moved by music or poetry, weep at a soppy film or gasp at the beauty of a painting, or be awed by the scope of human history and achievement. But he would never know what he was missing, so did that really matter?

Johnnie slumped down on the park bench, holding a take-away cup of coffee in one hand, warming his fingers. The park was full of wintery mist, the depleted winter foliage grey in the chill sunlight, and Johnnie was cold despite the heat he'd generated from running.

That's the thing, though. Do I love Bertie? Really love him?

The journey with his firstborn son played through his mind at rapid speed: the birth and the giddy excitement, the blissful early days before they knew the truth; the faint niggles as Bertie missed his developmental milestones and then the diagnosis, with all its brutal facts. Through it all, Johnnie had loved him, wildly and desperately; he had been prepared to move mountains for his little boy, full of protective passion. He was ready to take on anyone who looked askance when Bertie acted differently to most boys his age. Then Joe and Nathan had arrived, and he'd gone on a different fatherhood journey, closer to the one he'd dreamed might be possible with Bertie. It involved smiles, conversations, silly chatter, songs, jokes, hugs and kisses, bedtime stories, games and laughter. That was something that Bertie never did. He never laughed. He smiled, and made noises of pleasure – but he never broke into peals of laughter.

As Bertie grew up, Johnnie began to feel the pain of his unrealised potential, and instead of subsiding, the grief for the person his son would never be increased. He had tried to accept Bertie as he was, and he thought he had succeeded, but now . . . Bertie was on his way to becoming a man, and it was much, much harder than he'd expected. He hadn't anticipated his love changing from fierce passion to this new emotion: removed, wary, worried. Protective, still, but more like a guardian than a parent. It was nothing like the way he felt about Joe and Nathan, as their relationships grew and changed, as the boys matured and became their older selves, with opinions and personalities that intrigued and pleased him. They would be friends as well as sons. But Bertie . . .

Where has it gone? Where is my love for Bertie? Is that why I let Netta do most of the caring? She was right about that. I've been avoiding Bertie. I've been letting her shoulder it all. Because of the way I feel, and the fact I'm frightened of that, and what it means.

He stared out across the park, and felt the unaccustomed

sensation of tears in his eyes. Blinking them away, he put down his cup.

Netta was at home with the boys. It was time to get back.

In the potting shed, Alex was lost in her work making table arrangements for a wedding the following day. Her ear pods were in, and she was singing along loudly to the music only she could hear as she created tiny but delightful posies in tones of pink and green, arranging each one in a miniature mercury-glass bud vase. An unexpected movement in her peripheral vision made her look up and she shouted out in surprise, nearly knocking over a vase as she jumped. A man was standing there, his hands held up to her as if in a gesture of surrender. She yanked the pods out, recognising the man from the local enterprise party the other night. He was wearing the same faded red hoodie.

'What are you doing here?' she demanded, flushing. He must have been listening as she'd sung along to the track in her ears. 'You made me jump! What makes you think you can just walk in without asking?'

'Sorry, sorry,' he said quickly. 'I knocked but there was no answer. I came round the back on the off chance I'd find you.'

'Well, you have,' she said brusquely and went back to putting miniature pale pink roses into a vase. 'So, what do you want?'

'Hey.' He stepped forward, looking a trifle hurt. 'I thought we were getting on okay the other night, then I offended you.

I'm sorry if I made a blunder while we were talking – I obviously didn't know that you used to live in the house.'

She glanced up, feeling her antagonism soften slightly, partly as a result of the beseeching expression on his face, and partly because of his warm, rolling accent. *His name is Jasper.* She hadn't forgotten him. 'So you know about Tawray, do you?'

'Pam told me when you'd gone. She was a bit embarrassed, to be honest, that she'd not cleared it all up right away.'

'Hmm.'

'So as we're neighbours . . . well, I just thought it would be a good idea to build some bridges, that's all.'

'Right.' She felt a gathering of irritation in her stomach and looked away. 'Okay. Thanks for calling by.'

Jasper looked exasperated. 'What's the problem? I know I live in your old house, but is that any reason to be so off with me? I mean, it's not my fault you're not there anymore, if that's the cause of this chilliness. And I don't think I've done anything else to offend you.' He frowned as he saw her expression. 'Have I?'

'Well . . .'

'Uh-oh. What?'

She tied a pink ribbon around the vase she'd just finished, and looked up. 'If you must know, I was a bit put out by the way I got treated when I called round to the house.'

'You called round?' He seemed mystified.

'Yes. The woman who answered the door was very unfriendly. I only wanted to tell her about the flower tradition.'

Understanding spread over his face. He nodded. 'Oh right,

you talked to Polly, did you?' He made an apologetic expression. 'She can be a bit brusque.'

'Yeah. Rude, actually.'

'All right, rude. Sorry.' He looked abashed. 'That's no good. I'll talk to her about it. Honestly, I'm really sorry.'

'Okay.' She was slightly mollified. 'I appreciate that.'

'So.' Jasper smiled at her. 'Are we friends?'

She pushed out her lower lip thoughtfully as she gathered a fresh set of stems and started to sort through them. 'I'm not sure.'

Jasper pulled a stool over from the side of the room and sat down, up against the long pine table. 'Beautiful flowers. You've got a real artist's eye.'

She eyed him sardonically, but actually she was pleased. She liked to think of her arrangement as art: temporal, sure, but art nonetheless. There was something so pleasing about well-arranged flowers; they only had to be put next to a clumsy arrangement for the difference to be seen. In so many areas of life, quality looked easy. Whenever people said, 'Oh, it's just a . . .' it was a sure indicator that they didn't understand the vast gulf of skill between basic and brilliant.

'Is all this for a wedding?' Jasper asked.

She looked up, as if surprised that he was still sitting at her potting table. 'Yes.'

'Now, that's a brave time of year.' He shook his head gravely.

She couldn't help smiling at his mordant tone. 'You mean the weather?'

'Oh no. Not the weather. Let's face it, it's bound to be shit and if it isn't, that's just a bonus. No. Think about. It's the anniversary. Every year, just before Christmas, you've got to remember a bloody anniversary, a card and a present. When you have to send out hundreds of cards and buy dozens of bloody presents. Whenever people get married on Christmas Eve or New Year's Day, I think, good luck getting a table for that anniversary, mate!' He made a comical expression and shook his head. 'Nah. Get married in the summer like every-one else, and have a decent date for your anniversary. That's my advice.'

Alex laughed. 'I've never thought of that. It's a good point. My anniversary was in April but that was the month of my husband's birthday and then, through terrible planning, both our daughters were born in April. So that was an awful month.' She shook her head. 'God, I used to dread April. Whoever said it was the cruellest month wasn't wrong.'

'T. S. Eliot, I think.' He smiled at her. 'Unless someone said it before him.'

'Okay. Impressive.' She finished another arrangement, deftly tying the pink ribbon with a flourish before pushing the vase to the side and reaching for another.

'So why don't you tell me about this flower tradition?'

Alex looked up, startled, and found she was staring straight into blue, twinkling eyes. Nonplussed, she said hesi-tantly, 'Oh . . . well . . . yes . . . the flower tradition . . .'

'I'm all ears.' He folded his arms and crossed his feet at the ankle, adopted an earnest expression as if ready to absorb whatever she had to say.

She took a breath, just in case he was mocking her, and

when she saw he was waiting for her to speak, she said, 'Fine. I'll tell you all about it.'

When she'd finished, he was gazing at her with an unreadable expression. Then at last he said, 'I love it.'

Alex was taken aback. 'Really?' She'd expected an interrogation or a dismissal, not this complete acceptance of the value of a dried flower display.

'Yes. I want to do it. Is there still time?'

She thought. She had committed a lot of the dried blooms to other projects, assuming she wouldn't be working at Tawray this year. 'I'm not sure . . . It might not be as lavish as usual, but I could certainly pull something together. The baubles are the things that really make people smile, and I've got just about enough for those. I could order in extra dried stock for the garlands, which are more about quantity.'

Jasper clapped his hands together, pleased. 'I really do like this. I want to do something a bit environmental at Tawray, you know? And Christmas decorations from nature – that's really good. We've all had enough of plastic baubles and foil tinsel, right? Wrapping paper we chuck away after one day that can't be recycled. That's bloody awful. I like the idea of a sustainable Christmas. Why don't we try and turn the open day into a kind of Christmas fair for local environmentally friendly businesses?'

'Yes!' Alex exclaimed, enthused. 'I love that! Local produce, no plastic, sustainable decorations. That's brilliant!' Her face fell. 'But it's really short notice. *Really* short. To pull off something like that.'

'Let's not think too big then. How about baby steps? We'll

do the flower display, along with any local producers who show an interest and still have availability, and whatever else works.'

'There's usually a cream tea thing in the old orangery. It's small, only space for about a dozen tables. But people like it.'

'Great.' Jasper slammed his palm down on the pine table. 'You're a genius. I'm getting loads of great ideas right now.' He smiled at her. 'Shall we do this together?'

'Oh.' She blinked at him. They'd got a bit carried away with the vision of an environmentally friendly Christmas. The truth was, she would have trouble just doing the flowers. And then there was everything else. 'I'd love to,' she said lamely, 'but . . . there are family issues.'

He looked disappointed. 'Really? I'm sorry to hear that.'

'Yes. My father isn't well.' That didn't really cover the extent of what was happening but she didn't know how to say more to a relative stranger. 'And my brother is coming down with his family. It's just not easy. But . . .' She didn't want to pour cold water on a project that had already begun to excite her. It had never occurred to her that Tawray might play a role in all the things that concerned her: local trade, the environment, nature . . . But if Jasper was serious . . . well, that was really something. 'Look, can I think about it? I'll definitely do the flowers, if you're happy with my costings, but I'll need to work out what else I can do.'

Jasper smiled, his face brightening again. 'Great. Look, give me your number and I'll be in touch. If you're okay with that.'

Alex smiled back. 'Yes. I am.'

*

264

After Jasper had left, Alex's mood lifted. Tawray – and her mother's connection to it – was not, perhaps, lost after all. She was going to do the flowers, and that was brilliant. She imagined climbing the ladders to drape the great chimney pieces in delicate but surprisingly robust garlands of intense beauty, and to put strands of marigolds, dried to the colour of old brass, across the family portraits that still hung there.

Or will they still be there? Where have all the pictures gone? All the furniture? Pa had never said, and she couldn't ask him now.

She thought of him lying at home in the house he'd shared with Sally for the last few years. She'd been there when the ambulance arrived from the hospital, driving slowly, unlike most ambulances, to keep David stable. They'd carefully lifted him down on a gurney, before carrying him into the house, Sally fluttering around like a panicked mother bird, directing the bearers to go here, there, up, down – 'gently, now, gently!' – until David at last lay in the hospital bed in the study. He was, Alex realised, exactly as he'd been in the stroke unit, no more and no less responsive, but it was different to have him at home. In these familiar surroundings, despite the equipment around him, he seemed more normal and peaceful, as though this was an inevitable stage of his life and not a medical emergency. It was easier to accept that he might die this way, away from all the doctors, nurses and equipment that were supposed to keep him alive.

She knew that was counter-intuitive. She should want him in the place where they could best care for him, with drugs, operating theatres, resuscitation capacity . . . And yet, the feeling of having him home was good and felt so natural, how could that be wrong?

Sally had clucked around him, tucking him in, checking his equipment and summoning the nurse in a querulous voice to bombard her with questions about every aspect of David's condition.

Poor woman, Alex thought, watching as the nurse patiently and kindly dealt with the torrent, *I hope they're paying her a really good day rate.*

Putting up with Sally would be tough, on top of overseeing the last days of a man unlikely to regain consciousness.

I suppose he's not coming back. The consultant has been pretty clear about it. Alex found it was easier to deal with bitter grief if it was pushed firmly away from emotion to fact. *But he's not dead yet. Maybe he can still hear us. Maybe he's still thinking about all of us. I wonder what he'd have to say about us all. And what he would say if he had one last chance.*

In the kitchen after work, Alex checked her emails while she prepared supper for the girls. It was completely black outside, not so far off the shortest day of the year; Scarlett and Jasmine left for school and returned home in the dark. That was why it was all the more important to provide a warm, cosy home with hot food and welcoming beds.

She scrolled through her messages, dismissing the unimportant, and then saw one from Tim marked 'Christmas'. She opened it.

Hi Alex,

It's probably the right moment to talk about the most sensitive time of the year. I'd really like it if I could have the girls this year. You wanted this divorce and I didn't, so perhaps you would be generous and let me kick off the whole 'your place, my place' thing. Chloe wants us to go to her parents on the Isle of Wight, and I think the girls would love it. Can we say Christmas Eve in the morning until Boxing Day? If I'm honest, it would be great to have them all the way to New Year, but I realise that's a bit much to ask. As long as I can take them for Christmas, that's fine, thanks.

Hope your dad is okay.

Tim

Alex read it, convulsed with sadness. Christmas. Why was that one day so incredibly meaningful? One single twenty-four hours. And yet . . . the thought of it without the girls filled her with grief. She'd been with them every Christmas of their lives, from the first when they'd been oblivious bundles, to the frantic excitement of stockings and presents and all that went with it as they grew older.

He wants to take them away from me.

She caught herself up.

It's not about me.

But still, it caused her pain. He wanted them, she wanted them. One of them had to surrender.

She thought and then wrote a quick email to Tim:

I don't disagree in principle with what you want to do. I understand you'd like the girls with you. The problem is that Pa is desperately ill, and the doctors are expecting him to go at any time. I would prefer it if the girls could be here when that happens. Can we try and agree to be flexible? If they are here for that, and it happens before Christmas, I don't mind if you take them for the stretch between Christmas and New Year. If not, you can take them for Christmas Day and Boxing Day, but I'd prefer it if they can be nearby in case of any sudden changes. I hope you can see that this won't be repeated, and I'd appreciate your understanding.

Alex x

She read it through again, and felt that it was the best response she could give right now. It seemed odd to be bargaining with her father's life, but she had no other option: she didn't want the girls to remember their grandfather's death as a time of distance and confusion.

I lived through that. I know how awful it is.

They would know everything, every step of the way. That was the best thing for all of them, she was sure.

Chapter Twenty

David had been drifting in and out of consciousness for such a long time, he'd forgotten what it was like to hear a whole conversation. Certainly the idea of getting up, walking around and participating seemed so removed from his reality as to be closer to a dream than a memory. He was not exactly conscious even when he became more aware of his surroundings. It was like lying fast asleep while a radio played in the same room, and sometimes what was on it dropped into his consciousness along with the memories that floated like feathers around his mind.

He heard Alex and Johnnie. He was aware when Mundo spoke, the bass of his voice shimmering through his consciousness, sending things shaking and awry. It pounded like a distant rock track, booming away, hurting almost.

He knew Sally was constantly with him, and that comforted him. Throughout his life with her, she'd been assiduous about looking after him. No one could have been kinder to him, or more solicitous, and he'd accepted it gratefully. The calm of life with her was welcome after the tempests of his first marriage. How lucky he had been that Sally was there, supporting him, when the final, awful blows fell. She'd been prepared to devote herself to him for the rest of his life, because the two of them were bound together after that. He loved her, in a pleasant, friendly way that never scared him, or hurt him. If for some reason Sally had left him, he would not have felt that his soul had been hollowed out and his whole being drained; he wouldn't have suffered agony in the way he had with . . .

Julia.

Julia was with him too, but as a silent presence, somewhere nearby. He wondered how she felt about him now, if she had forgiven him, and if she still had love for him in her heart. They'd shared so much. Then they'd spun apart and it seemed that no force could bring them back together.

That was what had roped him and Sally together for the rest of their lives. They both knew the truth about Julia, and they both knew what had caused it. After that, they had to unite, both in marriage and in their pact of silence. No one else could ever know.

Oh Julia. I wish I could have told you that I'm sorry.

Chapter Twenty-One

1987

It was early summer when Julia drove down to Tawray with Greta. The sun was out and Tawray was bright with colour, the treetops swaying in the blustery breeze sweeping in from the sea, the gardens thrumming with colour and life.

'Oh, it's beautiful!' Julia cried as the little car approached the house. 'Beautiful. Look at that, Greta, doesn't it stir your heart?'

Greta panted in agreement, eager to be out and exploring.

It was strange to arrive alone, for the first time, to a house that was now wholly hers. She wished David could be there too, but if he could not, then she would just have to get on with it. She was sure that she needed to be at Tawray, that it was the only barrier between her and self-destruction.

Nevertheless, her first night there was difficult. She missed David desperately and didn't even dare to phone him, now that he was staying in the spare room of a friend who might not appreciate being woken by the telephone in the middle of the night. The house, which had seemed to be the symbol of safety and security, felt rather different once she was there

271

alone. The memories that came to her in the night were not ones of comfort but of the traumas she had known there.

Mummy.

The one room she had always avoided was her parents' suite, with the grand four-poster swagged with old-fashioned chintz, and the door that led into the bathroom.

No.

She wouldn't go there, not in her mind and certainly not in reality. She had taken her childhood bedroom as her own again, without even thinking about it, despite the fact that it was small and not very handy for a bathroom, necessitating a quick dash down the corridor to the old high-cisterned lavatory in an icy cupboard-sized room. Her old bed gave her some comfort and the feeling of Greta's warm body curled up at her feet offered the security she needed, alone in the great house in the dark. But she missed David desperately.

'Are you sure your daughter will have the time to help? I know she's got the children . . .' Julia was letting Mrs Petheridge out after their cup of tea in the kitchen. She had been a cleaner and cook at Tawray when she was younger and now hoped to take on the job of helping Julia keep the house.

'She'll be glad of the work, and there're plenty to help with the kids,' Mrs Petheridge said, pulling on her jacket. 'But what are you going to do with this old place? You're not going to live in it all alone, are you?'

'Oh no,' Julia said airily, 'I've got lots of ideas.' Though, really, she didn't yet have a clue what she would do. The accounts showed her that the house needed to make some more income.

'There's lots doing weddings around here,' Mrs Petheridge said. 'Hard work, though. And seasonal.'

'Yes, there're lots of ideas. Opera on the lawn, perhaps,' Julia said vaguely. 'We'll come up with something.'

Mrs Petheridge turned and smiled at her. 'Well. I'll be off. And you won't be on your own for long anyway, will you?'

'What do you mean?'

The other woman's gaze dropped to Julia's stomach. 'You're not far along. But I can always tell.' She gave her a kindly look. 'But I'm sure you already knew.'

Gasping and shaking, Julia stood against the big front door, her eyes unseeing. Fear had drenched her as suddenly and thoroughly as if a bucket of water had been thrown over her.

I can always tell.

Julia moaned softly. *Oh no. Oh no.*

But she was knew it was true and had already known somewhere in her mind, even though she had resolutely ignored it, pretending to herself that it was quite normal to be late with her period when it was usually on time, and that perhaps she had just forgotten having her last one, and that the extraordinary fatigue that fell on her at eight o'clock each evening was just the result of Tawray air and all the sorting out she was doing.

It's happened.

Something in her had hoped it would not. She had even rehearsed little speeches to David: *I don't know, there must be something wrong with me. Why don't we think about adopting?* In fact, it had been so deeply ingrained in her mind that her body would do what she wanted and refuse to conceive that she had even given up her contraceptive pill quite cheerfully.

Well, she had watched David take them out of her washbag and ceremoniously throw them away, even popping each foil blister, releasing the pill and dropping it into the loo.

'You're going to stop the poor fish from spawning that way,' she'd joked, trying to quell her sense of panic at watching them disappear into the bowl. Despite her faith in the power of her will, she knew that to be on the safe side, it would be better to be on the pill. *If I get too anxious, I'll just go to the clinic and get some more.* But she hadn't done that, unable to bring herself to practise that level of deception on David. Besides, the bargain of being allowed to keep Tawray was that she would at least try.

David had said, 'If we're going to live there, then we need to start a family. I want lots of little Julias and Davids to run around and grow up there and make it into a home. Don't you?'

'Yes, of course,' she'd said, and it wasn't that she didn't want that too, because she did. *I do, I want children.* She just didn't want to have them, physically to bear them. Was that so very strange? Who in their right mind would? The mystery to her was that so many women plunged into it as if it wasn't the most horrific and ghastly trick it was possible to play on a person: to take their body, implant an alien being inside it to grow almost to bursting point, forcing a skeleton to weaken and the muscle fibres to loosen and tear so that this new creature could be accommodated; and then, horrifically and agonisingly, swell open the lower body so the creature could be expelled in bloody torment. And that was if it went well. What of the many, awful problems? Twisted cords, breech births, ruptured placentas, prolapsed wombs, haemorrhage, suffocation, brain damage, birth defects, infections . . . *miscarrying a child almost formed.*

But she hadn't been able to tell him that.

Now Julia closed her eyes and tried to control her breathing. Her fingernails pressed so hard into her palms, it felt as though she must surely draw blood.

She hadn't gone back to the family planning clinic. She'd begun to believe it would never happen to her, almost as though her determination would prevent nature taking its course. She had instead started rushing to the bathroom after each time she and David made love, to rinse herself out with the shower head, thinking that would stop it. But it hadn't stopped anything. She was pregnant.

Oh God! What shall I do?

She ran to the kitchen and into the large cool larder. On the top shelf was a row of bottles. She reached up and took one down, then hurried out to the kitchen to find an opener. A minute later, she was pouring red wine into a glass and looking up at the clock over the door. It was eleven o'clock in the morning, too early for a drink, but she didn't care.

She lifted the glass to her lips, noticing that her hand was trembling, and held it there. Fumes, dark with grapes and toxic with alcohol, rose to her nostrils. She tried to take a sip and couldn't. She tried again and got some of the liquid into her mouth. It was bitter, mouth-puckering, revolting. She swilled it around her mouth and attempted to swallow, but her gorge rose against it and she retched. She rushed for the sink and spat it out, pushed the tap on and took a palmful of cool clean water to her mouth, rinsing it out. Then she went back to the glass and took a large swig, trying to swallow and managing to force the mouthful down. It sat in her stomach for only a moment before she was back at the sink, throwing it all up.

She cried out, 'What am I going to do?'

She burst into tears.

The doctor gave Julia the impression that tending patients was something he managed to fit into his hectic schedule of fishing and golf.

'Of course you're pregnant,' he said dismissively as she sat in his consulting room. He scribbled something onto her notes in fountain pen.

'Aren't you going to give me some kind of test?'

'There's no point, my dear.' He smiled. 'When a young woman, not long married, enjoying a healthy sex life and no longer on contraception, misses a period or two, then there really is only one explanation.'

'I thought you might just want to be sure.'

He glanced at her over his glasses as he wrote. 'I'm sure enough not to give you a test. Date of your last menstrual period?'

'Oh, I don't know. It was in . . . April? March?'

'Don't you keep track?'

'Not really.'

'You should. Well, I'll just have to estimate.'

Julia watched him calculate in his head, even though she had already done that herself and worked out that the baby would probably come in the new year.

'Let's say mid-January,' he said, scribbling it down.

'I wonder . . .' she said tentatively, 'if there is any way of having a Caesarean birth?'

'What?' The doctor stared. 'Why on earth would you want that?'

'Well, I don't like the idea of giving birth, you see—'

The doctor laughed. 'Oh, my dear girl, of course you don't. But it's quite natural. You'll take to it perfectly well, you'll see. By the time you're nine months pregnant you'll do anything to get the darned thing out, believe me. A Caesarean is a serious operation, we don't do it unless absolutely vital.' He gave her sympathetic look. 'Of course you're frightened, but this isn't the Dark Ages. We have pain relief now, hospitals, doctors. And your body is designed for this – you might even say it's your one purpose, as far as nature is concerned. Millions of women have done it before you, millions will in the future. Don't worry yourself. You'll be fine.'

She stared at him, unable to find the words she needed to explain her deep, dark fear, or the terror she already felt about the tiny creature floating inside her and what it would do to her. *It wants to kill me.* She bit her tongue. He was right. What made her so special? It was her lot to suffer. Only certain women were exempt: those who could not, or would not, like nuns or lesbians or old-maid aunts. Most had to do this. *Wanted* to do this. It was proud, vain and selfish to think of avoiding it.

'Thank you,' she said weakly, before getting up and walking out, no one noticing her sway with faintness or the deathly white pallor of her skin.

She went home more determined than ever to force down the wine, or the ancient bottle of gin she had found in the cellar, and to smoke the cigarettes she had brought with her. If she was going to miscarry, she had to do it now, while the thing was still a tiny bundle of cells, as close to nothing as possible. But her body rebelled and wouldn't let her. Every time she tried to induce a miscarriage, she was violently sick.

That only made her more afraid. Her body didn't care. It was going to do what it wanted, no matter how she felt about it. That thought horrified her.

Julia was dimly aware that it was a beautiful summer, that Tawray was blossoming outside. The pink and white, and emergent green of spring, turned to the deeper colours of summer and the gardens burst into magentas, reds, purples and creams. Beyond, the blue sea sparkled, blowing salt wind over the house and leaving the tang of the beach on the lips. The village was alive again with holidaymakers and tourists. Tents fluttered on the hillsides and caravans blocked the narrow lanes as they lumbered to their sites. Julia knew these things, she saw them when she went out, noticed the squawking seagulls riding the air currents and felt the warmth of the sun on her face. But she couldn't feel it.

Sleep eluded her and she had lost her appetite for almost everything. The thought of food made her feel sick, the taste of tea, coffee and anything dairy revolted her. Instead she was plagued by twin fears: losing the baby and not losing the baby. She was trapped. Every day that went by without a miscarriage she felt more terrified that she was condemned to lose the baby late, as her mother had. Or condemned to give birth, with all the horror that inspired. She longed for David but she was also afraid of seeing him and telling him, because then it would all be true, but more than that, the gulf between them would grow wider, she was sure of it. On the phone it was easy to say nothing, breezily answer, 'I'm fine!' when he asked how she was. It wasn't going to be so easy in person, when he could see with his own eyes that something was going on.

He had been away on yet another trip, with more booked for the autumn, and as soon as he returned, he headed for Tawray.

Julia was sitting on the front steps as the taxi came up the drive from the station. He had said not to come in case he didn't make the train and couldn't tell her, and now here he was, getting out of the taxi, his smiling, handsome, loveable self.

Julia was joyous – she'd forgotten how much better he made her feel just by being there. Why had she been afraid to see him, when he was the light of her life? *What is it with my stupid head, that I can't remember these things?*

They spent the first hours in rapture at being together, and with David having some proper leave, and there being no need for him to rush away on Sunday evening. They settled down to supper in the kitchen later that evening.

'Goodness, this is good!' David said, with evident surprise, as she put a beef casserole and mash in front of him. He sniffed appreciatively. 'It smells delicious. Have you been learning to cook?'

'Not exactly. Mrs Petheridge made this.' Julia grinned. 'I told her you were coming so she rustled it up. I think she guessed I don't cook all that much.'

'Well, lucky us to have her then.' David picked up his fork and tucked in. 'Oh yes, that's lovely.' He looked up and said, 'Aren't you having any?'

She pushed her own fork into the pile of potato in front of her. 'Oh yes.' But a moment later, she put it down. 'I don't think I'm very hungry.'

David stopped eating, and seemed to see her for the first time. 'Aren't you? You know what, you're looking a lot thinner. Are you all right? Are you ill?' He looked anxious. 'Come on, have something to eat.'

'I really couldn't,' she said faintly. The smell of the casserole was turning her stomach in any case. The idea of putting anything in her mouth had her on the brink of running for the sink.

David put down his fork. 'What's going on, Julia? Do I need to get you to a doctor?'

'No,' she said. Then took a breath. 'I can't face eating anything . . . because I'm pregnant.'

His mouth dropped open and his eyes widened as he took it in, then a burst of happiness illuminated his face. 'Oh Julia, really? Really?' He laughed with joy. 'That's amazing news! I'm so happy! How long? Why didn't you tell me?' He leapt to his feet. 'So many questions. Come here, darling.'

He was next to her in a moment and engulfing her in a hug, and then was almost comically anxious that he might be hurting her, or the baby, and that she ought to be sitting down, or lying down, or drinking something, or eating something.

Julia laughed. 'You don't need to fuss so much. I'm fine. Feeling ill is normal.'

'Of course it is. Morning sickness,' David said confidently. 'I just didn't realise you lost so much weight, that's all. They always talk about eating for two. I suppose that comes later.'

'Yes, I think it does. It all gets better.'

She hoped that if she kept her dark fears to herself, then it might all just get better. While David was there it seemed to improve. She slept properly for the first time in ages, and when the dreams came to torment her, as they often did, and she woke with a pounding heart and irregular breathing, she could hold tight to him and the panic subsided.

What she couldn't do was tell him that the thing growing inside her, the thing that was making him so happy and ecstatic, so full of plans for the future, was making her feel so very afraid.

When it was time to go back to London, David was palpably reluctant to leave her. 'I want you to come back with me,' he said firmly.

'I can't move into Robin's flat! He's only got his spare room, it's far too small even if he wanted us both.'

281

'Then I'll find somewhere else to live, where you can come back. I don't want you down here all alone while you're pregnant.'

She felt comforted by that. She hadn't realised how lonely and frightened she had been until David came down. 'All right then. Yes – look for a flat. That's a good idea.'

But even though she knew that being close to David again would help her, she couldn't imagine how it might combat the thick fog of panic that was beginning to engulf her.

Chapter Twenty-Two

David found a tiny flat in Battersea, and Julia returned to London. The worst of her pregnancy sickness was over and her energy started to come back a little, but she took things quietly. David set off across the bridge every morning, bound for the palace, while she walked Greta in the park, stopped for a cup of hot water, and ventured out in the afternoon to do some shopping. The rest of the time, she sunbathed on their little balcony, read and slept.

Sally came round to visit, bringing a big bunch of flowers, packets of chocolate biscuits and a bottle of fizzy non-alcoholic grape juice. But she gasped when she saw Julia even as she offered a congratulatory kiss.

'You're so thin!'

'Am I?' Julia looked down. She knew it was true. Her arms were slender, her stomach quite flat and her behind felt bonier than it ever had. 'I've had quite bad morning sickness. I'm getting better.'

'I hope so.' Sally frowned. 'There's nothing more to it than that?'

'No.' Julia shook her head. 'Well . . .' She felt a sudden huge temptation to tell Sally everything. But one look into the clear blue eyes and she couldn't. Sally seemed too pure for the dark imaginings in her heart. There was no way she would understand. Like David, Sally would only be able to think of the pregnancy and Julia didn't want to bring her own grim darkness into their world, or share the horrible fears she had. But when Sally went to the loo, she came back holding a plastic bag that Julia recognised.

'What's all this?' she asked, holding it out, her expression worried.

'Where did you find that?' Julia said crossly. 'Are you spying? That's rather sneaky.'

'I was looking for another roll of loo paper. I opened this bag because I thought there might be some inside.' Sally looked in as if to reassure herself she hadn't imagined it. 'Dozens of used pregnancy tests. Boxes more unopened.' She frowned and looked up at Julia. 'Are you worried that you might not be pregnant?'

'I . . . I . . .' Julia couldn't think of anything to say to explain. She sat down on the sofa and curled up, wrapping her arms around her head.

'Julia, what is it?' Sally sat down on the other end and gently reached out to touch her arm. 'Are you all right? Is everything all right with the baby?'

Julia felt a rush of claustrophobia and longing to run outside the flat, across the road and into the park, to run and run. She yearned to be free of this constant, appalling feeling as though she was in a room with dozens of doors, and she kept spinning around to see if any of them were unlocked and none of them were. 'I don't know,' she said. 'I think so.'

'But it might not be?'

'It's not the baby. It's me.'

'What do you mean?'

'I test every day to see if I'm pregnant, in case it's gone. I'm terrified of losing it.'

'Oh, you poor thing! Of course you're worried.' Sally looked sympathetic. 'But you're into your second trimester. You're safe now, aren't you?'

'No, no, I'm less safe than ever! This is when my mother thought she was safe and she wasn't, she wasn't at all. Every day took her closer to losing it, not further away!' Julia looked up at her with frightened eyes. 'That's what's happening to me.'

'Not necessarily! Julia, you're not bound to have a disaster because your mother did, it doesn't work that way. You're going to be fine, I promise.'

Julia bit her lip. Sally didn't know. She had no idea. It was easy for her to make these ridiculous promises when the truth was that she was no in position to do so. Everyone kept doing that. They kept saying it would all be fine, natural and easy. What did they know? And what did it really matter to them anyway? They didn't have to live through it. But each day, she felt more and more certain that she was on her way to disaster. She could barely eat and didn't sleep for more than an hour or two before being wakened by horrific dreams. Last night's nightmare had involved blood seeping through her pores, pushed out by the expanding baby inside her until she was as empty as a juiced orange. In the morning, once David had gone, deep depression almost overwhelmed her. It was only taking Greta out to the park that managed to lift her from a feeling that what she really ought to do was work out the quickest way to die and put them all out of their misery – herself, the baby, to whom she would be a terrible mother in any case and who didn't deserve the awful fate of being born to her, and David, who would be better off without her.

'All right,' she said and tried to smile. 'Yes. I'm going to be fine. I shouldn't worry.'

'Shall I throw these away then?' Sally picked up the bag. Then she said slowly, 'Are you sure you don't want me to tell David about this? You're really all right?'

'Of course I am. Throw them away. I don't mind.' She watched Sally do just as David had done when he took away her pills: the things she relied on were tossed away and no one knew how she really felt.

Whatever I do, I mustn't tell them.

There was a point when she couldn't hide it any longer. She ate, but couldn't prevent the compulsion to go to the loo and throw it all up again afterwards. Why, she had no idea, but she felt calmer and safer when she'd been sick. She found that once or twice during the day she would go to the knife drawer, pull out the small, sharp paring knife and pull it lightly across her skin until a trail of tiny ruby blobs appeared on her arm. If she couldn't quite bring herself to do that, she would find pencils or anything with an edge, and score it into her tender forearm until it was criss-crossed with pink lines. Each night, while David slept beside her, she thought about leaving the flat and going to the river, standing up on the parapet of the bridge and throwing herself off into the murky waters.

'I don't want to die!' she would hiss to herself, tears leaking out from the corners of her eyes. But a darker voice from deep inside her would respond. *I want to die. It's better that way. Better that way than the torment.*

She knew that she wasn't going to be able to bear it for much longer. It felt absurd on the day she waved David off to Royal Ascot, in his morning coat and top hat and with the elegant badge on his lapel, knowing he was going to drink champagne and spend the day with the glittering titled crowd in the royal enclosure, while she sat at home and wondered if today she would have the courage to end it. Instead, she called Mark and asked to meet him. He was surprised to hear from her, but readily agreed to meet her in the park to walk the dogs.

They met in a sunny spot not far from the Peace Pagoda in Battersea Park and mooched along together, the two dogs frolicking about, and talked of nothing for a while. Then he gave her one of his sideways looks.

'This is all very nice, Julia, and it's always a pleasure to spend a bit of time with you. But I can't help wondering why you called me. We're not exactly buddies these days, now you're respectable and I'm still a useless wastrel.'

She thought that even though he was dressed in a baggy shirt that covered up the wrecked skin of his arms, frayed denim shorts and a pair of battered deck shoes, he still some-how managed to look a bit like an off-duty rock star, maybe because of his messy fair hair and the Ray-Bans covering his bloodshot eyes.

Julia hesitated. Then she remembered that this was Mark, crazy, hedonistic Mark who had encouraged her on to all kinds of excess. If anyone was going to help her, he would. 'I was wondering . . . wondering about drugs.'

'Really?' He gave her a quizzical look, an eyebrow raised in the way that used to make her giggle. 'Drugs? Who for? Not for your saintly husband, surely. Have you got some mad party friends who are up for bit of zaniness? I can do special dinner party packages, you know. It's quite the thing in the best circles.'

'No. It's for me.'

'For you?' He took this in and shrugged, slapping the dog lead he was holding lightly across his leg. 'Okay. What do you want? Coke? Weed? I've just had a batch of these fabulous new pills from Ibiza. But you don't like tabs, do you?'

'I want heroin.'

Mark stopped and half laughed. 'Heroin? Why on earth do you want that? I tell you what, darling, if you've got this far in your life without taking it, don't start now. Besides, you're not looking well. You're too thin. God knows what it would do to you with that body weight. I've no idea how much you could stand.'

'You mean it might kill me?'

'All too easily.'

'But wouldn't that be a lovely way to go?' she said as

lightly as she could. 'You've told me how wonderful the feeling is. Why not let me have a try? We could go back to my
place now and do it, if you've got some with you. Why not?'

Mark stopped. He turned to her, his expression serious,
and took off his sunglasses. His eyes were worried. 'Okay.
Stop right there. What is this?'

She gazed at him defiantly. 'What do you mean?'

From the outside, she thought, they might look like a
couple having a minor tiff as they walked their two dogs on
a beautiful summer day. She was in a denim skirt and a loose
stripy shirt with the sleeves rolled up, and flat leather shoes
with cut-outs in the pattern of daisies. Her pregnancy was so
well hidden that Mark hadn't even noticed it. But actually
she was trying to persuade him to take her back to her flat
and kill her.

*That's weird. It's so weird. Maybe he'll get in trouble. He
might get taken to court, prosecuted and put in prison. That
ought to bother me.* But it didn't. Her only concern was her
own escape.

'Look, Julia, I'm dark. You're dark. I know that. But you're
not that dark, you haven't fallen as far as I have. You've got
the chance to make a proper life for yourself. Why do you
want to spoil it now? Take my advice – if you want to get
high, have some coke.'

'What do you care? Come on, Mark.' Her tone became
wheedling. 'I want to try this out before it's too late.
David's such a square, he'll never let me. I promise not to get
addicted.'

Mark snorted. 'Yeah, that's believable. That's what they all think. The people who don't get addicted are the ones who never try it, because they're not fucking bothered. The ones who want it are the ones who should be kept well away.'

Julia shrugged. She couldn't be bothered with all that. She put her hands on her hips. 'So, will you?'

He said nothing, then suddenly grabbed her arm and turned it so that the white inner forearm with its tracks of cuts and scratches was visible. 'What's this?'

'Nothing!' She tried to pull it away but Mark was too strong.

'Are you already using?' he demanded.

'No!'

'Then what are you doing? Are you . . . cutting?'

She snatched her arm suddenly from his grip and rubbed it, angry. 'None of your business.'

He looked at her again. 'You're too thin, Julia. You're cutting. You want drugs. What is it? What the fuck is it?'

Julia felt blood rush to her face. 'You're just like everyone else!' she screamed. 'I thought you would understand, you of all people! You said we were the same! But you're going to stand in my way, just like all the rest, just like all of them!' Panic washed through her, engulfing her and maddening her so she couldn't bear it any longer. 'Oh God!'

She turned round and ran to the wall that went along the park by the river. She had some crazy idea to leap up onto it and over into the Thames, but as she climbed up, she saw that the tide was out and she would only land on wet, stony sand covered in litter and river detritus. *I'll jump, and I'll run, and I'll get to the water, and I'll wade in and—*

'What the fuck are you doing?' Mark yelled, going after her. He reached her and grabbed her. 'Julia!'

'Get off!' She tried to push his arm away. 'Let me go!'

'Are you crazy, get the hell down! You'll break a leg.'

A passer-by stopped and called out, 'Is he bothering you, miss?'

Mark shouted over his shoulder, 'She's fine! Just playing silly buggers!' Then he hissed, 'Get down! Do you want us both to be arrested?'

She gave a dry half-sob.

'Come on, Julia, please.'

'Let me go,' she said, but she felt the impetus leaving her. She began to wilt.

'Come down.' He put up a hand to her and she took it, letting him help her off the wall. They stood close to each other, staring into one another's faces. Tears began to pour down Julia's cheeks. The passer-by moved away, satisfied she wasn't in danger.

'What's wrong?' Mark asked plaintively. 'I want to help you.'

'I want you to kill me, Mark! I don't want to go on. I want you to inject me with heroin and send me on my way. It's the kindest thing to do! Don't you understand?' She clasped both his arms in her hands. 'I want to die, I want you to kill me.'

'Why?' He was ashen with shock. 'For Christ's sake, Julia, do you know what you're asking me? Why do you want to die?'

'Because . . .' She stumbled over the words but managed

at last to say them before she found she couldn't speak at all. 'I'm pregnant. I'm going to have a baby and I'd rather die.'

Julia didn't know much about the rest of the day, only that Mark somehow got her back to the flat and inside, using her keys, and laid her down on her bed. He waited all afternoon. She sometimes smelled the tang of cigarettes as he lit up on the balcony. Other times she felt his presence in the room as he checked that she was all right, offered her water or tea. She didn't reply. She'd sunk down into somewhere far away.

David returned, astonished to find Mark there. She heard voices. Exclamations from David, Mark's murmuring as he explained what had happened. 'She told me to kill her.'

'What? Why?'

'She's pregnant and she wants to die.'

'Oh my God.'

Julia could hear the broken sound in David's voice and she felt guilty. More reasons to hate herself. How could she hurt David like this? Hurt the baby? What kind of a person was she, to even dream of it?

Wicked. Evil. Ought to die.

Oh, those damn voices, I wish they would shut up!

Mark said, 'She wanted me to inject her with heroin and let her die that way.'

'Christ. Surely she wasn't serious?'

'Oh, she was serious.'

'What am I supposed to do?'

'She's at risk and so is the baby. You don't have a choice.'

*

Julia knew that Mark had left. Someone else arrived. A soft female voice.

Sally.

Phone calls were made, and Sally came to sit with her, holding her hand. The same evening Julia was taken to a secure unit where she agreed, for her own safety, to be locked up and treated. David wept, and Sally held her hand, then the nurses came and took her away.

She knew she ought to feel bad but now, all she felt was relief. They would take it all away, she didn't have to bear it all by herself anymore.

The rest of the summer was spent in the cool confines of the hospital. They could only give her limited drugs in order to protect the baby, but they kept her calm and safe. When it was understood what was happening, the doctors said that when the time came, she could have a Caesarean. That began to help the great terror to subside. Her fear of miscarriage was still there but alleviated by the knowledge she was already in a hospital, even if not a maternity kind. And the gentle waves of medication took the panic away and let her, at last, sleep. The vitamin drips restored the chemicals she was missing from lack of nutrients and lifted some of her depression. She could sleep again.

The only thing that tormented her still was the knowledge of what she was putting David through. He came to see her almost every day, and when he couldn't, Sally came, full of concern and sympathy.

'You should have said,' was the closest she came to any

kind of rebuke. Otherwise, she talked cheerfully of the little things in life, what was happening in her agency and the dates she was going on. She had a new boyfriend, a solicitor, and it was looking promising.

Meanwhile, Julia's belly swelled, the baby moved and kicked, and at night, if she couldn't sleep, then she lay grappling with her terror of the thing inside either living or dying – both seemed equally terrible when she was in the grip of her fears.

Lala came too, arriving with David one afternoon not long after Julia was taken into the unit. She was pale with worry but full of words of reassurance. Julia was happy to see her but certain that Lala was angry.

'Is she cross with me?' she asked David anxiously, when Lala had left.

'No. Cross with me.' David looked tired and sad. He had lost weight too over the last week or so, and Julia had the impression that there were pressures on him from all sides. 'She thinks I should have seen what was happening. She thinks I shouldn't have left you alone at Tawray.'

'I made you.'

'She's right. You shouldn't have been alone. We'll work out a way that it won't happen again.'

Julia didn't know exactly what was going to happen to her and she was content to let others decide. Knowing that she would not now be going through childbirth had lifted a great weight from her shoulders. Other fears remained – that she would go into labour early, miscarry a late baby, that the baby would be sick or suffering birth defects – but the worst one was gone. She thought that they would probably let her out if she insisted but she was happy not to go anywhere. Here was fine. As the year progressed, David came to see her a little less.

'I'm going to put the hours in now,' he said, 'so that we can have more time when the baby is here. I've arranged to carry all my leave over.'

'That's a good idea,' she said with a smile, even though she couldn't really envisage a future with a baby in it, despite her swollen belly.

In the autumn, David was taken up with work and any number of away days, as he tried to bank as much holiday as he could, and Julia spent her days in the unit, visited by Sally and Lala, and David's parents; even Violet came when she heard that Julia was unwell.

'What does Aunt Victoria have to say about this?' Julia asked, as Violet sat with her in the day room. 'I expect she thinks I'm a chip off the old block – a maniac just like my mother.'

Violet's bright blush told her that she was not wrong.

The autumn days brought earlier evenings and the changing weather made her gloomy again, but still, she felt safe in the unit and had no desire to leave it, although she missed Greta and was overjoyed when David was able to bring her in for visits.

She was in the day room one Sunday, waiting for David to arrive with Greta, when her eye was caught by a headline on the Sunday tabloid. 'Baronet's son found dead.' Going cold, she picked it up, only to see a grainy black and white photograph of Mark and a short accompanying piece to say that he had been found dead at home of a drug overdose, thought to be suicide.

'Oh Mark!' She whispered, seized by grief. 'Oh Mark.' She closed her eyes. 'So you did it. You wouldn't let me. But you went on ahead.'

And she pushed the paper away, afraid suddenly of the thoughts swirling around her head, and full of despair for Mark and the path he had taken, whether he'd wanted to or not. And part of her envied him, that his journey was over and he was at peace.

Chapter Twenty-Three

Julia and David sat in the professor's consulting room at the unit, listening. Julia was only half paying attention; her real focus was the tiny bundle in her arms. Jonathan had been born by scheduled Caesarean section in the Chelsea and Westminster three weeks before, and she had spent a couple of days there recovering before she had returned to the unit. There had been no question of her being allowed home before the proper assessments had been carried out and she had recovered properly from the operation.

'We have to be sure that appropriate mother–infant bonding has taken place,' the professor was saying gravely, while David nodded, looking serious. 'Obviously we cannot risk any return of the previous conditions and everything points to a high risk of postpartum psychosis. It's a very real possibility.'

'Yes,' David said, 'but you can see that she's absolutely fine now.'

He looked over at his wife. Julia glanced up. 'What?'

'You're fine now, aren't you, darling?'

'Yes . . . oh yes. Fine.' She meant it. What was a great puzzle to her now was the memory of the utter darkness and sense of futility that had possessed her while she was pregnant. The terrors of growing a baby and awaiting its birth had faded like the memory of a nightmare on a bright, confident morning. Now she was entranced by the beautiful, perfect little being who had appeared in her life, and to whom she was already devoted.

David said firmly, 'I think you can see that the bonding has been successful.'

The professor observed Julia for a moment as she tended to Johnnie, tucking his blanket around him, stroking his head, murmuring to him and putting kisses on his swansdown-soft cheek. She looked up, suddenly aware of the silence. 'What is it?'

The professor gave a small smile. 'Yes, all the signs are good so far. We've been careful about the medications we've given your wife, in case of any transference through breast milk, which is why we've been extremely careful to monitor her condition. But we're happy with her progress. It's looking as close to normal as we think is possible.' He leaned towards Julia over his desk and said loudly, 'You're feeling all right, aren't you, Mrs Pengelly?'

'Yes, yes.'

'Then we'd like to go home,' David said firmly.

'That's looking possible. But it's an absolute prerequisite that Mrs Pengelly can't be left alone, so we'll need an undertaking before we can consider that.'

'I've got time off,' David said quickly. 'A good few weeks. I can be there to care for them both.'

'Good. But once you return to work . . . what then?'

'If necessary, I'll engage someone to be with her. I promise, she won't be left alone.'

'I'm right here, you know,' Julia said, but not crossly. She was still mostly focused on the baby and, besides, she had the obscure feeling that she had relinquished rights over herself because of what had happened. If people had to make her decisions for her now, well, that was understandable. She'd been lost for a while, she would have to re-earn their trust, she could quite see that. She only knew that she didn't want to be in London, or to return to the flat where she had been so unhappy.

Home to Tawray. That's where I want to be.

And that was something David couldn't refuse her.

Julia had left Tawray in the brightness of summer but now returned in the darkest part of the year.

The real year's midnight, she thought, remembering her aunt's objections to her choice of wedding day. *If anything feels like the lowest, coldest, most cheerless moment, it must be this. February.*

The weather was icy cold, the hours of daylight short and only differentiated from the darkness by a kind of yellow haze which seemed to be the closest to sunlight they were going to get. Johnnie was in his baby seat, which was strapped into the back with the seat belt wrapped around it, and Julia sat beside him all the way, his fingers wrapped around her thumb. She watched as he slept, fed and changed him when they made their stops at motorway service stations, and found the whole experience utterly exhilarating.

'I haven't seen you this happy for months and months. Perhaps ever,' David said as he watched her feeding the baby, the small warm body concealed behind an artfully draped baby shawl. They were sitting at a Formica-topped table over cups of nasty coffee with long-life milk in it, overlooking a car park. The hum of traffic came from the nearby motorway.

Julia looked up and was instantly moved by the love and pride on his face. 'I feel like myself again.'

'What happened to you?' he asked quietly. 'Where did you go?'

'I don't know,' she said honestly. 'I couldn't control it, you know. The guilt, the fear, the self-loathing. It wasn't something I could manage.'

'You never told me.'

'I didn't want to disappoint you.' She smiled at him, humble.

He leaned towards her. 'You never could.'

'I could. I did.'

'No.'

She smiled again. 'I can't believe we're talking about this in a motorway cafe.'

He reached over and took her hand. 'Promise me you'll talk to me if you ever feel bad again. If you ever feel low or useless, or need my help. Do you promise?'

She looked up, and found herself gazing into his dark blue eyes, touched by the intensity in them, and the desperate need for reassurance that she could see all over his face. 'Yes,' she said simply. 'I promise.'

Another midwinter promise. Like my wedding vow.

But she was sure she would never need to keep the promise.

It was pitch dark when they reached the house, but light glowed golden behind the great windows downstairs, making them appear like beacons against the night sky.

'But who's there?' she exclaimed, holding Johnnie close. She had taken him out of the baby seat for the last few miles, unable to resist keeping him on her chest, where she could inhale his beautiful baby smell.

'I asked Mrs Petheridge to get things ready for us. I couldn't have us turning up to a dark and cold house.' David pulled the car to a halt. 'Come on now. I've got something to show you.'

It was not simply that the lights were on; the house was warm and clean and a fire was burning in the drawing room, illuminating the panelling in a dark honeyed glow.

'This is wonderful!' Julia said, her eyes shining. 'It's properly homely!'

'That's not all. Come on.' David was obviously excited about something and he took her by the hand, and led her back to the hall and up the stairs.

'Where are we going? To my room?'

'Yes. Look.' David threw open the door of her bedroom and she went in, looking around in astonishment. It was transformed. Her bed was gone, and the old peach-coloured paint vanished. Now it was papered in a bright pattern of yellow and green hot air balloons soaring upwards in a pale blue sky, and carpeted in a thick-tufted ivory velvet. A cot took pride of place, a nursing chair nearby, and cream nursery furniture stood around the room, including a bookcase full of picture books.

She gazed at it, full of strange emotion to see her old room so transformed: it was life-enhancing to see it remade for a new young life. And yet . . .

'Do you like it?' David asked anxiously. 'We did it while you were in hospital.'

'We?'

'Sally and I.'

'Oh.' She looked around, taking it all in. 'Sally's been here?'

'She offered to help. Wasn't that kind of her?'

'Yes. Very.' She turned to David with a smile. 'It's lovely. Really. I love it.'

'Do you?'

'But . . .' The thing that had been troubling her leapt suddenly into the forefront of her mind. 'Where will we sleep?'

'In the main bedroom, of course.' David looked at her quizzically. 'Is that all right?'

'Of course.' It came out lamely so she followed it up quickly. 'That's . . . good.'

She felt that same emotion that had gripped her in the professor's consulting room: that she had somehow, obscurely, given up her right to make decisions for herself. She couldn't say, *The baby isn't coming into this room, it's too far away from me. And I'm too scared to sleep in my parents' old room because of what happened to me there.*

Instead, she said, 'Yes, that's good.'

And after all, she told herself sternly, the nursery was beautiful. It was perfect.

David did not object when she put their travel Moses basket next to the bed and laid Johnnie in it after his last feed, or say anything when she avoided their en suite bathroom and went instead to the one down the hall. She realised that he would not contradict her outright, that much of their communication had now been relegated to the non-verbal. By her actions, she was saying, *I won't use your nursery yet*, at the same time as her words said how much she liked it. And by not commenting on her decision to have Johnnie sleep by their bed, he was somehow endorsing her – *Very well, I understand, he's too young. Have him sleep with us for now.*

But they never said any of that.

Instead, as she lay in his arms that night, Johnnie in the cot beside them, she said, 'So Sally came down?'

'She's been so kind.' He pulled her close. 'The whole time you were in hospital, she couldn't do enough.'

'She came to see me practically every other day. It was good of her.'

'She's been a real friend to us. And she got such a kick out of helping me do the nursery, you'd have loved it.'

'I just . . . I suppose I always thought that I'd show her Tawray myself. It feels odd to think that she's been here without me.'

'You don't mind, do you?'

'No! No.'

There they are. The eggshells. Something had changed between her and David, that she couldn't quite identify. He watched her all the time, and got noticeably edgy when the baby cried, as though fearful that Julia would get hysterical and not be able to cope. He seemed constantly worried that something might tip her over the edge into the madness that had possessed her before. *Psychosis, they called it. But really, old-school madness.* David knew Mummy's death had scarred her but not how much, and she couldn't tell him the depth of her trauma. So they'd all agreed it was a strange circumstance brought on by the hormonal changes of pregnancy and whatever weird things happened inside women's brains when their bodies were annexed by their babies. She hadn't been able to explain it, because she didn't understand it herself, and she didn't want to revisit those awful feelings in any case. The experience was fading into a merciful blur and she had no interest in restoring it to focus. Now it was over and gone, she wanted to put it all behind her and let it go. So with tacit acquiescence, they said nothing. But it lay between them, delicately stepped over every day.

The weeks at home with David and Johnnie were some of the happiest she had ever known. The cold bleakness outside seemed to make the house all the more welcoming when the fires were blazing and the old radiators banging with effort as they warmed up. With David there, the nightmares receded and she was able to concentrate entirely on Johnnie and his all-absorbing needs: the feeding and changing, bathing and sleeping. He cried but she understood he had no other way to tell her what he needed, and it didn't panic her. She was exhausted but the night feeds and lack of sleep were sweetened by seeing his face when she woke, the feeling of him nestling into her and the contentment that flooded her when she nursed him.

He fattened and grew, and changed from a trembling red-faced little creature to a plump, chortling, kicking baby, bright-eyed and full of energy, and both of his parents adored him.

The time came, all too quickly, when David had to return to work. The flat in Battersea had been let go, and he was back to occupying the spare room in his friend Robin's flat. Without saying anything, he and Julia had known that she would not now be going back to London. It helped that spring was on its way, signposted with the banks of snowdrops along the drive and the emergence of clouds of yellow and purple crocuses across the lawn.

They took Johnnie out for a walk in his pram, pushing it along the gravel walks, pointing out birds and flowers and clouds, even though he'd fallen asleep as soon as they tucked him in and taken him outside. Greta scampered around them, dashing off on an adventure before coming back to them, then running off again.

'I don't want to go,' David said, as they walked side by side, muffled in scarves and overcoats. 'I really don't.'

'Can't you give up that job?' Julia said. She didn't want to lose him to that odd netherworld of the court, where she was not permitted to know what was going on.

'I can't right now.' David dug his hands into his pockets and stared at the gravel as they walked.

'Why not?'

'There's nothing to go to, for one thing. I don't want to go back to the navy, so I'm going to have to find a new career. And for another . . . well, she needs me.'

Julia felt suddenly cold. 'What?'

He hesitated. The habit of concealment was strong, and she felt him struggle as he considered whether to say anything. When he spoke, it was slowly and slightly halting. 'Look, I'll have to tell you a bit so you understand. Things are tough for her. I know that in many ways she's her own worst enemy, but she's having a hard time. The marriage has gone up in smoke. She hasn't a hope in hell of winning her husband back, and she can't understand why the whole world is in love with her but the one man she really wants is impervious.'

It was more than David had ever said about his employers, more than Julia ever dreamed he'd say.

'Is it that bad?' she ventured in a small voice.

'Very. Something has to change soon, or I don't know what will happen.' He sighed. 'It's making life very, very difficult. All of us – the staff – we're splitting into camps. Communication is becoming impossible with all the dissemination and scheming. It's tough.'

'That's awful.' She thought for a moment. 'But . . . why doesn't he love her?'

'Who knows? My guess is they are entirely unsuited to each other; you'd see that if you were in their company for five minutes. I think that whatever infatuation they had for one another wore off a long time ago, and it's left them wondering how the hell they can stand each other for the rest of their lives. Perhaps if she were more docile and submissive, and understood the rules of the game and was prepared to live by them, it might work. They could live more or less separate lives and appear united when necessary. But she doesn't want to do that. She doesn't want to submit. She's angry and resentful and she intends to remake things her way if she possibly can.'

'Why should she be the one to submit? Why not him?'

David gave her a sideways look. 'It doesn't work that way, as I expect you understand. The whole machine of court is too big, too entrenched. It doesn't change, not easily. It would be like trying to move a mountain.'

'Well, no wonder she's angry, if she's just expected to put up with it all. Is he doing anything in particular to upset her?'

There was another long pause before David said, 'I can't comment on that. But no one involved is blameless, I must say that.' He sighed. 'I do what I can, but it's not easy. The way things work at court – well, there's only so much that can be said or done, and if one oversteps the mark or slips up, it can quickly be curtains.' He slid a gaze across at her. 'I could be gone any day now. I could be forced out with silent treatment until I resign – that's the usual way. But until then, oddly, I want to stay and do what I can to stop the ship hitting the iceberg.'

'I didn't realise it was so bad.'

'It is.'

'Then I'll have to come to London.' A sense of bleak depression settled on her. David had made clear his priorities, and she came second, behind his work.

'No.' David reached for her hand. 'I've had an idea. Tell me what you think. How would you feel about Lala coming over?'

'Lala? How could she? She has her work!'

'Well, actually, she's thinking of taking a break for a while. She can tell you more when she comes. But what do you think? I'll still be here as often as I can, you know that. Every weekend, every holiday.'

Lala. Scenes of the past flitted in front of Julia's mind: their shared girlhood here. To have Lala back for a while would be sheer happiness.

'Yes. If she'll come, then yes.'

The pleasure at Lala's coming pushed out the bitter feeling she got when she thought about David's loyalty to his beautiful, charismatic and suffering employer.

Julia knew she was being guarded, watched over as though she were a helpless child, but she didn't mind. The handover between David and Lala was almost seamless. He left on a Sunday afternoon and before bed, Lala had arrived from the airport, as elegant as ever in a navy travelling suit, smart pumps and a rope of huge pearls at her neck.

Within half an hour, when the baby had been admired and put to bed, it was as though they had never been apart. By the drawing room fire, over cups of cocoa, they talked over everything that had happened, and Julia tried to give Lala an inkling of what it had been like, although she still shied away from describing the experience in-depth.

'It was like being possessed, that's the closest comparison I can think of. Although I've never been possessed, of course. And then the actual arrival of the baby, which I'd been so frightened of, was like an exorcism. I've been emptied of the evil. It's gone.' She smiled shyly at her sister. 'Does that sound completely barmy?'

Lala considered while she stirred her cocoa. She was curled up on a big armchair, her feet tucked up under her smart skirt. 'It sounds unusual. And hard to understand. But I'm just glad you are better. You look like your old self again. Are you eating?'

Julia nodded. 'I'm not much of a cook, but I seem to make mean scrambled eggs. Of course I'll do more once Johnnie is eating. I intend to learn.'

'And then . . . more children?'

Julia laughed, waving her hand in the air as if batting away the question. 'Oh really, one is more than enough right now, I can tell you! I can't imagine ever wanting more than Johnnie.'

Lala consulted her watch. 'Talking of your son, he'll be awake in a couple of hours. You should get to bed.'

'You're right. He's got a habit of waking on the dot of two a.m. Most ungentlemanly of him, I must say.' Julia finished the last of her cocoa and put down her mug. 'Let's go up. Mrs Petheridge will clear away in the morning.'

Lala was gazing at the space where the mural wall used to

be. 'Such a shame Quentin got rid of it. He really should have asked you first.'

'I know.' Julia looked over as well. 'I miss it every time I come in.' She smiled at Lala. 'Perhaps we should have another one done, when Johnnie's older. Wouldn't that be nice?'

'Very. Now off to bed.'

The next day they walked down to the beach, Johnnie strapped to his mother's chest in a sling, while Mrs Petheridge did the tidying and made them lunch.

'I can't pretend she doesn't make my life a lot easier,' Julia confessed as they went. 'I expect most mothers have it a lot harder than I do, with someone to clean up after me. No wonder I'm in such a good mood.'

They walked down the winding path with its steps cut into the cliff, and got down to the sea. It was a sombre green-grey, sporting foaming curls of crashing waves that beat down on the shore in their strange, irregular rhythm, a pounding syncopation against the battering wind.

'You're happy with David then?' Lala said, tying back her fair hair against the whipping gusts of wind.

'Of course.' Julia looked down to make sure that Johnnie was well protected; he lay tight against her, cosy and insulated inside her coat, which she'd buttoned over the sling.

'He's not going to be here very much. Will you be all right?'

'I wish it were different.' They strolled across the wet sand and stood looking out to sea. There was no one else around, not even a dog-walker. 'But he has a job to do.' Julia stared for a while, and then said, 'I trust him.'

Lala looked surprised. 'Good. Why wouldn't you?'

Julia shrugged. 'I worry sometimes, about his job. How much it demands from him. He gets so stressed over it. The phone is ringing at all hours these days – not while he's here, but in London. He told me it can be first thing in the morning or last thing at night. There's a terrible atmosphere in the office, suspicion and division. Not that he can tell me much about it.'

'Well, didn't I say all those years ago? I knew she was going to be trouble.'

'Did you?'

'I'm sure I did. It was bound to happen. I don't mean she is the problem; I just mean that it was inevitable there would be problems, with all the romantic dreams she had and the reality of his life and the way the world has always revolved around him. I expect he has a mistress and she can't stand it.'

Julia frowned with surprise. 'A mistress? But she's so beautiful, why would he want a mistress?'

Lala laughed knowingly. 'It's always about more than beauty. Beauty reels men in, but it can't keep them if their lives become too difficult. Believe me, there'll be someone loving and caring and full of compassion who makes him feel loved. That's what men want – to feel loved.'

'Women want that too!'

'Of course. But we're the ones who give more than we take. Men are the reverse.'

311

Julia stroked the top of Johnnie's woolly hat, staring out to sea thoughtfully. 'That doesn't sound fair. We should give and take equally.'

Lala shook her head. 'It doesn't work like that. Women are required to sacrifice to keep a man happy in a way that they can't ask for in return. Men expect women to be strong. If the woman starts to crumble, they usually have no idea what to do – so it's up to women to get on and cope as best they can. We have other consolations but we have to make them ourselves. I have a friend who goes to the theatre and opera three times a week, alone or with a girlfriend. Her husband is nice enough but he seems soulless and a bit cold, so she goes elsewhere for her fix of epic emotion and sense of being alive. That seems to work for her.'

'You mean, we mustn't look to men for support when things go wrong?'

'Maybe if your car battery is flat. But not if you are.' Lala shrugged and laughed wryly. 'I just think they're too needy themselves to give much, and when too much is asked, they look for an escape. It's not scientific, and of course there are exceptions, but I think that when men seek their consolations, they find another woman to give what they think you can't, and then love her and not you.' She looked suddenly sheepish. 'I'm not talking about you, of course. You and David are fine, I can see that, and he couldn't have been more devoted when you were ill. He probably isn't that kind of man.'

'But is Denis?' Julia asked shyly. There were whole parts of Lala's life she had never enquired about; the age difference between them seemed to make it impertinent, somehow, and Lala had never shown any need to confide. But then, she always seemed so confident and secure. Perhaps that was only a front.

'Yes, of course,' Lala replied frankly. 'The relationships between the sexes are much more pragmatic in France – it's a cliché but it's true. Women are expected to look after their husbands in a more giving way. We are made to understand early that what the English believe a man to be is the opposite of the truth. Over here, you all assume he wants to shag remorselessly and be unfaithful. Actually, most men are too lazy for that; they are happy with one woman and even if he strays once or twice, he will stay with her if the marriage is strong. And then sex. Supposedly for men, it is all about the physical act and the release of need, pure desire. But in my experience, they need it to feel loved and valued. Sex for them is love – just love for themselves and not for you.'

'This all sounds very depressing,' Julia said. 'Maybe that's how it is for some people, but surely not for everyone.' Then she said stoutly, 'David loves me completely, I know he does.'

'Oh yes, of course. But I think that, as time goes by and love changes, it becomes more true for us all.'

Julia felt annoyed. 'Everyone keeps trying to tell me that I have to compromise and accept that nothing is going to be what I want. I don't agree with that! After everything we've been through, I'm more certain than ever that David loves me no matter what.'

Lala turned and took her hand. 'I'm so glad about that, Julia, I really am. We need people like you two to show us what is possible. I'm sure you and David will be fine. Shall we take that little chap back home? It's cold out here and I need tea.'

They turned to go home, Julia's hand cupped over the woolly cap on her baby's head. She realised with something like horror that she had almost missed out on this. She had wanted to kill herself, and to kill Johnnie, this dear, precious little thing. It made her heart wobble and jump to think of it. She'd come so very close to never knowing this happiness.

I'll never feel like that again, she promised herself. *Not now that I know what motherhood can be like.*

She dropped a kiss on his warm head as they headed for home.

Chapter Twenty-Four

Present day

'Well? What do you think?' Johnnie asked, as he and Alex stood in the hall of the house he had rented. They'd just done a quick tour on the way to visit Pa.

'It's very nice.' Alex nodded. It was a roomy Victorian rectory that had been reconfigured for the holiday market with the kind of chrome and marble finish that she was fearful might one day happen to Tawray: attractive and tasteful but somehow bland, as though lifted from the pages of a style magazine. 'You could have stayed with me, you know.'

Johnnie shook his head. 'We couldn't inflict the whole family on you for such a long time. The reality of having Bertie around – and with Christmas to organise as well – would be too much. I've already had to agree with my mate who owns this that we can put extra locks on the doors.'

'I wouldn't mind!' Alex protested. 'I know Bertie, I know what to expect. I love spending some time with him, and Nathan and Joe too.'

It was a bit overwhelming to imagine a family of five staying with her for over a month at such a busy time, but she would have been more than willing.

'I appreciate that.' Johnnie shoved his hands into his coat pockets and sighed. 'Honestly, it would not be easy. I think it's going to help Netta and me to have our own space as well.'

'When do you move in?'

'When the family come down. I'll have to get it set up before then. I hope you don't mind me crashing with you until I manage to get it sorted.'

'Of course not. You're always welcome. You don't even have to ask.'

They went out and Johnnie locked the front door behind them.

'How are things?' Alex asked gently. She'd been aware of the strain on her brother's face since he'd returned, staying with her until he had the new house sorted out for the family, and she knew it was more than Pa's condition.

'Not good. She's not happy. In fact, she's talked about divorce.'

'What?' Alex put a hand on Johnnie's arm in alarm. 'I had no idea it was that bad!'

'Neither did I,' he said grimly. They went over to the car and got in. 'It's come out of the blue as far as I'm concerned.'

'Is there someone else?'

Johnnie shook his head. 'I don't think so. I mean, there might be, but I'd be surprised. I think it's about us, about her and me.'

'What's the problem?'

He started the engine. 'The usual. Communication. Feeling undervalued. Resenting the fact that I don't help enough.'

'Well, that's good,' Alex said, trying to be positive. 'You can change all that. You can learn communication and make her feel valued, and start to help more.'

'Sounds easy enough.' Johnnie pulled the car round to face the road. 'But it isn't, Al, you know that. I'm doing all I can and I just have no idea how I can do more. I help out at home, I try and reassure her about how much I appreciate her. Nothing seems to work.'

'Well, don't give up, for goodness' sake. I've been through divorce, and I can tell you, it's desperately horrible. The worst thing ever, except for Mum dying. Even though Tim and I have done all we can to be civil and grown-up and put the kids first, doing birthdays and school concerts together, never arguing in front of them and telling them all the time how much we love them, both the girls cried nearly every day for two months. Scarlett is still really unsettled, although Jasmine seems more stable. Do anything to avoid it, you have to.' She gave him a sympathetic look even though his eyes were firmly on the road in front of them. 'It sounds like Netta still loves you.'

'Does it? I'm not so sure. She said she doesn't think she can make me happy but I think what she was really saying is that I don't make her happy.' He bit his lip, misery over his face. 'And I don't know how to change that.'

Alex sat at her desk, frowning at her computer screen through her reading spectacles and putting together a costing for Jasper. He'd emailed just after their discussion in the potting shed, full of enthusiasm for the plan they'd concocted and eager to get a date in the diary and local producers on board. She'd written back to explain in more detail what the flower exhibition entailed, he'd replied with more ideas, and before long they'd hammered out a plan: the two main rooms on the ground floor would be decorated and the house opened for a full weekend. Refreshments provided in the orangery by a local cafe who prided themselves on using Cornish produce and providing vegan options as well as regular fare. Stands would be set up in the hall, with tasting tables in the dining room and gift stalls in the drawing room.

The only problem is that a lot of suppliers are booked out close to Christmas, so there might not be as many as we'd like. But it's a start. We'll have enough to make it worthwhile, I reckon. So if we're agreed on the date, just send me your costing, and let me know when you'd like to come up and do the decorations. I'm sorting out all the boring stuff – licences and insurance.

See you soon.

Jasper

It was odd to have this new force in her life so unexpectedly, one that was drawing her back to Tawray with such insistence. The major and Lady Clare, who had rented the house for eight years, had been kind enough but the door was firmly closed most of the time. They'd been gone for six months, and the house only sold at the end of the summer.

Mentally, Alex had made her farewells, and now Jasper was keen to get her up there to help him survey the rooms and make a floorplan, and he'd mentioned other schemes, which seemed to come pouring out of him in a flood.

She smiled at his email, then thought, *I wonder what Polly makes of this*. Jasper hadn't mentioned her. Polly hadn't given off even a whiff of the kind of enthusiasm that Jasper had in spades. She didn't seem the type to get excited about produce fairs and dried flowers. That might make things difficult. She looked at his email address: Jasper@jaspergardyne.com.

Gardyne. That's a nice name. It sounds like garden.

On impulse, she did an internet search of Jasper Gardyne and he popped up at once, so she clicked on a couple of links that mostly went through to Scottish news sites and a few business articles, but it was all quite dry and without much personal detail. He'd grown up in Scotland, gone to Edinburgh University and as soon as he left, started a media company with a couple of friends and a tiny start-up fund. Within ten years, the company had grown to owning several newspapers, a brand of local magazines, some websites, a production company and an online news channel. Then, quite suddenly, he'd organised the sale of the company to a larger media conglomerate and disappeared from view. There was nothing more she could find out about him, and he didn't appear to be on any of the usual social media sites.

Frowning, she went back to her search results. They went on for a couple of pages, but the results seemed to be repetitions of the same articles and reporting in different guises. Jasper was still a bit of a mystery. Polly Gardyne appeared on Instagram but her account was locked and there was nothing more Alex could find out about her.

Just then, she heard the front door slam closed.

'Is that you, Johnnie?' she called. She was expecting him back for a late supper, just the two of them as the girls were at Tim's.

Heavy footsteps came down the hall towards the study and she turned to the door.

'Johnnie?'

The door pushed open and she saw that Mundo was standing there, smiling at her in that odd way he had, as if only half his mouth would cooperate. She gasped.

'I'm so sorry. Did I frighten you?'

She stuttered as she pulled off her glasses. 'N-no. I thought you were Johnnie, he's due home any minute. Did you just let yourself into my house?'

'I knocked but you didn't hear. The door wasn't locked, so I came right in. You ought to get a decent doorbell.'

'I've got a doorbell,' she said coldly. 'You didn't ring it or I would have heard.'

'Sorry. My mistake.' Mundo strolled in, looking about at the piles of paper and the pin boards covered in pictures. 'You're keeping busy then. But you could be a bit tidier.' He threw her an amused look. 'But you were always rather messy, weren't you? Remember your bedroom at Tawray? Piles of shit everywhere.'

Alex swallowed, her mouth suddenly dry. 'What do you want? Why are you here?'

'I was driving past and suddenly thought I'd see if you

were in. We're supposed to be talking about the future, remember? The three of us? About my mother, and Pa's will.'

She tried not to show how much she disliked him calling her father 'Pa'. After all, he had a right to, as David had brought him up from the age of eight. 'We didn't set up a time or anything.'

'No. And my mother told me you and Johnnie visited Pa today while I was out, and you never even told me Johnnie was back.' Mundo gave her one of his sardonic looks, which seemed to be amused but also appeared to conceal anger. 'Didn't we agree that we had to have a chat as soon as we could?'

'Yes. I've been busy.' It sounded lame.

'Right. So Johnnie's due back now is he? Shall I wait?'

'I'll text him.' She pulled out her phone and tapped out a message.

Are you on your way back? Mundo's here.

She pushed send.

Mundo was gazing at the cards and pictures pinned to one of the boards. He looked dapper as usual, in smart cord trousers, a bottle-green jumper over a pink checked shirt. His dark hair was carefully arranged, his skin smooth and stubble-free. He was well turned out, handsome even. But there was something about the protrusion of his lower lip, with its hint of petulance, that repelled her. He glanced over, amused. 'How do you make sense of all this? It just looks like a giant mash-up to me. I could never sort out a case with this kind of confusion. I like order. Neatness.'

'I know.' Alex remembered Mundo's obsessively tidy room back at Tawray, his pleasure in organisation. She'd hated that room. So clinical and so cold.

'Is he coming?'

She glanced down at her screen. 'Nothing yet.'

'Hmm.' Now Mundo was at the side of her desk, pushing some pieces of paper into a neat pile, which sent a prickle of irritation over her skin. She caught a whiff of his aftershave – something rich and oriental. 'So what happened with you and Tim?' His voice dropped to a mellow note, honeyed and deep. 'Did he find out you like to sleep around?'

She felt sick again, the same pang of disgust as in Sally's kitchen the other day. '*What?*'

'Oh, sorry. Forgive me. I'm sure you don't sleep around anymore.'

The disgust swirled with something else, more noxious, in her stomach. 'Shut the fuck up, Mundo.'

'Calm down, Alexandra.' He smiled again, amused. 'We're all allowed our little peccadillos, aren't we?'

'I don't know what you're talking about.' Her voice sounded slightly strangled.

'I'm sure you don't.' He leaned over, too uncomfortably close for her liking. 'Who's this? Isn't she pretty.' He pointed to a photograph of Scarlett, her dark hair pulled back in braids, her blue eyes wide and innocent. 'She looks just like you.'

Alex stared at the photo and realised that Scarlett was the

age now that she had been when Mum died. That thought twisted something inside her with such pain she could hardly bear it. The idea of Scarlett suffering what she had, all that loss and grief, was almost too much. And then . . . she had a memory of her and Johnnie standing together, drawn close in their shared misery, and Sally pushing Mundo towards them. He was eight, pale and pudgy, with that sulky mouth and pale blue eyes that flickered with mischief.

'This is your brother,' Sally declared. 'Your new brother. Aren't you lucky? I'm sure you'll make him feel welcome, won't you?'

Alex had thought that she didn't like this exchange at all: losing a mother and gaining Mundo. And then it all began, that subtle and not-so-subtle crowbarring of Mundo into the family, the insistence that he must be treated with limitless kindness, patience and forbearance. Two children who had lost their mother, whose father had disappeared into a pit of grief, must put their new brother first at all times, no matter how he behaved towards them.

That was it. Pa left us to it. He was never there. We lost him too. I just never realised it.

Mundo leaned over to pick up Scarlett's photograph.

'Don't touch that!' Alex shouted, and went to grab it, but he pulled it away just in time, laughing.

'What's wrong? Can't I look at a photograph?'

'Put it down,' she shouted, more loudly, more frantic.

'All right, all right.' Mundo put the photograph down, and shrugged, still laughing. 'You're a bit of a tigress, aren't you?

I'm just admiring your peach of a daughter. You should be proud of her.'

'I am. I don't need your approval.'

'Oh, come on.' He edged a little closer again, his cool blue eyes looking at her appraisingly. 'She got her good looks from you. You're still attractive, Alex, and I can remember a time when you didn't use to be so fussy either. Can't you?'

Her heart was pounding, and she could feel her breath coming faster. 'I'm warning you, Mundo. Don't start.'

'What are you trying to say?' He looked hurt, and then his mouth turned down at the corners. 'You're being a bit unkind. I don't like it when you're unkind.'

She stared at him, his face unpleasantly close to hers. He was so powerful. What was it about him that made him so strong and so frightening? Her phone beeped and she looked down. It was a text from Johnnie. The words danced in front of her eyes but she managed to read it.

I'm stuck in traffic outside town. Won't be back for a while.

She looked back at Mundo and tried to sound stronger than she felt. 'He's going to be late. I think you should go.'

'But now we've got some time to catch up properly, haven't we?'

'Please go.'

'Why?' He reached and tucked a strand of her hair behind her ear. 'I'd like to stay.'

Alex leapt up. 'Get out, Mundo, I mean it!'

'Woah! All right. Don't get het up. I'm just being friendly.' He moved away and shook his head. 'Anyone would think you're frightened of me.'

'I just want you out. Johnnie and I will find a time to meet you and talk about the inheritance issues. Until then, please go.'

Mundo's expression turned sour. 'I see. Fine. You and Johnnie were always the same – ganging up on me. Treating me like an outsider. I see that nothing's changed.' He went to the door. 'You'll both regret it in the end. I haven't forgiven or forgotten, and we're all grown-up now, aren't we?'

She couldn't say anything, just longed with everything she had for him to walk out the door. He looked back at her, and gave another of his sardonic, half-amused looks.

'I mean it, Alex. You're not going to get away with shutting me out. I'm here to stop that. Understand?'

Then he was gone and a moment later, the front door closed with a bang. Alex sat shaking, staring unseeing into the room and remembering.

It had started in little ways. Right from the beginning, when Sally had moved herself and Mundo into the house. Aged only eight, Mundo seemed to have a talent to provoke way beyond his years, and a desire for it. What he hated most was to be ignored, thriving on attention and getting reactions. She would never understand why he wanted to attack her and Johnnie, but he'd been the same since the day he arrived. As soon as the grown-ups' backs were turned, he'd not be able to stop himself, doling out kicks and pinches, or whispering nastiness and spite. He liked to torment Johnnie by targeting his favourite possessions, often stealing or breaking them or making the grown-ups force Johnnie to hand them over in the name of sharing. Or he'd tease with mean songs and rhymes and nicknames, or repetitive tricks, like tiny balls of paper lobbed over and over at someone's face.

With Alex, he had similar methods. He liked to sneak into her room and read her private journals and writings, and then tease her, and he always found what she hid. He put horrible things in her bed: dirty, slimy crawling things. He played practical jokes that left her soaked, filthy or even hurt. He would threaten to drop favourite things down the loo or off the roof, and he was adept at the sudden and painful twist on a wrist, or a flicked towel, delivered swiftly and just out of the eyeline of the grown-ups. He discovered that horrible names and nasty rhymes worked better on her than on Johnnie, so he concentrated on that for a while, provoking her to tears of misery by calling her Smelly Alex and acting disgusted by her smell whenever she was in the room.

And then they grew up and something changed. She hadn't thought Mundo could be any more horrible but he found a new seam to mine. It started with pictures from dirty magazines, ripped out and left in her bed: crumpled photographs of naked women or couples engaged in vividly portrayed sex acts. She saw her first naked, aroused man that way and was unable to shake the image for weeks. Alex didn't want to see them, but he left them where she couldn't help it. She was too ashamed to tell anyone what he was doing, in case they thought she was somehow complicit in it, so she could only rip them up into tiny pieces and flush them away.

Then the pictures began to come with notes, printed in capitals.

DO YOU DO THIS?
DO YOU LOOK LIKE THIS?
DO YOU AND YOUR FRIENDS LIKE DOING THIS TO EACH OTHER?
WILL YOU DO THIS FOR ME?

It revolted her. Once, sickened by it, she'd run into his room, thrown a crumpled picture down on his bed and shouted, 'Will you just stop it?'

Mundo had picked it up with an air of surprise. 'Stop what? What's this?' He looked at it in faux bewilderment and then, in a shocked tone, said, 'Alexandra! Why are you showing me this? Where did you get it?'

'You put it in my room!'

'Of course I didn't. That's disgusting.' He'd narrowed his eyes at the picture. 'Although, actually, she's quite nice, now I look closer. I like those tits. Have you got tits like this? Why don't you show me?'

'Shut up!' she'd screamed and run back to her room, her eyes stinging with frustrated tears.

The pictures kept coming but she grew used to them, able to shut their contents out of her mind as she ripped them up and threw them away. One day, Mundo would leave.

He'd go to university and then she'd be free. It wasn't long to wait now.

It was a Saturday in the Easter holidays and she was in the small sitting room, curled up on the sofa watching television. Mundo had just got back from skiing with some of his rich friends. Johnnie was out somewhere. Alex felt her heart sink as she heard the sitting room door open and a minute later, Mundo was sitting on the sofa too, at the other end. She ignored him, watching her programme in studied silence in case he decided to start teasing her in any of his favourite ways, until she became aware of a regular movement out of the corner of her eye. Looking over, she was confused, unable for a moment to understand what she was seeing, until she realised that Mundo had exposed himself and was gently rubbing the erection that rose from his flies.

Alex gasped in shock and froze, suddenly terrified. He didn't look at her, but continued caressing himself as though he was completely unaware of her presence. She quickly looked back at the screen but saw nothing on it, aware only of the awful movement at the edge of her vision.

Then, with a rapid movement, she scrambled away, getting off the sofa and out of the room as quickly as she could. She ran to her room, appalled and incredulous. She was also scared. What did this mean? What was he doing?

Alex knew she ought to go to Pa and Sally at once and tell them. But she couldn't. How would she find the words? It was too shameful, embarrassing, mortifying. And what if they didn't believe her? What then? No. She had to hope it was just a one-off, a moment of madness on Mundo's part. Perhaps he hadn't seen her, hadn't realised he wasn't alone.

But she knew in her heart that wasn't true.

Alex ran to the front door as soon as Mundo had gone through it, and locked it. The girls were with Tim. Johnnie was still out in the car somewhere. She was alone, and now she was scared. Mundo's vileness that had scarred her teenage years. It had been the awful secret that he had forced her to share with him, and even now, she couldn't bear to think about it. A huge part of the guilt was that she was complicit. She'd let him get away with it, and that made her feel wretched, as though there was no way she could be innocent in all this.

Leaning against the front door, she tried to get her breath and be calm, but panic was still gurgling through her. It had taken years to act normal around Mundo, to be able to pretend that they were simply normal step-siblings. She did it by blanking it out. She had told no one about what he'd done, not even Tim.

Tim.

He'd been so different from Mundo, and that was a huge part of what had drawn her to him. Tim might have been a bloody pain in so many ways, but she knew it would never occur to him to treat any girl the way Mundo did. Tim was kind, gentle and safe. He was loving and straightforward and had no idea that love and sex could be nasty, twisted games that were all about punishment and power. When she'd met Tim, his attitude to her – sweet, normal, unthreatening – had been like water in the desert to Alex, and their relationship had done a huge amount to heal and reset her, restoring her real self and giving her back her faith in people. It was just that, when she had been healed, it had become clear that Tim wasn't right for her after all. His sweetness and straightforwardness were, in the end, not enough.

Somewhere between the two of them, Tim and Mundo, these two extremes and everything they represent, there has to be something else. The thing I'm looking for.

But what was it?

Someone with kindness and sweetness, of course, but also with some vital dynamism, some element of sympathy with her that went beyond romantic feelings and was all about a shared outlook, a shared vision and passion for the same essentials of life.

Alex couldn't remember much about the relationship between her parents, so her only pattern was Pa's second marriage, and what she understood about Sally and Pa was that they were in harmony. Alex had always felt in some vague way that Pa loved Sally, but as a best friend. She was not his great passion, she was sure of it. That had been Mum, she felt it in her core. But a best friend was a wonderful thing to travel through life with. If Tim had been her best friend, instead of an amiable housemate, it could have worked.

But it hadn't. And here she was alone. And Mundo was back. Was he up to his old tricks?

She breathed out slowly, trying to calm her pounding heart.

Oh God. I hope not.

Chapter Twenty-Five

When Alex called at the house to see Pa, Sally stood at the front door, white-faced, a little hunched inside her baby-blue sweater, and said, 'I'm sorry, Alex, it's not a good time.'

'What?' Alex half laughed, as if Sally was joking. How could it not be a good time for a man who was completely unconscious? She'd seen Pa virtually every day now, sometimes with the girls, and he had never changed at all, unless being in a different position counted. The nurse turned him from time to time to prevent bed sores or to allow her to wash him.

Sally looked worried and her gaze slid away from Alex to the evergreen shrubs by the front door. It occurred to Alex that by now Sally usually had decorations and fairy lights up, but not this year. The house showed no sign of the fact that Christmas was so close.

'Is something going on?' Alex asked. She'd felt that she and Sally had found a new bond over the last few weeks in their shared anxiety for David. For once, the prickle of antagonism that had existed between them for so long had

331

faded a little. The barbed comments and tart remarks had stopped almost entirely and Alex felt for the first time as though she might be seeing the real Sally, the woman below the act. It made her wonder why on earth she had kept it up for so many years.

The stupid thing is, we might have been friends.

For years, Alex had wondered what it might have been like if Sally had loved her, and what it would have been like to have a kind, caring stepmother to replace, just a little, what she had lost. She sometimes imagined a world where she had a motherly figure to turn to, to confide in and be guided by. But Sally had rejected that role. When Alex's first period arrived, Sally had given her a box of tampons and shut her in the bathroom, with no instructions or explanation. Alex hadn't had the first clue what to do, and had ended up putting wads of loo paper in her knickers to deal with it. It was only the other girls at school and Matron who had explained what she needed and helped her get sanitary towels instead of tampons.

She wondered what it might have been like to have a step-mother who hugged her and kissed her and wished her real happiness. It had never been like that. Even on Alex's wedding day, Sally had claimed a bad headache that meant David had to sit with her at all times, and not walk Alex up the aisle after all. Mundo would do it. Alex had protested that she'd rather walk alone or with Johnnie, but no one would listen, and in the end she'd bowed to the general insistence that this must happen, and had taken the arm of the person she hated most in the world in order to be married. Her main memory of her wedding day was that awful walk, the smile on Mundo's face, Tim's bewilderment, Pa's refusal to stand up to Sally. Sally had even suggested that Pa not give his speech but he'd said he would do that, and Sally should go home and lie down if she wasn't up to the rest of the day. So Sally had left before the speeches, walking out shakily, helped by Mundo. Everyone was asking if she was all right. All the attention, all the concern, all eyes on her.

Alex had felt as though she was engaged in a battle she had never wanted to fight, against an enemy she wished would be her ally, whose main aim was to divide and rule. Keeping Alex and Jonathan away from Pa seemed to be her overriding concern.

But why?

That was always the question. What did she want to gain from it? Tawray? Sally had been the main force behind getting rid of it. Money? Surely she had enough to be content. Advantages for Mundo? He had the best education money could buy, he had a brilliant legal career and a glamorous life – he was by far the most successful of the three children. What more could she want for him?

It was as though she was obsessed by making Pa choose her over his children, and she would only be satisfied by erasing Alex and Johnnie altogether. Alex thought of all the school pictures and family photographs that had disappeared over the years, so that only Mundo was represented in silver frames on the sideboard. Mundo was immortalised in an oil painting in his graduation robes. Johnnie's graduation picture was a photo in a frame propped up in the small sitting room bookcase, half obscured by holiday postcards.

And now, on the doorstep of Alex's father's house, Sally was denying her entry.

'Well, when can I come back?' Alex asked. 'Later today?'

'I'm not sure. I'll text you.'

'What shall I say to Johnnie? He's expecting to visit.'

'Tell him the same.' Sally was evidently itching to get away. 'I must go now. I'll text you.' And she slipped back inside and shut the door.

Alex stood there, bemused. There was not much to be done, she could hardly force her way in. Pa must be all right. She would leave it for today and come back tomorrow. Actually, it would be a good idea to get up to Tawray with some of her decorations. Jasper had sent her a message to say that the Christmas trees had arrived and were in their stands, and she'd begun to see notices of the opening of the house for viewing.

She shrugged. *I've got plenty to do. If Sally wants to play a silly game with me, that's fine. I'll come back tomorrow.*

But she knew that niggling sense of anxiety about Sally from of old.

Alex drove up to the house in her small van, painted in the company colours: duck-egg blue with 'Tawray Flower Company' on the side in chocolate brown lettering. The back was stacked with boxes that held the baubles in tissue paper and straw, along with strands of tiny fairy lights that would nestle among them.

She got out and rang the bell, then went back to start unloading the van. A few moments later, the front door opened and Jasper came bounding down the front steps, followed by a pair of small but very hairy dogs, their eyes obscured by fringes and pink tongues hanging out. He was casual as usual, in jeans, a shirt and a blue tank top, his expression bright and welcoming.

'Hello! You're here, fantastic. Let me give you a hand with those. Out the way, Krystal, you idiot, you'll trip us over. Ignore the dogs, they're mad.'

'They're sweet. What are they?'

'Shih tzus. Nutters. That's Krystal and that's Alexis.' He raised his eyebrows. 'Don't ask.'

They started unloading the boxes. It had rained overnight and everything was damp so they carried them straight inside and put them down in the hall where two large unadorned Christmas trees stood on either side of the staircase.

'Goodness,' Alex said, looking around. 'It's just the same.'

'Yeah, we haven't changed much.' Jasper followed her gaze around the large hall with the staircase leading away in the middle. 'I don't really know where we'd start. I like it as it is, if I'm honest.'

'No, I mean . . .' Alex glanced all around, surprised. 'Everything is still here. The pictures, the furniture. Even the suits of armour. Just the same.'

'Oh yeah, well . . .' Jasper laughed. 'Of course.'

Just then a woman came walking up from the back of the hall, holding a cup of steaming coffee. She was attractive, or would have been if her expression had been less sour. She had a fine-boned face, clear eyes and brown hair pulled messily back into a bun.

'What are you doing?' she asked.

Alex recognised the flat voice from the last time she'd been here, but said nothing, just stacked the boxes neatly against the wall.

'Hi, Polly,' Jasper said. 'I think you met Alex already.'

'Did I?' Polly looked over without interest. 'Okay.'

'She's doing the flower display. Remember? I told you all about it.'

Polly rolled her eyes. 'Christ. I can't believe you've been talked into this; I can't think of anything worse. The sooner I get on a beach the better.'

Jasper said lightly, 'Well, some of us are working. Do you think you could make us some coffee while we bring in the boxes?'

'All right.' Polly looked over to Alex without a spark of interest. 'How do you like it?'

'Just milk, please.' She looked down at Polly's hand where she was holding her cup and saw the glint of a gold band. *Married. Oh well.*

'Thanks, Pols,' Jasper said, one of his broad, infectious grins spreading over his face. When Polly had sauntered off down the hall towards the kitchen, he said confidingly, 'Don't mind her. She's a wee bit gloomy at first but she gets better when she knows you.'

'Right,' Alex said, finding that hard to believe. 'Shall we get started? I've brought some extension plugs for the lights, so we could begin with those. Have you got ladders?'

'Right here, just like I promised.'

They worked together for an hour, stopping for a few minutes to drink the coffee that Polly delivered wordlessly, and at the end of that, they'd got the lights arranged around the two Christmas trees in the hall.

'Let's take a break,' Jasper said, after they'd stood back to admire their handiwork.

'Fun stuff next,' Alex said cheerfully. 'Decorating!'

'I want to show you the orangery first.'

They walked through the house. It was still all so familiar. Despite everything, the house remained essentially itself.

It's hard to remember that it isn't ours anymore. It's gone forever. I'm only here because I'm invited in.

That thought was painful. She didn't want to live here – she loved the Old Barn, and Tawray was far too big for most families in any case – but the old house felt part of her own self, and of her mother. How could she not feel nostalgic for it, even if so many of her memories were bitter ones?

'Oh goodness, this is wonderful!' Alex said as she followed Jasper into the orangery, which was connected to the main house by a small passageway that opened out into the glass-walled room. It had been thoroughly cleaned, and tables and chairs were set up at intervals. Along each wall were small Christmas trees decorated only with tiny twinkling lights. The furniture looked like rattan, neat and elegant against the faded orange of the terracotta floor tiles.

'It looks amazing,' Alex breathed. 'Much better than the major's efforts! He put palm trees everywhere, along with rusty garden furniture that always wobbled. This is miles better.'

'Glad you like it.' He looked pleased. 'I want your garlands up there, where the glass meets the roof. They'll look fabulous. The cafe furniture is sustainable bamboo and I've got chinaware from a local potter – you'll love it. It'll all be for sale. The cafe people are setting up this weekend – you should taste their vegan lemon drizzle cake, it's incredible.' He caught sight of Alex's expression. 'What? Have I said something wrong?'

'No. It's just that I had no idea you'd take all this so seriously! I mean, you're going to make it better than it was before.' She was surprised by the happiness that welled up inside her, to see the orangery looking so good.

Jasper smiled. 'I hope so. That's what I want.'

'Environmental issues mean a lot to you then?'

He nodded. 'Yeah. I have my reasons. They just sound kind of weird.'

'You can tell me.' She sat down at the nearest table and looked up at him. 'I've got time.'

Jasper laughed, but looked awkward. For the first time since she'd met him, he didn't seem so sure of himself. Slowly he sat down opposite, not meeting her eye. He looked boyish, despite the fact that he must be in his mid-thirties, and uncertain. After a moment, he spoke slowly. 'I grew up pretty poor in a crappy town just outside Edinburgh, with two younger brothers. It wasn't great. Our lives were blighted by lots of things, but drink and ignorance and mental illness were all part of it. I wanted to get out so badly. I had a mentor at school who told me I could make something of myself, and through him I got into university to study law. I was going to be a hotshot lawyer and never be poor again. That didn't happen because I met my mate Stephen, and the two of us set up a university paper with the kind of stuff we wanted to read in it. It was lively, funny, intelligent, unpretentious. It had jokes but it also tackled the difficult stuff from a position of common sense. We weren't like the ideologues and the political crazies and the soapbox preachers with an agenda. We were straightforward and funny. People loved it. We rolled it out to other universities, like a franchise, funding it by advertising.' Jasper shook his head as if in disbelief. 'It just worked. We thought we were geniuses. I was going to be a media tycoon, and I fucking loved it. I chucked in any ideas of law, and Stephen and I set up our business. Great. The sun shone on everything we tried, it just got bigger and bigger. But then . . .' He stopped and seemed lost in his own thoughts.

'Yes?' Alex pressed gently.

'I kind of ignored what was going on at home. My dad died of drink. One of my brothers emigrated to Australia. The other, Duncan, stayed at home with Mum. It became obvious that he wasn't just slow or lazy, but he was never going to be normal. He lived at home with my mum in our old house, even though I offered to buy them something else. They wouldn't have it. I should have visited more but I was totally caught up in my work and my exciting new life. I had a shit-hot flat in Edinburgh and I put them out of my mind and concentrated on having a good time. I barely slept for five years, flew all over the world, ate and drank and partied and womanised like it was the end of days.' Jasper's expression grew harder as if in disapproval of his old self. 'I had no idea what was going on back home. Later I found out the local kids made my brother's life hell. They jeered at him, threw stones, tormented him. He was just a bit of amusement for them, but it terrified him, he hated it. He retreated inside the house and became a total recluse.'

'Your poor brother,' she said.

'I know. I'd ring up and say come and see me. They'd always have a reason why not. When I went back, I'd let Mum talk me into meeting them at a pub or a cafe. I didn't mind, I hated that awful house.' Jasper pulled in a breath and released it on a long, sad sigh. He looked up at Alex with a wry smile. 'Well, I finally got round to visiting. I didn't let Mum put me off any longer. I'd been sending her money, plenty of it, so I just assumed she was fine. But she'd coped with the stress of looking after Duncan by shopping – nothing fancy, stuff from the market, the high street, online. But it had got completely out of control. The house was a disaster zone, packed to the gills with stuff. Duncan liked science fiction toys – spaceships and aliens and characters from films – and she'd bought him thousands of them.' Jasper hesitated. He couldn't look at Alex now, his gaze fixed on the table, his fingers knotted together. 'I mean, the house was packed. It was un-fucking-believable. They were climbing over it to get around. Drowning in it.'

Alex pictured it. 'Oh my God.'

'It took weeks to sort it all out. Mounds and mounds of

newspapers and magazines. An avalanche of stuff, some of it never opened or used – clothes, books, dolls, toys, hats, shoes, bottles, furniture, you name it – countless *things*.' Jasper shook his head slowly. 'I realised, of course, that my ma was suffering from a severe psychological condition, most likely as a result of looking after Duncan. I got them both out of there, and got her the support she needed. But something turned in my stomach when I saw that volume of useless objects and the piles and piles of rubbish and litter scarring everything. We chucked away skips full of it. It was one house in one small town in one country, and when I tried to multiply that to fill the world, my mind couldn't cope. I thought of the slums built on rubbish piles, the rivers and seas thick with it, the great pits of it being buried in the earth, and I felt with all my heart and soul that it had to stop.'

She nodded, seeing it with him, feeling an echo of what he must have felt.

'I hadn't really considered it before, how much useless tat there is in the world.' His eyes burned and he looked suddenly passionate. 'I don't care if the system needs us to buy endlessly, if the markets require more and more consumption. It has to stop, Alex! We have to do something about this! That house became a symbol to me of us all, of the world, being buried in that mountain of pointless, useless rubbish.'

'Yes, I see that.' She was moved by his intensity. It made her feel so angry and helpless when she saw the litter on the beach: the detritus of bottles, cans and packaging; the sloppy, wrinkled mess of abandoned plastic bags. 'I get it.'

'I wanted to do more. Once Mum and Duncan were sorted out, I decided to sell my part in the company. I already had enough money and I just couldn't go on with my old life. I needed change.'

'So that's how you ended up here?'

He nodded. 'I wanted to get away somewhere completely new. I saw this place advertised and I thought, maybe that's the answer. I was burned out, and didn't realise it. So I'm taking baby steps, you know? Baby steps. While I work it all out, find my purpose.'

Alex nodded. 'Yes. I understand. I hope you find it here.'

He gazed at her, solemn. 'You don't mind that I'm doing it here, in your old home?'

'Of course not. I'd love to see this place come alive.' She looked about. 'It has its stories, you know, not all of them happy.'

'I hope you'll tell me about it one day.' He smiled, looking more like his usual cheerful self. 'Now, shall we start hanging those beautiful baubles? I really want to see what they look like on the trees.'

She followed him out of the orangery, realising that he hadn't told her how Polly fitted into the story, or what she felt about his new start.

I don't know him well enough to ask. I'll just have to wait until he tells me.

'Here we are!' shouted Johnnie as he pulled the hired van to a halt in front of the rectory.

Nathan was wide-eyed. 'Is this really all ours?' Their house in town occupied a narrow slot in a long terrace of identical properties, all tall and thin to take up as little space as possible.

'Yes, for now,' Johnnie said.

Joe was already climbing out of the sliding side door. 'Come on, let's go and explore,' he said, his eyes on the expanse of garden surrounding the house. Nathan followed him. Bertie stayed in his seat, well belted in, and gazed out of the window, making vague chewing noises.

Johnnie turned to look at Netta. 'Well?'

'It's very pretty,' she said, then turned to look anxiously over her shoulder at the piles of boxes in the van. It had made sense to hire a vehicle big enough to take all the luggage they would need for such a long stay; even so, it was crammed with stuff. 'We should get unpacked. We'll make the beds, get Bertie sorted . . .'

Johnnie put a hand on her arm. 'Relax. We've got plenty of time. It's going to be okay. We're on holiday now, both of us. I don't have anything to do but look after you and the kids.'

'And support your father,' she reminded him swiftly.

'Of course. But you're my priority right now.'

She blinked at him as if doubting the sincerity of what he was saying. 'All right. But we can't sit here all day, can we?'

They got out, and Netta took Bertie inside while Johnnie started unloading, calling to the other two to come and help. By the time the boxes were out of the car, Netta had found the kettle and made everyone tea or squash, and put out biscuits.

'It's great, isn't it?' Johnnie asked, coming in breathless. 'Do you like it? I've sorted out the locks for Bertie's room, we can put up the temporary cameras later and I'll get the network going.'

Netta breathed out slowly. 'Yes, I do like it.'

'Great.' Johnnie felt a welling-up of hope. 'I just want us to take some time out, try and refocus ourselves.'

Busying herself with wiping down the surfaces, Netta said nothing for a moment, and then she said, 'You just have to realise that if we slow down and stop being frantic, then we might see things we don't want to see. You might have to face something unpleasant.'

'I'm prepared for that,' Johnnie said simply. 'I want this to work.'

Since that day on the road, when he'd been inches from death, his mindset had changed. Something about that near miss had made him realise that time was precious and life was fleeting. Alex's words about Netta's issues being something he could work on had stayed with him and he had started making a real effort to address them all. He had to save this marriage. The idea of him and Netta separating was dreadful, a world he didn't want to live in. He had spent too long building this life and this family to have it shattered back into a million pieces. The thought of Joe and Nathan suffering was more than he could stand. Whatever Netta wanted was worth it. But despite his best efforts, he couldn't seem to break through Netta's reserve. The chilliness still stood between them, like a brittle, transparent wall of ice.

'Okay.' Netta turned away. 'I'd better start unpacking. We've got a lot to do.'

Johnnie walked towards the market square in the town centre, where a local choir was singing carols around the Christmas tree, shops were open for business and everything glittered and sparkled with tinsel and lights.

We'll have to get sorted out for Christmas, Johnnie thought. But Netta had probably already done most of it. She usually discussed the children's presents with him, but she knew what they wanted, and did all the shopping for their extended family. She kept a box that she filled with stocking gifts throughout the year. The cards were written and posted by the start of December, and she usually managed the food and drink situation as well, although Johnnie did the actual cooking on the day. He liked to don the apron and chef's hat, and play the role of the provider.

So far so good in the new house.

Only a day in, but the twins liked the new place and were still giddy with the size of the garden, Bertie seemed settled and Netta was good-humoured, if still somewhat absent.

But this is weird – walking through town to the pub. I haven't done this since I was about nineteen.

Alex had called the previous day asking to meet up for a chat. It hadn't seemed politic to go out on the first night in the new place, but now here he was, striding through the winter darkness to his old haunt, not quite sure if the experience was a pleasant one or not.

He went into the pub, an old-fashioned place decorated with fishing nets and crab baskets. It was busy inside, the air heavy with the scent of mulled wine. Alex was already at a small table tucked away by the fireplace so he queued up for a drink and then went to join her.

'Thanks,' she said as he put a glass of mulled wine in front her. 'I'm driving, though.' She stood up to greet him with a kiss on the cheek.

'There won't be much alcohol in that, it's mostly apple juice and cinnamon. But don't drink it if you don't want it. I got it for the seasonal feel as much as anything.' He sat down, taking off his coat. 'How are you?'

'I'm okay.' She took a sip of the mulled wine and made a face. 'Yuck, you're right. I think I'll stick with my cup of coffee.' She sat back to regard Johnnie. 'Have you been round to Pa's house today? Only Sally wouldn't let me in yesterday and she said she'd text me when I could come over. But she hasn't been in touch.'

'Do you think she's forgotten?'

Alex shook her head. 'That's not like her.' She looked worried. 'My alarm is going off.'

'Ah.' Johnnie knew it was time to pay attention when Alex's alarm went off. All their lives, she'd been an excellent barometer of the state of Sally's moods. When Johnnie was unaware of a change in atmosphere, Alex would warn him that a storm was coming.

'But how do you know?' he would ask, mystified. 'It's like you're a clairvoyant or something.'

'I have no idea,' Alex would reply. 'I can just sense it. It's an aura around her that changes when she's angry or upset. The mystery to me is why you can't feel it when it's so bloody obvious.'

Now he said, 'What do you think the problem is?'

'I think it might have something to do with Mundo. Sally and I have actually been getting on quite well. But Mundo's been banging on about seeing you and me together; maybe he's been complaining about us to her and it's had an effect. I've been so busy I haven't sorted it out. Sally told me he's commuting up and down to London in any case.'

'Why does he want to see us?'

'The assets, Sally's future, inheritance. Typical Mundo concerns.'

Johnnie frowned. 'Right. I don't like the sound of that very much.'

'He came round to the Old Barn hoping to ambush us but you were out. I don't think he left very happy with me. Then Sally wouldn't let me in.'

Johnnie heard the note in his sister's voice that meant she felt panicked and under attack. It always happened when Sally turned on her for no obvious reason, leaving her flummoxed and trying to work out what she had done to offend.

Alex went on: 'I was thinking about it all yesterday, and then I was at Tawray and—'

Johnnie was surprised. 'You were at Tawray? Why?'

'The new owner has agreed to do the Christmas flowers.

And I suddenly felt it all coming back and that maybe Sally wasn't going to let us be with Pa and he might die without us there and—'

He heard the rising note of anxiety in her voice and put his hand out to her. 'Hey, calm down, it's okay. I can see you're worried, but what would Sally gain from shutting you out?'

'I know. She's been desperate to have me around up until now. She seems to think I'm the only one who understands what she's going through and who cares about Pa as much as she does. The nurse is fine, but she's strictly professional and when she's not on duty, she goes up to her room and watches telly. Sally's been lonely.'

Johnnie sipped his drink. 'But she's got her little friend with her now, hasn't she?'

Alex nodded. 'Mundo.'

Johnnie leaned towards her, lifting his shoulders in confusion. 'I mean, what's all this about assets and inheritance? The will is the will, it's all decided now. Until Pa actually dies, we have no idea what's in it. Sally is probably the only one who has a clue, if she and Pa even discussed it.'

'I just assumed everything would go to Sally, with maybe a bequest or some mementoes for us and the grandchildren. And Mundo too.'

'Yes. I don't like it.' Johnnie frowned. 'I agree with you, something's up.'

'What can we do?'

'See Mundo? Hear what he's got to say?'

Alex looked pensive. 'I suppose that's all we can do. And

I'll keep the pressure up on Sally – text her, call round. Are you going over?'

'I planned to take the children and Netta over tomorrow. They haven't seen Pa yet.'

They were both silent for a moment, thinking about how Sally might react to having three noisy boys in her well-ordered house, with Pa lying there ill.

'I could take Bertie for the morning, if you like,' Alex suggested. 'It might be easier if it's just the four of you the first time. Sally might work herself up into a bit of a state otherwise.'

Johnnie nodded. 'You're right. Well, if you could, that would be great. He's perfectly easy if you know how to deal with him. I hate the way Sally acts like he's about to murder her, or destroy the house, or both.'

Alex's gaze had slid away and she was staring across the pub, through the mass of bodies. Johnnie followed her gaze but couldn't see what she was looking at. She went completely still, then suddenly leapt to her feet and marched away, pushing through the crowd.

'Alex! Where are you going?' He got up to follow her, and saw that she was standing over a table on the other side of the room where two people were sitting. As he got closer, he saw that one of them was a petite blonde woman and the other his former brother-in-law.

'What the hell are you doing here, Tim?' Alex was exclaiming as he neared. 'Why aren't you at home with the girls?'

'They're perfectly all right,' Tim replied, but he looked

defensive. 'They were fine with us going out. The woman next door is sitting with them while they watch telly.'

'That's not what we agreed! You shouldn't leave them with someone I don't know!'

'She's my neighbour, she's completely reliable.'

'That's not the point! They shouldn't be on their own with a virtual stranger, not with everything they're going through right now with Pa so ill! He could die any minute.'

'Don't play that card, Alex,' Tim said in a bored tone. 'They're fine. They know how to call me if there's a problem.'

Johnnie had reached them now, and he could see that Alex was white with fury, her eyes blazing. Tim looked up at him.

'Hi there, Johnnie, how are you?'

'Fine.' He turned to his sister. 'Al, are you okay?'

'No! I'm furious!' she snapped.

'For crying out loud.' Tim rolled his eyes. 'It's a storm in a teacup.'

'That's what you think!' Alex shouted. 'It's actually really important to me. You said you would look after them, and you're in the pub! With . . . ' – she shot a scornful glance at the woman, who'd sat watching silently – '. . . her.'

'Excuse me, I do have a name!' Chloe said indignantly but Alex ignored her.

'It's not just that you're not looking after them,' Alex said, dropping her voice but retaining her tone of outrage. 'They're your daughters, it's your night to be with them. You only see them three nights a week. Why the hell would you rather be in a pub with your girlfriend than spending time with Scarlett and Jasmine?' Her eyes filled with tears and she looked on the brink of weeping. 'Why wouldn't you want to be with them?'

'He sees them plenty!' Chloe remarked.

'Shut up,' hissed Alex, turning furious eyes on her. 'This has nothing to do with you!'

Johnnie took her arm. He could see that she was on the edge of losing it. 'Come on, Alex, leave it now.'

She shook him off. 'I will not leave it! I'm not going away quietly, knowing that my girls are alone with a stranger in his house! Jasmine is only five!'

'They're fine!' Tim said loudly. 'They're absolutely fine. Do you honestly think I'd leave them if I thought they'd be in danger?' He picked up his glass and drained it. 'Look, we'll go home if it will make you feel better. We only popped out for half an hour anyway.'

Alex couldn't speak, almost choking on her outrage.

'Come on, come on.' Johnnie pulled her gently away. 'Leave him.'

Back at their table, Alex was shaking and furious, stammering out her anger at Tim.

Johnnie put a hand on her arm. 'Look, it's just possible that you're overreacting a tiny bit. I know he shouldn't have left them, but he's right, they're more than likely fine, watching some telly and perfectly happy.'

'It's not just that!' Alex said, pulling out a tissue and wiping her eyes. She looked over at her brother, agonised. 'Don't you understand? I can't bear it happening to them too!'

'What happening?'

'Their father . . . their father rejecting them, because he's got someone.'

'Oh.' Johnnie looked at her, understanding. When she saw Tim and Chloe, she also saw Pa and Sally. When Tim chose to leave the girls in order to spend time with Chloe, Alex felt the same pain she had when Pa chose Sally over her. Johnnie had seen it so often when they were growing up: Alex begging for Pa's attention only to find that he was focused on Sally instead. There had been school plays and concerts he hadn't turned up for because it clashed with Sally's bridge tournament or her charity gala. He hadn't gone to Alex's graduation because Sally had been ill that day and didn't want to be left alone. And Pa hadn't even walked her up the aisle at her wedding. Johnnie felt a sudden rush of anger, but instead of being directed at Sally, as it usually was, it was for Pa. *Why did you always, always let her down? No wonder she feels so desperate when she thinks Tim's doing the same.* The outrage she felt was a manifestation of the raw rejection she'd been dealing with all her life. He grabbed her hand and said, 'I get that, Alex, I really do. You were shoddily treated. Pa did that. I'm sorry.'

Alex hardly seemed to hear him. 'I can't bear it. This whole thing – Pa so ill, the girls being abandoned . . .' She blew her nose. 'I just don't understand why it all seems to be starting again.'

'What is?'

'You know what I mean, Johnnie! The pain. The pain of all of it. Mum. Pa. Sally.' She seemed to stumble as she said, 'And Mundo.' She stared at Johnnie, agonised. 'All of it.'

Johnnie stared back, everything churning inside him. 'Yes. That's why we need to find out the truth about Mum. It's the only way to understand it.'

'Is it too late?' she asked, her eyes red. 'What if Pa never comes back, and can never tell us?'

'I don't know.' He shook his head and smiled wanly. 'I guess he just has to get better.'

Chapter Twenty-Six

1989

Julia stared with joy at a row of three big green plastic tubs that sat in the corner of the kitchen garden, tucked against the warm brick wall.

'That's fantastic. How does it work, Colin?'

'It's very simple, but you have to keep your ingredients right, or it won't the do the job.' Colin, who had worked in the gardens at Tawray for years, as a boy helping his father and now as a man, had become her partner in crime. She loved his broad Cornish burr and the way he seemed to know everything about gardening. She was also glad he seemed to want to pass his knowledge on to her. Colin lifted the black lid off the top of one of the tubs and looked into its insides. 'You want to put in your organic matter – kitchen waste of all kinds except meat, your weeds, leaves and grass clippings – and you also need a bit of roughage and something dry, like old newspaper and cardboard. You can add coffee grinds if you've got them. Stick it all in the top and wait. You'll have to wait a while at first, but then you'll soon have a good supply of compost you can take out of the bottom, you see? And you can keep the three of them running on rotation, so as you empty the third one, the first should be about ready again.' He smiled at her, pushing his hat back on his head. 'It's satisfying when you get them all going right. These tubs will keep your flowers and veggies going beautifully.'

'That sounds marvellous.' Julia peered inside the nearest tub but there was nothing within that gave any indication that it was anything more than a big container. 'How does it turn into compost, though?'

'It's mostly because the heat increases in here, through the plastic, and speeds up the rot. And if it's not too hot, you get your worms as well, squeezing it through their bellies and making it all rich and lovely.'

'Rich and lovely.' She savoured the words.

'The plants love it, it feeds them. It's wonderful for them here – the air is full of minerals from the sea.' Colin grinned. 'Bring back some seaweed from the beach when you go down, and chuck that in the tubs as well. You'll make it really special then.'

'Oh yes,' Julia said, then her eye was caught by a movement over by the artichoke patch. 'Whoops, there goes Johnnie!'

She raced over and swooped him up from where he was about to stumble into the tall plants, and kissed him. 'You're filthy, aren't you? Have you been eating soil again?'

Johnnie babbled about the garden and showed her his dirty hands. Soil was smeared across his face and sat in lumps in the soft strands of his fair hair.

'Never mind,' Julia said, bouncing him onto her hip. 'We'll clean you up inside.' She caught a glimpse of the time on her watch. 'Crumbs, I had no idea it was so late. Colin, I have to go in! I'll come back tomorrow. I'm going to be busy with a guest for now.'

'Right you are,' Colin replied, untroubled. 'Whenever is fine.'

Julia pulled Johnnie to her and headed back to the house, checking on the progress of everything as she went. The rhythms of the garden suited her, she found. Things had to be done, there was plenty to keep her busy, but the needs of plants were fairly slow. What couldn't be done today could be done tomorrow or even at the end of the week, and it would all still be all right. It balanced her, knowing that this calmer, more sedate state of affairs existed alongside Johnnie's intense schedule. He needed to be fed and looked after constantly, and if his needs weren't answered, it could be disastrous. She knew well the frantic screams of a boy hungry for his dinner which was not ready. And David's work life moved at a similarly frantic pace, hours and minutes accounted for and considered vital to the smooth running of operations. Julia felt it too, when he told her about his day. They'd recently had a car phone put into his Vauxhall, and he phoned her from it at odd moments when he was stuck behind a parade in Horse Guards or in the knots of traffic in Hyde Park. Just hearing about what he was doing and would do in the course of a day put knots in her stomach.

She'd stumbled by accident on gardening as a way to

counter her anxiety and to repel that great invisible hand at her back pushing her through life and into the dark. She and Johnnie had been outside so that he could get some fresh air – he'd just started walking, and his snail's pace meant she had time to look – really look – at what was going on around her. Then she got talking to Colin when he was mulching the roses and the next moment she was helping him.

Before long, she was out there whenever possible, sometimes with Johnnie and at other times without him, when he was napping inside. She felt certain that it was going to help in the next stage of her life, the one she had been preparing for over the course of a couple of months now.

It was almost pleasant to be out of the warm May sunshine and in the cool of the house, Johnnie babbling away on her hip as she went to the kitchen. Mrs Petheridge had put out Johnnie's lunch on his plastic plate, and Julia slipped him into the highchair and tied on his bib.

'Is this the chicken casserole I made last week, Jackie?' she asked.

Mrs Petheridge nodded. 'Yes, it is. And very nice it smells too. Your lunch is ready as well. I've laid it in the morning room like you asked.'

'Thanks. How was the asparagus?'

'The best I've seen for a while.'

'Oh good.' Julia was pleased. She had grown it herself under Colin's direction and Mrs Petheridge had promised to make it into the most delicious quiche. She started feeding Johnnie. 'And is the guest room ready?'

'Yes, it is. All done.'

'Thank you.'

The next moment, as Johnnie chomped down another spoonful of his lunch, she heard the doorbell chime loudly. She put down the spoon. 'Would you mind taking over? I'll be back in a second.'

Hurrying to the front door, she threw it open and there on the doorstep stood Sally, pretty and fresh in a pink and white checked sundress and white-framed sunglasses, her fair hair loose around her shoulders.

'Julia!' she cried and they hugged. 'I'm so happy to see you!'

'Me too. Come in!' Julia's gaze slid downwards to the unmistakable bulge in the front of Sally's dress. 'Oh!' She looked up at her friend, astonished. 'Sally, are you pregnant?'

Sally took off her sunglasses, looking sheepish. 'I know,' she said. 'I should have said. I . . .' Her cheeks became stained the same colour pink as the squares on her dress: rosy and demure. 'I just . . . I didn't quite know what to say.'

Julia led her into the hall. 'Not because of me, I hope! You know I have no problem at all with pregnancy.'

'Well . . .' Sally's gaze slid away again and she looked more embarrassed. 'It was partly that. And partly because . . . obviously . . . I'm not married.'

Julia burst out laughing. 'Oh Sally, as if that would bother me! I don't mind in the least! Have you had some stick for it? I'm sorry if you have. Wait, let's go and see Johnnie, and then I want to hear all about it. You are a dark horse, though. Fancy not saying anything! I'm almost offended.'

They went through to coo over Johnnie and Julia finished

giving him his lunch. They didn't talk about Sally's pregnancy in front of Mrs Petheridge, but once Johnnie had been put down for his lunchtime nap and they were on their own in the morning room with their lunch, Julia said, 'Well, I think you'd better tell me all about it. Is it Arthur's baby?'

Arthur had been Sally's boyfriend for two years now, and Julia had been expecting to hear any day that Sally and he were engaged.

Sally pushed some asparagus quiche around the plate with her fork before saying quietly, 'Arthur isn't going to have anything to do with the baby. We've finished, you see. We finished before I knew I was pregnant.'

'Oh Sally! I'm sorry.' Julia felt dreadful. This was not what she'd been expecting. 'But shouldn't you tell him? Doesn't he want to be involved?'

'He doesn't want to be involved in the slightest. He's not interested.'

'Are you sure?'

'Absolutely certain. So I made up my mind to do this without him.' Sally looked suddenly defiant. 'My parents wanted me to get rid of it, of course. My mother was quite horrible and said I'd never get a husband if I had another man's baby – used goods and all that – and my father said no one wanted a cuckoo in the nest. But I can't do it, Julia. I've always wanted a baby and I just can't kill this one because I'm not married to the father. The way I see it, Arthur and I would have split up at some point in any case, so I'm sparing the baby that experience. I think divorce is a lot more painful than simply not knowing one's father. So I'm doing it alone.'

'You're so brave. And you look marvellous. You're glowing,' Julia said, her voice heartfelt. 'I'm delighted for you, if this is what you want.'

'Thank you.' Sally smiled. 'I'm excited. Only two months to go now.'

A shadow passed over Sally's face and Julia said, 'What is it? Is something wrong?'

'Well, I can't say my employers are thrilled about it. In fact, they want me to leave in a month.'

Julia gasped. 'Can they do that?'

'I'm afraid they can. They're not saying it's because of my pregnancy, of course, but they're a couple of old dinosaurs. They clearly disapprove heartily and think there's no way I either could or should keep working with a baby.' Sally sighed. 'And I don't know if I could in any case. A nanny is going to be out of the question on my salary.'

'What are you going to do?'

'I'll move back to my parents'.' Sally smiled again but it was tight-lipped this time. 'That will be fun, I'm sure. I'll be looked after as long as I can take the daily moral lectures about what a disappointment I am and how I've blighted the poor child's life by not being married.' She sighed. 'Anyone would think it's the nineteen-fifties or something.'

Julia blinked at her, her mind whirring. 'Don't be too downhearted. Perhaps we can think of something.' She glanced at the bottle of Sancerre chilling in the cooler on the table, which had been meant to set off the quiche perfectly. 'I don't suppose you'll be having any of that now.'

'No. But you go ahead, I don't mind.'

'No. I won't either.' Julia felt herself redden slightly.

Sally gave her a quizzical look. 'Julia . . . do you have something to tell me?'

'Well, I was going to mention it but your news rather took precedence.'

Sally smiled. 'So you're pregnant.'

'Yes.' Julia felt oddly undercut. She'd thought her news would create more of a sensation, but Sally had sprung a much bigger surprise.

'That's wonderful too.' Sally carefully ate a mouthful of salad and then said, 'I just hope you've made the right decision. Considering what happened last time.' She looked earnestly at Julia. 'I'm only thinking of you.'

'I know, I appreciate that.'

'Did David put pressure on you?'

'No!' Julia thought about how the decision had been made. They'd done it together, although it had been David who had said it was time to think about another baby. Left to herself, she would have been content with Johnnie. She could understand, though, that a brother or sister would be best for him. David had said she could do it, and she was sure she could. The nightmares that had consumed her seemed so remote now, and hardly real. This time she would be able to stay in control and manage the whole thing rationally, knowing the outcome would be positive. She'd had a baby now. It was fine to do it again. David had said she could, and she was sure she could. 'I want to do it,' she said firmly. 'Honestly.'

'Just be careful. We don't want you back in hospital.'

'No. But that won't happen. I've got Johnnie now.'

'How far along are you?'

'Oh, just at the start. Eight weeks.'

Sally smiled, her expression merry. 'Isn't this fun? We're both pregnant together! Our babies can be friends, won't that be lovely?'

'Lovely!'

But Julia felt obscurely guilty that she had David and this house, and beautiful Johnnie, while poor Sally was all alone.

'I think there must be something we can do for her,' Julia said to David when he came back from London for the weekend. Sally had stayed for a couple of days' holiday with Julia but she had not overlapped with David, heading back to town on the Friday morning for an antenatal appointment at the hospital.

'She sounds determined to do it by herself,' David said. They were sitting on the terrace after dinner, watching the sun sinking slowly into the distant sea. David had a cigar and was sitting downwind of Julia so as not to turn her stomach with the smell. She couldn't face any tobacco when she was pregnant.

'I know, but she isn't looking forward to going back to her horrible parents at all. They're so nasty and judgemental.'

'Does she have a choice? It might be the best thing with a small baby, so she has help with it.'

'It sounds miserable to me.' Julia sipped her tea and shivered slightly in the cool breeze. It was still very early to be sitting outside. David saw it.

'You're cold. Shall I get your coat?'

'No, no, we can go inside in a bit. I'll be fine.' She hesitated, then decided to come out with the scheme that had been cooking in her mind all day. 'I think we should ask Sally to live here, with me.'

David looked over in surprise. 'What?'

'Think about it, David, it makes complete sense. Sally and I can be pregnant together. It's not as though we haven't got the room, because we have. Tons of it. And there's Mrs Petheridge and Hayley to look after us as well. It's completely obvious and I can only wonder why you haven't already suggested it.' She thrust out her lower lip obstinately. 'Don't try and tell me it's not a good idea, because I know it's a brilliant idea and that's that.'

'I don't think it's a bad idea,' David replied, laughing. 'Though I can see that you wouldn't allow it if I did. I actually think it's a stroke of genius. I should have thought about it myself when she told me.'

'Told you?'

David looked suddenly uncomfortable but quickly recovered and said lightly, 'Yes, she told me in London. About the baby.'

Julia stared. 'You already knew? And you didn't say anything?'

'Well, she asked me not to – so that she could tell you herself.'

'But when did you see her?'

David shrugged. 'I often see her in London, you know that.'

'Really?' *Do I know that?*

'Of course. She works just near the palace and I see her occasionally for lunch, just like you used to when we lived in Kensington. That will all stop once she gives up the agency, I'm sure. So of course I noticed that she was having a baby.'

'Noticed, but didn't tell me.'

David looked faintly exasperated. 'I explained that, she didn't want me to. She wanted to tell you herself. Besides . . .'

Julia couldn't help feeling hurt and affronted. She'd been deceived and made a fool of. She felt stupid. 'Besides what?'

'She was worried, and so was I. We were both wary of what might happen if you were exposed to pregnancy again. This is before you showed me how brave you are by deciding to have another baby yourself. The last thing we wanted to do was trigger another attack.'

Julia looked away. Perhaps they were right. But something about the whole thing made her feel wary.

'And . . .' – David took a puff on his cigar, letting the wind take the long trail of grey smoke as he exhaled it – 'don't forget, I kept your secret from her too.'

'Yes.' She remembered how unsurprised Sally had been by the revelation that she, Julia, was also pregnant. 'Yes, I suppose you did.'

'So having her here is an excellent idea. The sooner, the better, I say. Call her tomorrow and find out what she has to say.'

Sally thought it was a very good plan. So good that she made arrangements with her employers to leave at once, a suggestion they were only too happy to go along with, bearing in mind the advanced state of Sally's pregnancy, which wasn't looking good to the clients of the agency, especially in the absence of a wedding ring.

Sally's aunt, too, was relieved to be free of her heavily expectant niece and the looming threat of a baby in the house, and promptly promised Sally's room to a young guards officer looking for lodgings.

'So I'm afraid you may be stuck with me for a while,' Sally said, arriving in her little car and only just fitting behind the steering wheel. 'I really don't have anywhere to go now, except my parents.'

'You're welcome for as long as you need, you know that.' Julia kissed her cheek, and put a hand on Sally's swollen stomach. It felt tight and full under her palm. 'Gosh, you're nearly there, aren't you?'

'Just a few weeks now. Apparently the bump will drop a little and then we'll know the baby's engaged and on its way.'

Julia smiled, suddenly rueful. She hadn't felt any such pleasure in her body's ripeness when Johnnie was on the way. The only thing she could cling to in the torrent of confusion and revulsion was that she wouldn't have to give birth. A chime of those feelings seemed to echo across time and sound in her ears. She quietened it down instantly. She didn't want to let that happen to her again. *It won't. I forbid it.*

'You don't have much with you,' Julia remarked, looking at Sally's small overnight bag.

'David said he'd bring the rest; his car is so much bigger than mine.'

'Yes, of course it is. Now come on. Let's get you settled.'

Sally took over the main guest room, handy for the large bathroom next door, and when Julia popped her head in to see how she was getting on, she was impressed at how quickly Sally had made it her own. The furniture had been slightly rearranged to make it feel cosier, and lacy cushions decorated the two small armchairs. Her white candlewick bedspread covered the bed, along with some floral cushions, and the dressing table was neatly laid out with her brushes, potions and bottles of scent.

'All I need is a cot,' she said cheerfully.

'You'll want it in here, I suppose.' Julia looked about. 'You can get a Moses basket next to the bed quite nicely.'

'Yes, that will work,' Sally said. 'But only for the first few weeks. Then I thought the baby could share with Johnnie.'

'Really?' Julia was surprised. 'Don't you want the baby with you?'

'I don't think so, not after it's strictly necessary. Once I've got them on the bottle and sleeping most of the night, I'd rather they were in the nursery like a normal baby.'

'Yes,' Julia said uncertainly. She hadn't thought about having Sally's baby in with Johnnie. But, she supposed, it could do no harm.

Sally turned and hugged her hard, her bump pressing against Julia. 'This is so lovely, Julia! We'll have such fun together. Thank you so much for having me here.'

Julia felt warm and happy. 'Yes, we will. Lots and lots of fun.'

Sally settled in very quickly and soon Julia couldn't imagine what life had been like without her. She was wonderful with Johnnie, acting almost like a second mother to him, taking him for walks, putting him down for naps and always singing and chatting to him.

'He's an angel,' she would say to Julia, 'and he looks just like his dada too. I hope my little one is as good as Johnnie is.'

'It's bound to be,' Julia said. 'Arthur was pretty good-natured, wasn't he?'

Sally shrugged. 'Yes, he never frightened the horses, let's put it that way. But it's no guarantee, is it?'

They got everything ready for the new arrival and sorted out the transfer of Sally's care to a new set of midwives and a new hospital. The closer her due date came, the more nervous Julia felt of the responsibility of getting Sally to the hospital at the right time, but Sally's own serenity helped. Nothing seemed to faze her. She was quite convinced that everything would go off without a hitch and that calmed Julia down, even though she woke sometimes in the night with a violent sense that things were about to go horribly wrong. She would be breathless and sweating, recalling how useless she had been the day her mother had needed her, and how awful, how gruesome it had been. In one terrible nightmare, it was the same as it had been with Mummy and the frightful sight on the floor, but this time Mummy had Sally's dead-white face, and it was Sally's terrified eyes staring into hers and Sally's hands reaching out to her, red with blood. Julia had been unable to sleep for the rest of the night, shaking and afraid.

'I'm going to be fine,' Sally would declare. 'And I've half a mind to check in to the maternity ward early, so I'm on the spot when it all starts.'

'I don't think they let you do that,' Julia said doubtfully.

'I'll talk them round! Just you see.'

Julia said half guiltily, 'I'm sorry, Sally, I know you don't have anyone else, but I don't think I'm up to going to the hospital with you. To keep you company for the birth, I mean.'

Sally looked astonished that she'd even considered it. 'Don't be silly, why on earth should you? I'll be fine on my own. I'll have a midwife and doctors on hand. I'm fully intending to have one of those epi-things in the back so I don't feel anything. My dream birth is to be reading Jilly Cooper with a nice of cup of tea while everyone else is busy at the business end.'

As it was, Julia didn't have to worry. When Sally went into labour early one morning, she was so calm she didn't tell anyone about it, and when she did, David was there to drive her slowly and carefully to the local hospital.

Julia waited anxiously at home, while David called every few hours with any updates he managed to glean from the midwives, and at ten o'clock that evening, he rang to say that Sally had safely delivered a baby boy.

'That's wonderful!' Julia said, overjoyed. 'Is he all right?'

'Fine. A thumping great boy too, very healthy. Sally's fine, it was all very straightforward, just as she said it would be. I've seen her, and she's blooming. I'm going to come home now. Sally will be in for a few days at least, I should think. If there's any soup or something going, I'd be very chuffed – the food here is atrocious.'

'Okay, I'll heat something up. Oh, and David, does she have a name for the baby?'

'Yes, she wants to call him Edmund.'

'Edmund. Yes, that's nice. Little Edmund.' Julia sighed. 'The happiest days are when babies are born.'

'Yes,' David said. 'Yes, they are.'

Chapter Twenty-Seven

Sally's return and the arrival of the baby was a joyful occasion and Julia was nothing but delighted to have them back, both healthy and almost rudely blooming. The baby was fat, much larger than Johnnie had been at the same age, and had a pair of crystal-clear blue eyes. He also had a strong pair of lungs and bellowed out his desire for food every three hours on the dot, whereupon Sally would let him suck down a bottle of creamy formula milk and he'd sleep, satisfied.

'I couldn't do the breast thing,' she explained to Julia. 'I tried but it didn't work.'

'Thank goodness for bottles then,' Julia replied. 'It certainly makes him sleep well.'

'It's heavier in the stomach, or something.' Sally looked curiously at Edmund. 'I think that's what – who cares, if it helps him sleep!'

She was a hands-off mother in some ways, wanting to get the baby into the nursery as soon as possible, and onto a strict routine of naps, walks and meals. But she also wanted only the best for her boy, and soon parcels and packages of all sorts were being delivered from London: beautiful baby clothes, handmade toys and crisp white linen for his cot.

'It's just that I think quality matters,' Sally would say gravely when another expensive little outfit appeared. 'And I also think he really notices! He's got very high standards.'

Julia felt disloyal laughing about this behind Sally's back, but she couldn't help it. She told David all about the various standards that Edmund had. 'Very high for someone of less than six weeks,' she said, giggling. 'He doesn't like plastic toys, nylon or outfits that are too garish. He does like the colour mauve, and anything with cats on it. He's on the fence about pirates – bit violent – but we'll see how he goes with that one. Beatrix Potter is the clear favourite so far, original Frederick Warne editions if possible, obviously.'

David laughed too. 'I have a feeling he's going to be spoiled.'

'You could be right.'

Julia started calling the baby Mundo, short for Edmund, but also as a private joke with David. Mundo meant 'world' in Spanish, and it was quite clear that he was going to be Sally's entire world from now on. She worried constantly that he might be too cold and was always wrapping him in layers of coats and blankets; or she was nervous about his insides working properly and she inspected his nappies with a forensic interest before throwing them away. She hated that he might be unhappy; if he cried, she would do anything to soothe him.

'Mundo is going to be a handful if she goes on like this,' Julia remarked, but that wouldn't be her problem. He was still so tiny. By the time he became a toddler, Sally would have made other living arrangements for the two of them.

In the meantime, Johnnie found a new baby in the house a strange addition to his life, and he was quieter for a while, and much more clingy than he had been. For a period he couldn't bear to be away from Julia, and cried all the time, begging to be picked up. So she took him out to the garden with her and the two of them would spend happy hours together, Julia digging, weeding and planting, and Johnnie making mud pies and collecting snails or stones or whatever took his fancy.

While things were outwardly harmonious, Julia tried to push away the growing sense of unease she was feeling. After her last experience of talking to the doctor and having her concerns dismissed so easily, she hadn't even considered asking about her options for a Caesarean, and no one so far at her appointments had mentioned it, so she was steeling herself to manage the ordeal of childbirth that must, inevitably, be her lot. The fact that Sally had had such an easy birth and a healthy baby was a cause of pleasure for her, and yet at the same she had an awful feeling that Sally had somehow got all the luck and that meant there was none left over for her. She was doomed to agony and disaster.

Don't be so bloody stupid, she told herself crossly, when she woke in the night, afraid. *Of course she didn't take all the luck. And anyway, your baby isn't due for months. Plenty of time for the luck to refill, even if that were true. Which it isn't.*

But as the weeks went by and the pregnancy inside her became more certain, and she passed into her second trimester, she felt the fluttering of bad feelings and dark thoughts flitting past her conscious mind like bats swooping in the twilight. The baby was growing. She was past the time when it could disappear easily in a clot of blood and a stomach ache. Now she was for it again, in that horrible dilemma of losing each way, if it lived or if it died.

She found herself, quite suddenly, repelled by food again.

Why am I doing this? she asked, as, despite everything in her protesting, she went to the downstairs loo, bent over the old wooden throne seat and threw up her lunch. She could not explain and she could not stop it. The more she saw how happy and normal Sally was, the more inadequate and condemned she felt, and the more she kept her darkness to herself.

If it doesn't get any worse than this, then that's okay, she told herself. *If it does, I'll tell David. I'll tell him and I'll get some help.*

But she was determined to show him that this time she was going to be all right. The thought of birth still filled her with mind-spinning fear but she dealt with that simply by refusing to think about it. The nightmares, unpreventable, that came to her when she slept were frightful: her body bursting open; a baby of hideous deformity; a dog or a snake or a calf emerging, slimy and blue.

Just dreams, she told herself. *Sally did it, with no fuss. She did it, and I can do it too.*

'I won't be long, love!' sang out the hairdresser as she went past Julia, who sat waiting on one of the plastic seats by the door. 'I'm just waiting for Mrs Morton's do to set, and we can start on you. Have you got a cup of tea?'

'I'm fine without one, thanks.' Julia picked up a magazine from the pile of well-thumbed, tired old things next to her. Johnnie was at home with Sally and Mundo and she'd taken a few hours to herself to get her hair cut, thinking she would try out a new salon in town. But most of the local ladies had had the same idea, and the place was packed.

She looked at the cover of the magazine, intrigued. It was the kind she never saw, except when in a hairdresser's or dentist's waiting room, full of gossip and true-life stories. The front cover had a picture of the latest royal event: the Queen Mother's eighty-ninth birthday. Inside, the article was lavishly illustrated with pictures of the gathering of the clan outside Clarence House for the traditional appearance and collection of cards and flowers.

There she is.

In a neat, narrow-waisted blue summer dress, with big splodgy flowers in pink and yellow; large gold and pearl earrings nestled into fluffy blonde hair; blue eyes made bluer by the dress. She was standing to the side, as if happy to cede centre stage to the main attraction of the little old lady in the lavender hat. She was smiling, apparently at ease, her beige-suited husband by her side.

They look happy enough.

She noticed suddenly that in one of the pictures she could see David, just back through the open gate of Clarence House, unobtrusive in a black suit, almost out of shot. But his eyes were fixed on the figure in the blue dress with a fervent intensity she'd never seen before.

'I have to look out for her,' David had said lately. 'I can't shake the feeling she's in danger.'

'Danger? But she's got bodyguards, hasn't she? Police detectives?'

'Yes, but it only takes a moment. Ever since that nasty little pervert jumped out at her in Northumberland, I haven't felt easy.'

She remembered him telling her about the incident: some sex pest who leapt out of the crowd to get a hug and had quickly been wrestled away. 'You told me he said he didn't mean any harm.'

'Maybe not. But he touched her. He could have had a knife or a gun. Then it would be a different story.'

'David,' she'd said soberly. 'That's not your job, you know. You organise the diary, you're not in charge of saving her life. There are plenty of other people to do that.'

He'd shrugged. 'You're right. She just seems so vulnerable at the moment.'

Julia said nothing. After a moment he said, 'Maybe I'm getting too sucked into the whole thing. Perhaps I ought to think of doing something else.'

'You've been saying that for years, and you never do.'

She gazed at his image now, caught forever in the August sunshine, staring at the back of that fluffy blonde head, and felt a twist of jealousy. All week he was in that other life of his; only at the weekends did he come back home. All week at the beck and call of his boss, smoothing her life out for her, supporting her, keeping her company . . .

I won't look anymore.

She flicked the page over, getting away from the article, not wanting to see those pictures. Exasperated, she tossed the magazine down and picked up another, opening it at random. It was some kind of shock-horror rag and after a second's bewilderment, she realised she was looking at a photograph of a huge exposed belly pictured from below, its owner's face looming over it. In the centre of the belly was a kind of terrible, weeping wound, a purple puckering that glistened and shone. What on earth was it?

Her eyes went to the headline.

My stomach started leaking through my Caesarean scar.

Julia gasped, going ice cold all over. Her eyes flicked down over the text but she found it difficult to absorb, with the giddy, sick feeling in her stomach and the loud buzzing in her head. She only managed to glean that one day this woman had woken up to find a fistula had formed from her bowel and pushed its way through the delicate skin of her scar, leaking out the contents.

Julia stood up, dropping the magazine to the floor. She started to walk to the door.

'Are you all right?' the receptionist asked. 'You're next, dear.'

'I have to go,' Julia said in a blank voice, and she walked off in a daze, oblivious to everything around her. All she heard was the scream of terror in her head.

*

How did life change so suddenly from one minute to the next? How could something as inane as an article in a cheap shock-and-scandal magazine change her life so rapidly and so thoroughly? It shouldn't be possible and yet it was.

A switch had been flicked and all the ghouls and horrors that she'd been studiously ignoring were suddenly there, illuminated in all their vile, visceral contortions, showing her the stuff of her terrors in full technicolour.

I'm going to die. Any moment, something terrible is going to happen to me. My scar is going to burst open, the baby will come out, my intestines will leak out, all the gore and the blood will spill everywhere.

She was in the car, starting the engine to drive home. As she went, she clutched one arm across her belly, which had swollen as she settled into the second trimester, as though she was afraid that at any moment she would have to hold in her own stomach. A flutter inside her made her shout out loud, certain it was all beginning. The car veered over into the opposite lane and she wrenched it back, one-handed.

The terror was almost too much to stand. It occurred to her to drive to the clifftops and take the car over the edge in order to end this frightful situation, but she couldn't think clearly enough to work out how to get there or how to find a place where she could get access to the edge. The confusion was too much to fight against, so instead she did only what she could do and drove home to Tawray.

When she got there, she was gibbering and shaking, clutching her stomach. All the while another voice in her head was telling her she was being stupid and that she shouldn't listen to the cacophony of doom, but it was all too raw and too terrible. She stumbled up to her room, not stopping to find Sally or minding about where Johnnie was, and when she found the dark peace of her bedroom, she climbed under the sheets of her bed and lay there shivering violently, despite the summer heat.

She was already grieving for what had gone: she'd lost her peace of mind in one extraordinary second. She didn't know if or how she would ever get it back.

When Sally knocked on the door a little later, Julia was strangely calm again. The fact that her stomach had not yet burst through her scar was helping her to grasp on to some small piece of normality, but she felt dead inside, numb and beaten. All she was sure of was that something pulsed deep within her, with its own beating heart and its own will, and it wanted her dead.

She climbed out of bed and went to the door. 'Yes?'

'Are you all right? We didn't know you'd come back until we saw the car.'

'Yes.'

'Don't you want to see Johnnie? He's going to have his tea in a moment.'

'No.' She pulled each word out of the slurry of her mind with the greatest effort.

'Julia, open the door, please.'

Julia tried to work out whether she wanted to open the door or not, but the effort was too much so she simply obeyed.

The expression on Sally's face told her that it was obvious something was amiss. 'What's happened? Is the baby all right?'

'Yes, yes. I'm fine.' Julia could hardly summon up the energy to speak. 'I'm just very tired, that's all. I have to sleep. Can you look after Johnnie for me?'

'Yes.' Sally was frowning, not sure if Julia was simply tired or if it was something more extreme than that.

'Thanks. I'll be better tomorrow.'

She shut the door and went back to her bed.

Julia managed to get up the next morning, but she was still consumed by the lifeless, draggy feeling of the previous day. When she got downstairs, Sally was already up with Johnnie and Edmund, the baby on his bottle in her arms and Johnnie flinging porridge around his highchair and sometimes into his mouth.

'Julia, are you all right? I was just coming to check on you. Are you ill?'

Julia shook her head. 'I'm fine,' she said and tried to force out a smile.

'Do you want some coffee?'

Julia felt a swirl of nausea and shook her head. 'Nothing, thank you. Listen, can you help me with Johnnie? I need to do some gardening today.'

'Yes, of course.' Sally frowned. 'Are you sure you're okay?'

'Yes. But I have to get to the garden. Sorry.'

All day long she worked manically, feeling the calm return as long as she was in the garden, dealing with the weeds, tending to the flowers, harvesting the vegetables, turning the compost heaps or emptying the bins, squashing the bugs or collecting snails. Sally brought Johnnie out to play in the morning and again in the afternoon but she seemed to sense that something in Julia required isolation and the release of manual labour to help her get back on track.

As soon as she came inside, she felt the darkness drop on her, the terrors of the approaching birth and the compulsion to hurt herself. She understood she had changed but she simply couldn't help it. She was hanging on by her fingernails, and she knew it.

David came home a day earlier than expected and Julia suspected that Sally had phoned him and told him that all was not well. He looked strained and pale, worry all over his face.

They went upstairs together and lay a long time on the bed. David put his arms around her, and stroked her hair as she lay pressed close to him, pulling comfort from the warmth of his body and the beating of his heart and his breath against her head.

'Julia, are you getting ill again?'

I don't want to let you down. You don't deserve it. 'No,' she said.

'You could go back to hospital, you know. That would be fine, if it's best for you.'

'I don't want to do that.' She meant it. The safety of the hospital was enticing, and she remembered the blissful feeling of all responsibility being lifted from her, but the thought of leaving Johnnie and the garden was too terrible. The only

two things that gave her life meaning. *And David, of course.*
That was what made this different from the last time. She
didn't want to leave now, she had too much to stay for. But
those gruesome sights in her head, the compulsion to get rid
of what was in her, the fear of what lay ahead . . .

'We haven't really talked about the birth,' David said
gently. 'If you need to have an elective Caesarean, we should
start the process now.'

'I . . .' A vile sick feeling kicked in her stomach. 'I don't
know if I can have a Caesarean.'

He pulled away from her. 'What? But last time you were
so very frightened of giving birth.'

'I still am. But Sally did it. I should be able to do it.'

'You're not Sally. She has nothing to do with it. You have
to do what's right for you.' His blue eyes were so frank, so
determined. David knew best and he wanted the best for her.

'So you think I should have a Caesarean?'

'Yes, I do! It worked last time.'

She wanted to tell him that if she had another operation,
she was convinced she'd wake up with her insides leaking
out, but that sounded so ridiculous she couldn't bring herself
to do it. He would bat it away, tell her she was being stupid.
He didn't know it could happen, that it was a real thing. He
hadn't seen that picture.

'All right, if you think so,' she said helplessly, and he
seemed happy with that.

Julia knew the darkness was descending on her. It didn't
mean that she loved David and Johnnie any less desperately,

but that the feelings she was battling had become so strong that she had to turn all her resources inwards simply to stay alive. Her great fear now, besides that of the approaching birth and the realisation that the solution of a Caesarean birth had been taken from her, was that she might lose this battle.

Her anxieties returned in double measure but now with a new twist. Even though her scar was nothing more than a thin silvery line below her stomach, she was afraid that it would become infected and she cleaned it compulsively every day, graduating from soap and water to disinfectant to a solution of bleach. Her hands too had to be clean, and she could no longer go into the garden in case she caught something from the germ-laden soil all around. She imagined spores of some kind, minute wriggling worms that flew under her clothes, found the scar and burrowed in, head first, to infect her. The only thing that had been her consolation and salvation was now taken away from her.

Julia knew that David and Sally were talking about her, that they were worried by her state of mind. Her insistence that nothing was wrong was soon done away with. They all knew that the illness was back, as strong as ever.

'I don't want to go back to hospital,' she told David when they were able to talk about it. She couldn't look at him, though. The worry and pain in his eyes were too much to bear.

They were sitting together in the bedroom, the curtains drawn against the bright day outside, where she felt safe from infection, despite the stifling heat.

'They can help you there,' David said. 'They did it last time.'

'No.' Julia shook her head. 'It's different. There's Johnnie now. If we get them involved, they might take him away from us.'

From his worried frown, David had not considered this. 'Would they? Are you sure?'

'They might. Or they might never let me out.' She wanted to hold his hand but couldn't be sure that he'd washed it, so she made a vague gesture towards him. 'We can't risk it, we just can't.'

He studied her for a moment and saw that she was getting agitated. 'Yes, all right. But if it gets bad, Julia, if you want to kill yourself or hurt the baby, you won't have a choice.'

'I don't want to hurt the baby!' she cried in torment.

'All right, all right! I understand.'

She started to cry, twisted up by the knowledge that she didn't want to hurt the baby, but she might not be able to help it if the terror got too great. *I'll do everything I can to force myself to be all right. I will tell him if it gets too bad.*

David said gently, 'I'm saving up my leave just in case you need me here later. Sally will stay with you until then. She knows everything, Julia, she'll look after you. And I'm only a few hours away.'

She nodded. 'Yes.'

He smiled at her, though his eyes were sad. 'You're being brave.'

'I'm weak. I'm a coward.' Her voice was faltering as she spoke.

'No. You're trying to conquer your fear. That's the defin-
ition of bravery, my darling. But I'd do anything to take all
this away from you.'

'I know that.'

'Can I hug you?'

The voices in her shouted that she mustn't touch him, but
she struggled against them and won. In his arms, she felt a
vestige of the love and comfort she used to get from him.

'I love you. You can do this, Julia,' he said softly. 'I know
you can.'

Chapter Twenty-Eight

As Julia's time to give birth drew near, she found a new place to hide. Now, the pregnancy did not exist. There was no baby. Her fears of infection and desire to keep clean remained, as did her need to purge after eating, and her now chronic insomnia, but her mind drew a protective veil around her and allowed her to occupy two contradictory positions at the same time.

David took leave from his job as the nights grew dark and the time approached when Julia could go into labour at any time. Sally was there constantly, and Julia was aware, dimly, of the new alliance between her husband and her friend. They'd been bound together by her situation, and their duty to her.

Christmas was coming once more, the days were short and cold, and their lives retreated inside. The gardens were put to sleep and everything became about the house. A tree was put up and presents soon gathered at its base. David wrestled in armfuls of holly and ivy and great bunches of mistletoe with their pretty pale green berries, so they could decorate the old rooms.

'It needs something bright really,' Julia remarked as she looked at the swags of green she'd laid across the chimney piece. She was sitting on the window seat where she'd once had a hidden nook, soaking up the warmth from the old radiator underneath. 'Flowers, or something.'

'Yes, that would be nice,' Sally said idly as she turned the page of a magazine. The natural look wasn't really her thing, Julia knew. She preferred metallic sparkle and artificial lights.

David came into the drawing room. 'A present has arrived for you, Julia.'

'Has it? I didn't see the postie's van.'

'This one came by taxi. Didn't you see it come up the drive?'

She shook her head.

David stood back, pushing the door open wider behind him, and there was Lala in the doorway, in a fur-collared coat and hat, pink-cheeked and smiling.

'Darling Julia. Happy Christmas,' she said.

Astonished, Julia tried to get off the seat, but her huge bump hindered her, and she moved slowly. 'Lala, you never said!'

'I wanted to come before now, but I haven't been able to.' Lala came forward. 'You look wonderful. Wonderful.'

Julia laughed wryly. 'I don't think so. I've got so fat, I can't think how.'

Lala blinked at her. 'Well, the usual way, I expect!'

'Yes, far too many cakes. Mrs Petheridge made her famous Christmas cake and I can't stop eating it.'

Lala exchanged a quick look with David as if to show that

she now saw what he said was true. 'Cake is allowed in your condition,' she said briskly.

Sally stood up, smiling but a little shy. 'You must be the famous Lala.'

'Well, yes. And you must be Sally, the companion. Hello.' Lala's gaze swept over Sally but didn't linger. She turned back to Julia. 'Now the exciting news is that I've brought someone with me from Paris.'

'Denis?'

'Oh no, not Denis. No. He and I are no longer together. I've found a very charming new friend called Lisbet. She is waiting outside to meet you.'

'Outside in the hall? You must bring her in!' exclaimed Julia. 'Don't leave her in the hall, she'll freeze.'

'Lisbet!' Lala called, and a petite younger woman with jet-black hair in a curly bob came in. 'This is my sister Julia.'

'Welcome,' Julia said, with a smile, and she kissed her on both cheeks. 'I'm so glad you could come to spend Christmas with us.'

'I am very happy,' Lisbet said in a strong French accent. 'Thank you.'

Sally went to fetch the children and the babies were exclaimed over and tea offered. It was all so delightfully normal. No one could mention the strangeness of the unacknowledged presence of Julia's pregnancy.

Julia tried hard: she drank a cup of tea, talked to Lisbet, kissed Johnnie on his soft cheek. She was afraid. She felt the delicate fabric of her mental world shimmering when she saw Lala look at her bump. It might tear at any time, and she couldn't risk that. Blessed oblivion and freedom from the terror she knew was coming were all she craved. Like an inhabitant of Pompeii who went to a room and sat and waited, knowing death was coming in a toxic cloud but who could think of nothing else to do, she decided that she would stay in bed now, if necessary for the rest of her life, and only wait.

'I'm just going upstairs,' she said quietly, and lumbered slowly out of the room, and up the staircase, leaving them behind her in the warmth and light. She did not come down.

Julia missed Christmas and Lisbet's return to Paris. They brought Johnnie in to open his stocking with her, but she never saw the presents under the tree opened, or did any of the usual Christmas things. She was only glad when it was all over on Boxing Day, and the whole family went out to spend the day outdoors. Only Lala remained, and she came upstairs to sit with Julia and hold her hand. Julia was grateful to her, and even more grateful that Lala said nothing about all the problems, but was only with her, quiet, comforting and loving.

On New Year's Eve, the pains began. As soon as she felt the first contractions, Julia's fragile construction of fantasy collapsed and she fell headlong into blank, bleak terror. Her memories afterwards were vague: she knew she called for David and begged him to help her, to get the gun from the gun cupboard and shoot her, now, quickly, while there was still time. She recalled being in the back of the car with Lala holding her tight and soothing her, that she screamed hysterically with each contraction and, as they gathered force, she lost more of what little control was left.

Julia had no memory of arriving at the hospital, or of the frantic attempts to calm her, and the decision that she would need to be sedated as quickly as possible and the baby removed by Caesarean section.

She only knew that she crawled back to the world, battered and bewildered, on the first day of the new year, feeling as though she had been through some kind of epic battle that spanned the midnight of the year. She was alive; she had, somehow, survived. And in the plastic cot by her hospital bed was a tiny, perfect baby girl.

Julia was welcomed home like a conquering heroine and while she smiled and appeared perfectly happy, she felt like a fraud.

The baby was beautiful and, just as Johnnie had, she banished the demons. They faded into whatever hell they'd come from and Julia was free again. At least, the terrors that had tormented her throughout the pregnancy were gone, but she was not able to return to herself again as easily as she had the previous time.

'You're tired – exhausted!' Lala decreed. 'Of course you are, that's only natural. You're recovering from an operation. You need rest and time with the new baby.'

She guarded Julia carefully, making her eat, get up, walk, rest and sleep as regularly as clockwork, while preventing her even from lifting the baby until she was properly healed.

Alexandra was brought to her for feeding and cuddles, then taken away again.

David was happy, overjoyed with his new daughter, with her thatch of dark hair and navy eyes, and relieved that Julia was back with him. The madness was in retreat.

'No more babies,' he said, gazing down at Alexandra with love and pride. 'This little one completes us. We don't need any more.'

Julia smiled as she watched him gaze at their daughter. 'Yes. No more babies.'

She was utterly wrung out, mentally drained by her experience, and it was hard to imagine having any real strength again, but the knowledge that this madness never need come back was a comfort. *No more babies. No more babies.*

But she was afraid that it was something they could not control.

With Lala's arrival, Sally had faded tactfully into the background. She'd gone off to her parents' for Christmas, taking Mundo, and had returned in the dark days before New Year and the drama of the baby's arrival. Now, with Lala still here, she kept to the edges of family life, making herself useful looking after Johnnie but giving Lala and Julia plenty of space together.

The sisters were in the drawing room, close to the warmth of the fire, the baby nursing contentedly as Julia relaxed into the calm that feeding brought on.

'I'll need to go home soon,' Lala said. She bent forward to

poke the fire, sending a flurry of sparks upwards. 'There's work. I have to get back to that.'

'And . . . Lisbet?' Julia raised her eyebrows enquiringly.

'Yes. She was – is – rather a surprise, but a good one. I didn't expect my life to take this turn.' Lala smiled, flushing slightly. 'But I like it. I wonder now why I wasted so much time with Denis, long after it was obvious he and I weren't really suited.'

'You were waiting to find the right path.'

'Denis doesn't see it like that at all. He sees betrayal, lies and deception. He's very, very angry.' Lala shrugged. 'What can I do? I can't live my life to please him. We had our time and it's gone. I didn't lie to him, I didn't know myself what lay ahead. I tried to treat him with kindness and respect but what I couldn't do was turn time back. So now, we don't speak.' She laughed. 'I don't mind that much, to be honest.'

'I liked Lisbet. She seemed lovely.'

'She is. And very talented too. But don't get me started, or I'll not stop. You should meet her properly now you're well.' Lala looked over intently. 'You are well again, aren't you, Julia? Like last time?'

'I . . . I think so. I hope so.'

'Last time you were so flushed with joy. You're not like that now. There's something about you – as though you're very tired. Is that right?'

'I do feel tired,' Julia confessed. She stared down at the movement of the baby's tiny jaw as she suckled with her eyes tight shut, one small fist resting on Julia's chest. 'The old Julia feels like she's gone far away and left me here to cope. And I will cope. It was just easier when I was my old self.'

'I'm sad to hear that. I'm sure you only need time to regain your energy and your *joie de vivre*.' Lala looked at her questioningly. 'Do you think so?'

'I hope so. Yes, you're right. Time will do the trick.'

Lala looked back at the fire and pulled her cardigan a little tighter around her. 'I wonder, though . . . about your friend, Sally.'

'Sally?' Julia was surprised. 'What about her?'

'She's helped you, I can tell.'

'Yes, she has.'

'But perhaps it's time for her to start thinking of moving on. How long has she been here?'

'I don't know – six months or so, I think.'

'Her boy is growing up. She can't stay here forever.'

'There's no hurry. We have plenty of room.'

After a moment, Lala said, 'Oh, I think perhaps it might be for the best.'

'What are you saying, Lala?' Julia asked sharply, looking over at her sister.

'I'm not saying anything except that it's much better for a husband and wife not to share their lives with a third person. Marriage is for two people.'

Julia gasped and her skin across her forearms prickled unpleasantly. 'What do you mean?'

'Nothing – I don't mean anything nefarious is going on. But it's common sense, Julia.' Lala gazed back, serious. 'Just be on your guard. She's settled in here, to help you. Just don't let it get to a stage where you can't get her out. That's all I'm saying.'

'She does help me,' Julia said, feeling obstinate suddenly. 'She's been the best friend ever, the best I could possibly wish for. Are you trying to insinuate that she's worming her way in or something? Because you can see how hard she works, how much she does for me. I couldn't have coped without her. I'd probably be dead.'

'Then we owe her all the thanks in the world. But you don't owe her all of this – your house, your life. Your husband.'

'That's too much,' Julia said, angry. 'She's helped David too. She's been a friend to both of us, and God knows he needed it when I started to lose my bloody mind. He deserves someone to support him through all of that.' She shook her head. 'No. She can stay as long as she likes.'

Lala looked back to the fire. 'If you say so. But I had to say something. I wouldn't have been easy in myself if I hadn't. Now, shall I go and get us both some tea?'

Lala's words stayed with Julia, resonating through her thoughts. Later that evening, when she lay in bed under orders to sleep until the baby needed her next feed, she heard a whispered argument going on in the hall, of which she could make out very little, except that it was David's voice and, she thought, Lala's.

The next day Lala announced that she would be catching the evening flight from Exeter back to Paris. When she left, she hugged Julia tightly. 'Ring me if you ever need me,' she said. 'I'll be here as soon as I can.'

Then she kissed her and kissed the baby, and climbed into the taxi to take her to the airport.

After she'd gone, David said, 'I think it might be best if Lala doesn't come back for a while. I think she's disruptive and tires you out. You're much better being looked after by Sally.'

Julia didn't have the strength to argue.

It was, Julia thought, an intervention of fate when old Mr Kelsey died and his cottage on the edge of the home farm came up for a new tenancy. It lay on the other side of the estate, only two miles as the crow flew, but five miles round by road.

'This would be just right for Sally, don't you think?' she said to David. He was back from London for the weekend, but strangely distracted. They were having breakfast in the morning room, with Johnnie playing at their feet and the baby in Julia's arms. Sally had taken Mundo for a weekend at her parents'.

'What?' He looked up from his newspaper, owlish through his reading glasses.

'This cottage.' She pushed the report from the estate managers' office towards him across the breakfast table. Tawray had been run by the same company in town for years, and she had kept them on to administer the usual routine of collecting rents and taking care of the various properties on the estate. All available properties and land were rented out on long-term leases, and the income from them paid Tawray's bills and kept everything ticking over. 'It would need to be refurbished, but it could do for Sally, couldn't it?'

David took the paper and regarded it, frowning. 'Yes, I suppose so.' He looked over at Julia. 'You want her to move out then?'

'She has to some time. I mean, she can't stay here forever, can she?' She returned his gaze with something like defiance in her own.

'I suppose not.' He stared at the report. 'Will it cost much to sort out?'

'I don't know. The office will manage it. It's an investment.'

'They'll charge her rent.'

'Perhaps a small one. But she can do something, can't she? She told me only the other day that she was getting requests to work on manuscripts from her old agency. That sounds like a perfect job. Easy to fit around looking after Mundo.'

'I suppose so.' He shrugged. 'It all depends if you feel you're up to it.'

'Me?'

'Being on your own.'

'I have to learn how to manage eventually, and I can get help with the children, if I need it. There are lots of lovely girls in the village who would come up.'

'Yes, but they don't know the situation.' David took his glasses off and put them on the table, frowning. He looked much older suddenly, she realised. 'They won't be able to help you in the way Sally does. She understands. You feel safe with her.'

'But she can't stay forever. I have to look after myself.'

'But you can't pretend things are normal, Julia. They're not! You're not your old self yet, you're just not.'

She felt a stab of hurt. 'I'm doing my best.'

He hesitated, visibly gathered his patience, and said, 'I know you are. But things aren't right yet.'

She stared at him mulishly. 'You mean in bed.'

'It's not just that. But that's part of it, yes.' He stared back, a look of defiance in his blue eyes. 'That's part of it.'

It had been three months since the baby was born. Julia's wound had healed and she was quite capable of making love. But she couldn't do it. She loved being close to David, hugs and kisses and all the feelings of nearness and intimacy, but when it came to it, she couldn't go through with what he so clearly desired.

'I don't want to have a baby,' she said helplessly. It was almost insulting that she should have to say it, after everything she'd been through.

'You don't have to – you can go on the pill. You are on the pill already, aren't you?'

'Not yet. But it doesn't always work, you know.'

'We can use condoms.'

'They get torn. They're not reliable either.'

'If you're on the pill and we use condoms, the chances are tiny – tiny! And if you get pregnant again, we could think about terminating this time. I don't want to go through that baby business again, and I'm sure you don't.'

Anger boiled inside her. So she should take that awful risk, and perhaps endure a termination, because of what he wanted. He'd put her through having children in the first place, although of course she was happy the babies were here. Now he wanted sex. His needs were more important than everything she'd been through: the trauma and suffering and major operations; the madness and horror and the closeness to death. That all counted less than his physical needs.

'I can't do it, not right now.'

'Then you're not better. And I think in that case, you still need Sally.'

'I need Sally?' Her tone was menacing. 'Or you need Sally?'

He frowned. 'What?'

'Sally can go when I start fucking you again, is that it? But until then, she stays? Why is that? In case you get overcome with need and there's someone willing in the house?' She couldn't help spitting it out, feeling reckless, as though she wanted to see what would happen next.

David looked appalled. He went as white as paper. 'What?'

'You heard me. Why are you so bloody eager to have Sally around?'

His expression turned to outrage. 'I can't believe you're saying this, Julia! Are you accusing me of something? If you are, it's below you.'

She stood up, clutching the baby to her chest, one hand on the table. 'Then why does it matter? Why can't she move out?'

'I told you, you need her!'

'And I told you I don't! Listen, David, Sally needs to move out. This is the perfect opportunity. I'm sorry I can't snap back and be the wife you want, I'm sorry I'm ill and

397

inadequate and a failure. I've been through hell to give you the children you wanted. I can't risk that happening to me again, and if that means you have to bloody well be celibate, then I think you should put up with that. I don't think it's too much to ask. Unless you'd rather see me dead.'

She walked out, shaking, holding the baby close.

I mean it. I really do.

David explained the situation to Sally at some point when she returned. Julia was almost ghoulishly amused, wondering if David had interpreted what she said as a threat not to have sex with him again while Sally was in the house, and suspecting that he half hoped that if Sally went, Julia might relent. He had no doubt heard jealousy of Sally in her words, perhaps assumed that Julia was feeling that her friend was a sexual threat. *Typical male vanity. He can't hear what I'm actually saying to him. It doesn't seem to occur to him that my suffering is worth him making a sacrifice.*

Whatever David thought, he had acted on it. He told Julia that Sally was fine about moving out and certainly she seemed completely normal. She would be staying for as long as it took to renovate the cottage in any case, and that would mean some months more.

Sometimes, as the year moved into spring, Julia watched Sally with the children, or spent a happy afternoon with her, and she wondered if she was doing the right thing. Perhaps Lala was being ridiculous, warning her about the effect of having Sally in the house. Lala might be progressive and very French and pragmatic in some ways, but sometimes that came out as highly conservative and perhaps regressive. The family could be a flexible unit; maybe there was room for Sally.

But still, there was something strange about David coming home to be welcomed by the two of them; the two women sitting at the dining table with him, the little pack of children. Sally was always so glamorous, with her blonde hair recently cut short, and her bright blue-green eyes. She was always perfectly turned out, in smart, expensive clothes, even though she hadn't worked for a year. And she was warm and almost exaggeratedly pleased to see David, hanging on his every word, treating him like some kind of returning hero.

Has she always been like this? Or am I only seeing it now?

She wondered if Lala had dropped poison in her mind, the way that picture in the magazine had poisoned her last pregnancy.

Am I just prone to ideas that take root and then I can't distinguish them from reality?

But what good did it do to know that? She still wouldn't be able to tell the difference.

Life seemed to settle down to an easy rhythm while they waited for the Kelsey cottage to be finished. Sally was as good-tempered and helpful as ever and if she resented being made to move out, she didn't show it. If anything, she seemed excited about her new home and all the ways she could make it cosy, comfortable and charming. But underneath, Julia was thinking obsessively about her problem. A trip to the doctor had been of little help; when she'd asked for a hysterectomy, he'd not just told her it was an awful idea, but that it was immoral.

'What if you lose one of your children, God forbid?' he'd said sternly. 'You'd never be able to have another. And there are plenty of women forced to have hysterectomies who'd do anything to be in your shoes – healthy and young and fertile. You can hardly expect us to waste taxpayers' money on you!' He smiled kindly. 'You'll change your mind. You'll see.'

'What about my husband having a vasectomy?' she asked timidly. The idea had only just come to her, while David was away, and it seemed like it might be a solution.

The doctor looked scandalised. 'You can't ask a young man like him to do such a thing! What if you divorce and he remarries? You could be condemning another woman to infertility.'

Julia blinked at him, confused. It seemed odd that she should risk everything to enable an imaginary second wife to have David's other family, but perhaps the doctor was right and it was entirely unreasonable to put such a condition on David.

'The operation is not one hundred per cent reliable in any case,' the doctor remarked, reaching for a pen. 'I've heard of several cases where it's failed.'

He wrote out a prescription for the pill, suggested a coil as a backup, and told her that she might have an early menopause which would solve everything. The message was clear – contraception was her responsibility. David had a right to remain untouched by the process, and his needs must be fulfilled.

She'd gone away, downcast and ashamed for voicing her

suggestions, wondering if her doctor had even read her medical records. A hysterectomy was extreme, but it was the only way she could think of to be totally certain she wouldn't get pregnant again, especially if vasectomies sometimes didn't work.

It was when she was lying in bed with David one night, a week or so before Sally was due to move out, that the idea came to her. She'd tried several times to make love when he wanted it, usually after a few glasses of wine. But where once they had enjoyed mutual pleasure and satisfaction, Julia had felt unaroused to the point of discomfort, unable to let go and give herself over to the experience. Her fear of what might happen if their contraception failed had overridden anything. All subsequent attempts had gone exactly the same way. She felt both defensive and ashamed, as well as sorry for David, who was suffering because of her.

I can't bear to sleep with David anymore. I've tried and it's hideous. But what if I tell him that he's free to sleep with someone else if he wants to? There must be women in London who he can see, without me ever knowing. I wouldn't mind that. As long as he stays safe and keeps it discreet, that would be fine.

As soon as she had this idea, it seemed brilliant. The sense of relief that engulfed her was intense – relief that she would be free of her awful fear of pregnancy for good. She could be abstinent. David could satisfy his needs. They would still be a family, and at last, the future would seem bright again.

Chapter Twenty-Nine

Present day

In his bed in the house he's lived in with Sally for ten years, David Pengelly is moving closer to death. From the start, he's felt it circling him, hungry for him, keen for him to join the great tribe of those who've left the earth forever; but his life force has clung to his physical form, not ready to detach, float free and take the final journey to wherever awaits him. Although it seems that darkness wants to consume him, he also feels that there might be something beyond that, a state or a dimension or a place where something new might begin. It's so hard to imagine extinction, even though he knows he came from nothing. Or does he know that? Perhaps he came from a place like the one he is going to, he simply can't remember it.

For a while, he has thought he might stay indefinitely in this twilight existence, floating to the surface occasionally and then sinking down again into a washing silence. Then, just recently, as he has begun to spend longer listening to the world around him, he suspects that he's making a very long and slow return to it. He has heard Sally and Mundo talking,

402

and that has given him an impetus to come back and make things right. He needs to find his voice, his clarity, and tell them what he knows to be real and true. They all have to love each other! Time is short. Life is beautiful. Love is everything. Be kind.

There's also something else he needs to do. It flickers in and out of his mind. It impels him to anchor himself into his body for a while longer and travel back to the conscious world, to rejoin them all again and make everything clear.

I want to tell them the truth about Julia, about how I loved her and how I love them.

He knows and understands everything now; he sees it all and he's filled with compassion, infinite pity and understanding for all of them. And the heartbreaking love is almost too much to stand. He wants to come back so that he can taste the sweetness of that human love one more time before he gives it up forever.

But he senses death is close again. He was wrong to think it was in retreat. It is very close now. It is not how he expected death to be.

He can do nothing. There is no fighting, there is only surrender. He sends out everything he has to those he loves, hoping that somehow it will move through the universe and find them.

Love one another. Be kind. Goodbye.

Chapter Thirty

Alex woke suddenly at four thirty. It was completely dark but the numbers on her alarm clock glowed pale green and showed her how early it was. She sat up, alert for anything that might be happening in the house. Hadji hadn't made a sound in the kitchen, which meant there was no intruder. Johnnie was ensconced in the rental house, so it wasn't him. The girls were at Tim's.

She listened hard, but there was only silence.

As she realised just how alone she was, there in the dark, the bedroom cool without the heating on yet, she felt suddenly spooked. She pulled her covers up around her and nestled into the warmth, then lay down and tried to clear her mind. Morning would be here soon enough, if she could just sleep again.

After a few minutes, she drifted off and slept soundly until her alarm went off at six thirty.

Johnnie was roused the next morning by a cry from Netta. She was in another room but it pierced his consciousness.

'Is everything okay?' he called, instantly alert.

'Yes!' she shouted back. 'It's just that Bertie's emptied out everything in his bathroom, it's total chaos in there. I'll have to clean it up.' She came along the hall and poked her head around the bedroom door. 'He's really gone to town with the shampoo.'

'That's annoying.'

'I'll clean it up. We can go into town and get some supplies. And I thought we could get the tree today.'

'Tree?'

'Christmas tree. We're having one, aren't we? The boys will want one. I brought the decorations, by the way.'

'Did you?' It hadn't crossed his mind to bring the Christmas decorations with them but he could see now that it was a good idea. He said nothing, feeling as though he'd been rebuked for being thoughtless.

There was a pause. Netta said, 'Don't thank me or anything.'

'Thank you,' he said. 'Thank you for remembering the decorations.'

'It doesn't really mean much when I have to tell you to do it,' she said coolly, and disappeared back into Bertie's en suite to start dealing with the mess.

Johnnie grimaced in frustration. He wanted to say the right thing. He could always see with hindsight exactly what he should have said. Why did it never pop into his mind when he needed it? Instead of feeling criticised for not remembering the decorations, he should have congratulated Netta on doing it. It was obvious now. But clear as it was, he was sure that next time he would get it wrong again. He felt helpless, doomed to fail over and over. It demotivated him. It felt as though there was no point in trying. His faith that he could work this out started to waver.

He picked up his phone and began scrolling through his work emails. In a minute, he'd get up and make some coffee, take it to Netta with a smile on his face and try to make amends. He'd told her last night that Alex was taking Bertie this morning, but that had annoyed her too. 'Why shouldn't Bertie be allowed to see his grandfather like the other two?' she'd asked, and when he tried to explain about Sally, she'd snapped back, 'Sally will just have to deal with it.'

So he'd said no more. But Alex was expecting Bertie this morning, so he needed to make that happen, and the best way was probably just to assume it was going ahead as he'd said, get Bertie ready and put him in the car. If Netta said nothing, she was fine with it.

Just then a text popped up on his phone. It was from Sally. She never texted him, and had only phoned maybe twice in twenty years, both times from the car when Pa was driving and couldn't use his phone. It was all in caps:

JONATHAN PLEASE CALL ME AT ONCE SALLY

Something turned over in his stomach, and his heart started pounding. He had a bad feeling, a sense that things had suddenly spun out of his control. His thumb was trembling as he managed to get her number up and press to connect to it.

It rang only once.

'Jonathan!'

He knew immediately. It was the raw pain in her voice. 'Pa.' He said it like a flat statement of fact, even though part of him still wanted her to contradict him. 'He's dead.'

'He's gone, Johnnie!' wailed Sally. 'You have to tell Alex.'

'Yes.' He closed his eyes, trying to be businesslike. Why had he been so stupid? This was bound to happen. He should have known. 'Did he have another stroke?'

'We don't know. The doctor is coming to certify the cause. Miss Thomas is helping me. We don't know what's happened! It's a stroke, I think, we don't know!'

'Okay.' She was obviously teetering on the edge of hysteria. 'I'll ring Alex and come over. Please don't do anything until we get there, Sally. Do you understand?'

'Yes, yes. We won't do anything. Oh David, David.'

'Is Mundo there?'

'He went out this morning, I don't know where he is.'

'I'll be there very soon.'

He ended the call, then lay back on his pillows, stunned. A moment later, Netta came in, talking about what the boys needed for breakfast. She stopped when she saw Johnnie's face. 'What's happened?'

'It's Pa.'

She stared, her eyes wide. 'Is he . . . ?'

He nodded.

'No, Johnnie.' She rushed to him and hugged him hard, then pulled back, her eyes full of tears. 'I'm sorry.'

He stared at her, his lips dry. 'How am I going to tell Alex?'

'I'll drive you. Come on. We've still got that van. I'll take you to her, and then both of you to your father's house.' She took his hand and held it. 'Johnnie, I'm so sorry. I thought he might be recovering, at least a little. Are you okay?'

How do I feel? Emotions were whirling through him, but most of all he felt numb. 'Fine. Thank you,' he said. 'I'll get dressed.'

There was no answer at the front door of the Old Barn, and Hadji came trotting in his sideways way around the house, yapping a welcome, so Johnnie guessed that Alex was in the potting shed.

He walked slowly around the barn and across the yard, letting her have a few more minutes without the knowledge he had to impart. The door was open, strains of music coming out of the shed along with Alex's tuneful humming.

He went in and saw her at the table, well wrapped up against the cold and wearing her fingerless gloves so that she could push tiny flower heads into bauble shapes. She looked up, and a smile broke over her face. 'You're here! Where's Bertie?'

'He's outside in the car with Netta.'

'Aren't you bringing him in?'

'Alex.' He drew in a breath and his face contorted in pain. Her scissors fell on the table.

Johnnie never forgot the expression that spread over her face and whenever he thought of it, he saw the face of a statue carved into utter torment.

PART TWO

Chapter Thirty-One

Three weeks later

Alex was getting out of her car in the marketplace when she heard her name. Turning, she saw Jasper coming towards her, puffing as he wove between the parked cars to reach her.

'Alex! Hi! How are you?' he asked, his eyes questioning. 'Are you okay? I'm so sorry about everything, about your dad. It's just awful. Of course you're not okay, what am I thinking?' Jasper's liquid Scottish accent came rolling rapidly out as though he was worried she'd disappear on him. He was a little red in the face, but looked just as she remembered from before Christmas, except that he was now dressed in a long dark coat with a bright green scarf wrapped messily at his throat, and his black hair stood up in a soft ruffle on the top of his head. 'I'm just really sorry.'

Before Christmas. She could vaguely recall that carefree day at Tawray, decorating the trees. *That feels like an age ago now. A different life*. They were in the dead period now, the cold dark time that followed the New Year festivities.

'Thanks,' she said. She'd not thought about him since Pa had died and it was almost like seeing a stranger.

Jasper looked awkward. 'Are you busy? Do you have time for a coffee or something? I could tell you how the flower day turned out, if you want to hear about it. And there's something else I want to talk about. Though of course it's perfectly understandable if you'd rather not right now.'

She blinked at him. The flower day. The first one she'd missed. 'How did it work out?'

'We missed you, but your decorations looked fantastic. People seemed to enjoy it and the local traders were thrilled. They definitely want a rerun next year.'

Alex smiled. 'I'm glad. Really, I am. I'm sorry I couldn't be there.'

'Don't be silly. I wouldn't have dreamed of expecting it.' He thrust his hands in his pockets and smiled back. 'So . . . do you want to get that coffee?'

'I'd like that, but I can't right now. I'm afraid I've got an appointment at the solicitor's. We're reading my father's will this morning.'

Jasper flushed and looked embarrassed. 'God, I'm sorry, how awful of me.'

'You weren't to know. It's fine.'

'I won't hold you up. But can I give you a ring maybe tomorrow? There's something I want to talk to you about.'

'Of course.' She smiled. 'I'm around.'

'Great. I'll talk to you then.' He nodded his farewell and headed back through the marketplace.

Alex hadn't been sure how formal the meeting would be, but the process of reading the will seemed like an important one, so she'd put on her navy work suit and a pair of heels, pulling her dark hair back into a sleek ponytail. She'd left the girls with Netta, who was packing up the rectory and seemed to be raring to get home, before driving into town.

Now she walked across the square towards the solicitor's office housed in the old Corn Exchange.

The last few weeks had been terrible. For the first time, she'd been glad of Tim being able to take the girls over Christmas, and she agreed that they would actually be better off with him. She was floored by her grief for Pa in a way she hadn't expected, and flagged even more under the burden of Sally's needs.

That was one of the strangest things: Sally's volte-face. After years of condescension and barely concealed scorn, Sally clung to her like a child to its mother. She needed reassurance about the most basic things, and seemed bewildered by everything that had to be done, and frightened of the future.

'Why doesn't she rely on Mundo?' she had asked Johnnie, when the two of them were sitting at Sally's kitchen table drinking tea. Sally had gone off to find a hymn book so that they could select David's favourite hymns for the funeral.

'My question exactly,' Johnnie had said, raising his eyebrows. 'Where is Mundo anyway?'

'Sally says he's been called back to town. Great. Just when he could actually be useful.' Alex sipped her tea. 'I've offered to stay with her until he gets back tomorrow.'

'That's very good of you.' Johnnie gave her an admiring look. 'She doesn't deserve this, you know.'

'She's a woman on the brink of getting old who's lost her husband, and she's grieving.'

Johnnie leaned towards her intently. 'Yeah, but she wasn't always like this. When she had the power, she didn't offer you kindness, did she? And you're grieving too – for the father she kept you from. Don't forget that, Al. It's great to be all forgiving, but don't push yourself back on this, I think you'll regret it.'

'I hear you. But Pa would have wanted us to be kind to Sally. And it's not for long. Once the funeral is over, I doubt she'll want to hear from us again.'

The lead-up to Christmas was awful. Alex found all the carol services and school events with the girls unbearably moving, and each one inspired deep grief and regret. She was devastated that Pa wouldn't see the girls grow up and that he'd miss all these stages of their lives. As a result, she became so upset during Jasmine's nativity play, another mother had to help her out into the playground and then hug her until she stopped weeping great choking sobs of loss. Saying goodbye to them on Christmas Eve had left her in one of the blackest places she'd ever known.

Johnnie was grieving too, but his way was less visible. He clammed up, retreated inwards and focused on the practical aspects of the whole thing.

'You're coming to us for Christmas, Alex,' he'd declared, in a tone that brooked no dissent. 'You can't be on your own in the barn without the girls, that's no good at all.'

Then Sally had said, in her new, quavering voice, that she

wanted Alex to come to her on Christmas Day. 'I need to get to church,' she'd said. 'And the company will be nice.'

'Won't Mundo be here?'

'Oh no, he's in London with Isabella. He has commitments there.'

Yeah, I can guess what kind of commitments those are. Smart parties, work dos, shopping on Bond Street for something nice for his girlfriend. She felt sorry for Sally again. All these years, her world had revolved around Mundo. She'd done everything she could to guarantee him a successful life, and now she needed him, he'd vanished without a trace. 'Okay. I'll come in the morning and take you to church. Then we'll go to Johnnie for the rest of the day. How does that sound?'

Sally had looked so pathetically grateful, Alex felt sorry for her all over again.

Johnnie was not so pleased when she told him, but although he grumbled, he accepted it. As long as Mundo was not part of the package, he could just about cope.

'Where is he, though?' Johnnie wondered.

'God, don't ask. You'll summon him up like some kind of evil spirit. Let's hope he stays away.'

Christmas Day itself wasn't as awful as she'd feared. Alex missed the girls like crazy and found the online chat with them during the day was almost worse than nothing at all because the connection was so bad, and they were so giddy with excitement anyway that it was hard to follow their thought processes. At least, as far as she could make out, they liked the presents she'd entrusted to Tim.

'I'll see you very soon,' she said. 'Happy Christmas, love-lies.'

It was good to be with her nephews, though, and their joy helped to make up for what she was missing. Netta and John-nie produced an excellent Christmas lunch, and they watched television over a big box of chocolates for the rest of the day. Sally sat quietly through most of it, and only occasionally was seen crying silently into a white cotton handkerchief.

As they did the washing-up, Netta said to Alex, 'All the fight's gone out of her.'

'I know,' Alex said, drying up a plate. 'All this time, she's been a monster and now . . . she's so broken. I never would have predicted it. Honestly, I've never seen her so diminished. She's literally got smaller. And she's so helpless too.' She shook her head. 'It feels weird that she's calling me up, rely-ing on me, deferring to me. Anything I say goes. She's pathetically grateful for anything.'

'You're good to her,' Netta said solemnly. 'Better than I would be.'

Alex shrugged. 'How are you and Johnnie getting on?'

Netta looked thoughtfully into the soapy bubbles in the sink. 'All right,' she said. 'I thought it was a terrible idea, but this escape from the rat race has helped. Bertie usually has bad eczema, and it's cleared right up. Maybe the air is cleaner or something. And it makes a difference having Johnnie here, I won't deny it. He's been able to spend so much more time with the boys and they've loved it.'

'That's all good, isn't it?' Alex ventured, picking up a glass to polish with the tea cloth.

Netta nodded. 'Yes. But it's not the here and now I'm worried about. It's the future. It's what we're going to go back to. It's how we're going to cope.' She looked at Alex solemnly. 'I don't think Johnnie and I agree on what we want our future to be. And that's a really, really big problem.'

'Right,' Alex said, uncertain how much Netta wanted her to ask about it. Then, more brightly, 'You could just stay here!'

'That only shifts the problem here. It won't go away.'

'But there might be other solutions here. Or things might just change . . .'

Netta smiled one of her reserved, closed-mouth smiles, as though she nursed secrets none must know of. 'I don't have any faith that anything will change.'

'Don't you?' Alex asked, concerned. 'That sounds really serious, Netta. I know Johnnie can be thoughtless and a bit self-absorbed. He got used to looking after himself when he was a boy. Sally could be so cold to him at times, when he really needed a mother figure to make it right for him. So he shut off a bit. Maybe he still has that habit.'

'I'm sorry about that, but I can't be a mother to him, Alex,' Netta said coolly. 'That's not my idea of a healthy marriage, even if I wanted to take on that role.'

'I know,' Alex said hastily, 'I'm just saying. I know that Johnnie wants to work on that aspect – on taking more responsibility and not just thinking of himself. He wants to make it work so badly.'

'If only that was all it takes. Our future is about more than

417

just us. I don't think Johnnie understands that. In fact, I know he doesn't.'

'Can't you talk to him about it?'

'Now is not the time. Johnnie's grieving and needs me to support him. We have to get through the funeral and out the other side.' Netta plunged her hands into the sink and pulled out another soapy plate to put in the rack. 'That's the priority at the moment.'

When Alex arrived at the solicitor's, Johnnie was already in the waiting room, more informal in jeans and a jacket. He looked nervous.

'Are you all right?' she whispered as they sat together in the quiet reception room.

'Yes. Just wondering what we're going to find out today, that's all.'

A moment later, a plump, elderly man with a round face and steely grey hair came into reception, dressed in David's style: a navy blazer, shirt and tie and well-pressed trousers. He nodded an awkward hello, before giving his name to the receptionist and settling down to wait. Another man of the same vintage and in almost the same outfit came in a few minutes later, and the two clearly knew one another. They talked in a half-whisper until the door opened and a middle-aged man in a grey suit stood there.

'The Pengelly family, please?'

Alex and Johnnie stood up, and so did the other two men.

The man in the grey suit frowned. 'Aren't we expecting more than this?'

Johnnie spoke up. 'My stepmother hasn't arrived yet.'

'Ah, yes, well, let's go through, get some cups of coffee and so on, and no doubt she'll be here soon. I'm Simon Warburton, by the way.'

They followed him into a conference room, which was dominated by a large table with bookshelves holding legal tomes. Along one wall, a small sideboard was laid out with tea and coffee.

The elderly gentlemen collected cups of coffee and came over to Alex and Johnnie.

'How do you do,' said one politely. 'My name is Williams, Eric Williams.'

'I'm Philip Hansel,' said the other.

'Okay,' Johnnie said, a little terse. 'How do you know our father?'

'We're executors,' Eric Williams said. 'Of the will.'

'But we know him from the golf club. Excellent player. Sadly missed. Our commiserations. We'd like to look into some kind of memorial bench, if you're of a mind with us—'

Johnnie was staring at them with a look of disbelief on his face, when the door opened, and Mundo strode in, almost dragging Sally, who was hanging off his arm, looking small inside her fur coat.

'I hope nothing has been said!' Mundo boomed. 'I assume you've waited for Mrs Pengelly!'

Simon Warburton stepped forward. 'Hello, Mrs Pengelly, so glad you're here. Of course we were waiting. If you'd like to get some coffee, we'll get started.'

'Thank you,' Sally said in a high, tense voice, and her gaze flicked anxiously to Alex and Johnnie, but she said nothing beyond a murmured hello. They all sat down.

It's not like the films, Alex thought, as proceedings got underway. She'd imagined a formal reading of the will like something in a murder mystery but this was quite ordinary and rather boring. A gathering around the table and discussions of probate, codicils, beneficiaries, taxes, costs and HMRC.

'So what are the actual terms of the will?' Johnnie asked, a little impatiently, after quarter of an hour of administrative discussion. 'I realise there's lots of red tape to deal with, but I want to know about my father's assets and how they'll be divided up.'

'Of course, of course, that's quite normal.' Warburton turned a few pages on the stapled wedge of paper he was holding. 'Yes, let me see. As there is a death certificate provided, we can move to the next stage of agreeing the terms.'

He began to read out the relevant paragraphs. Alex listened, trying to concentrate. Johnnie was scribbling hard on a notepad just beside her and he seemed to be following it all perfectly well, but she found the words slipping and sliding about, turning into a stream of legal terms that meant nothing. Then she heard, 'To my natural children, Jonathan and Alexandra, according to the terms of their mother's wishes set out in her will of . . .' and she became alert, listening hard. 'The ongoing trust of the Tawray estate entrusted to my care on my wife's death until such time as I would deem them capable, or they reach the age of forty, whichever is sooner, is to be passed to them along with all outstanding assets including properties, after due taxes and fees have been paid.'

'What does that mean?' Alex whispered to Johnnie.

Johnnie blinked, obviously stunned. 'Wait!' He held up a hand. 'The house was sold earlier this year.'

Warburton scanned the document in front of him. He flicked over a couple of pages. 'I don't think so,' he said. 'I've got a full report pending from the estate administrators, but as far as I can see, it all remains intact. It looks as though the house is let on a long lease. But not sold.'

Sally gasped and Mundo frowned. Alex turned to Johnnie, her heart racing. 'Did you hear that?'

'Yes.' Johnnie looked at her, his face screwed up with surprise and disbelief. 'But . . . why did Pa let us believe it was sold?' He looked over at Sally. 'Did you think it was sold, Sally?'

'Yes,' she said faintly. 'I did.'

Simon Warburton was watching them. 'I'll proceed if that's all right?' They didn't demur, still lost in their surprise. 'Right then.' He read out again from the will. 'To my wife, Sally, I leave the sum of fifty thousand pounds after taxes and fees, and an annual income derived from my naval pension and private investments to maintain her in comfort. And to my stepson, Edmund, in recognition of his many benefits and successes, the sum of ten thousand pounds after taxes and fees.'

He looked back at the family. 'Those are the main bequests, though there are several other smaller ones, including to the golf club and the children of Alexandra and Jonathan. And there is a great deal of information about the Tawray trust, which will take some time to pass through probate, not least because of the complex inheritance tax issues. But . . .' The lawyer smiled over at Alex and Johnnie. 'The control of the trust is a major bequest. You will have quite a responsibility, with all the associated properties and business.'

Alex glanced at Johnnie, who looked jubilant, and then at Mundo, whose expression was thunderous, his face the dark red of old brick. Sally looked lost and confused and she clutched at her son's hand.

We've got Tawray, she thought wonderingly. *So after all this, all the losses and sadness and disappointment, Tawray is coming back to us.*

Not long after, Mundo got up and took Sally away, his face still set in an expression of dark fury. Sally went with him, obedient, and paying no attention to her stepchildren. Alex and Johnnie stayed to discuss issues of the trust's possessions and how it would be administered, and then they excused themselves, leaving the executors to continue their meeting.

'I'm afraid probate can take many months,' Simon Warburton said apologetically as he showed them out. 'There's no saying when legal transfer will be completed.'

'We understand,' Johnnie said. His eyes were shining with a light that Alex hadn't seen before. 'But can I get something straight? All my father's property belongs to the Tawray trust?'

The lawyer nodded. 'I believe so. All purchases were made

with money from the trust. All assets belong to it. Well, goodbye. Please do be in touch if you have any questions.'

Outside, in the dank January air, Johnnie put his hands in his pockets and whooped, doing a little dance on the pavement.

'It's exciting, isn't it?' Alex said, half laughing at the silliness of it. 'We've still got Tawray!'

'You betcha!' Johnnie laughed.

'Come on, what's making you so jolly? I know it's wonderful, but I see a lot of paperwork and admin in my immediate future.'

'Yes, yes. But . . . don't you get it?'

'I suppose we're going to be quite well off,' she said slowly. 'Not with money but with the house and so on.'

'Oh, there'll be some money too. You'll be okay – you'll have the barn and the business, and some money from the trust. That's not what I mean, though.' His eyes glinted at her. 'Don't you see? He didn't leave anything to Sally.'

'He left her fifty grand!'

'Yes, but that's not enough for a house, not of Sally's standard. The house she's in belongs to us now.'

'Oh.' Alex began to see his point. 'And Mundo got almost nothing.'

'Did you see his face?' Johnnie whooped again and laughed. 'He must have thought Sally would get at least half of everything, and that would eventually come to him. And instead he's got ten grand and a "thanks very much". Ha! That's made my day.' Then he grabbed Alex's hand and stared at her, excited. 'But can't you see the real deliciousness of it all?'

Alex shook her head.

'We can chuck Sally out. Don't you see? After all this, we can finally give her a taste of her own medicine.'

Chapter Thirty-Two

The rectory was in a state of flux as Netta gathered together the things she wanted to take back to their old house. It was time to return, with the new term approaching. Johnnie was staying for now and Netta would come back for the funeral.

'I wish you would stay here,' Johnnie said, leaning against the hall table as she came in with a bag full of the boys' toys.

'You know that's not possible,' Netta replied, dumping it by the door. 'The boys have to get back to school.'

'They could go to school here.' He went over and took her hands. 'Look at how much happier we've all been since we got here. Obviously I don't mean with Pa, but as a family. The kids love this house, the garden. Bertie loves it too. He seems calmer somehow, and his allergies have definitely improved. Why don't we just escape and come down here?'

Netta flushed and pulled her hands away. 'You know why. I've got a job, the children are settled. Bertie's in his school and you know how hard it was to get that place and how we had to fight the council. I can't just give it all up and come down here!'

'But, Netta.' Johnnie spread out his hands as if in supplication. 'It's all different now!'

'How is it different?'

'I'm going to be responsible for Tawray, the estate, all the business Pa built up on the quiet when it looked like he was playing golf and drinking port. It's a new opportunity. We can use this, Netta. It's our chance to change our lives.'

'I see,' she said tartly. She scooped up her notepad and pen from the hall table and scored some deep lines on the paper. 'And we should dance to your tune, should we?'

'But you hate your job, you could easily find something else down here. There's bound to be a school for Bertie if we start looking. I know we'll find something.'

Netta's face seemed to set hard, and her eyes flashed with anger. 'I found the last school, I did the application, I got Bertie in. I fought the council, and I got the twins into their school, and sorted them out too: uniforms, sports kit, stationery, school bags, shoes – all of it! But because you want to move, I should give up my job and do all that work all over again.'

'No!' Johnnie wanted to bite his stupid tongue. 'No, I don't mean that. We'll do it together this time. I just think we could be happier here. And I thought you might feel the same way.'

'The thing is, Johnnie, I have the burden of looking after Bertie and running the massive admin of our family life. I always have, and I always will.' Her face went redder. 'And I know very well that one day you are going to make me choose between you and him. Between staying married to you and looking after Bertie. And I can tell you this: he will always come first. Always. You might want to get rid of him, but he's my son and I intend to look after him until I die, or he does. That's my intention. I can't do anything else.' She stopped, clearly fighting for control, her breathing coming rapidly.

'Where has all this come from?' Johnnie said, bewildered. 'I don't want you to choose between us.'

'Don't lie to me! I know you do. I know very well.' She looked furious and outraged. 'That's why I'm not going to change my life to suit you, like you seem to think we all have to do. And you can't make me. I'm taking the boys back home and you can stay here.'

He stared at her, flummoxed. Why did he always get it so wrong? When he thought she'd be happy, she was cross. A gift of fate in the form of his legacy from his mother via his father was not a wonderful thing that could set them free of the life that was stifling them, but something he was going to inflict on them all. He couldn't win.

'I thought you might be pleased,' he said.

Netta put down her pen and when she spoke, her voice was ominously quiet. 'Why don't you ask me what I want? Why don't you ever say, "Netta, what would make you happy?" You present me with all these outcomes like they're the answer to my prayers. But you don't know my prayers, my hopes, my dreams! Because you never ask me!'

'You want what's best for the children, don't you?'

'Yes!' Her eyes flashed as if he was somehow accusing her of the opposite. 'Yes, I do.'

'Well then?' He tried to sound reasonable, unselfish. 'What could be better than a life down here for them? And we might even move into Tawray eventually, if you liked that idea.'

'Oh yes,' Netta said sarcastically. 'I can just see how I'm going to find it easier to cope in a house like that. Looking after Bertie will be a breeze with forty rooms for him to hide in!' She stood up. 'I can see where this is going. You're pretending that it's about the children and their best interests, when actually it's all about you. We're going home and that's that.' She stopped in the doorway and turned to stare at him, her eyes fierce. 'And don't think I don't know what you really intend. Because I do! I've known for ages. And I'm not going to let it happen.'

She stalked out and Johnnie felt a kind of strangulation in his throat but one that came from the inside. The sense of inadequacy came rushing up inside him and felt like it was crushing all his internal organs, pushing his breath out of his body. The sensation of being trapped was overwhelming and he had a sudden urge to beat his head against the wall, and start to tear his skin off. Why couldn't he manage this situation? Why couldn't he make her happy? Why couldn't he tell her things in words that would not set her off and make her angry?

Had Netta always been like this: sarcastic, cross, distant and hard to reach? He knew it wasn't so. Once she'd been sweet and loving and caring and cherishing. What had changed? Was it him, or was it her? Whose fault was it?

Johnnie fought for control of his breathing.

How can she treat me like this when I've just lost my father?

He picked up his phone and texted Alex, hardly able to make the letters work with his shaking fingers.

Can I see you Al? I need to talk about Netta.

The reply came at once.

Of course. Come now.

Alex was in the polytunnel looking at the seedlings. For the first time in weeks, she was beginning to feel restored. It was partly being surrounded by growing things, and partly that the girls were back home safe and sound. She had begun to feel better the moment they arrived with Tim just after New Year and they had been ecstatic to be home with her again despite their sadness about their grandfather. Hadji had leapt about, yapping, thrilled to see them.

'We've got birthday cards and presents!' Scarlett had shouted. 'Hello, sweet Hadji! We've missed you.'

'Happy birthday,' cried Jasmine. 'Open mine first.'

'Oh yes.' Alex laughed. 'My birthday.' She'd practically forgotten it. It was never exactly the main event, as it happened on New Year's Eve, but this year she'd ignored it completely, though Johnnie and Sally had remembered cards and presents: bath oil from Johnnie and the usual gift voucher from Sally. She opened the girls' cards and gifts, and kissed them both. When they'd gone rushing off, excited to be home, Tim had stayed with her in the kitchen.

'Did you do anything nice for your birthday?' he asked conversationally.

'Not really. I wasn't in the mood this year.'

'Of course.' He looked sympathetic. 'I'm sorry about your father, Alex. Really.'

'I know.'

'How are you?'

She managed a small smile. 'I'm coping. But I never got to say goodbye – that's the hardest bit.'

Tim shook his head sadly. 'That's terrible. I'm really sorry. And it was another stroke?'

'No. Heart failure. It just gave out in the night. The doctor said that can happen.'

'How's Sally?'

'In a bit of a bad way. She's still in shock.'

'Give her my best, won't you? I was fond of your dad.' Tim coughed a little awkwardly. 'Listen, I wanted to say sorry about that time when the girls were left with a sitter you'd never met, and without checking with you. I shouldn't have done it. I get that now. I won't do it in future.'

'Thanks, Tim,' she said, touched by his frankness. She felt a load lighten. To hear Tim make sure she knew the girls were his priority was like a balm to a troubled soul. She hadn't realised how very afraid she was that the girls would go through what she had with Sally until that night in the pub. And he could have shut her down, gone on regardless. But he'd listened. On impulse she put her arms around him and gave him a quick hug. 'That means a lot. You can't know how much.'

'Eh up,' he said, laughing awkwardly. 'Glad to make you happy.'

They smiled at each other, almost ruefully. *I think we're going to be friends*, Alex thought. *And we'll be much better as friends than as husband and wife. We are definitely on the right path.*

'Right. I'll be off. Bye.' He patted his pockets for his car keys. 'And happy birthday for the other day.'

'Thanks again, Tim. Take care.'

Alex brushed her hand over the soft velvet surface of a tiny green leaf, and looked up. Through the polyurethane wall she could see a figure muffled in a scarf and overcoat approaching, and she came out of the fuggy warmth of the tunnel.

'Hey,' she said, as Johnnie got closer to her.

'Hey there.'

'You look pretty miserable.'

Johnnie nodded, his mouth turned down, his eyes dark with misery. 'It's not good. It's really not. Netta and I are making each other sad, Alex. I don't know why.'

'Come on. Let's walk.'

They went out of the back garden gate and across the fields towards Tawray, skirting the edge of the park and going along the woods until they came to the clifftop. Beyond, the sea crashed stormily onto the beach. As they went, Alex listened as Johnnie poured out all the difficulties of the last few months.

'So it hasn't got any better?' she ventured, her hands tucked into her pockets even despite her woollen gloves. 'Have you been trying to communicate?'

Johnnie nodded. 'Maybe I haven't been doing it right, I don't know. Whenever I talk to her, she gets angry and sarcastic, and acts like I'm trying to railroad her into things – like thinking about living down here. She gives the impression that I'm pushing her into it. And I'm not! I'm just pointing out the advantages.'

'Okay,' Alex said gently. She couldn't help thinking of the way she and Tim had communicated. So often they replayed the same discussion, exactly the same way, even when it was about different topics. And time and again, they grew frustrated with the way the other handled it. 'So here's what I think, for what it's worth. You need to ask Netta more questions. Rather than tell her, ask her. So ask her how she would feel about making a permanent move, rather than trying to sell it to her. And if she expresses worries or doubts, don't dismiss them by trying to give her the solution straight away. What she'll hear is, "Your problems are easily solved! I've just done it, so now you should be happy and excited like me!"'

Johnnie nodded, obviously listening hard.

'So you need to acknowledge her: "I hear you. I can understand why you're worried. That's a real problem – do you think we can find a solution to it?" It's diplomacy. Make her feel like the two of you are solving her very real problems and issues together. But she has to know you've heard and understood. And that her problems are also *your* problems. If she's worried about her work, you should be too. And if she's nervous that there won't be a school for Bertie, you should show her that's your concern as well. Otherwise, she'll think you're just foisting all the work on her to deal with on her own.'

'That's exactly it!' exclaimed Johnnie. 'That's what she thinks. But that's not what I'm saying!'

'You might not be, but my guess is that in her experience, you leave all the spade work to her. Am I right?'

Johnnie pushed his face down into his scarf against the buffeting wind. The gales blew unhindered across the Channel here, and took the cliffs at speed. There was something crazy about being pummelled by this invisible force, but also fun, pushing their bodies against its strength.

Alex took his silence for acquiescence. 'My biggest piece of advice is this: never assume you know what she's thinking. You probably don't. And never assume she knows what you're thinking. Because she doesn't know that either.'

'Yeah,' Johnnie mumbled into his scarf. 'I see that.'

'Good. Just try it. I think you're right – life down here could be perfect for all of you, and I'd love it. But why not do some research into schools for Bertie? Why not ask what she thinks of them, instead of presenting them as the perfect solution? Why not show her that you're prepared to do the work, and that the trade-off of this new life is that you'll share more in looking after Bertie?'

Johnnie smiled at her. 'You're good at this. I should have come to you sooner.'

'But, Johnnie, can I say something? My feeling is that the

real problem here is Bertie. I think – and I might be wrong – that Netta is afraid for his future.'

'Really?' Johnnie frowned.

'You said yourself that you've been thinking about what's going to happen to him eventually, and that you need to talk about it with Netta. Have you done that?'

Johnnie shook his head. 'I've been avoiding it.'

'Does she have any clue what you might have been thinking – that he might not be able to live at home in the future?'

Johnnie thought, and then, quite suddenly, his expression changed, as realisation swept over it. He turned and looked out to sea, shaking his head slowly. 'Oh my God,' he said quietly under his breath. 'Of course.'

'What?'

'Around the time of the court case with the council we were discussing what we needed to ask for, and Netta said something about when Bertie turned nineteen, and I said, "If he's still living with us," or words to that effect, and she went a bit quiet. I didn't think about it again. But she's been cold and distant ever since. I hadn't made the connection. That's where it started to go wrong.'

Alex watched him processing it, then said quietly, 'She's afraid you're not committed to him. If you can show her that you are, I think you'll find that will make things a lot easier.' She turned her face to the wind, feeling its invisible punches to her face. 'Are you, Johnnie? Are you committed to him?'

Johnnie's face creased and he buried it into his scarf again. When he pulled it out, he said in a broken voice, 'I love him. I really do. I'd never ask Netta to send him away. We'll learn new ways to cope with him as he gets older. I'm committed, Al.'

'It's not me you need to tell. You need to let Netta know you love Bertie. And you love her.'

'I'll do that,' Johnnie said, his voice heartfelt. He put an arm around her. 'Thanks. I mean it.'

Chapter Thirty-Three

Jasper was obviously trying to be considerate when he left it a couple of days before ringing Alex. She took the call on her mobile as she worked in the potting shed, planting out more seeds in plugs of soil set into biodegradable trays.

'How was your meeting the other day?' he asked. 'Was it all right?'

Alex thought back. Was it really only the day before yesterday that they had read Pa's will? It seemed like a lifetime. One aspect of living with such heightened emotions was how slowly time seemed to pass, as though it was in thrall to the surges of grief and the darkness of despair. 'Yes, it was fine, thank you. We found that the house – Tawray – isn't sold after all.'

'Oh,' Jasper said, his tone surprised. 'I could have told you that. I acquired a long lease. Didn't you know?'

'We didn't, strange though it sounds. From the way you talked, I thought you owned it. You had so many ideas about how to change it.'

'Long leases are like that. As long as you get permission, you can make really big alterations. In fact, sometimes it's actively encouraged. The Tawray estate office hinted that they were pretty keen for me to overhaul the old place and make it viable.' He sounded sheepish. 'I'm sorry if I misled you, I assumed you knew.'

'It's not your fault. Crossed lines. But what did you want to tell me about?'

'Oh yes. I think you'll be interested in this.' His voice brightened, and she remembered how infectious his enthusiasm was. She liked the way his energy buzzed off him, and how he exuded good humour and interest in everything. 'So we've been up exploring the attics. My brother Duncan and my mum came down over Christmas and I gave Duncan the job of sorting through it all. I know it isn't our stuff and you'll be claiming it back at some point, but it can't hurt to have it nicely packed up.'

'Yes, I suppose that's right.'

'And Duncan found this huge roll wrapped in brown paper and blankets. At first we thought it was carpet, then we thought it was a rug, then we thought it was an enormous square of linoleum.'

'It gets more and more fascinating!' she said with a laugh.

'Give me a chance. Well, you'll never guess what it was.'

'I never will, so you'd better tell me, hadn't you?'

'A painting.'

She frowned as she listened. 'A *painting*?'

'A painting the size of a wall. Huge. Life-sized. And there are life-sized people all over it. It's a trompe l'oeil, and a really good one, from what I can tell, but it would need to be in place to see it properly. I've had a look and I think it was supposed to go in the drawing room. The proportions are right and there are definitely signs the room was once cut in half. And my motion is that this painting went there.'

Alex was astonished, leaning on the potting shed table as if to get support from it. 'But I've never heard of the room being divided. It wasn't when I was little. My parents never said anything about that. How extraordinary.'

'Do you want to see it?'

'I'd love to.'

'Then come round and take a look. Now. Why not?'

Alex drove to Tawray, thinking about how energising it was to be around someone with so much verve and good humour. She found it irresistible, though she could imagine that some people could find it annoying. *I like it, though. It's like a jolt of caffeine, or a rush of endorphins. It just gives me a boost. And that's what I need.*

She turned the car into the drive that led up to Tawray, following Jasper. She was intrigued. What could this mysterious painting be? She'd definitely never heard of any such thing.

Inside, the giant roll was on the floor in the library, where the furniture had been pushed back to make room for it.

'We need to weight it down at one end,' Jasper said, so they put piles of books on the corners and then carefully unrolled the painting, pulling it across the floor so that it revealed the bright jewel colours beneath. When it was almost fully extended, with the central part revealed, they piled books on the far edge to keep the whole thing from rolling up again. Then they stood back to study it.

'What did I tell you?' Jasper said, excited. 'It's fantastic, isn't it?'

'Oh yes!' Alex stared at it in astonishment. There was a family in front of her eyes, spread out in the room she knew so well, frozen in time but as fresh as if they were all there yesterday. 'That's my mother,' she said, and her voice choked her suddenly.

Jasper followed where she was pointing, to the figure of the lively-faced girl with thick tawny hair spreading over her shoulders, sitting with her feet crossed at the ankle at the front of the painting. Her tigerish eyes sparkled with life and mischief, and she was surrounded by tokens of her girlhood: books, apples and her dog.

'She's beautiful,' Jasper said quietly. 'I don't mean her face – though she is beautiful – but her spirit. The artist has captured her life force.'

'Yes.' Alex's eyes were damp. Seeing Mum like this, young and alive and untouched by the tragedy yet to befall her, was intensely moving. A thought appeared, strong in her mind. *She didn't have to die. It didn't have to happen.*

All their lives, she and Johnnie had accepted that Mum's death had been inevitable. She wasn't well. She had an accident because she wasn't well. But what no one said was *why* she wasn't well. What was wrong with her? How did she end up having that accident?

The thoughts had occurred to her before, but she'd never been able to get close enough to Pa to talk about it. Sally had never permitted that they spend enough time alone to get close to such a sensitive subject and she had always quickly redirected conversation if it included references to Mum.

But why did she die? What made her so depressed?

The accident had been suicide. It had never been said, but as she and Johnnie grew up, they understood that Mum's depression had led directly to her accident and the link became obvious.

'Your mum will love to see this!' Jasper said exuberantly 'You must show her.'

'I'm afraid she died when I was a child.' She saw his mortified expression. 'Don't worry, it's fine. But that's why this is lovely to me, to see her again.' Her eyes searched the rest of the canvas. 'So this must be my grandfather, and this is my grandmother – goodness, she looks sad, doesn't she?' She cocked her head to one side so that she could read the letter being written by her grandmother. 'My darling Julia, you are my joy. Oh, that's lovely.' Tears stung her eyes. 'What a beautiful thing.'

'Who are these other people? Who's this stunner?' Jasper pointed at the figure in the middle of the painting.

'I don't know,' Alex said uncertainly. 'I think I know who the others are – that's my mother's aunt, Victoria, and her children Violet and Quentin, and that must be my great-grandmother but she died when I was a baby. I can't think who this is . . .'

'She's got the centre stage, so she must be someone important.'

'Yes.' Alex's eyes went back to her mother. 'But this is the one that matters to me.'

'You should have it.'

'Have it?' She laughed. 'I don't have the space for it.'

'Well then, let's put it back up here. We'll put the wall back, and remount the painting. I think it would look fabulous.'

She gave him a quizzical look. 'You wouldn't mind that?'

'It's not up to me,' he said. 'It's up to you. Well, to whoever is in charge now. I guess you and your brother will get the final say over it. Personally, I'd love it. But it's your call.'

'I don't know if I can ask you to do that,' Alex said, frowning.

'You haven't asked. I offered.'

'I'll think about it.' She smiled at him. 'I'd like to show Johnnie first. Would that be okay?'

'Of course. It's here as long as you need it.'

'Thanks, Jasper.' Impulsively she went to him and gave him a kiss on the cheek. 'You've given me a gift today. You don't know how much it means.'

Johnnie found that the rectory was horribly empty without his family. He had loaded up most of their possessions into the car and driven them back to their old house, which seemed cold and small by contrast with the house in Cornwall. The boys hadn't been very excited to be back but rather listless, and within moments they had settled in front of the television instead of going out to play as they had at the rectory.

Netta said she was pleased to be back, but Johnnie got the feeling that she too didn't feel as happy to be home and facing the old routine as she had expected. He tried to stay upbeat and supportive, though, keeping Alex's words close to mind at all times. He had even written down everything that she'd said when he got home so he could try and hold on to it. *Listen to her. Acknowledge. Don't try and solve her problems without empathising and showing you understand.* At the end, he'd written in capital letters: *COMMIT TO BERTIE.*

They had put the boys to bed and were sitting down to a glass of wine together, and Johnnie said, 'I'm sorry I have to leave you here, but I have to be on the spot in Cornwall for a while.'

'I know that,' she said, and smiled wanly. 'We'll miss you.'

'I'll miss you like crazy.' He looked at the surface of his wine and the way it curved away from the glass. 'I know we have a lot to consider, but I am thinking seriously about how we might relocate. I know it means giving up your job and finding new schools for the boys but I'm prepared to start looking into it, if you are. If it's something you like the sound of.'

Netta sighed but without rancour. She looked so tired, he thought. In fact, she'd been looking tired for years now. 'I know it's a good idea in theory . . .'

'And it's useful that we've just had a taste of the practice too,' he said and then paused and rephrased what he had been going to say, which had been to tell her he thought it had gone well. 'How do you think it worked for you?'

'I can't pretend I didn't like having you around more.' She looked at him thoughtfully. 'But if we moved, wouldn't you just go back to your old ways, and get bound up in whatever new work you had?'

'I would try to be aware of that, and I would listen if you

tell me the balance is going wrong. I would definitely commit to being there for you and the boys – and to taking more of the workload where Bertie is concerned.'

'It's true you did more over Christmas,' she conceded.

'I wasn't sure you'd noticed.'

'I did. I saw that you were trying harder to take care of him and give me a break.' She smiled again. 'Thanks.'

'You're welcome.'

Netta looked away, then back at him. 'It doesn't mean all our problems are magically resolved because you get Bertie dressed a few times. I need to know you're going to be there for us all the time. For the long term.'

'Of course.' Johnnie frowned. He was many things, but not a quitter, and he was fiercely loyal to the family.

'I mean it – the long term. Joe and Nathan will grow up, get jobs, move away, have families. But Bertie is going to be with us for the long term. Our whole lives. I need to know that you're committed to that. But he isn't always going to be a cute little boy, Johnnie. One day he's going to be a man – a man who isn't like other people, who's always going to be stared at and different, and . . .' She sighed again. 'You know what I mean. I don't want us to put him away.'

Johnnie was quiet. He knew that was his challenge. To commit to Bertie no matter what, forever. *And to make sure Netta knows she can rely on me.* He put down his glass and looked at her seriously. 'I made a stupid, throwaway remark a while back, when we were battling the council. The whole thing made me very anxious and bleak. I know I hinted that I was thinking about putting Bertie in a home. I've had time to think that through, and I didn't mean it. I love him, Netta, just as he is, and as the man he'll become. He's with us both for life, I know that, and I'm glad about it.'

Her expression softened, and he saw something on her face he hadn't seen for a long time: a mixture of hope and vulnerability. 'Do you really mean that?' she asked.

'Absolutely.'

'Then' – she hesitated – 'perhaps we could think about a move. It will mean losing my support network, moving away from my friends, finding new ones. We're going to have to be a unit, a really strong unit, if we're going to survive down there. There will be fewer resources for Bertie, so we will have to provide more of what he needs.'

'Of course. I'll do some research and we can both think about it.'

'But one more thing.' Netta gave him an ironic look. 'No stately homes, please. I've got enough on my plate.'

Johnnie laughed. 'I promise.'

She put her hand over his. 'And I'll be there for David's funeral. You can count on me for that.'

'Thanks.' He smoothed her palm with the fingers of his other hand. 'I know I can. And it means a lot.'

Having returned the keys to the rectory to his friend, Johnnie moved back in with Alex and the girls when he returned from London.

'How was the big smoke?' Alex asked, coming out to greet him as he climbed out of his car.

'Horrible. The sooner we can get back down here, the

better.' Johnnie came in with his luggage. 'Thanks for having me again, Al.'

'You're welcome. I'd be offended if you went anywhere else.' She led him through to the kitchen where there was fresh coffee in the pot.

'Any word from Sally or Mundo?' Johnnie asked. 'They had a few days to let the contents of the will sink in. I'm surprised we haven't heard from them.'

'Me too.' Alex poured out the coffee into two mugs. 'I would think Sally wants to talk about the future at some point.'

'Mmm,' Johnnie said cryptically. 'I should think so.'

She eyed him. 'We should talk about it. What's going to happen. What we're going to do.'

'Yeah. We'll have to do that.' Johnnie continued to give nothing away.

'Well, we can leave it for now, I suppose. The funeral is so soon, I imagine Sally is focused on that. I was expecting her to ring me, though, if only to talk through arrangements. She was calling every day after Pa died, wanting to know what I thought about hymns and readings, and, "How about 'I Vow To Thee My Country' because"' – Alex did her Sally voice – '"it was a great personal favourite of the princess?"'

Johnnie accepted the mug of coffee and added some milk. He rolled his eyes. 'As if Pa would care about that.'

'Well, you know. After Pa died, Sally lit two candles on either side of that framed photograph Pa got when he left the palace, and put the open box of his ceremonial cufflinks next to it, like a shrine or something.'

'Bit weird. A shrine to who? Pa wasn't her friend. He was her employee. Sally ought to put out a photo of Pa if she wants to start lighting candles.'

Alex nodded. She took a sip of her coffee and said thoughtfully, 'What do you remember, Johnnie, about Mum dying? I don't mean afterwards. I mean . . . at the time.' She looked at her brother, who stared down at the shiny white surface of the kitchen bench. 'I don't remember that day at all, the last day, but I was only seven and you were ten. Do you remember?'

'A little.' Johnnie looked uncertain. He dragged a hand through his thick tawny hair. 'Not much. I remember that it was sunny. We were in the garden for some of it. It was a normal day.'

'Did we see Sally? Or Pa?'

'I don't think so. I don't remember.'

'Was Mum normal?' Alex persisted.

Johnnie sighed. 'I'm sorry, Al. I don't remember. That's what makes me think she must have been normal. Because I'd remember if anything weird or out of the ordinary happened, I'm sure I would.'

'Just a normal day at Tawray,' Alex said slowly. 'Except that Mum decided to kill herself.'

'Yes.' Johnnie looked solemn. 'And everything changed. Forever.' He sighed again. 'I'd give anything to see her again, just once.'

Alex gave him an odd look. 'Well, you know what, Johnnie, it's funny you should say that. There is a way. But you'll have to come to Tawray.'

446

Chapter Thirty-Four

August 1997

'What are the purple ones called?' piped up a small voice.

Julia looked over to where the sound came from, rubbing her damp hair out of her eyes with the back of her wrist. She saw Ali, small brown limbs, short dark hair, big blue eyes as she pointed to a tall flower with a dark round head.

'Those ones are alliums,' Julia called back.

'They look like pom-poms.'

Julia smiled. 'Yes, they do.'

Johnnie whizzed past them on his bike, churning up gravel under his tyres as he went. He was obsessed with his mountain bike and rode it round and round the gardens, up the steps, along the colonnade, round the orangery and back, making engine noises as he went. 'Brr, brr, brrrrrr.'

Julia looked back at Ali, who was almost lost among the tall growth at the centre of the border. 'How are your flowers doing?'

'They look very nice,' Ali said gravely. 'And there are lots of bees. Lots.'

'That's good. Bees help us get fruit in the orchard.'

'One stung my foot,' Ali remarked.

'What, just now? You were very brave about it, you didn't make a squeak.'

'Last week. Remember?'

'Oh yes, I remember that.'

Ali came over, jumping over the lavender bushes at the front of the border. 'What are you doing?'

'I'm cutting flowers for the Christmas garlands. You know how pretty they are, don't you? Well, we have to plan ahead, and grow our flowers in the summer, then save them so that they can still be used in the winter.' Julia held out her trug. 'You see? I'm going to save these pretty ones. We'll hang them up in the back pantry and let them dry out in the dark. They should be all ready by Christmas.'

Ali leaned companionably against her thigh. 'What's this called?'

'It's love-in-a-mist. Also known as nigella. One of my favourites. Come on, my basket's nearly full. It's hot out here and nearly time for tea. Shall we go in?'

'Can I have an ice cream?'

Julia took her hand. 'You won't eat your tea.'

'I will!' Ali looked up with pleading eyes. 'I promise I will.'

'Well . . . all right.' She called Johnnie over, the lure of ice cream enough to stop him spinning around the garden. He dropped his bike on the grass and came in after them.

'You'll have to put that away later,' she reminded him.

'Course I will.'

'You left it out in the rain last time.'

'That was Mundo,' he protested. His face darkened. 'He told me he'd done it on purpose.'

'I'm sure he didn't,' Julia replied. 'He was probably just showing off. Maybe he didn't want to admit how stupid he'd been.'

'He is stupid,' muttered Johnnie as they made their way into the house.

Julia felt strangely unaffected. Yes, Mundo was turning into a nasty little sneak, that much was obvious, but she was confident that Ali and Johnnie were safe enough from him. Sally had not managed to give her son any sense of how to do the right thing but she knew that somehow her two were turning out all right.

They went into the kitchen and found Mrs Petheridge had gone home, leaving out a cold supper for them: chicken and what she called salad, which was sweetcorn and lettuce haphazardly mixed together with some chunks of tomato. The children went into the larder to dig in the freezer for the ice creams Julia got in bulk from the cash and carry.

She put the basket of flowers on the counter so that she wouldn't forget to hang them up, and looked over at the food sitting under the pink fly nets. Nausea swelled up in her stomach at the sight of it.

I'm not hungry. Not in the least. I think I'll give that a miss.

She was serene, though. There was nothing wrong with not being hungry. Plenty of people had no appetite, particularly in the summer. There was nothing unusual about that.

449

The children came out of the larder, already licking pink and white ice creams. 'Where's Pa?' asked Ali.

'He's working,' Julia said brightly. 'He might be down at Sally's house.'

Ali nodded and she and Johnnie wandered out to eat their ice creams in the last of the evening sunshine.

Julia poured a large glass of white wine and took it out onto the terrace. She lit a cigarette and exhaled the smoke into the warm air. She had recently begun to smoke again; she didn't know why. It seemed like a good idea. She was careful to smoke when the children weren't there to see it, but it gave her a small sense of release, just as this ice-cold white wine did as it slid down her throat and hit her empty stomach.

The realisation that David was sleeping with Sally had come slowly but surely, and now she was absolutely certain. He was with her today. The sight of David's car, parked with an attempt at concealment by putting it around the side by the oil tank, had made it quite plain.

'Work,' he would have said, if she had asked him. 'Work.'

So convenient. They had been working in close proximity to one another for years, she saw. In London, where Sally's office was just around the corner from the palace. And then here. David had given up his job at last, only a few years ago. He'd resigned, he said. He left with a pair of royal cufflinks that came in a box from Asprey, a curling D on each circle of blue enamel, and a signed photograph in a silver frame.

Had he resigned? She wasn't entirely sure. There had been huge changes at his establishment. Once his employers had officially separated, there was great work to be done splitting up a household that had previously been united, on the surface at least. The truth was that the fissures had run deep for years, but the opportunity to start afresh had meant a general reorganising and refreshing.

'I resigned,' David said firmly. 'It was time.'

Why was it time then? That's what she didn't understand. By then, though, with Mundo almost five and Sally settled into the cottage, it was clear that she wasn't going back to London. Johnnie and Ali were growing up. Perhaps David felt that his life had to move, if he wasn't going to miss out on it. Still, Julia felt that he never would have gone if he hadn't been somehow pushed, one of the many casualties of his boss's sometimes capricious nature.

They never spoke of her, even when her life was splashed all over the newspapers in all its epic, absorbing scandal. Only now and then, usually when she was on official business – doing what she did best by highlighting uncomfortable issues, bringing her bright spotlight of fame with her – did he say anything, but only to comment on the organisation or the press pack, most of whom he knew well. He muttered when he saw her facing them alone; he would frown and appear cross, as though all the hard work he'd put into his job was being wasted.

Julia read all the papers with a kind of fascination, still under the spell, even though it had turned out that it was another frosted elegant blonde who had been her rival all along. When she read that that suntanned, swimsuited figure had gone out to confront the paparazzi in a boat, she hoped that David hadn't seen it. She knew it would hurt him almost personally to see her do such a thing.

'You're going to be surprised by the next thing I do,' the princess had said to the press.

Julia had stared at the pictures of her facing them down and wondered what on earth she meant. *What? What are you doing to do? What will it be?*

Julia took another drag on her cigarette and saw that a layer of grey was forming on the underside of the puffy summer clouds. Perhaps it would rain this evening – the gardens would be pleased. It was a dry end to the month, and a good soaking would be appreciated.

She wondered how long David would be down at Sally's house. Perhaps she was feeding him, hanging on his every word in the way she had when she'd lived here. 'Oh David, that's fascinating! You are clever!' The eyelashes fluttering, the lips moist.

It seemed laughable, but it obviously worked. It was evidently enough to take David away.

That's not fair. You know it's not.

All right, it wasn't fair. Julia had her own part to play in it all, she acknowledged that.

So David had left court and come back to Tawray, to settle down to life as a country gentleman. He'd taken a job heading up the estate management company that administered this estate – his royal connections made him eminently employable, it turned out – and soon several new clients had joined, lured by the sparkle of his second-hand star dust. After having chuntered along for years, it began to flourish and bring in money, and David was hailed as a canny businessman, which brought in more business. Once Mundo had started at nursery, Sally joined the company as his PA and assistant, and she was an excellent worker – assiduous and intelligent, with an eye for detail.

And I suppose we all benefitted. There was money to repair Tawray, and Julia had plans for the future that would need funds: she wanted to restore the old barn and set up a proper flower farm there – it seemed like the perfect place. The management of the flowers here at Tawray had been going so well; the flower festival held at Christmas was growing every year, and she thought it could be a viable business.

On the surface, then, life looked sweet. But nothing was what it seemed. In the heart of it was the canker of David's infidelity.

But can I blame him?

She, after all, had taken the decision to make their marriage a celibate one. What healthy man could live with that? When she'd told him to seek solace in London, with women she didn't know and never would, he'd wept. He told her he didn't want that, he wanted only her. He said it had always been her, and always would be. But he didn't know if he could spend the rest of his life loveless.

'I love you,' she'd said. 'But I can't go through it again. I cannot do it. I want to, but I can't.'

He hadn't understood, she could see that on his face. What was so hard? Millions of women did it every day without necessarily wanting to. What made her so special?

Julia took a long drink of her wine, and another drag of the noxious cigarette.

What makes me so special?

All her life, they had told her that she needed to think a little less of her own needs, and more of others. You are terrified of having a baby? What on earth makes you so special? Get on with it. You want a marriage of happiness and mutual support? Why on earth should you be any different from anyone else? Your husband's work comes first, and rightly so. Control your horror of pregnancy and sleep with your husband. He's entitled to it.

She wrote to Lala. Her sister had not been back in years. She and David had obviously fallen out badly enough not to want to see one another, and she had not come back. Julia's world had shrunk down to Tawray and its immediate environs – there was no way she could go to France and see Lala herself, so they relied on phone calls and letters. Letters were best, somehow, and she liked to write things she found hard to say:

> *I think that David is sleeping with Sally, just as you said he would. I don't know what to do. I've pushed him away but I never wanted him to go to her instead. I'm afraid I'll lose him forever.*
>
> *He's never been mine. For all our marriage, I've had to share him. If it was just sex with Sally, that might be all right. But I'm afraid she doesn't want to share. I'm afraid she'll take him away, for good.*

Lala wrote back:

*I'm so sorry to hear this. I was afraid it might happen.
I could tell you lots of things about what men are like
but I hoped that David was different. He is a simple
creature, as they all are. He wants to be loved. If you
want to save your marriage, then I believe you must try
and give him that. I think it's the only way. I'm sorry.*

Well, she had done what Lala suggested. She had tried.
And what good had it done? None. She had been more certain than ever that her destruction lay that way. Perhaps,
when nature had taken its course and she was no longer able
to conceive, then she'd be able to feel differently. Until then
it was an impossibility.

She finished the cigarette and drained the glass, then stood
up slowly and went back to the kitchen for more, stumbling
just a little. The wine on her empty stomach had gone quickly
into her bloodstream.

In a moment, she would feed the children, put them to
bed, all the while thinking of David down at Sally's house.
She knew he was there, though today he'd said he was going
fishing. It was too beautiful a day not to enjoy, he'd said.
Almost the end of the summer. The children back to school
next week.

Julia poured out another glass of wine. Her hands were
shaking.

What's wrong with me?

She wondered why, exactly, she had been chosen for the

devil to torment. While others walked happily and naturally through life, she took this burden with her: her incubus. Her filthy, horrible, personal devil sat with her day and night, whispering profane horrors into her ears. The wine sometimes blotted them out, but it could also do the reverse: amplify them to a point where she couldn't stand the noise a moment longer.

She went to the back door. 'Children! Your supper is ready, come in now!'

The white wine sat cold and inviting on the counter. She gazed at it and wondered, *What will it do tonight? Will it blot everything out? Or will it sharpen it unbearably?*

After all, her personal devil had been coming out more and more frequently, to sit across her shoulders. It liked it when David was with Sally, in particular. It told her things she didn't want to hear. It made her remember things she didn't want to remember. It reminded her of her secret.

My dark, dark secret.

The children came scampering in to sit down, chatting merrily. She sat down with them, and lifted the glass to her lips.

Chapter Thirty-Five

Present day

Standing at her father's graveside, Alex couldn't help remembering Jasper's words about wedding anniversaries and what a terrible time of year the winter was.

Does that make it good for funerals?

It certainly ramped up the atmosphere of gloom and misery, to stand in the freezing cold by the ice-bound ground with sunset a few hours away even though it was only just noon. The service was well attended, with lots of local dignitaries, landowners, farmers, townspeople and villagers, who had all had a connection with David or with Tawray at some time. It was a sombre and traditional programme, with beautiful music that Pa would have loved. Johnnie delivered the eulogy. He spoke eloquently of David's life and career, first in the navy and then in royal service; he talked about Julia briefly and the difficult time surrounding her death; and mentioned Sally too, paying tribute to the long and happy marriage she and Pa had shared. His voice shaking just a little at the end, he wished his father Godspeed on his journey, on behalf of his children and grandchildren – neatly avoiding having to mention Mundo's name.

Alex glanced over at Mundo now. He was perfectly turned out as always, in a long black overcoat with an expensive cut to the shoulders, brilliantly shiny shoes and a dark navy tie worn with a white shirt. His hair was neat and his demeanour one of the successful city lawyer with complete self-confidence. He had come with Sally, who was resplendent in a black coat with a huge diamond brooch on the lapel, and a hat of soft black feathers on her hair, now coloured its usual icy blonde. The two of them stood at the graveside, tears pouring down Sally's face, which she dabbed away with a white handkerchief. It was the first time Alex had seen either of them since the news about Pa's will.

She looked away. She was holding Scarlett and Jasmine's hands as they watched, wide-eyed, the last moments of the burial service. They weren't crying but they were quiet and solemn, and she tried to stay strong for their sakes as she watched the coffin lowered down into the earth, its brass plate inscribed with Pa's name. That was the end now, forever.

I never got to say goodbye.

Johnnie stood across the grave from her, holding hands with Netta, his face etched with grief. They had decided not to bring the boys and Alex felt it was the right thing. She rarely saw them as united as they looked right now, Netta pressing close to him as if to give him the extra comfort of her nearness.

Alex looked over to where she could see her mother's

headstone, able to make out some of the lettering on it. *Julia Pengelly. Much loved and missed wife and mother.* She thought of the tiger-eyed girl in the mural and her delightful smile. When Johnnie had said he didn't want to go up to Tawray quite yet – 'I can't face it, Al, I'm sorry' – she had shown him the picture of the mural she'd taken on her phone. He'd zoomed in to look at their mother and when he'd glanced up, his eyes were bright with tears. 'That's amazing,' he'd said, choked. 'She looks so alive. Will Jasper really put it back up?'

'If we want him to,' Alex had said. 'I think he means it.'

They'd put off that decision, along with so many others, until after today. *Including what to do about Sally.* No matter what Johnnie felt, they had to bear in mind what Pa would have wanted, and he must have assumed they would do right by Sally.

Which means, I suppose, that he never really saw how she treated us. Was that because he didn't want to see it? Alex remembered Sally and Pa's wedding day, when he came in to find that Sally had slapped her to the floor, having torn off her T-shirt. He never said a word about it, or rebuked Sally for that action. In fact, Sally was never brought up on anything she did. Pa never said anything.

You wanted a quiet life, didn't you, Pa? And you didn't want to be left alone again. You needed Sally, that much was obvious. I just wish you could have stood up to her a little bit more. I wish you could have shown us that you loved us too.

Pa's will seemed to be that message: he had not given his

possessions to Sally, he had given them to his children, as if in recompense for all the years they had been short-changed at Sally's hands, and put second behind Mundo. In the end, David had decided that blood was thicker than water, and put Sally's fate in their hands. It was a neat little twist.

I couldn't possibly have foreseen that.

She looked over again at Sally and Mundo. The service had come to an end. Sally stepped forward and threw a red rose into the grave. Then she turned, and let Mundo lead her away, as she sobbed.

That's it. It's all over. I really don't need to see her ever again after today. The tie between us is cut forever.

The wake was held at the village hall, and when Alex came in, Sally was there already, her eyes red and her lips shaky even while the feathers on her hat nodded jauntily as she moved her head.

'Alex,' Sally said in a wobbly voice when she saw her, and held out her cheek for a kiss.

Alex kissed it coolly and passed by. Thinking over the past had kindled the old anger and resentment, now inflamed by the knowledge that she would never have the chance to talk to her father again. It was hard not to blame Sally for that. *Just hold on till this is over. Then you can cut her out of your life if you need to.* The girls went off to look at the food on the tables at the side of the hall. Alex collected a glass of wine and went over to join Johnnie and Netta, who were in conversation with a local couple but giving off every vibe that they wanted to be left in peace. Alex managed to disentangle them, and they went out a side door to stand in the car park for some respite from the growing noise in the hall.

'I wish I still smoked,' Johnnie said feelingly. 'This is just the kind of time for a fag.'

'This is going to be the hardest bit,' Alex said, 'and then we can go home.'

'This is our father's funeral, for God's sake,' Johnnie said crossly. 'Why should we have to talk to people we don't want to see, eat horrible sandwiches and shop-bought Battenberg when we've just had to bury Pa?'

'I think some people think of it as offering a bit of consolation,' Netta said gently.

'They don't console me. They bloody bore me – all the talk of golf clubs and knitting groups and rambling associations.'

'They mean well,' Alex said. 'They're just people like Pa. His friends. We'll be like that one day.'

'I won't,' Johnnie said emphatically. 'Because I'm going home to drink a bottle of whisky and smoke a cigar to make sure I never get old.'

Netta looked shocked but Alex laughed. 'Come on, we all rail about becoming old and boring but it's better than the alternative.' She turned to Johnnie. 'You are right, though, about leaving. Let's get the girls and go back to my place. We'll remember Pa as we wanted to.'

'Great idea,' Netta said. 'I'll drive, Johnnie. Let's go back.'

Just then the door to the hall opened, and Mundo stepped out through it. He glanced over at them, his blue eyes flinty. 'I wondered if I'd find you out here,' he said. 'Don't you think it's rather rude to sneak off like this? My mother has no idea where you are. She's been asking for you, Alex.'

'Oh dear,' Alex said coolly. 'I'll make sure I say goodbye on the way out, but it won't be because you want me to.'

He gave his little mirthless half-smile. 'I see. The worm has turned. You've got what you wanted, so my mother can go hang. Nice. Very nice.' He nodded, looking at their wine glasses. 'I guess you're toasting your newfound riches, are you? Pa's not even cold in his grave.'

Alex glanced at Johnnie, whose expression was closing down into anger.

'What did you say?' he demanded.

Mundo gave him a cool look. 'You heard me, Johnnie. I'm sure you're delighted by the prospect of being able to turn a woman – who's been nothing but good to you, by the way – out of her home. I expect you think you've done rather brilliantly, hiding the fact from her that her future security lay in your hands, and you've let her walk right into a trap. By being a brat all your life, you can now say she wasn't the perfect replacement mother to you. Well, she did her damn best with a couple of spoiled little kids who made her life hell right from the start. It was no picnic being married to Pa and looking after him. She took all that off your plate and you never had to be bothered with it for a second. And this is the thanks she's going to get.'

Alex heard a noise that sounded almost like a growl coming from Johnnie's throat. Like two dogs squaring up for a scrap, the men were staring at each other menacingly, daring the other to make some kind of move and set their enmity free.

She held up a hand. 'You know that's not true, Mundo. None of us were perfect, but Sally could be unkind. We were kids who had lost our mother – she could have been a bit more understanding of what we were going through.'

'She did more than a lot of people would have,' Mundo rejoined. 'And it was hard for her when she saw how you treated me.'

Alex's eyes widened in surprise. 'Er . . . how *we* treated you?'

'Two against one,' he said. He looked from one to the other slowly. 'I was the outsider, and, boy, did you make sure I knew it. You never accepted me.'

Alex felt a cold chill of horror as his blue eyes fell on her, remembering the way he had tormented her. 'That's rubbish,' she said in a tight voice.

'No, it's not. You both excluded me. Always trying to get me into trouble.'

'*You* were the troublemaker.' To her horror, her voice was quavering. 'Right from the start. You were always telling lies about us. You know what happened . . . what you did.' Now, she realised, her hands were shaking. The effect of Mundo's cold blue stare and all it brought back was almost too much.

Johnnie said nothing, but one fist was clenched tight, his fingertips white around the stem of his wine glass as though he was about to snap it.

Mundo gave another of his tight half-smiles, one side of his mouth smiling while his eyebrows lifted sardonically.

'I don't know what you're talking about, Alex, but aren't we a little old for all this? Whatever you said to the old man was certainly effective. You've got the estate and all the cash – I've got ten measly grand. And my mother is entirely dependent on your charity, in which I don't have a great deal of faith.' He shook his head. 'I might have to have a drink too, to toast you. Congratulations. You did well. I didn't see it coming. If I had – and I had that kind of mind-set – I might have been able to do something about it and look out for my mother and me. After all, I was brought up as his son. I kind of expected that he might think of me that way.'

Johnnie was keeping control with difficulty. He drained his glass and said tightly, 'Well, I guess he didn't. Who knows, but hey ho, those are the breaks, I guess.'

'Calm down,' Netta whispered, putting her hand gently on his arm.

'Well, that's the thing,' Mundo said slowly. 'Maybe those are the breaks, and maybe they aren't.'

Alex found the sight of him disturbing, almost loathsome. His black coat and air of mourning made him ghoulish, and besides, he represented so much she never wanted to remember. Without meaning to, she shuddered.

Mundo saw it. He looked amused, as though he liked to see her revulsion. It seemed to fire him up again. 'I don't intend to take this lying down. I believe you put undue influence on Pa to exclude me and my mother from the will.'

'The Tawray estate wasn't his to give away!' snapped Johnnie. 'You obviously don't know your trust law. You'd

464

better start being nice to us, Mundo. We've got the power to evict your mother if we feel like it.'

'We'll see.' Mundo gave them all a look of scorn. 'You better enjoy your little celebration while you can. Just in case it doesn't last.'

He turned on his heel and marched back into the hall.

Alex turned to Johnnie, horrified. Her brother looked pale and angry. 'What do you think he means?' she asked. 'Do you think he's going to challenge the will?'

'Anyone can challenge a will,' Netta said gravely, 'but that doesn't mean they'll succeed.'

'I don't think he cares about that,' Johnnie said, white about the lips. 'He probably wants to hold up probate and stop us being able to administer the estate or receive our bequests. He can do that for years.'

'But that means he and Sally don't get their money!' Alex exclaimed.

'He probably thinks that's worth it. Sally can stay where she is, as long as she has money to pay the bills. Mundo isn't going to care about ten grand – he must earn twenty times that a year.'

'On what grounds can he challenge any of it?' Alex asked. 'I thought the estate was all part of Mum's bequest.'

'I suppose that's what we're about to find out,' Johnnie said, the fight going out of him.

'Don't worry,' Netta said, putting an arm around him. 'We can take him on together. You told me he was obnoxious, but wow. He gives a whole new meaning to the word.'

Johnnie managed a grateful smile.

Alex straightened her shoulders. 'We won't let him win,' she said with vehemence. 'We just won't. We can't.'

Netta and Johnnie headed off, saying they would meet her back at the Old Barn. Alex went back into the hall to gather the girls together and get their things. She was tired: on top of her sadness from the funeral, the encounter with Mundo had left her troubled. She concentrated on getting the three of them out without bumping into too many of Pa's old friends, or attracting the attention of Sally, who was with Mundo at the far end of the hall.

She was just at the double doors at the entrance when a soft voice stopped her.

'Excuse me . . . are you Alexandra?'

Alex turned to see a well-groomed woman in her late fifties, smart in an expensive black suit and heels, with a boxy black handbag hanging on a silver chain over her shoulder. She had a glossy swinging auburn bob, light blue eyes and a long bony nose over slim lips.

'Yes?' Alex stared at her, seeing something faintly familiar in her face.

'I wanted to say hello, and introduce myself. I don't know many people here but I saw that it was David's funeral today and I wanted to come. There aren't so many of us left, after all. I think we need representatives of the family where we can get them.'

Alex smiled at her, confused. 'I'm so sorry, I don't know . . .'

The woman laughed awkwardly. 'I haven't said my name,

how silly! I'm Violet Hamlyn. I was . . . I am . . . your father's cousin by marriage. I wanted to express my condolences to you on his passing.'

'You're related to Sally?'

'No. To your mother. To Julia. I'm her cousin Violet.'

Alex gaped at her, and the image of the mural burst into her mind. She saw the meek, bland figure of Violet, small and dumpy, at the back of the picture where Julia dominated the foreground with her tawny, vivacious glamour. It was not immediately obvious, but now she could see traces of the younger face in the older one. 'Of course. Cousin Violet!'

'That's right.' Violet looked interested. 'Did your mother talk about me?'

'I don't think so. But I was a bit too young to remember if she did.'

'Of course you were.' Violet flushed and looked apologetic. 'I'm so sorry. That was clumsy of me.' She smiled and her gaze flicked to the door. 'I can see you're heading off so I won't keep you. My condolences again. It's been so lovely to meet you. Goodbye.' She turned to go back into the room.

Jasmine pulled on Alex's hand and muttered that she wanted to go home. Scarlett kicked lightly at the skirting board as she gazed at the posters on the wall. Alex stammered out, 'Wait!'

Violet turned back. 'Yes?'

'I need to ask you something – if you don't mind, if there's time.' Alex turned to the girls. 'Go and get some biscuits if you like.' They scampered off as Alex pulled out her mobile phone and opened up the photograph file. 'We've recently found an old painting – a mural – that used to be in the drawing room . . . Here it is. Maybe you remember it?'

Violet gasped as she looked down at the image. 'The old mural! How fabulous! I haven't seen that for years! Last time I went to Tawray, it was gone. That was decades ago. Oh, how marvellous.' She took the phone and spent a few moments exclaiming over it, her eyes bright, then handed it back. 'That's lovely. Thank you for showing me.'

Alex took the phone. 'You should come and see it when we put it up again. But I have a question . . .' She pointed to the woman in the middle of the mural: young, fair and blue-eyed, with fine features, wearing a mustard-yellow blouse and a denim skirt with some seventies chunky-heeled slip-ons.

Violet looked. 'Yes, that's Lala.'

'Who?'

'Don't you know? Your mother's older sister, Lala. Well, her half-sister, from her father's first marriage.'

'Half-sister?' echoed Alex, astonished.

Violet seemed surprised. 'Do you not know about her?'

'No.' Alex looked back at the figure in the painting. 'Not a clue! How bizarre. No one has ever mentioned a half-sister.'

'I think there was an argument of some kind,' Violet said vaguely. 'I'm not sure really, I wasn't close to Julia. I only heard what was going on from my mother. But I know she told me that Lala left Tawray after a bad falling-out, and didn't go back.'

'Do you know where she is now?' Alex asked, and her heart began to beat faster.

'Not exactly. We weren't close and we've never been in touch. I can tell you what I know. I'm sure you could track her down if you want to.'

Alex beamed at her, the smile growing broader as she realised the implications of what Violet was saying. *Mum had a sister. I can find her.* 'That would be absolutely brilliant, Violet. Yes please. Tell me everything you know.'

Chapter Thirty-Six

Johnnie and Netta walked along the beach hand in hand. It was freezing but the majesty of the sea crashing on the beach in ceaseless motion made the cold worth it.

'That meant a lot to me, Netta,' he said to her, squeezing her hand. 'What you said to me yesterday with that bastard Mundo right there.'

Netta looked at him, the wind ruffling her cropped hair into little dark feathers. She smiled. 'I know we've had our problems, but you're worth a hundred of him, Johnnie. I thought about how horrible it would be for the boys if a man like that were their father. They're so lucky to have you. They adore you, and I know you love them.'

'I do,' Johnnie replied. 'All three of them.' He emphasised that. She had to be completely certain that he was committed to Bertie. 'I want a life down here for them if at all possible – but only if it works for you.' They strode along on the sand, matching their footsteps so that they made prints in exact pairs.

After they'd been walking out in long strides for a while,

each lost in thought, Netta spoke. 'There are definitely some advantages to moving. I like the idea of clean air and a spacious home for Bertie. The pollution around London is awful. You can taste how pure the air is here. I think that'll be good for him. And I've found a couple of schools that look interesting. Worth investigating. No promises,' she said quickly, seeing his delighted face. 'But my mind is open.'

'Oh God, I'm sure you wouldn't regret it, Netta,' Johnnie said fervently. 'I'll do everything I can to make you so glad you agreed. I reckon I could get Robert to rent us the rectory again, if you'd like that. Or we could find somewhere else if you'd prefer.'

'I haven't said I will yet,' Netta cautioned. 'Don't rush me.'

'Of course . . . take all the time you need.'

They walked in companionable silence for a while, and then Netta said, 'We've got to stay in any case.'

'Have we?'

She smiled at him. 'There's no way I'm letting that vile little man win. You told me about what happened when you were growing up, and I didn't believe a word of what he said yesterday – about you two ganging up on him. I know you and Alex, and I can see that you're not like that. If anything, you've both been struggling all your lives with the result of the way you were treated as children. Mundo's arrogance and coldness were blindingly obvious. So I'll be damned if he gets to cheat you and Alex out of what you're entitled to. We'll stay here and we'll fight him.'

'Atta girl!' cried Johnnie and he broke into a run, pulling

her after him until she started running too and they careered around the beach, laughing and breathless.

I'm alive, Johnnie thought. He remembered screeching to a halt just feet from the bonnet of the oncoming car and the sense of helpless despair as he'd contemplated his life being over. The profound, overwhelming knowledge of how precious it all was, how much he wanted to live. He'd felt differently ever since. Life and death were so very close, the barrier between them so fragile. Pa had lived, loved, made children and died. Death would come for Johnnie one day, and then for the boys, and then for their children, and so on forever. But right now, he was here. With Netta.

He pulled her into his arms and kissed her hard, tasting the salt air on her lips, feeling her soft skin against his, inhaling her warm, sweet scent.

'I love you,' he said fervently when they'd separated. 'And our boys, and our life. It's not perfect but it's ours. Let's not waste it. Let's be happy.'

She smiled, the warm, open smile of the old Netta. 'You know what? I think we can do that.'

In the waiting area for the afternoon Eurostar departure to Paris, Alex felt her spirits lift. The girls were with Tim for the weekend and this journey away – an impulsive, last-minute one she'd only decided on last night – meant stepping out of normal life and leaving it behind.

It's exciting. And I have no idea what's waiting for me at the other end.

On the train, she settled into her seat and watched as they

slid slowly out of St Pancras and away through Kent, headed for the tunnel. She got out her notes and her laptop and checked everything she meant to do. There was an email from her friend Gita, a journalist, who had set everything up, just in case the name Pengelly was not a welcome one. Gita had contacted Lala under the guise of wanting to interview her for a newspaper, about her life in fashion. But it would be Alex who turned up on her doorstep. When she felt on top of everything, Alex leaned back and rested, falling asleep and not waking up until they were almost at the Gare du Nord. It was dark and cold, and she took a taxi to her hotel, an eccentric little place on the Left Bank that she'd found years before on a trip with Tim. She'd loved it but he was doubtful, so they'd never gone back. Despite her nap on the train, Alex had only enough energy to change and get ready for bed, then she went soundly to sleep again.

The next morning was a bright and crisp January day. Paris looked enticing but she turned her face against its charms and went to the station to catch the RER train for the hour-long journey to Versailles-Chantier instead.

Am I doing the right thing? she wondered as she watched the Paris suburbs glide past the window. She'd been so sure when she booked this impulsive trip. Violet had given her enough information to track down her elusive aunt and now here she was, and she would have to face her. *I couldn't not try to find her. She's got the answers we need, I'm sure of it.*

At Versailles, she walked from the pretty glass-and-iron station into the town, following the directions on her phone. The nerves were kicking in now, causing a sick sensation to swirl in her stomach. Was this cloak-and-dagger approach the right one? Perhaps it would have been better to be more upfront. Surprises were not always welcome.

Ah well, it's too late now.

Her phone led her into the town centre and to the fashionable Montreuil quarter, and from there, off the busy main road and down a quiet little street with modern buildings and shops on one side, and old shuttered houses on the other. Halfway down on the right, a small house was tucked between two larger ones, like a child between two grown-ups. It was grey and looked battered and worn, but there was a charm to its dark shutters, red-tiled roof, and the climbing plant curling its way up and over the blue front door.

This is it.

Alex's heart began to beat faster as she stood on the door-step, trying to gather up the nerve to knock. Her courage was rapidly failing her, and she was just about to turn on her heel and head away when the door opened and a slender woman in late middle-age stood there in a tartan coat dress, her jet-black hair rather magnificently awry. '*Oui?*' she said crisply. Then said something very fast in French that Alex didn't understand.

'Um,' she said lamely.

A voice from within said in English, 'Don't be so impatient, Lisbet, I think it's this Gita lady, coming to interview me.' Another woman came into view, a little older than the first. She peered at Alex through a pair of rimless spectacles. She was tall, elegant and her short hair was a soft white shot through with blonde. 'Are you Gita?'

'I . . . yes . . . I mean . . . no.'

'Yes or no?' the older woman said. 'Which?'

'Gita sent me,' Alex replied. 'But I'm not Gita.'

A look of impatience crossed her face. 'Why did she send you? If she couldn't come, she should have rescheduled.'

'I asked her to contact you, because I was afraid you wouldn't see me if you knew who I am.' Alex licked her lips and took a breath. 'I'm Alexandra Pengelly.'

The woman went still and stared at her, evidently taken completely by surprise. 'I see,' she said, her voice fainter. Then it regained its strength. 'Well, Alexandra Pengelly, you'd better come in.'

The rather dour exterior of the house successfully concealed the beauty within. Each room was exquisitely furnished in a mixture of rustic French and English antique styles, and alive with colour and vibrant fabrics. The walls were hung with modern art and the old tiled floor covered in herringbone coir rugs.

'Please sit down. Lisbet, would you get us some tea?' Lala Teague fixed Alex with a bright blue stare. 'It's a little early for wine, isn't it? Even though I quite feel the need for some.'

Alex took her seat on a sofa decorated with magenta and yellow ikat cushions. She was afraid and yet exhilarated: she'd been invited in. That was positive. Lisbet went off into a galley kitchen at the back and started boiling a kettle, while the woman Alex knew was her aunt continued to stare at her, drinking her in.

'You look like David,' she said at last. 'But I can see

something of Julia in you too. So, tell me. Why are you here? My guess is that it isn't to interview me about my career in fashion.'

'No,' Alex admitted. 'I got my friend to say that, just in case you didn't want to see me.'

'Why wouldn't I?'

'I don't know. That's why I'm here. Because I don't know much, and I'm hoping you can give me the answers I'm looking for. You're one of my only relatives on my mother's side, and we've never met, even though you're my mother's half-sister. My aunt.'

'Yes, your aunt.' Lala hesitated, as if considering where she could start with this unknown, unexpected niece. 'Well, if you want to know why we haven't met before, the answer is very simple. First, we have met. When you were just a baby. And the reason why we didn't meet again was that your father banned me from the house and from having anything to do with my sister. We had a fierce argument not long after you were born. I was bad for her, apparently. Sally was much better. Well, I was busy myself, and newly in love and setting up a home. I let time slip by, feeling hurt and rejected. I spoke with Julia, of course, but I never went back to Tawray. Then . . . after she died . . . I was so heartbroken and I couldn't bear to return.' A sad expression crossed her face. 'It was my home once as well. You probably don't know that, but it was.'

'I do – that's how I found you. You're on the mural.'

'The mural?' Lala sounded astonished. 'How do you

know about that? Did you find a picture of it? It disappeared years ago.'

'No. We found it again. It wasn't destroyed, it was taken down and rolled up for safekeeping. And when we unrolled it, we found you.' Alex handed over her phone with the photograph on its screen and Lala took it, putting on a pair of rimless glasses and squinting through them.

'Oh my goodness,' she whispered. She stared at the picture for a while, and when she looked up, she was smiling, her eyes bright. 'I never thought I'd see that again. And I never thought I'd see you either. I thought all that was gone for good and that you would have been trained to hate me by that woman.'

'You mean Sally?'

Lala nodded. Lisbet came through with a tea tray which she set down on the low table. She poured it out and handed it around, then went quietly away, leaving the other two to talk. Lala continued to talk all the while.

'I warned your mother about Sally. I told her what would happen if she continued to let her live in the house and pay such obvious court to David. It astonished me that she couldn't see it. It was flirtation on a mammoth scale – on a monstrous scale! And the wife was letting it happen right under her nose; she was letting her husband be stolen from her while she watched, and in her very own house!'

Alex felt sick. 'So that's what happened, then?' She realised suddenly that she had badly hoped that wasn't the case. 'Why was Sally living in our house?'

Lala waved a hand and picked up her tea for a sip. 'Sally

had got pregnant outside marriage, and your mother hadn't been terribly well when she had Johnnie and was worried the same thing would happen when she had you.'

'Morning sickness?'

'Something like that. David worked in London for the royal family, busy all the time, only there at weekends. So with Sally pregnant and virtually homeless, it seemed an excellent arrangement for her to come and keep your mother company. Poor Julia couldn't see what a viper she was nestling to her bosom. My belief is that woman had her eye on David from the start. She couldn't be bothered to go and get her own man. She wanted him, and she wanted everything Julia had.' Lala looked suddenly fierce, her scorn for Sally evident.

'But the house was Mum's,' Alex pointed out. 'Not Pa's. If he'd left her, he and Sally would have been out on their ear together.'

'But if Sally didn't know that, perhaps she thought she would get the house, the lifestyle, the security. If she did know – well, maybe her love for David was genuine. Or maybe she intended to hound your mother to death.'

Lala said it flatly but the horror still came through and Alex gasped, appalled. She had never once, in all her days, thought Sally might purposefully have tried to drive her mother to her death. *It's a terrible thought!* She realised afresh how little she knew of the past.

'What happened to Mum?' she asked, leaning forward towards her aunt. 'We were never really told. And now that Pa is dead—'

'David's dead too?' Lala's face softened. 'Oh. I didn't know. I'm sorry, my dear. And now you're looking for answers.' She eyed Alex curiously. 'Are you married?'

'I'm divorced – almost – and I've got two girls.'

'You're at a time in your life when things need explaining – you bring two new people into the world and suddenly your own life and your own childhood are thrown into relief. You wonder what was going on around you when you were little. I understand that. Now you've lost your father, your thoughts are returning to your mother. That's understandable too.' Lala leaned back against her cushions. 'I can't tell you much from the time you were born. I wasn't there for those years. But I know your father was unfaithful with Sally, and Julia knew about it. Julia was beautiful and spirited and emotional and she'd had her own demons – a mother who died in late pregnancy. It left her both fragile and idealistic – a very, very toxic combination. If you're tough and pragmatic, life is easier for you. If you're the reverse, life is a series of desperate disappointments, frightful setbacks and broken dreams. And if, like Julia, you're desperate for love and tormented by fear and mental problems, life can become overwhelming.'

'She had depression,' Alex said quietly, but her mind was reeling from the knowledge that Johnnie had been right. There had been an affair between Pa and Sally, and Mum had known. No wonder she'd wanted to die. Bitter hatred towards Sally rose up inside Alex, a hundred times stronger than anything she'd ever felt before.

'Yes, a certain sort of depression. It probably started from her experience with her mother dying but it grew to encompass all aspects of her life. Eventually, she couldn't cope at all. She tried, though. She used the garden to help her.' Lala smiled at her. 'And you children. She loved you both so desperately.'

'It's hard to understand why she left us.' Alex's voice quavered. 'That's always been the hardest thing.'

'She wouldn't have wanted to. They found high levels of toxins in her blood – she'd drunk a lot. She wasn't in her right mind. Leaving you would have been her nightmare.'

'What happened?'

Lala looked suddenly desperately sad. 'She went out onto that horrible lake, with all its weeds and stems, in the rotten boat. She was alone, so no one saw it, but somehow she ended up over the side, tangled up in all of that weed. And she drowned.' Her expression misted as she remembered. 'That morning was surreal. Bizarre. I lived in the middle of Paris then and that night the world turned on its head. I woke up to hear of that car accident, the one that killed the princess. The news was full of it, the streets were crammed, reporters everywhere, it was mayhem. My telephone went and when David told me the news, I was so confused. I thought he was mixing up Julia with her. I kept saying but no, she's in Paris! It's here that she's dead! He was so stunned by both events – he knew the princess too, of course – and he was almost overwhelmed by their coinciding. Within a week, he was at the funeral in Westminster Abbey. A little while later, after the post-mortem and the release of the body, he was at Julia's. Sally was at his side, of course.'

'Were you there?'

'No. I didn't come. I was too angry. I couldn't bear to lay eyes on them because I believed they'd killed her.' Lala lifted her chin obstinately. 'I still believe that, if I'm honest. I was too angry to come back, even if they'd wanted me, which they didn't. David said to me over the phone I should leave you children alone to have a normal childhood. I was desperately offended – I thought he meant Lisbet, you see, and that he was worried I might infect you in some way with my decadence.' She looked suddenly repentant, her chin going down and her shoulders slumping. 'That was possibly wrong. I probably owe you an apology for leaving you alone all this time.'

Alex smiled sadly. 'Who knows? We can't tell what might have been.'

Lala was looking at her almost as if for the first time. 'You seem like an impressive young woman, Alexandra. Julia would have been very proud if she were here now. She would love to know you and your children. I don't believe she would ever have left you if the pain of staying weren't too great.'

There was silence for a moment and their mutual sadness filled the air.

'Are you sure Pa and Sally started their affair while Mum was still alive?'

'That's certainly what she believed.'

'And you think that's what drove her to her death?'

'What else could it have been? She had everything to live for – apart from that.' Lala's expression was sombre. 'That's what I've believed all these years.'

Alex gazed at the tiled floor in contemplation, then spoke softly. 'I still feel like there are questions to answer. I don't think I understand yet.'

'Perhaps you never can. Maybe the answers aren't there.'

'They are,' Alex said. 'I'm sure of it. Sally can tell me. You can tell me.' She leaned forward. 'Lala, would you come to Tawray? I want your memories and stories and everything you can tell me about my mother. The answer might be in there, even though you don't know it. Johnnie needs it too. He's still suffering. It would help us. Will you?'

Lala stared and said nothing for a long while. Then she got to her feet and walked around the room pensively. 'Tawray,' she said at last. 'I have such mixed feelings about it. I was happy there, though. And so was Julia.' She smiled. 'So very strange that you found the painting. I'd love to see it again.' Then, suddenly decisive, she nodded once. 'Yes. I will come. Very soon. I'll come and I'll try to tell you everything you and Johnnie need to know. I owe you that.'

Chapter Thirty-Seven

When Alex got home on Sunday afternoon with the girls in the back of the car, tired from their weekend with their father, she was surprised to see a car parked in the driveway. Then she spotted Jasper outside the house, inspecting the view out over the fields.

'Hello,' he said, as she got out. 'You're back!' His eyes went to the girls as they climbed out with their overnight bags. 'Sorry, is this a bad time?'

'It's fine,' Alex said with a smile, though she felt exhausted from her whistle-stop trip to Paris. She'd got back that morning, having spent the night in a cheap London hotel before catching an early train home. 'These are my daughters, Scarlett and Jasmine.'

'Hi, girls!' Jasper said with a smile and a wave. They chorused their hellos, and then waited impatiently on the doorstep for Alex to let them in. 'They're gorgeous,' he said to Alex as they disappeared down the hall once she'd opened the door. 'You must be so proud.'

'I am. Come in. Would you like a coffee? You want to see me about something?'

'Always.' Jasper smiled as he followed her in. 'A little bird told me that you just had a birthday.'

'Well, it was a while ago now. It was on New Year's Eve. I didn't feel like doing much, with Pa just having died, so it went under the radar.'

'No, no, I quite see that.' He looked solemn as they went into the kitchen and Alex put her bag down. 'But what a date for a birthday. Always a party!'

'Yes, but never a birthday party,' she replied, and they laughed.

'So next year, you should do a Scottish Hogmanay,' he said conversationally. 'I think you'd love it. Proper reeling and everything. *I* love it.'

'Do you wear a kilt?'

'Of course. I've got the full outfit. It's a crowd pleaser.' He grinned, then went on. 'So I called by on the off chance to see if your brother wanted to come up and see the mural. It's a bit large to leave in the drawing room indefinitely. I'm going to put it back in the attic until you decide what you'd like done with it.'

Alex gasped. 'I'm sorry, I completely forgot we'd left it rolled out for him to look at! You must have been walking around it for ages.'

'It's been no bother,' Jasper said with a friendly shrug. 'But maybe it's time to put it away.'

'Johnnie would love to see it.' Alex smiled at him. 'It looks like my brother is going to be moving down here permanently. He's taking over running the estate. You two will probably have a lot to do with each other.'

'Ah.' Jasper looked thoughtful. 'Well, I hope he doesn't mind dealing with a stubborn Scottish git.'

'He can't wait. Says it's always been his dream. Actually, he is really interested in some of your schemes. I told him about your plan for ground-source heating and he loves it. He wants the whole estate to move towards environmentally friendly methods of living – he thinks Tawray could be a model for the future.'

Jasper looked excited. 'Really? Ah, that's great! And I've got some plans for your old house – always assuming you guys are happy with them. Listen, what do you think of this? Totally carbon-neutral wedding receptions.'

'Great idea.' Alex smiled at him. Her spirits rose and her tiredness lifted. Talking about the future and what they could do to make it better always cheered her up. It helped her put the worst of the past away for good. 'It sounds like we've got a lot to talk about. My brother's in London with his family, but he's coming back tonight. Can I bring him up tomorrow?'

'Of course.'

'Great.'

There's a lot to spring on Johnnie before then. I hope he's ready for it.

Johnnie sat on the sofa close to the fire, a glass of wine in his hand, and listened astonished as Alex told him about her trip to Paris. When she'd finished, he said, 'You didn't think to tell me about this before you went?'

'It was such an impulsive decision. We were all still reeling from Pa's funeral and Mundo's behaviour, and I wasn't thinking all that clearly. But the first thing I've done is tell you.'

'I could have come with you.'

'I thought about that. But I wasn't sure how we'd be received, and one person is less intimidating than two. As it turned out, she was absolutely fine.' Alex remembered her afternoon with Lala in the house in Versailles. 'In fact, she didn't turn a hair. You'd have thought it was an everyday occurrence, having a long-lost niece turn up out of the blue. But afterwards she sent me this.' Alex pushed her phone across the table to show him the email she'd received from Lala, in which she poured out the emotions she felt on being reunited with Alex and the feelings of guilt and regret she had about their separation.

Johnnie read it, his expression blank.

'She wants to come and see us, and visit Tawray – it used to be her home too, she grew up there.' Alex looked at him pleadingly. 'Imagine what she can tell us about Mum. Don't you want to know? I want to, very badly. I feel as though people have tried to keep us away from her for so long. Lala can tell you about what happened, the way she did me. I feel as though that will somehow bring Mum back just a little.'

Johnnie nodded slowly. Then he closed his eyes. When he opened them, he sighed. 'It's hard to let go of anger,' he said. 'Why didn't she come and help us when we were only young? How come everyone left us to Sally's tender mercies?'

Alex nodded. 'What happened, happened. Everyone made mistakes.'

'But aren't you angry, Al? Angry at Sally and Pa? If what Lala said is true, they started their affair right under Mum's nose.'

'I know.' Alex felt the bubbling of her fury. It had been eating at her ever since she'd seen Lala. All the way back on the Eurostar, all through the night in that cheap hotel and on the train home. *They killed her, they killed her, they killed her.* Something deep inside her had changed. The pity she'd had for Sally, the desire for them to forge a bond – that had gone. Lala's words rang in her ears and played over and again in her mind: Sally had been a viper in the bosom. Perhaps she had intended to hound Mum to her death. She had been sleeping with Pa before Mum died, maybe for years, and Mum knew it. 'I am angry. I'm furious.' She shook her head. 'I think that perhaps she deserves what Pa did to her – leaving her without security and a home. Maybe we should do exactly what we want, and chuck her out. Let Mundo take care of her. I expect she'll soon see that he wasn't worth everything she did for him, the way she tried to further his interests over us all the time. Maybe we should do that.'

Johnnie stared at her and she could see reflected in his eyes her own feelings of rage and desire for revenge. 'Yes,' he said grimly.

Alex pictured Sally – the blue-green eyes, frosted blonde hair, powder-soft skin. The strangely old-fashioned clothes, the desire for everything to be neat and tidy. *She's a mystery.*

A hateful, horrible mystery. And she deserves to suffer for what she did.

Johnnie said slowly, 'Maybe she should get what's coming to her.'

Alex drove them both up to the house the next morning. It was Johnnie's first trip back to Tawray in a very long time, and it was odd to know that the pain he'd felt at its loss had been that of a phantom bereavement. It was still there, and while they might not live there, they were still its owners, entwined with its past and its future.

Alex talked excitedly on the drive there. 'I'm sure you and Jasper are going to get on. He's so enthusiastic, he's got loads of ideas for encouraging environmentally friendly living, and supporting local business. He's got piles of inspiration for how we can work together.'

Johnnie raised his eyebrows. 'Oh, I say – has he now? And who exactly is this Jasper? Sounds like he's a little more than just the occupant of Tawray.'

Alex laughed, flushing slightly. 'He's a friend. And he's married, actually, so don't get any ideas. But I think he's a good thing for Tawray and he certainly wants to work with us, not against us.' She told him how Jasper had turned the flower festival into much more than she imagined. 'So he's worth cultivating, especially if you're going to be running the estate. You two could come up with some brilliant schemes. Jasper was saying he wanted to get Tawray running on an all-natural reed bed system, and cut out non-organic products in the water system entirely. Nothing but biodegradable cleaning products, shampoos, soaps, you name it . . .'

'I like that idea,' Johnnie said thoughtfully. Alex's positivity was catching. 'We want to move Bertie entirely to organic and biodegradable products, to help with his allergies.'

'Good idea. And here we are.'

They were welcomed by Jasper, who came out onto the front steps before they'd even had time to ring the bell.

'So you're Johnnie.' Jasper shook Johnnie's hand heartily. 'It's an honour to make your acquaintance. I think we've got some fun times ahead of us, according to Alex. Lots of people think these old houses don't have a place in the modern world. But I think they're wrong. We need community more than ever, with the virtual world taking over so much of our lives. We need places, we need spaces. We need gardens and other people.' He waved his arm in the direction of the house, with its many windows, its turrets and gracious proportions. 'That's what we can do here. People. Nature. Harmony. That's my dream.'

'Wow,' Johnnie said with a laugh. 'And all before we've had coffee.'

'Sorry, mate, sorry – come in! I can get carried away sometimes, can't I, Alex?'

'A bit,' Alex said dryly. She smiled. 'But that's what we like about you.'

Johnnie was looking up at the big house. For so long, he'd thought of it as the place where Sally had made his life a misery, where Mundo had tormented him and where Pa had appeared to turn his face against him and not see what was going on. And it was the place where Mum had died, with all the terrible changes that meant.

But what if we remake it? What if we can do what Jasper says, and bring people in? He thought of Bertie and the way he needed safe spaces to occupy, room to be taught and room to live. Once he grew up and could no longer be in full-time education, he would need somewhere he could live and breathe and be occupied. Could that be somewhere like this?

Just then, Polly came marching out of the front door. ''Scuse me,' she said briefly, not looking at the visitors.

'Where are you off to, Pols?' Jasper asked in a friendly tone.

'Shopping,' she said shortly, and went quickly down the steps to her car. A moment later, it was pulling around on the gravel and heading for the gates.

'Charming, isn't she?' Jasper said, shaking his head as he watched her go. 'I'll never get what my brother sees in her.'

'Your brother?' Alex said, looking surprised. 'Duncan?'

'No. The other one. Hugh. He and Polly went off to Australia to find a new life, didn't like it and came back penniless. So they're living with me until they get back on their feet. Well, Polly is. Hugh is out on the oil rigs, making some money.'

'So she's your sister-in-law,' Alex said slowly.

Johnnie gave her a quizzical look and a smile. Alex was clearly not in possession of that bit of information.

'Yes. And a right bundle of laughs she is too. Our very own little ray of sunshine.'

Johnnie glanced back at Alex, who had flushed light pink. *I can help her out here.* 'Are you married, Jasper?' he asked casually.

'Nope. Polly's put me off the idea, if I'm honest. Now, you'd better come and see this painting,' Jasper said, leading the way to the door. 'We need to decide what to do with it.'

'Absolutely,' Johnnie said, following him into the house. 'Lead the way.'

Once he was actually in front of the painting, Johnnie realised he was in no way prepared for the scale of it. It was enormous, the people life-sized, the proportions perfect and the effect of realism astounding. The full effect would only be felt when it was upright, he could see that, but even so, it was wonderfully real.

'Look at the mice!' he said, pointing them out wherever he saw them.

'Why are there boxes of matches everywhere?' Alex asked wonderingly.

'I think it's full of messages,' Jasper said. 'I see more and more of them – I just can't work out what they mean.' He pointed to the window in the painting. 'I mean why is there a parrot on the curtain rail? There must be a reason, don't you think, Ali?'

Johnnie looked at his sister, surprised to hear her called by her old childhood name. She was evidently startled. 'Did you just call me Ali?'

'Did I?' Jasper looked surprised. 'I don't know why. You just look like an Ali to me. But I'll make sure I call you Alex from now on.'

'No, no, it's fine. you can call me Ali. I don't mind it.' She smiled.

'You're right, Jasper,' Johnnie said firmly. 'She does look like an Ali. I'll call you that too, if you like.'

'I think I do,' Alex said with a laugh. 'Try it out, and we'll see.'

While Alex and Jasper talked about all the possible hidden meanings in the painting, Johnnie stared at the picture of his mother. She was just a girl but unmistakable as his mother; he remembered with sudden vivid clarity things he had forgotten: the shape of her eyes, the colour of her hair that was so like his own, the way her hands looked. He could hear her voice again after years of forgetting it. He heard her calling him in across the lawn, reading him a story, singing to him. He felt her soft touch and a kiss on his cheek.

This was her place first. Before it was Pa's and before it was Sally's.

The thought was comforting. They'd tried to shut her out of Tawray, but they never could. It was her place and her home. She was here and always would be.

'I think this whole painting is a message to Mum,' he said suddenly. 'She's the only one looking out and look at that smile – it's so collusive. I think the painter was telling her story in this picture. We just have to work out what it is.'

'That's a lovely idea,' Alex said softly.

'Aye,' Jasper said. 'I like the way this study of grown-ups is full of the elements of a child's imagination. That's something really special. And she' – he pointed to Lala – 'is gorgeous.'

'You'll get to tell her that in person soon,' Alex said with a laugh. 'Though she won't quite look the same and her girl-friend might be a bit protective of her in that respect.'

'A man can dream,' he replied cheerfully. 'Then I guess we know the answer to the dilemma of whether we put it up, or we put it away . . .'

'Of course,' Alex said.

'Up,' Johnnie said. 'It's the only way to go, after all.'

When they got back to the Old Barn later that day, Johnnie found his spirits swooping downwards once more. It had been wonderful to see his mother again, and to experience that flood of vivid memory. Now sadness was setting in.

He looked over at Alex as she started to make them both some lunch. The girls were back at school, the house was quiet, apart from Hadji's snores as he slept in the basket by the door.

'I've been thinking,' Johnnie said. 'Seeing Mum again . . .' He felt that burning anger reignite inside his belly. 'If Pa and Sally really drove her to it . . .'

Alex looked back, her eyes apprehensive. 'I know what you're thinking.'

'If they really did . . . ' – Johnnie took a deep breath – 'Sally should get what's coming to her.'

'We have to be sure,' Alex said solemnly. 'We have to be absolutely certain we know the truth.'

'Sally would never tell us,' Johnnie said dismissively. 'She's a completely unreliable witness. She'll protect herself, like she's always done.'

'Maybe. But we ought to give her the chance.' Alex turned back to the soup she was stirring. 'If we're planning to take everything away from her, then we owe her that.'

Chapter Thirty-Eight

1997

David felt numb. The service was over. All around him, people were sobbing. Unbearably sad mourning music filled the ancient abbey, discordant yet beautiful, as the choir entreated the Lord to give rest to his handmaiden, who had fallen asleep.

David watched the procession approach slowly down the central aisle. The boots of the guardsmen carrying the lead-lined coffin crashed to the ground in perfect time as they bore it out towards the September sunshine. With each step, the trumpets of the lilies on top of the coffin shuddered. The world was watching, it seemed. Watching and weeping.

May flights of angels sing thee to thy rest.

The shock and agony in the abbey were palpable. She was too young. She was beautiful.

The pallbearers passed him, slow, steady, their faces set in strained concentration as they bore their heavy load. The colours, to David, seemed too bright for this despair: the scarlet of their uniforms, the vivid gold, red and blue of the royal standard draped over the coffin, the pure white of the lilies, the green of their leaves.

She's in there. Inside there.

How had all that light and life and promise been extinguished? What had it all been for?

What does it matter?

He remembered her now as a flash of quicksilver, a marvellous melange of smiles and tears, of temper and joy. The moaning, the laughing, the jokes. The self-pity, the rage, the happiness, the adoration for her children. The magical radiance, the special star quality that came from beauty mixed with an inner vulnerability. Everyone had felt it.

But I didn't really know her. She wasn't really connected to me. I was in her life for a time, I saw one facet of her existence, and then I was gone. Once I'd served my purpose. Gone like all the others. No real malice in it. That was just how it was.

It was all long ago. Her death was terrible. But it meant nothing to him in comparison with losing Julia. That's why he couldn't feel anything now. Life had lost its colour, its meaning. He had lost his own self. There was nothing more to go on for, he could see that with utter clarity.

The coffin procession disappeared through the abbey doors and into the sunshine beyond.

'David, I'm scared!' Sally's blue eyes were wide, her fear obvious. They were in the drawing room of Tawray, the late summer sunshine streaming in through the windows, burnishing the armour of Julia's two knights who now stood either side of the fireplace.

David was standing there, his head on his arms which were folded on the chimney piece. He didn't reply. He could barely hear her.

'David!' she begged, going up to him, putting her hand on his back. 'Please speak to me. You're frightening me.'

He turned his head to her, opening his eyes. They felt red and dry, a legacy of the sleepless nights he'd suffered since . . .

Oh Julia.

The memory of her lying there on the stainless-steel table, marble white with eyes closed, her spirit gone, her marvellous tawny hair limp and lifeless. It haunted him, it stayed on his eyelids after they were shut, it was everywhere he looked.

Julia. Why?

He knew why.

I did this. I did it to her. It's all my fault.

He had never comprehended what unbearable torment might be like until now. All pleasure in life was gone and nothing had meaning. All beauty and joy had been leached from the world, its colours drained, its purpose gone. But that was not the worst of it.

I can't look at the children.

Johnnie and Ali were living reproaches. He couldn't bring himself to look into their eyes, innocent, stunned, grieving, confused, knowing that he had done this to them, he had killed their mother, and he couldn't live with the guilt. He wanted to run through the house screaming, 'I loved her!

I didn't want her to die!' He wanted to find Julia wherever she must be hiding and shake her till her teeth rattled. 'How dare you, Julia?' he'd shout. 'How dare you do this to us? To them? To me?'

But that was impossible because she was dead and he had done it, and now he couldn't bear to look at the children. In his head, he knew that was wrong. They needed him, as they sobbed for her. Their eyes pleaded with him for an explanation and for comfort. They were desperate for love, and they needed twice as much from him now.

And I have nothing to give them. Nothing.

It was not that he didn't love them. He loved them too much. Far too much to stand their grief and the guilt it engendered. As a result he could see no future, nothing for himself. He had nothing to offer them either. There was no point to anything at all.

Sally had drawn back, but she was still staring at him with those wide, frightened blue eyes. Her simplicity and straightforwardness had given him such comfort when he was confronted with Julia's complex problems. She had offered him what he'd needed from Julia: warmth, affection, the embrace that welcomed him into her body and gave him solace. If only he had had that from Julia, he never would have needed Sally. But Julia practically pushed him into Sally's arms. Even though it was never said, he'd come to believe that in some obscure way Julia was giving him permission to sleep with Sally, in the knowledge that, at the end of it, he loved her, Julia, best.

But had she?

She had certainly suggested that he sleep with other women. She had never named Sally. Perhaps she hadn't meant Sally after all. When she'd suggested he meet his needs elsewhere, the pain had been indescribable. She was closing her physical self off from him forever. He knew why, intellectually, and he had every sympathy with the horror she had been through. But he couldn't divorce love for his wife from physical love. It didn't seem possible, nor did it seem fair and right to ask it.

How can she have meant Sally?

But she knew about Sally, he was sure of it. In the spring – was it so recent? – Julia had taken him back into her bed. His heart had lifted and sung with joy when he realised that she wanted to make love to him. He knew for certain that he would abandon Sally in a heartbeat if Julia wanted him back, if he could share the love he had in his heart with her body. Four nights. It had been a dream of passion for him, full of the kind of shuddering bliss he had known in the early days of their relationship.

But it hadn't lasted. He'd known that it wasn't the same for her. He could feel her struggle, and he knew that she had fought valiantly, but lost the battle. She'd said that the last time, her voice freighted with sadness, 'I'm so sorry. I can't. I wish I could with all my heart. I can't do it.'

It had broken his heart but he'd known for certain that was the end. And although he had tried to resist, he'd ended up returning to Sally's arms: warm, simple, uncomplicated.

And Julia couldn't live with it. She killed herself because I betrayed her.

'David, you can't blame yourself,' Sally said in her quavering tones.

'Of course I can!' he shouted, and he saw her flinch, and was glad because she was guilty too. They'd both betrayed Julia. 'Who else is there?'

'Julia wasn't well! She had a mental illness!'

'She was fine, you know that. She hadn't been ill since Ali.'

'That's not true, she wasn't able to sleep with you,' Sally protested. 'She was still sick, you must see that!'

David shook his head, looking away in disgust. 'No. She was fine. I put an unbearable burden on her, and the two of us caused her terrible pain. You know that, Sally. So do I.'

She stared at him, biting her lip, scared. 'What are you going to do, David?'

'I have no idea. We haven't even buried her yet.' He dropped his head on his arms. 'I don't know how I can go on, how I'll look after the children. I can't even fucking look at them!' Hot tears stung his eyes and he blinked them away. He wouldn't allow himself the luxury of tears. He didn't deserve even them.

Sally put her arm across his back again, and leaned close to him. He could smell the floral scent of her perfume. 'Let me help you, David. I want to. I can look after you and protect you, and make it all right again, I promise.'

'I don't deserve happiness,' he said wretchedly. 'You shouldn't be around me, not when I'm like this. I'm no good for anyone, including you.'

'David, I love you. I want to help you.' She was urgent, insistent. 'I'll make sure no one ever hurts you again. I promise.'

There was a long pause and she said again, almost on a whisper, 'I love you, David. I loved Julia too, we both did. But we couldn't help her in the end. We need to go on with our lives. The children need that too. Let me help you, David, please.'

He lifted his eyes to her. He could see her sincerity all over her face.

She really means it. She wants to do it.

It would be easy that way. He could give all the responsibility to Sally, while he took on the lifelong wrestle with the knowledge that he had killed Julia and destroyed her children by taking their mother away. Sally would sort it out. He saw, quite suddenly, that only she could enable him to carry on in any meaningful way.

'Do you mean it? It's a burden for you.'

'No, it's not,' she said firmly. Her arm tightened around him. 'It's what I want. You'll never regret it, I swear.'

Chapter Thirty-Nine

Present day

In her study, Alex took a deep breath and picked up the phone. Sally answered, as she hoped she would. She was pretty sure Mundo was too lazy to answer the telephone, even if he was there.

'Sally, it's Alex.'

'Oh.' Sally's voice dropped to a whispery quaver. 'What is it?'

Alex blinked in surprise. This was the first time she'd made contact with Sally since before the reading of the will. She suspected Sally had noticed a little chilliness from her at the funeral. She'd expected more of a reaction than this to a phone call.

'I'd like to come and see you.'

'I don't think . . .' Sally said quickly, her voice still low. 'I don't think that's a good idea.'

'Well, there are some things I'd like to discuss with you. I think we need to talk. I have to warn you that Johnnie is thinking seriously about the terms of Pa's will. I think we should get everything out in the open and clear the air, so

501

we can move forward. No one wants conflict or extreme solutions.' Alex hoped she was being clear but it was hard to say out loud that Sally was risking her house if she chose to refuse offers of mediation.

'You can't come here,' Sally said urgently. 'Mundo won't allow it.'

'Mundo?' The name was bitter on her tongue. 'Why not?'

There was a pause as if Sally was looking over her shoulder to make sure she was not observed. 'He says he's going to challenge David's will. He doesn't care how long it takes. He's told me I can't see you or Johnnie anymore.'

To her surprise, Alex heard distress in Sally's voice. Despite her newfound fury towards her stepmother, she felt indignant on her behalf. 'He can't do that. You can see who you like!' *And I need you to tell me your version of what happened. I need to hear your story.*

'That's what he's said. I can't go against Mundo, Alex. I'm sorry, you can't come here. Please don't call again.' Sally put the phone down, leaving Alex listening in astonishment to an empty line.

Alex lay awake in the night. The thoughts flying around her head were keeping her adrenaline coursing long after switching her light out. She tossed and turned on the pillows, her eyes stubbornly open, and she stared wide-eyed into the darkness.

I can't let this happen. I can't let him get away with it.

Memories of what Mundo had put her through during those awful years kept bubbling to the surface of her mind, and she pushed them down, not wanting to see them and feel their force again.

Control. That's what matters to him. He only wants to win. But how is he going to challenge the will? It obviously came as a surprise to him, that's why he's taken his time before telling us what he intends to do. He's been coming up with a plan. What is it?

It was impossible to get any peace, and even though she was exhausted, she couldn't sleep. Then, suddenly, a thought floated into her mind.

I'll ask him not to do it. I'll go there and I'll ask him not to. Maybe that's something no one has ever tried.

For some reason, it seemed to make perfect sense. A blanket of calm fell over her and a few minutes later, she was asleep.

The next morning, she dropped the girls off at school, stopped to pick up some things in town and then went straight to Sally's house. Mundo's silver-blue Aston Martin sat in the driveway – typically ostentatious and yet also extremely covetable.

Sally answered the doorbell, and she gasped when she saw Alex. 'I told you not to come!' she said, her expression anxious. 'What are you thinking of?'

Alex still found it hard to accept this new, vulnerable Sally, the one who worried about who she was allowed to see, who perhaps even missed her. 'Can I come in, Sally? Just for a moment.'

Sally opened her mouth to protest, then closed it again and stepped back to allow Alex in.

Alex stepped into the hall. It was just the same. It felt as though Pa had popped out and would be back at any minute. *But he'll never come back.* She thought of Lala's words again and she felt her coldness to Sally harden further. 'Is Mundo here?'

Sally blinked nervously. 'He's upstairs. He isn't up yet.'

'I'd like to see him. Can you ask him to come down?'

'Why do you want to see him?'

'I just want to have a quick chat, that's all.' Alex smiled blithely as though it was perfectly normal to turn up first thing in the morning to talk to her good friend Edmund.

'Well . . . all right. I'll ask him.' Sally went slowly up the stairs, evidently nervous.

Alex wandered about the hall, looking at the pictures in their silver frames: Mundo in his barrister gear, his little horsehair wig perched on top of his head. Mundo and Isabella in a variety of smart outfits depending on the season and the occasion. One of the bigger ones had them climbing out of a helicopter dressed for Ascot, clutching at their hats, their badges for the royal enclosure visible on their chests. Mundo everywhere, and if not him, then Sally and David – at the golf club, at a reception at the town hall, on the beach in Italy from when they went to Positano for a holiday. Two tiny frames held pictures of the girls and a set of photos of Johnnie's boys were in a box frame on the wall – all sent by Johnnie and Alex rather than requested.

It reminded her of the injustice they'd had to put up with all those years.

Mundo told it exactly the reverse of the way it was. We

weren't spoiled, he was. He got everything and he can't stand the fact that now it's our turn.

But, she reminded herself, she wasn't here to command, rather to ask, even if that had only the remotest chance of succeeding.

Sally came back down. 'He's just coming. I'll make some tea.' She disappeared into the kitchen and a moment later, Mundo came down the stairs. The first thing Alex saw was a pair of hairy calves and then he appeared in a short grey silk dressing gown which he was ostentatiously tying at the waist as if to emphasise that it might open at any minute.

'Miss Pengelly – if that's what you are again now you're divorced – to what do I owe this pleasure?' There it was – his little half-smile as though he could only spare a bit of the energy of a regular smile.

'I'd like a chat,' she said calmly.

He reached the bottom of the staircase, and gave a massive yawn, rubbing his hand through his hair so it stood on end in a way she suspected he thought was endearing. 'All right then. Although why you can't wait until a civilised hour, I have no idea.'

'It's nine forty, Mundo.'

'Exactly. Come in here, where we can be private.' He led her into the dining room at the front of the house. It was pin neat, with the large table covered in a baize cloth for protection. A cabinet of china and ornaments stood against the wall. Mundo pulled out a chair and sat down, crossing one leg over the other. 'Now. How can I help?'

Alex looked away from where the silk gown seemed it

might slip open at any minute. She felt sick and suddenly unsure of herself, reminded against her will of all the times Mundo had put her in horrible situations. She had promised herself it would never happen again, and here she was, of her own free will, in a room with him, alone, and he was wearing almost nothing.

Just say what you have to say and leave. Don't give him the satisfaction of knowing how uncomfortable you are.

'I guessed from what you said at the funeral that you intend to challenge Pa's will. I want you to withdraw it.'

He snorted. 'Forget it. I intend to go through with it and use maximum force to disrupt everything. Why not? It'll be fun.'

'You and Sally won't get your bequests either.'

'Oh deary me!' Mundo pretended to wipe his eyes. 'I don't get my ten thousand pounds? Boo hoo! Well, guess what, I don't care. I'll fund Mummy for as long as she needs me or has to go into a home – this place is rent-free, so I'll only be paying the utilities, and that's only if she needs it. She's got a nice little pension of her own, and some stocks and shares. She'll be okay.'

'Then why are you doing this?'

'Because I can,' Mundo said, sticking his chin in the air and crossing his arms, his air of smugness infuriating as he no doubt hoped. 'I don't want you to win, and I don't want Pa to win. So I'm going to throw a little old spanner in the works.'

'What kind of spanner?' Alex asked. 'What on earth can you say to challenge it? Warburton thinks the will is genuine, there's no evidence of a different will or any missing addendum or codicil. So what are you objecting to?'

'I'm objecting to the fact that my daddy hasn't treated me the same as he treated those other children.'

'Because the properties and businesses are in the Tawray trust, which was my mother's, and because he's not your father.'

Mundo smirked. 'That's what you think.'

Alex gaped at him. 'What?'

'That's right,' Mundo said. He looked tremendously pleased with himself. 'My mother is going to admit that she started her affair with Pa after Johnnie was born, or maybe even before. And that she got pregnant with his child – me – and I was born before you, but before she and Pa were a couple.' He shrugged. 'Easy peasy. See?'

Alex stared at him in horror, unable to speak.

'Yes indeed. He's my father.'

'Of course he isn't!'

'How do you know?' Mundo shrugged. 'I'm not tall, but otherwise I look quite like him – brown hair, blue eyes.'

'They'll make you take a DNA test.'

'No. They can't. I won't agree and as Mummy is going to testify in my favour, we won't need one. Come on, Alexandra. See it from my point of view. It's going to be fun. Mummy will do and say anything I ask her to. And in any case, it's probably true. We all know David and Sally were hard at it for years before they got together and became respectable.'

A nasty swirl of nausea rose in her stomach. She felt faint. 'Then all the times you exposed yourself to me. That terrible time . . . that thing you did . . . You're trying to tell me that you believe now that you're actually my brother.'

'Yes . . .' He made a face. 'Spicy!' Then he laughed. 'Oh, come on, all teenagers experiment! You know that. We were finding out the facts of life a bit, that's all. You were as willing as I was.'

'That's not true.' She began to shake. 'You know it's not. You tormented me. You forced me.'

'You liked the chase,' Mundo said. 'You've always been up for it, I found that out from your diaries.'

Suddenly she noticed that his dressing gown had slipped open and she could see everything that lay nestled between his legs. It twitched and jerked lightly as he became excited.

'Come on, Alex,' he said, seeing where she was looking. 'Let's see how much you want that money, eh? A test for you. Touch my cock and I'll know you don't believe I'm your brother. But if you won't touch it . . . well, there we are. We must be related. So, what will it be?'

Alex closed her eyes, feeling her gorge rise. She was fourteen again, stuck on the roof with Mundo. He'd followed her up to the turret where she liked to hide and read on sunny days. He blocked the way out. He told her he would throw her off the roof if she didn't do exactly as he wanted.

'Oh God,' she whispered. The feelings of panic, despair and fear came racing back as clearly as if they had happened that morning. It felt as if the walls were closing in, the floor was rising up to meet her. *Oh my God*.

Mundo was standing up, he was coming towards her, his robe hanging open, his erection now in his hand. 'Come on,

Alex,' he was saying, half laughing, half urgent. 'Why don't you touch it?'

He reached for her hand and she snatched it away. 'No,' she said but she was frozen, helpless. She was fourteen, in the turret, and he was going to show her what it was all about. That's what he said. *I'm going to show you how it works – you want that, don't you? Girls pretend they don't, but they do.* 'Go away,' she whispered. 'Leave me alone.'

'Can't hear you!' sang out Mundo. He was close to her now, almost pressing up against her. She could smell his fusty morning smell – unbrushed teeth, sweat – and her stomach churned again. 'Don't pretend you're fussy.' He reached out for her hand again. 'You always used to like it, even when you said you didn't. Remember? Come on!'

'No!' Alex cried. She tried to move away from him but he already had her hand in a vicious grip. 'Not again! I won't let you force me again!'

The door to the dining room burst open and Sally stood there, her eyes blazing. 'Stop it, Mundo!' she screamed. 'Stop it this instant! Leave her alone!'

Mundo stood still, stunned for an instant, then dropped Alex's hand, fumbled his robe shut and gave a feeble laugh. 'We're just fooling around, Mummy. Nothing real. Nothing serious.'

'Don't you touch her!' Sally flew into the room, her expression furious, and delivered a hard slap across Mundo's face. Trembling with rage, she confronted him, her fists clenched. 'You think I'm a fool! I always wondered if you did anything to her. I saw the way she loathed you and couldn't bear to be near you, and I wondered. But I gave you the benefit of the doubt. I didn't believe you'd be capable of it!' Her face twisted in a mixture of despair and revulsion. 'Well, I was wrong. I'm ashamed of you, do you hear me? You're disgusting. Disgusting!' She was panting, irate, glaring at him with fire in her eyes. 'I heard what she said, and I believe her. You'd be up for a charge in a heartbeat if Alex chooses to go to the police and where would your legal career be then? In the bloody gutter, that's where! You idiot. You've always pushed for too much, you've never been satisfied with what you have. But to do that to her . . . to that poor child. I'm so ashamed. Get out!'

Mundo was rubbing his face in amazement, his smirk gone. He turned and walked out, not looking at Alex or his mother.

Alex took several deep breaths, trying to calm herself. Sally put her hand on Alex's arm, concern and apology on her face. 'He's gone. I'm so sorry. I'm so terribly sorry.'

Alex's trembling began to subside. *He's gone. Sally stopped him. Sally slapped him!* She felt as if she had been having an awful nightmare that had suddenly taken a weird blackly comic turn. Sally, slapping Mundo! Sally taking her part over Mundo's! It was unbelievable.

'I heard it all through the hatch.' Sally pointed at the almost invisible pair of white shutters in the wall through to the hall. 'I always hoped it wasn't true.' Her expression was penitent. 'I don't know what to say. I won't stand in your way if you want to take it further.'

Alex let out a long, shaking breath. 'Thank you, Sally. That means a lot – in fact, I can't tell you how much. Let me think about it. What I really want is for him to drop the challenge to the will – the grounds are so awful.'

'There won't be a challenge,' Sally said at once. 'And certainly not on the grounds that he's David's son because he isn't, that's for sure. But don't let that stop you. If you want to complain, please complain. He can't do that, Alex. He just can't.'

Unexpectedly, she put her arms around Alex and hugged her. She said again, 'I'm so sorry.'

Such simple words. But honestly meant, they are so powerful.

The hatred for Sally unlocked, like a padlock with the right combination, and released her. Sally had atoned for all of it in this moment of listening, believing and supporting. She had put her beloved son's comfortable life and prestigious job at risk, for Alex's sake.

'Thank you, Sally.' She clutched the other woman's hand and squeezed it. 'That means more than you'll ever know.'

'We're family,' the older woman said. 'It's been hard at times, but we're family. And I know what's right. I couldn't let him do that to you. I just couldn't let him do it.'

'There's one thing I want, Sally.' Alex gazed into her stepmother's blue-green eyes. 'Will you talk to me and Johnnie? Please? I mean, really talk to us?' She squeezed her hand again. 'That's what we need now, more than anything.'

Chapter Forty

The atmosphere in Sally's house was the most striking thing, Alex thought, as she and Johnnie sat down with her. There was no sign of Mundo and Alex suspected he'd gone. The aura was solemn, almost church-like. There was going to be a confession of some kind, a revelation, and she and Johnnie were both on edge, wondering what they were going to hear and what it would mean to them.

I feel closer to Mum than I have since she died. Julia seemed to be with them, in the painting, in Lala, in the house. *She's in us all the time, we're her children. As long as we're here, she hasn't left.*

And yet, she had gone, years before, ripped away from them for reasons they didn't understand, and which no one had explained to them.

Sally took them into the sitting room and they all sat down. She took a deep breath, knitted her hands in her lap, and began to speak, her tone low and calm.

'Alex has explained to me that you want to know about your mother. What you need to understand is that Julia's death was very difficult for David to handle, and he never wanted it spoken of. The wound went very deep, for so many different reasons. After Julia passed, he was destroyed and he blamed himself. We both blamed ourselves. It was easier to draw a veil over it and never speak of it. That's what we did and I made sure it stayed that way because I wanted to protect him. But he's gone now. So you deserve to know the truth.'

Alex's heart was pounding and she could see that Johnnie was alert to every sound Sally made.

Sally went on: 'Have you heard of tokophobia? It's a fear of pregnancy and childbirth, and in its extreme forms, it can cause psychosis. It's not as well known as post-natal depression. I'm afraid, for reasons we never understood, your mother suffered from it very badly. When she was pregnant with Johnnie, she was hospitalised until the birth. She couldn't face natural childbirth, so she had a Caesarean. Afterwards, she appeared to recover completely and she was adamant that she could manage to have another child. I was living with her by then, looking after her, and you, Johnnie, when David couldn't. At first, she seemed to be able to cope, but the illness came back worse than before with you, Alex. And she never fully recovered. It left its mark on her and she became mortally afraid of getting pregnant, so much so that she forbade your father her bed.' Sally swallowed, evidently uncomfortable. 'And I'm afraid that was when your father sought comfort elsewhere and we began our affair.' She darted quick looks at both of them. 'You'll no doubt think that was a terrible thing to do, and it was. All I can say is that I loved your father and I hated to see him in pain. I didn't wish to break up the marriage and I honestly thought that Julia might even prefer that he slept with me and stayed with her. That's what I understood. But we never talked about it, so perhaps it was wrong. I was in the cottage by then, and we stopped being such close friends.'

Alex could see it as she talked: Pa, slipping away to see Sally because he needed relief from Mum's emotional problems. It wasn't right, but it was perhaps understandable. He couldn't know what it would mean. At least, she hoped not.

Johnnie only said, 'Go on.'

Sally hesitated, then said, 'This is the hardest bit to tell you. I'm sure you understand why. Julia and David attempted a reconciliation and it was a disaster; she was unable to be a wife to him ever again. Her phobia was just too great. So David and I resumed our affair. That summer, Julia changed again. Not outwardly. David told me afterwards he had no idea that she was so depressed, so down. But from what happened, she must have spiralled down into the worst despair of her life.'

Johnnie said sharply, 'Was it because she found out about you and Dad? Was that what drove her to it?'

Sally looked helpless. 'I don't think so, Johnnie, I really don't. I think she'd known for some time that David was finding comfort with me. And what you have to understand is . . . she told him to do it.'

'What?' Alex said, stunned. 'Mum told Pa to have an affair with you?'

Sally blushed. 'Not with me, perhaps. But she told him to sleep with other women because she couldn't do it. It broke

514

his heart.' She looked down and then up again at her step-children. 'I'm under no illusion about this. If Julia had wanted David back, she could have had him with a flick of her fingers. He never loved me one tenth of the way he loved her. If she'd told him to drop me, he would have. Just like that.'

They both stared at her.

I never thought I would hear Sally say such a thing, Alex thought with amazement. It was completely out of character, a sign of a humility she had never before displayed. *It must take a great deal for her to admit that*. She felt a rush of happiness at the idea that Pa had loved Mum so much all along, and then bitter sadness followed, at how it had all turned out.

'Did you intend to steal Pa away from her?' Johnnie asked sharply. 'Was that always your plan?'

Sally's blush deepened and she hesitated before she answered. Then, with a quick glance at Alex, she said in a small but firm voice, 'No. It's true I always hero-worshiped him. I was impressed by his job, his contact with the royal family. He was older than Julia and me, and so handsome and glamorous. I probably made it obvious how I felt about him. But I never dreamed he would leave Julia for me. Why would he? She was very special, I knew that. A man like David would never choose me over her. I didn't think I had a hope. Even when he started sleeping with me, I knew it was only the crumbs from Julia's table.'

Johnnie frowned, still outwardly stony, but Alex could see a flicker of something like compassion in his eyes. He was touched by Sally's humbleness too, just as she was. It was so unlike her, and what she said helped make sense of everything. 'Then you didn't want her out of the way?'

'Of course not,' Sally exclaimed, evidently appalled by the suggestion. She looked at them both, her eyes suddenly clear and candid. 'I loved her. She was my friend. I loved her, and I loved you too.'

Alex felt her heart contract with pain. 'Then why did you treat us so badly?' she asked, her voice plaintive. 'Why did you come between us and Pa?'

Sally's eyelids fluttered and she bit her lip, looking down at her hands twisting in her lap. They both waited for her to speak, to tell them at last what they had longed to know. 'Perhaps I wasn't the best stepmother, I can see that now. I was so focused on David. My greatest fear was that he would realise I wasn't as good as Julia and he'd decide to leave me. I was desperate for him to stay with me, and for him to love Mundo as much as I did.' She flicked a glance up at them and then away. 'I knew he could be naughty. I suppose I was afraid that if I didn't push him forward and make much of him, David wouldn't love him as much as he loved you, and Mundo would suffer. So I overcompensated. I spoiled him. I pushed you away. I see that now.'

'Pa let you do it,' whispered Alex. 'That's what hurt the most. The sense that he didn't love us.'

'Oh, he loved you,' Sally replied, almost as if surprised at the suggestion he might not. 'He loved you too much, that was the problem. He was so full of despair at what had happened to Julia and that you'd lost your mother . . . well, I was frightened for him. I thought he might kill himself. He felt so terribly, awfully guilty.'

'That's why he pushed us away?' Alex asked wonderingly.

Sally nodded. 'I know it's counter-intuitive. But people are strange, aren't they? Because he loved you so much, he couldn't get too close to you. And I promised him I'd keep him safe as long as I lived. I put myself between you and him to protect him.' She paused and then said awkwardly, 'I'm sorry if you suffered because of me. I loved you in my own way. Julia would have been furious with me if she'd thought I'd let you down, and I know I did. I feel awful about it.'

Alex felt a stirring of sympathy. *All we need to do is understand. Then we can forgive.* 'It's all right, Sally,' she said.

Sally cast her an agonised look. 'I owe you the biggest apology of all. I'll do everything I can to put it right.'

Alex smiled at her. 'Thank you.' She hesitated; something was nudging at the edge of her mind. 'I have a question. Is there any chance Mum could have been pregnant when she died?'

Sally frowned, thinking. 'I . . . I don't know. The autopsy didn't mention a pregnancy. Surely it would have if she had been. She slept with David in the spring, it was August, there would have been a clear sign if she was expecting a baby, I'm sure of it.'

'Yes, I suppose that's right,' Alex said thoughtfully. 'I just wondered . . . what you said about tokophobia . . . whether she had a new attack triggered by getting pregnant.'

'It's a possibility,' Sally said slowly.

'We could request the autopsy report,' Johnnie said. 'That would tell us if they looked for a pregnancy.'

'Good idea,' Alex said. 'It was a long time ago now but they should have the records still.'

Sally nodded. 'Julia's death got rather lost in the great fuss over the princess. They died the same weekend. But actually, we were glad that everyone was focused elsewhere. David couldn't bear the idea that Julia would be an object of gossip and scandal, her life ripped apart by other people with no one really knowing the truth. Only those of us who'd loved her knew. She could be remembered the way we wanted to remember her – vibrant and loving and alive. Before her illness claimed her.'

There was a long silence. Alex was gripped by so many conflicting emotions, she didn't know how to start processing them. She put them to one side, to take out and study later. Time was needed, she could see that at once. Time to process all this extraordinary information. Instead, she said, 'Thank you, Sally. Thank you for telling us this at last.'

'There's no one left to protect,' Sally said with a small smile. 'They've all gone. I don't have to keep their secrets anymore.'

Alex nodded slowly.

Johnnie spoke, his voice gruff. 'Yes, thank you, Sally. I appreciate it.'

'I'm sure you'll have more questions. I'll do what I can to answer them.' She stood up and patted her hair, her expression changing as she adopted one of her bright smiles. 'Now, would anyone like a piece of Victoria sponge? I made one specially when I knew you were coming.'

Alex and Johnnie were both muted on the drive home. When they arrived, Alex suggested a walk to the beach and they followed the old familiar route to the clifftop and down the rugged path to the shore. It was calmer today, with lots of jagged white edges on half-formed waves instead of the epic crashing of the previous week. They sat down on the rocks near the water's edge, and gazed out over the sea.

Johnnie said, 'I just never thought of Sally protecting anyone except herself. It's so weird to think that she thought she was protecting Pa.'

'And Mum.' Alex nodded. 'But I was touched by the way she obviously loved them both. It had never occurred to me that she might love Mum too. Anything can make sense when you see it from a different point of view. Some of the crazy, weird, unkind things people do.'

'Unless it's Mundo.'

'Yes, well . . . there's always an exception to prove the rule.' They smiled at each other.

'We need to forgive Sally,' Alex said. 'We need to let go of thoughts of revenge and be kind. I believed what she said today. Didn't you?'

Johnnie hesitated and Alex could see something of his internal struggle. Then he spoke. 'Yes. It was hard to hear some of it. But I did believe her. I don't think she actually caused Mum to kill herself – it was clearly way more complicated than that.' He paused, took a deep breath and looked at his sister. 'But I'm still angry, Al. Not so much at Sally anymore, though it will be hard to forgive it all just like that. I'm angry at Pa. He let all this happen. He let Sally push us away, no matter what her motives. He must have seen how unhappy we were and how unfairly she treated us, and he didn't stop her. He didn't step in. I've blamed Sally for the house being sold and all along it wasn't. What a waste of bloody time and effort.' A surge of hot, furious grief flooded through him. 'For fuck's sake. He's dead! I can't say any of this to him. I can't ask him why he lied, or why he didn't help us more, or what it all meant.'

Alex leaned over and put her arms around him. 'I know. We're going to have to come to terms with what happened, and why. What Pa's role in all of it was. But from what Sally said, he was deeply hurt by Mum's death. Maybe irreversibly. He blamed himself and he punished himself for the rest of his life. It just didn't look like that to us.'

Johnnie lifted agonised eyes to her and found some comfort in the sympathy and love he saw in his sister's. 'We'll never know for sure, as Pa's gone. He can't answer us.'

'But Sally can still tell us more. She'll talk to us now, I'm sure of it. And something's happened you need to know about.'

She told him, slowly and with some difficulty, about what had happened with Mundo at Sally's house, and what he'd done to her in the past. She had to go slowly, so that she could let Johnnie process each revelation as it came and help him deal with the onslaught of powerful emotions her story evoked: there was the fury she was expecting, but there was also the guilt, sadness and disgust at what Mundo had done.

'I never saw it. I never stopped it.' Johnnie's voice was broken. 'What kind of a brother was I? I didn't protect you. God, Al, I'm so sorry.'

'It wasn't your job to do that. It wasn't your responsibility.'

'I want to fucking kill him.' The words burst out of Johnnie with the force of bullets and she knew that his anger came from deep within him, in the place where he put all his hurt and fury about the past.

'I know you do. That will pass. I wanted to kill him myself. But when Sally did what she did – when she came blazing in and confronted him . . . well, that set me free. I know slapping someone is wrong, but that slap – I felt that for Mundo. That slap from Sally was the only punishment he could have in this life that would mean anything to him. All the rest he could live down or convince himself was unjust. But from his mother, it was real. He couldn't pretend she didn't know him or understand him, or that she was jealous or anything like that. She knows him inside out and she was so disgusted.' Alex looked over at her brother, who was still hunched inside his coat, staring out to sea, his eyes hard. 'She said sorry to me, and she meant it. And she meant it when she said it today. We have to let her keep that house for as long as she needs and look after her till she dies. You know Pa would have wanted that.'

Johnnie went still. He had not thought of this before, she could tell, and he was silent for a while as he absorbed it. The gulls wheeled overhead, screeching as they rode the air currents. The waves rolled ceaselessly on and the sea breeze was tangy and fresh. The milky midwinter sun tried to make its way through the clouds.

'You're right,' Johnnie said. 'I understand.'

'There's one more thing, Johnnie. If you want to move forward, and start to let it all go, we need to forgive Pa. I'm angry because he wasn't the father I longed for him to be. He was selfish and locked away, and he should have been there for us. I've got to let go of all that. So have you.'

'Yeah.' Johnnie got up and climbed off the rock onto the wet sand. 'I know.' He smiled at Alex. 'That's what I'm working on, I guess. I don't know how long it will take, though.'

'Take your time.' Alex smiled, climbing down to join him. 'That's what I'm doing. It's going to be a life's work.'

As they strolled along the beach, Johnnie seemed suddenly more at peace than Alex had seen him for a long time, perhaps even for years.

'I'm going back to Netta tonight,' he said as they walked. 'I'm handing in my notice, and we're going to start sorting out a move down here.'

'That's fantastic.' Alex smiled. 'I'm going to love having you guys here. And you know there's room at the Old Barn whenever you want it.' She checked her watch. 'I'll have to get a move on. I said I'd meet Jasper in town for lunch.'

Johnnie gave her a sideways look.

'What?' She laughed shyly. 'I know what you're thinking.'

'Just be happy, Al. That's all I want for you.' He hugged her.

'It's all I want for you too, big brother.' She hugged him back hard.

Chapter Forty-One

1997

The secret, the terrible secret.

It's there in the darkness, deep inside her. She knows exactly what will happen, just like the last times except that then she was lucky. Then, she managed to escape. But only just.

She won't be so lucky this time.

She can already feel it coming back: the knowledge that swimming there, inside her, is an alien, a malevolent force growing with every passing second, which has only one thing on its developing mind. To kill her.

She's kept it hidden from everyone. That wasn't hard. No one sees anything amiss in her concave stomach. They don't see the scratches and cuts on her upper arms and thighs, or hear the choking and retching in the bathroom.

Sometimes a voice says, 'What about the poor little secret? Doesn't it deserve a chance? Why not see if you can both survive it?'

But then the hissing horrors start again. The terrible nightmares. The fears that turn her inside out with their force.

She's tried to be brave. The children need her, and she loves them so much. But she also knows how it goes, and how it feels to be sucked into the pit. Nothing matters there – husbands, children, life itself. Everything good is consumed and disappears in there. And that's where she's going. It's inevitable.

Tonight, though, she knows. This cannot go on. This has to end. She will find a different kind of courage.

She goes down to the lake with the secret, in the cool night air. She props the envelope that holds the letter she has written against a stone. It is addressed to David. The letter says, I'm sorry. *It says,* It's not your fault, it's not Sally's fault, it's my fault. *It says,* I don't know what to do. I think there's a baby coming, and I can't go through it again. I'm too afraid. *It says,* I know I made a promise to tell you when things got too bad but I can't do it and I don't know why. That's my fault, not yours. *Then it says,* Look after Johnnie and Ali and tell them I love them. I'm so sorry.

She leaves the letter by the stone and climbs into the rotting skiff. She uses the pole to push it away from the jetty and out over the black water.

The madness that has brought her here is unbearable. The secret is unbearable. She has been so terrible, so wicked, so evil. Her devil is back, whispering in her ear, telling her that she deserves to die.

I cannot fight him anymore.

The old skiff floats into the middle of the lake. The envelope is lifted by a breeze and deposited in the water where it floats away. But she doesn't see that.

I'm sorry. I've been so afraid. If I stay, there will be much worse to come.

She is looking one last time at the outline of the old house, the turrets piercing the sky.

Goodbye, Tawray.

Goodnight, sweet children.

But the relief that it is now all over is also wonderful. Release from the terror – that's what she needs more than anything. To be free. Yes, to be free will be everything.

She takes the secret with her and vanishes.

Epilogue

Present day

Tawray showed itself off to its absolute best when Lala finally returned, thirty years after she had last been there. The May sunshine was bright, the sky blue and dotted with clouds of fluffy white, and the fresh-minted flowers nodded their heads in the light breeze.

'It's just as I remember,' she said, as Alex drove her up to the house. 'But even more beautiful.' She gazed out over the dazzling sea. 'That view. It's heartbreaking, it really is.'

When she climbed out of the car, she looked up at the house. 'It's a little more spruced up than I remember.'

'Jasper's been restoring it. Or at least, he's got other people to do it. He's more of an ideas man,' Alex said.

Lala looked at her questioningly. 'He's your friend.'

'Yes, he's my friend.' Alex smiled and couldn't hide the pleasure she took in saying that. The friendship was growing all the time and she knew that one day, it was going to blossom into something more. They both did. But at the moment they were enjoying the delicious anticipation, the slow dance that was building towards some time or place yet to be decided when they would confess to each other that they were going to be together now. It might be the trip to Edinburgh that Jasper had suggested, to see all of his old stomping grounds. She could imagine that in that ancient and romantic city, something might happen between them. 'I might even wear my kilt if you're lucky,' he'd said with a smile, and she'd teased him about it, but there was an undercurrent to their joking: serious, questioning, laced with a glorious excitement and happiness.

'Is your friend here?' Lala asked knowingly. 'I'd like to meet him.'

'Not today,' Alex said. 'Just us and Johnnie to start with. Netta and the boys have gone to the beach but you'll meet them later. Scarlett and Jasmine will be here this evening. But for now, it's only us three. It seemed best.'

'Yes, you're right. Come on then, let's go in.'

Johnnie was waiting for them in the drawing room. 'You must be my aunt,' he said, coming to greet Lala with a kiss, a big smile over his face. 'It's a pleasure to meet you.'

'The pleasure is all mine.' Lala looked him over carefully, and tears glistened in her eyes. 'You are still that little boy I loved. And you have her colouring.' Her gaze slipped past him to the wall beyond. It had not long been restored and the room still felt a little odd to Alex, reduced down as it was. But on the other hand the mural looked magnificent, back in the place it was meant to be.

'Oh!' gasped Lala. 'Oh my God – I never thought I would see this again.'

She came forward to stare at it, the extraordinary representation of the room behind it, peopled with those she remembered from over forty years before. 'My father! Oh, that's exactly him, exactly! It's like he can talk to me any second. My brittle old grandmother and frightful Aunt Victoria – you didn't miss anything there, believe me. Ah, Quentin. Likeable but not much to him, as a man. Clever but . . . you know the type. Violet never made much of an impression; I'm glad if she turned out more interesting than she looked. And oh . . .' Lala put out a hand and, with one fingertip, delicately touched the portrait of Julia. 'Here she is, my lovely girl. This is exactly as she was. Exactly. Merry and funny and imaginative. Probably too imaginative.'

'We think the painting is full of little messages to Julia,' Johnnie said.

'Oh yes, you're right.'

'Can you explain them?'

'Well, I'll do my best. Look at that book on the shelf. *A History of Morotania*. Did your mother ever talk to you about that?'

Alex shook her head.

'Well, let me tell you a bit about it. It involved both of those sets of armour, for a start. Let me see – what were their names?'

Lala was off, a flood of reminiscence falling from her lips, each memory bringing their mother alive a little more. They listened and laughed while they looked at the picture of her, staring back at them from the painting and looking as though she were about to break into laughter herself at the silliness of all her childhood tricks and games.

Yes, she seemed to say. *I was happy once. And I want you to be happy too.*

Much later they walked down to the lake and stood together, the three of them, looking out at the water. It was cleaner now, because Jasper had thrown in hay bales to act as a natural defence against algae. But they could see that under the surface, the tangle of deadly weeds still lay, ready to take an unwary swimmer down forever.

'Of course, we don't know what happened,' Lala said sadly.

'There's nothing on the autopsy report about a pregnancy,' Johnnie said. 'They would have noticed if she'd been three months pregnant, surely. So perhaps it was all in her mind. If that's what caused her to do it.'

Lala looked agonised. 'I feel so terrible about it. If she did imagine it, she should never have had cause if she hadn't slept with David. That was my idea. I told her to do it if she wanted to save her marriage.' Tears sprang to her eyes. 'And look what happened.'

'Everybody can blame themselves,' Alex said softly. 'Pa did. Sally did, a bit. But no one knew what might happen. Hindsight makes everything obvious, but it wasn't at the time.'

'No. You're right.' Lala sighed. 'But regret is a terrible thing.'

Johnnie said, 'We can't change it. We can only learn.' He pointed to a small flowering cherry just near the lake, its young trunk still protected by meshing. 'We planted that in memory of Mum.'

Lala smiled. 'That's lovely.'

Johnnie looked over the gardens and up towards the house. 'Everything we do here is for her. Even just trying to be happy.'

Lala looked at Alex and Johnnie. 'She would have been very proud of you, you know. She would have said you made her existence worthwhile. What a shame she has missed all of this – you, the house, the grandchildren. But I can still hear her laugh and see her smile. She will never be forgotten. She'll always be here.'

They looked out over the water one last time, and then turned to walk back towards the house.

Acknowledgements

Thank you, as always, to everyone at Pan Macmillan: my marvellous and very supportive editor, Wayne Brookes; Alex Saunders, who is always unflustered, patient and endlessly helpful; and the wise and wonderful Jeremy Trevathan. Also to Alex Lloyd from Pan Australia, whose suggestions were so helpful and whose enthusiasm meant so much. You are a wonderful team and great fun to work with.

My thanks to Rosie Wilson, my fab publicist; Lucy Wai, who masterminds the marketing; and Stuart Dwyer and his team who get the all-important sales. Thank you to Neil Lang for another beautiful cover. I am so grateful to everyone in-house.

Huge thanks to Lorraine Green, who copy-edited with so much skill and sensitivity. Your encouragement, good humour and understanding mean so much.

Thank you to Mandy Greenfield, who proofread, and Samantha Fletcher at Pan Macmillan, who desk-edited. We can't do without these dedicated, precise and painstaking people, who make the books so polished and complete.

Special thanks go to Maddalena Cavaciuti for her sensitive reading, incisive editorial suggestions and heartfelt encouragement.

Thanks as always to my superstar agent, Lizzy Kremer, at David Higham Associates, and her team: Harriet Moore and Maddalena Cavaciuti. I don't know what I'd do without you.

Love as always to the SWANS – the South West authors who celebrate books, toast success and offer comfort in the dark times.

I'm very grateful to the staff of D'Urberville in Sherborne, who provided such delicious coffee, cake and a calm, welcoming environment while I was doing my rewrites.

Thank you to Paul Laikin for reading the first draft and giving me a warm, thoughtful and helpful critique, and to my mother, Kate Adams, for sending me the inspiration for Julia's illness.

Lots of love and thanks to James, Barney and Tabby, and to my friends and family for their support. I couldn't do it without you all – readers, book-buyers, bookshops, festival-goers and followers on social media. Thank you seems too small a phrase.

Lulu Taylor
Dorset 2019

The Winter Children

Behind a selfless act of kindness lie dark intentions . . .

Olivia and Dan Felbeck's dreams of a family are finally fulfilled on the birth of their twins. The longed-for babies mark a new and happy stage in their lives.

Soon after, Dan's oldest friend, Francesca, offers them the chance to live at Renniston Hall, an Elizabethan house she is renovating. They can stay rent-free in a small part of the unmodernised house, which was once a girls' boarding school.

The couple accept, and just as they are enjoying the family life that they have craved for so long, Francesca arrives at the Hall and doesn't seem to want to leave. What exactly happened between Dan and Francesca years ago at Cambridge? As Olivia wonders how well she knows her husband, she starts to suspect that her perfect life could be built on a lie.

Meanwhile, Renniston Hall holds dark mysteries of its own, and slowly the old house starts to surrender its long-held secrets . . .

Praise for Lulu Taylor

'I raced through this gripping tale about secrets and lies and long-buried emotions bubbling explosively to the surface'
DAILY MAIL

THE SNOW ROSE

I know they think I shouldn't keep her . . . That's why I've
escaped them while I can, while I still have the opportunity . . .

Kate is on the run with her daughter Heather, her identity hidden
and their destination unknown to the family they've left behind.
She's found a place where they can live in solitude, a grand old
house full of empty rooms and dark secrets. But they're not
alone, for there are the strange old ladies in the cottage next
door: Matty and her sister Sissy. They know what happened here
long ago, and are curious about Kate. How long can she hide
Heather's presence from them?

When an eccentric band of newcomers arrive, led by the
charismatic Archer, Kate realises that the past she's so desperate
to escape is about to catch up with her. And inside the house,
history is beginning to repeat itself . . .

Praise for Lulu Taylor

'Pure indulgence and perfect reading
for a dull January evening'

SUN

HER FROZEN HEART

Caitlyn, there's something I have to tell you. About Sara.

Caitlyn thinks her marriage to Patrick is a success. For one thing, he is one of the few people not to fall head over heels for her beautiful friend, Sara. Life is lived on his terms, but they are happy. Aren't they?

When a devastating accident turns her existence upside down, Caitlyn is forced to reassess her marriage, what she truly knows about Patrick, and his real feelings for her best friend. In the refuge of an old manor house, she begins to discover the truth.

At Kings Harcourt Manor in 1947, the worst winter in decades hits England, cutting the inhabitants off entirely. For Tommy Carter, widowed at the start of the war, it is particularly hard: the burden of the family falls on her. She has the solace of her children, and the interesting presence of her brother's friend, Fred. But there is also Barbara, a mysterious figure from her past who appears to want a piece of Tommy's future as well.

Praise for Lulu Taylor

'Interesting characters, well researched detail and a dash of romance. Perfect for a winter's eve'
SUNDAY MIRROR

THE WINTER SECRET

'My dear boy, the place is cursed. It always has been and it always will be . . .'

Buttercup Redmain has a life of pampered luxury, living in beautiful Charcombe Park. Her older husband, Charles, is wealthy and successful, and proud of the house he has painstakingly restored. Buttercup is surrounded by people who make her life delightfully easy. But the one thing she really wants seems impossible.

There are other discomforting realities: her husband's ex-wife Ingrid still lives nearby, although Buttercup has never met her. And it soon becomes clear that all the people who make Buttercup's life so carefree are also watching her every move. Does she actually live in a comfortable but inescapable cage? And what is the real story of her husband's previous marriage?

Xenia Arkadyoff once lived in Charcombe Park with her father, a Russian prince, and her mother, a famous film star. Life seemed charmed, full of glamour and beauty. But behind the glittering facade lay pain, betrayal and the truth about the woman Xenia spent her life protecting.

Now Charcombe Park is calling back people who were once part of its story, and the secrets that have stayed long hidden are bubbling inexorably to the surface . . .

Praise for Lulu Taylor

'Don't you just want to grab this, switch off the phone and curl up on the sofa? Winter bliss from Lulu Taylor'
Veronica Henry, top ten bestselling author of
Christmas at the Beach Hut